LEAVES OF THE TREE

LEAVES OF THE TREE

THE THIRD BOOK OF THE CHRONICLES OF DEBORAH

Maggy Whitehouse

A *Tree of Life* Book

Copyright © Maggy Whitehouse 2007
Jacket picture © José Luis Muñoz Luque
Colección de la Casa de Sefarad, (Córdoba, Spain).

The moral right of the author has been asserted

*All characters in this publication are fictitious and any resemblance
to real persons, living or dead, is purely coincidental.*

All rights reserved.
No part of this publication may be reproduced, stored in a
retrieval system or transmitted, in any form or by any means,
without the prior permission in writing of the publisher, nor be
circulated in any form of binding or cover other than that in
which it is published and without a similar condition including
this condition being imposed on the subsequent purchaser.

A CIP catalogue record for this book is available from the
British Library

ISBN: 978-1-905806-10-2

Tree of Life Publishing, UK

About the Author:

Maggy Whitehouse is an expert in metaphysical interpretations of the Bible and on the lives of women in Biblical times.

She studied the Toledano Tradition of Kabbalah with Z'ev ben Shimon Halevi from 1992, learnt New Testament Greek at Birmingham University, trained as an interfaith funeral minister and, in 2007, she was ordained in the Apostolic Church of the Risen Christ, a branch of Liberal Catholicism accepting of all faiths and traditions. She specialises in ancient wisdom for the modern day, melding Christian mysticism, First Temple teachings and the Toledano Tradition of Kabbalah. As well as *The Chronicles of Deborah*, she is the author of *Kabbalah and Healing*, *The Marriage of Jesus* (O Books) and the *Blue Panda* trilogy (Tree of Life Publishing).

As well as her writing, Maggy teaches workshops in Metaphysics, Bible Interpretation and Kabbalah worldwide. She is also a stand-up comedian.

She began her career as a journalist working in print, radio and television and started her spiritual quest after the death of her first husband. Maggy was producer of BBCi's spirituality website *360, Changing the World by Degrees* and host-moderator on the BBC's Religion and Ethics message boards in 2001 during the Iraq war.

She lives happily with her husband, Lion, in England and is the author of twenty-one published books.

Also by Maggy Whitehouse

Fiction:
The Book of Deborah (Tree of Life Publishing)
Into the Kingdom (Tree of Life Publishing)
The Miracle Man (O Books)
For The Love Of Dog (Tree of Life Publishing)
Tales Of The Blue Panda (Tree of Life Publishing)
Hounds Of Heaven: Another Tale Of The Blue Panda (Tree of Life Publishing)
Some Velvet Morning: The Final Tale Of The Blue Panda (Tree of Life Publishing)

Non-fiction;
Living Kabbalah (Hamlyn)
Total Kabbalah (Chronicle)
The Little Book of Prosperity (Tree of Life Publishing) Kindle only
The Spiritual Laws of Prosperity (Tree of Life Publishing) Kindle only
China By Rail (Century)
The Secret History of Opus Dei (Lorenz)
The Complete Illustrated History Of Kabbalah (Lorenz)
Kabbalah, The Heart of Jewish Mysticism (Lorenz)
From Credit Crunch to Pure Prosperity (O Books)
Kabbalah Made Easy (O Books)
Prosperity Teachings of the Bible Made Easy (O Books)
The Marriage of Jesus: The Lost Wife of the Hidden Years (O Books)
A Woman's Worth: The Divine Feminine in the Hebrew Bible (O Books)
Kabbalah and Healing (O Books)

One

In the beginning, God created the heavens and the Earth. Why?

To create a cradle for the baby that the One Holy wished to bear. For Adam Kadmon, the Son of God.

'But what is that to do with us?' I asked my mother as I sat at her feet in the firelight so many years ago.

Imma smiled and said: 'Everything. It is all about you and me. It is why we are here. Listen; I will tell you a story.'

Yeshua and I cuddled up beside her and sighed contentedly. Imma often told us stories. Every time we had a question, she would make us a story to tell us the answer. She told good stories.

Each one of us, she said, is one cell in that miraculous child and the baby will not be born until each of us—every one—has become perfect. It may take thousands of lives but that does not matter. There is enough time.

But why would God want to bear a baby? Isn't God the Absolute? The All-knowing, All-being Oneness? Perfection? All that is?

'For the same reason as your father and I wanted children,' Imma said. 'Somehow, even in the heart of perfection, there is a call to more; to create; to see another come into being and grow into its own self.

'But listen,' she said. 'There is more.'

*

When the Elohim created the heavens and the Earth it created also the angels and the archangels. It created animals and fish and birds—and man and woman.

They lived in a matchless world; an endless world of perfection and beauty and all was very, very good.

But nothing changed and nothing grew and the soul of Adam Kadmon had no being and was lifeless for it had nothing of its own; nothing that made it unique. Nothing to strive for. Nothing that made it conceive of any moment that could be separate from God where it could make a decision for itself.

For God did not know how to create separation; all God knew was Absolute and perfect. And so there was a stalemate.

Then, one day, as God passed over the waters of the Earth and observed the glories of creation, something caught the Holy One's attention. It was an oyster with its shell open on the sands at the bottom of the sea. But it was not the oyster itself that drew the Holy One; it was the pearl within it; silver and purple and milky and shining and smooth.

God spoke to the oyster who carried this pearl and said: 'O Oyster, I give you the greetings of this perfect day and I beg you to tell me, what is that which is inside your shell? For I know that I made you and, for certain, I did not make that.'

And the oyster looked at God and said, humbly, 'My Lord and my Delight, it is a pearl that I made myself. I hope that it does not displease you.'

'Displease me?' said God in surprise. 'How could anything displease me? All that is, is of me and all of me is perfection. But how come you created this pearl, O Oyster? I have seen no angel, nor archangel, nor animal, nor fish, nor bird, nor human create in this world of paradise but you.'

'Well, my Lord and my Delight,' said the oyster, 'I opened my shell to drink and a grain of sand—of perfect sand—flowed in with the water. And it caused me to be uncomfortable.

'I tried to expel it but I could not do so. So I covered it with a part of myself to make it smooth and comfortable instead of irritating. Now I take pleasure in it instead of pain. Is it not beautiful?'

'Beautiful?' said God. 'It is more than beautiful. It is the most wonderful thing that I have ever seen. Thank you, O Oyster, you are my teacher and I am truly grateful.'

Then the Holy One spent time in contemplation, for the new knowledge that the oyster had given was a treasure which required full enjoyment. And then, God made a decision and knew that it was very good.

The Elohim moved to the place where the man and the woman lived in peace and harmony with themselves and with the creatures and he called them to him and he spoke to them.

'Adam,' he said. 'Eve. The greetings of this perfect day to you. I have something to tell you. Do you see that tree over there?'

The man and the woman greeted the Holy One in turn, and in great happiness, and they looked over there and surely enough there was a tree—a new tree—which they had not seen before. It was tall and elegant and it carried luscious-looking fruits. They laughed for they had great joy in anticipation and they knew how much they would enjoy those fruits.

'You are not to eat of the tree,' said Yahveh Elohim. 'Not one fruit. Never.'

Now the man and the woman had never heard such a command before. All the Elohim's previous words had been 'yes' to them. They did not understand.

'It looks good,' said the man, perplexed. He felt uncomfortable and he did not know what was happening to him.

'This is our country,' said the woman. 'Everything here is ours to enjoy.'

'Not that,' said Yahveh. And the Elohim's heart melted with compassion for his creations for he saw that they experienced distress at his command. But the Holy One also knew, with the greatest of joy, that what the oyster had taught was true.

'You can do anything else,' said the Holy One. 'Anything. But do not eat of that tree.'

And Yahveh Elohim left the man and the woman alone to consider.

'Now,' said my mother. 'Come back for a moment into our home and think. And tell me, Deborah, what would you have done if you were Eve and you had been given such a very strange command.'

'Left the tree alone?' I said cautiously.

Imma laughed. 'I doubt it,' she said. 'What did you do when I made those honey cakes last week and left them by the hearth to cool?'

I blushed. 'I only took one,' I said shamefacedly.

'And you, Yeshua?' said Mother, looking at my brother. 'How many did you take?'

'Me?' said Yeshua. 'Me? I didn't even know they were there! Besides, you didn't tell me not to!'

We all laughed.

'Imagine then,' said Imma. 'Imagine that there was a tree with the most delicious fruit on it in our garden and I told you not to eat any. A tree with hundreds of fruit; so many that I would never know that one or two had gone. What would you do then?'

'Be good to start with. And then eat just one,' Yeshua said.

I nodded. I wouldn't have dared confess it on my own; but if Yeshua had already told the truth it was safe to acknowledge it. 'Anybody would,' I said. 'It's not that we want to be bad … it's just … how could it hurt anyone if we only ate one or two?'

Imma smiled at me. 'I know,' she said. 'The temptation would be just too great. Well, I'll tell you a secret—in fact I'll tell you two. I had one of those hot honey cakes too, even though I'd forbidden myself to do so. And the other secret is that the Holy One knew full well that Adam and Eve would eat from that tree.'

'Yes, of course,' said Yeshua with satisfaction. 'God wanted them to create a pearl.'

'Exactly,' said Mother. 'Would you like to hear the rest of the story?'

We nodded and settled back down at her feet. I sighed, for these times with just the three of us before the others came home were always my favourite moments.

The Holy One left Adam and Eve in the Garden with the tiny grain of sand that he had slipped inside their minds and waited patiently for the moment that they decided to act to create their own lives.

The Elohim knew immediately that it happened; for Adam Kadmon's soul quickened and life surged into it. The Divine Child began to grow at last.

But the Holy One also knew that every tiny part of Adam Kadmon would have to know of grit for the baby to thrive so Yahveh steeled the Elohim's heart and returned to see the humans and told them that it was now time for them to leave the world of paradise and to be born into a lower world of physical life and death. There, they would have to make choices every moment of every day and, through their choices, they would become unique and different. And their belief in their separation from God would cause them to choose always whether to seek the Holy One or to turn away.

As they left the Garden to take on their coats of skin and live in the physical world as we do now, Eve was carrying a twig from that wonderful tree in her hand. It was a piece of twig that came off when she pulled at the fruit and it had a couple of leaves on it.

And as she left, she bent down and planted that twig in the ground so that it would grow, tall and mighty, becoming a Tree of Life that could show all of humanity the way back home.

My mother told us this story every year of my childhood and I taught it myself to my son and to my daughter. And at the end of the story I also add the words that Imma always used whenever we questioned what she had said:

'I don't know if it happened and I don't know if it didn't happen. But I know that the story is true.'

Her name was Miriam. She was not my blood mother as she was Yeshua's but my own blood mother died when I was six and from the day that Imma and I met, I knew that I was her child.

She died last spring. I didn't know the day and it is easy to be imaginative in hindsight, yet I can remember stopping for no reason one afternoon while I walked from the Serapeum to the harbour to see what catch had come in with Kasaki's blue fishing boat. I paused by the waterside of Alexandria's great harbour and looked out, past the great lighthouse to where another distant fishing boat dipped its sails across the horizon. Imma's face came into my mind; a drop of comfort that I had not known I needed slid through me and, for a strange reason, I thought of the story of the pearl and for a moment I saw myself telling it to my own daughter—a daughter that I didn't have; a daughter whom I could name Marguerita—pearl.

I carried the thought for a moment, idly, feeling pleasure in it and then dismissed it—I was already too old for childbearing and, in any case, had been warned, by Imma herself, never to conceive again after my son Luke's birth. I always took great care for I loved my husband deeply and our life together was passionate so there was no thought of a daughter in reality.

But even in dismissing it, I wondered where that thought had come from and why. I was always quite fey and I had learnt to notice such moments in my life of adventure. It was six years since I had seen Imma and very little news reached us from any Eastern port.

John wrote to tell me of her death. That was kind. The letter took seven months to reach us and travelled via Rhodos and Kreta and Apollonius had to pay six whole drachmas to the ship's captain to gain custody of it, not to mention a tip for the messenger.

He brought it home to me in the early evening of a cool autumn day and handed it to me unopened before he had given me his usual greeting and kiss. He knew the rare missives from my homeland were momentous.

I cried as I read and my husband stood with one hand on my shoulder to offer comfort. She had died in her sleep, John wrote, and she had spoken of James, Salome, Yeshua and me only the previous night. She had been talking to John's grandson and telling him the story of Adam and Eve and the pearl and how she used to tell it to us, so many years ago.

'She was a good woman,' said my husband and I looked up at him, my eyes swimming with tears. Of course, he had met her all those years ago in Jerusalem and she had given her blessing to our marriage. Another lifetime; another world.

I bowed my head in acknowledgment and then stood and brushed my dress down and rearranged my *palla* over my hair. We had guests for dinner that night and there was work to be done.

There is an ancient curse: 'May you live in interesting times.'

I have lived in interesting times.

I was the adopted sister of a Jewish prophet who was crucified. He was a great teacher of the mystical tradition and his work continues after his death. My husband's name was Judah and he was Yeshua's best friend. Some stories circulate nowadays that he betrayed his friend. It is not true; I know for I was there but that story has been written elsewhere.

A year after Judah's death I married Apollonius, a centurion, later elected to senatorial class and now an official in the legislature of Alexandria. He knew my brother for Yeshua had healed Apollonius's son Vintillius in Kfar-Nahum. Yeshua said he had never met anyone with such faith, not even in all Israel.

Luke is not his blood son, just as I was not Miriam's blood daughter. I never knew who his father was. It could have been Judah or it could have been one of a group of Roman soldiers, including Vintillius, on the night of Yeshua's crucifixion. That is past; Luke is our son.

We live in Alexandria; I am a herbalist and a scholar. We once lived in Rome but Apollonius was not popular with the Emperor Gaius Caligula and we were glad to come back to Alexandria. That also has been written of elsewhere.

How my daughter Sarah came to be conceived, I will never know.

She made her presence known one day while I was walking with Philo to the Alexandriana for a meeting of Platonists and Merkabah teachers. Very few—if any—women were permitted in the Serapeum, let alone the great mother library by the harbour side. Philo thought little of women in general and wholeheartedly disapproved of learned women in particular. His brother was

Alabarch of Alexandria so he was a powerful man with influence who had done much to alleviate the lot of the Jews in Alexandria. In Jewish society, on the edge of which Apollonius and I hovered respectfully, he was unacknowledged King. One of our 'true' king Agrippa's daughters had even been married to one of Philo's sons.

He would no more have allowed his wife, Giacinta, to have learnt to read as to permit her to attend any of our meetings at the library. And to be fair, Giacinta thought such meetings a time-wasting self-indulgence in a world where there was bread to bake, fish to gut and grill and grandchildren to raise. But I had earned my scholar's privileges through my blood, my education and my beliefs and, in fact, Philo regarded me as one of his teachers. He had no knowledge of Hebrew, which Yeshua had taught me to speak and write, and he loved to compare his research with me. In turn, he instructed me in Greek and Etruscan philosophy and we were fast friends, enjoying the merging of traditions and faiths within the mystical structure of the Jewish Merkabah.

Walking along the colonnades and dodging in and out of the market-day crowds heading for the evening's races, we were discussing the *Kallimachos*—the self-castrated priest/priestesses of the cult of Cybele in Rome.

We had begun with a comfortable argument over the life and re-birth tradition of gods and goddesses and were comparing Yeshua's death and resurrection with the Cybele-Attis legend. As usual, we were being far from respectful of the older traditions— as with Isis and Osiris and so many other resurrection stories there was rather too much incest for Philo's taste and I enjoyed leading him into his ego's prejudices before suggesting that the symbology was more important than the reality. Even so, the need for the repeating myth century after century—and our own knowledge of its physical reality within our lifetimes—was always a source of great fascination to us.

The conversation moved on to the ecstatic priests of Cybele who dressed as women and 'pranced' said Philo. 'Pranced is the only word you can use' through the streets of Rome.

'Our mutual friend Paul has been forced to ban all the women in his new Christian cult from speaking, let alone go bare-headed to their meetings,' he said. 'Romans are now having sport in killing the Kallimachos on sight, they are considered such an abomination and, according to my sources, Paul is afraid that the Christian women will meet a similar fate through misunderstanding.'

'He would probably do the same in any case,' I said. '*You* don't approve of women speaking or going uncovered. Having met Paul and knowing a little of his attitude towards his ex-wife, I can't see him being liberal with women.'

'Ah, but you forget the people he is attracting,' said Philo. A strange feeling in my gut caused me to place my hand there. Probably indigestion, I thought, walking on. 'Slaves, ex-prisoners, rejects, renegades, the unwanted, the unappreciated, the unwashed.'

'You exaggerate!' I said, slightly taken aback by his vehemence.

'I don't my dear,' said Philo. 'New religions which promise freedom and do not require you to follow strict rules are bound to attract searchers for immediate bliss. People want an easy answer and Paul is giving them just that. Would your brother approve of what he is doing?'

'That's not a fair question,' I said. 'For a start, I don't know what they are doing and anyway, Yeshua had no intention of starting any new religion. He didn't set down any new ground rules or anything like that. I'm sure he would say there was nothing wrong with the old ones! I know Paul is said to have had that revelation on the road to Damascus—and he may well have done so—but the rest of it, he seems to be making up as he goes along.'

'My point exactly,' said Philo. 'You went to one of their meetings when you were in Rome. You know what they say about your first husband. Deborah—what is it?'

I had stopped listening and was standing stock still with one hand out on the base of the statue of Neptune. The other rested on my stomach which, I noticed for the first time, was becoming slightly taut. I believed myself to be somewhere around my fortieth year and had experienced all the symptoms of an early onset of the woman's change since the previous spring. I had assumed that I was just getting fatter. Even though this change was a little earlier than the norm for most women who had survived childbirth, my feminine constitution had never worked well and it had been a relief when menstruation had stopped. I was taking stinging nettle tincture for night sweats and red clover for nutrients but suddenly I remembered that red clover boosted fertility.

'Oh Vesta!' I swore. 'Philo, I'm pregnant. I can feel her quickening.'

My friend reacted swiftly. We were just next to the back door of the Alexandriana where the food was delivered to the kitchens. He guided me through the gate into the courtyard with his hand under my arm and sat me down on the low stone wall where Achmed's donkey had his lean-to stable and the chickens laid their eggs.

Achmed, our favourite of the library's stewards, would know what to do, I could almost hear Philo muttering to himself. Hot tisanes; compresses. Achmed would know, in the absence of any other women.

'Philo, I'm not ill,' I said. 'I'm just shocked.'

'But my dear, you need help.' He patted me nervously. 'I won't be a moment.' And then he was gone, leaving me reeling from this strange knowledge as the donkey, used to her treats, quested gently at me with her hairy, rubbery nose.

Sarah quivered again inside me. Sarah? I would never call a daughter Sarah! Sarah might have been the mother of our people but she had doubted God and seethed with jealousy over her handmaiden's son. Marguerita if this were really true—but not Sarah!

Achmed was there with his gentle, laconic style before I had time for further thought.

'Come with me, Madam,' he said. 'Are you well? Even so, we need to rest you a moment so as not to frighten the men.'

I smiled at his terminology. I liked Achmed. He didn't say silly things but he knew the truth about life. He realised, as I did, that my outburst had been embarrassing for Philo and anything to do with feminine things was anathema in the Alexandriana.

'I am well, Achmed,' I said. 'Just shocked.'

'Understandably Madam,' he said. 'Come sit with me in the pantry and I will instruct the gentlemen that you will be up in five minutes once you have had a healing tisane.'

'To cure me of being horribly female,' I giggled. Suddenly I was in a very good mood.

'Exactly.' The perfect servant's cheek dimpled and the light in his eyes flickered as if dancing as he bowed me in through the door to the kitchens.

Treats from the great library's kitchens were a glory in the lives of we Alexandrians, so few of us cooked ourselves at home, and Achmed's cronies excelled themselves with home-cooked sweets and cakes as well as savoury nibbles that tantalised the tongue with spices and herbs. I did have cooking facilities in the home that we shared with Apollonius's extended family but even so, my cooking was not greatly admired—it was peasant food from Galilee as Luke so often reminded me! We ate out much of the time or had food delivered.

If I were a true mother I would tell you that the meeting passed my by, unattended to due to the miracle of new life. In fact, I stuffed this impossible baby's existence into the back of my mind and, after placating my colleagues by taking in with me a plate of Achmed's baklava and seed biscuits, I enjoyed a rousing argument with Aristophanos and Philo. Their interpretation of Logos as a way of accounting for creation and the relationship between the infinite God and the finite world included the insertion of a whole realm of beings and potencies to bridge the gap between creator and creation and, although I could see their point, I thought it was dangerous ground in balancing Jewish and Greek belief.

'Deborah, is this safe? Because I will not have you risk your life. You of all women know if enough can be done to ensure your safety.' Apollonius, loving man that he was, was more concerned for his ageing wife's health than any additional heir to carry on his line.

'I don't know,' I said honestly. 'We have both always taken precautions that were so dosed to be on the edge of danger simply because we feared for my life. So if this child has come through despite that, then she means to come.'

'She?' Apollonius was alert to my intuition and rarely denied it. 'Well, if so, we shall call her Apollonia Marguerita Miriam.' You'd like that, wouldn't you?'

'No you won't,' Sarah sang, her voice like tiny bells in a breath of wind. I heard her but said nothing, just smiling at my husband in acknowledgment.

'What must we do to ensure your safety?' my husband went on. 'Your knowledge now is far greater than it was when Luke was born. There must be much that can be done. Modern medicine too. Luke will be able to tell us!'

I grimaced at the thought of my son's reaction. Not only was Luke approaching an age where the idea of sex itself was embarrassing but the idea of his elderly parents indulging in it was going to be repulsive to him. I sighed. 'We'll wait a little longer before we tell him, I think,' I said. 'There is still time for the baby to miscarry. I shall go and see Constanzia and see what is best to be done.'

'And you will stop taking the preventative herbs?'

'Oh yes.' And I will note the power of red clover too, I thought rather sheepishly.

'A Pearl,' said Apollonius, who had heard the story on the evenings when I told Luke. 'A pearl in our lives. So unexpected. When do you think she might be due? I'll cast a chart.

'Five months?' I said. 'I really don't know.'

A pearl, I thought as we made ready for bed that night and Apollonius was extra gentle and loving. Why do we need a pearl? There isn't any grit.

Two

Never were the miracles of the herb garden that I shared with Constanzia at the back of our apartment more apparent to me than that winter. My friend dosed me every week—and sometimes every day. It took some time to persuade the volatile Spaniard that it was the right thing for me to go ahead with the pregnancy but, when we had debated exactly what had gone wrong around Luke's birth, we realised that it was not the pregnancy that was the problem; it was the birth.

'And so it is with so many mothers,' said Constanzia. 'And those young and supple unlike you, my ancient one! So, we must build your strength and your blood and do everything that strengthens you. You may have to have a puny baby; no matter. If she wants to come, she will come. But she will not take you away!'

I should have been afraid but Luke's birth seemed a lifetime ago and a healthy quickening body knows how to dull the senses. And the soul of the baby was very clear and very strong and I knew that she meant me no harm.

'Who are you?' I asked her once. Could she be Imma coming back so soon?

No answer but a bright, excited silence.

'Why now?' I asked. 'What grit must you cover?'

'I am Sarah, not Marguerita,' she said and danced around me so that my whole body felt suffused with rainbow colours.

The only difficult part of the pregnancy was Luke's attitude. For eight years he had been an only child and, no matter how Apollonius and I tried to explain to him that we had not planned to have another baby, he was outraged. He thought it was all my fault and his attitude towards me was often openly hostile. Part of that might well have been the natural desire for separation that a boy experiences from his mother as he begins to grow up but there was a streak of unkindness which I found very painful. Luke always hated change and had been miserable when we moved to Rome and, again, when we moved back to Alexandria. Now he thought Alexandria provincial and missed his friends and his tutor from Rome and I know he worshipped his father too much to place any blame on him.

The boys he had begun to mix with in Alexandria's medical school were all older than he and, true to Greek fashion, despised all women. This was perfect to fuel the fashionable flames against me.

'It is unfitting for a woman to be with child at your age,' he would say over and over again. 'I am ashamed of you. It is bad enough that you tell me that you do 'God's work' and you study. You know perfectly well that our ways are strange to my friends and no woman should be doing the work of the gods. That's men's work.'

All I could do was bite my tongue, be loving but firm and hope that the storm would weather its way out. I was not going to rise to the bait for Luke was not going to listen to reason and I did not care to waste my breath.

I had never been a naturally maternal woman and maybe that helped. I loved Luke, and I enjoyed his company when he was willing to give it, but he was not the reason for my existence. So, despite that uncomfortable aspect to life, I was still happy even though the growth of the child inside me was tiring and limiting.

Our accommodation was fairly cramped for we now lived in a smaller apartment than our original home in the family-owned complex, having moved away and given up our original space to younger relatives. But we had enough money to travel out to the forested areas to the south when we needed some peace and quiet—and I was always happy in the silence and coolness of the great library, transcribing texts or just reading and learning. There was a welcome in the stillness of acceptance of scholars of the great works. Sarah liked it there too and, with a wisp of guilt, I began to love her and to rejoice when I felt her soul linking in to its temple and dancing in and out of my body. She had a way of lifting my spirits with a whisper of silver. It had taken me nearly a year to love Luke.

Apollonius was busy, continually working with the other Senators and religious leaders trying to calm the ever-volatile racial outbursts and fights in our cosmopolitan city. It warmed my heart to see how gently he dealt with the Jews, Egyptians and Greeks at each other's throats from custom and ever-fed resentments. He studied, too, at the library and we both enjoyed our happy routine of meetings and discussions with the 'hidden Alexandria' of the inner faiths.

Two people we did greatly miss—our old friends Rizpah, Lucius and their children. Rizpah had travelled with me from Judaea and was like a sister to me. She had once been married to Paul of Tarsus—in the days when he called himself Saul—but he had divorced her because he disapproved of her fervour for Yeshua's teaching and healing. In those days, Saul was a very orthodox Jew and Rizpah never was that.

She was a tall woman; fifteen years younger than me; well built and handsome with striking grey eyes and straight, dark hair. She loved to learn as I did and together we outraged the disciples in the days of miracles after Yeshua's death and resurrection. Once it was certain that we were not welcome there, it was a terrible step to leave behind our home and our life to come with Apollonius to Alexandria but Rizpah was always brave and I took strength in relying on her.

Rizpah and Lucius had become very much a part of Alexandrian society and, in fact, with the birth of her two children, she had put her studies to one side. We had even quarrelled a little over that but, even so, our parting when Lucius was posted abroad was a sad and lonely time. We believed that they were now in Gallia, in a port called Massalia. Sometimes a brief message would reach us or a little news from someone known to Philo. I thought of my friend often and sent her thoughts and prayers. I believed that despite the family pressures she had, after all, managed to maintain her interest in the faith and that she was happy because one fragment I heard was of a woman with a holy scroll who was teaching other women in the Roman settlement about the one God. They called that woman Maria or Magdala and that's how I knew that it must be Rizpah. It could not be Magdalene herself for her body lay hidden in the tomb from which her Lord and Saviour had risen, at peace with him and herself for many years now.

Rizpah had taken with her a copy of a scroll written by Magdalene after Yeshua's death and she would be using that in her teaching and studies. It was no surprise that people might confuse her with the woman we had both loved so much.

Just after the festival of Saturnalia, a rumour began to spread through the streets and markets of Alexandria. Word was out that there was a plot to kill the Emperor. Gaius Caligula's initial popularity had faded rapidly and some people now thought him quite mad. Although most people discounted talk of assassination plots as idle thinking, this particular rumour was surprisingly persistent. Some wondered if an attempt had already taken place and we had not heard of it. Others speculated that Caligula was already dead. People took to standing on the wharf when a ship from Rome was expected so as to be the first to hear the news. The Procurator became agitated and an announcement was made that those who continued to spread this rumour would be taken, in chains, to Rome to face the Emperor himself.

As always happens at such times, the rumour simply went underground. Apollonius was interested for he thought it must have been started by some prediction within the occult section of the city. There were many people practising strange kinds of necromancy and witchcraft and both clairvoyance and prophecy were commonplace both inside and outside of the temples if you knew were to look. We tended to avoid such areas for, although there was a certain amount of knowledge there, it was unusual for it to be being used for the good of all or in service of the Holy One. With some exceptions the magic was generally used to further people's desires and ambitions. Love potions were common and what predictive powers there were used to determine business deals and marriage contracts rather than leading people towards the Divine Plan for their life and teaching them that they had free will to direct their path as they chose.

Nevertheless, Apollonius took to visiting several groups, particularly consulting the star-gazers among them. His own study of this science had been thorough, as all his dealings were, and at first he came home from his searching horrified at what he saw as sharp practice and faulty reckoning. However, he did discover two men who had the higher good at heart and, through them, he discovered that the source of the rumour might well have come from the study of the stars. Some aspect of the heavens was, apparently, indicating a major change or death and Apollonius decided to study the matter further.

I was slightly nervous at this decision though I knew him to be a man of discretion and that all the work he did himself on the signs in the heavens was within the comparative safety of the great library. There were about twenty men who gathered there regularly to study the stars and, together in secret, they began to consult and cast charts for Caligula's fate.

When Apollonius told me that the rumour had a foundation I touched his lips with my finger and we agreed never to speak of it again outside the library while Caligula lived. I thought we were safe. I thought that all those in the library could be trusted.

Life continued happily and, when the streets were quiet from the now habitual race riots, peacefully. After the first tiring months I bloomed, losing my angular looks and gawky walk; my hair obeyed the oils with which the servants dressed it for once and my skin darkened and became rosy with health. Apollonius was proud of his beautiful, mature and feminine wife whose sharp tongue was stilled by the inner wonder of a healthy pregnancy and more laughter entered our lives than for many years. There was no grit to speak of.

The governor's guard came for Apollonius in the heart of the night in the eighth month of my pregnancy. The pounding on the door woke everyone in the villa and the portal was open before anyone could work out what was wrong.

The splitting of timber broke into my dreams and nightmare took hold from the moment of waking as soldiers surrounded our bed and seized my husband by force. My bulk prevented me from doing much but 'No! No! No!' I screamed, hitting out at them and spitting like a cat possessed by terror. It took two of them to hold me and one of the soldiers must have been an angel in disguise. 'Madam, you already have a son,' he said. 'You can do nothing for your husband but think of your son and the child you are carrying.'

Luke was standing beside him, white-faced and held tightly by one of the soldiers. At a nod from his superior, the soldier let my son go. He ran into my arms; still a child at a time of crisis. His father looked back at us both in despair as the soldiers led him from the room. The look engraved itself on my heart.

I watched until he was lost from sight and a great stillness descended through the fear. I looked up at the guard. 'Let us go,' I said. It was not a request but a statement using the element of power that Yeshua had taught me so many years before. Speak as if it were true and it is true.

The officer bowed slightly. 'We will leave now,' he said. 'But we will return in the morning for I have orders to take all the family of this man. If I see you again, I will take you too. And your son. Be warned.'

Then they left, all of them, vanishing through the shattered door with just the sound of echoing footsteps fading away and I was standing there, bulky and shaking in my shift, with tears running down my face and Luke's forlorn figure holding tightly around as much of me as he could reach.

We stood in silence for a while. No neighbour nor member of the family stirred; they knew better.

Then: 'It's *your* fault,' cried Luke, hitting out with his fists. I caught those flailing arms easily enough and held them firmly by the wrists. It seemed as though I was watching myself from a distance as I shook him just enough to startle him and then knelt down, drawing him as tightly as I could into my arms. Luke resisted fiercely for a minute and the baby lurched within me. He felt that movement and then relaxed, sobbing and nestling into my embrace as he cried out his shock and fear. The soldier was right. I had Luke; I had Sarah. I had to go on living whatever the cost.

'Why?' I called silently to the Lord. 'Why this? Have we not done enough? Why this cruelty? Why?'

It's the grit, came the answer—and rage filled me from head to toe. I cursed the name of the Lord and then I put tears away for later. This was time to act not weep.

'Pack quickly,' I said, through gritted teeth. 'We each can take one sheet-full of possessions with us. We have to go or our lives are in danger.'

'What do we take?' Luke stood hopelessly.

'Clothes; anything light of value; any gold or silver; any precious stones,' I said thinking quickly. 'Your sandals; your scrolls for school. Cups for water. My box of herbs and medicines. That will do, I think.'

We crept out of the house together. For a moment, I considered knocking on Constanzia's door but I did not know what time we had—or what spies were watching. And I did not want to implicate or embarrass her.

Where could we go? It was not yet dawn. What would we do?

'The library,' I said. 'The Alexandriana. The donkey's stable. We can hide there. Achmed will help us when he comes to work in the morning. He can get a message to Philo.'

The labour pains started before we left the villa and I stood still in the street rigid with shock as I felt my waters break. Now? When I had no friends nor family and I was alone with my son? Now? How much more cruel could this be?

I set my jaw and began to walk again. I had faced worse. Luke looked up at me frightened. 'Has the baby started?' he said.

'Yes,' but there's plenty of time yet,' I said smiling at him reassuringly. 'We'll get there.'

I will not die! I said to God and all the angels. It was not a prayer but a command. I could not die now and leave my son.

No death, they said. *Life.* But I know how easy it is to delude yourself.

Perhaps walking is the best thing a woman in labour can do, for Sarah was born incredibly swiftly and easily in the straw of the donkey's stall as the beast stood sulkily by the far wall, its ears twitching with curiosity and offence. My boy, too young by far, helped me through the birthing; his face bleached with concentration and fear. He broke the lock on the kitchen door and found me water and cloths and he cleared the blood-soaked straw as I lay, slumped around the tiny mucus-covered morsel who had slipped out of me so early and who still took her breath through my body for long moments before take in the air for herself.

It was Luke who cleaned her and who, grimacing, cut the umbilical cord with a vegetable-cutting knife once the placenta had birthed itself. He heated water for me too and stole milk for me to drink from the cool shelves inside the walls of the well in the courtyard. By the time Achmed had arrived and found us, Luke was deeply, exhaustedly asleep in the straw, holding his sister as if his life depended upon it.

If they survive at all, the family of those arrested by the city guard become invisible as fast as they can. Keep heads low; don't draw any attention; deny all knowledge. Jobs disappear; friends look right through them on the street. Homes are repossessed and lives fall apart. There were strangers living in our apartment within a week; we no longer existed.

Of course I turned to Philo and, even though he was brother of the Alabarch, he found us shelter in rooms at the back of his home. Giacinta cooked us food and did all that Sarah needed with all the natural affection of a born grandmother. I grieved, panicked and tried to take stock and decide what to do. The confusion of thought from new motherhood and the fear for Apollonius's life created a mad woman in me for quite some while and all I could do was rest and nurse my daughter—and force myself to eat. Luke wanted to run to the government building every day and bang on the door to try and get information but

Philo soon persuaded us that all that would do would be to irritate those who might be able to help and add to the risk of my being arrested too. What could be found out would be found out by Philo's brother and brought to us as soon as it could.

Even without Luke's anger and grief that time would have been terrible but my son's anguish added to the pain. The father he adored had been taken away. To add to that, he was trapped in someone else's house and all his pride in his rank and freedom was gone in one swift moment. But Apollonius and I had taught him well and his manners were exemplary, in public at least—and through God's mercy, he now had a baby sister to take care of. Giacinta was very wise when it came to children and, without a direct word, she let Luke know that he *did* still have status; that Sarah and I (but mostly Sarah) relied entirely on him as the head of the family. Once the first shock was over, he found love in the tiny hand that would hold his finger tightly and he remembered that strength could be drawn from God and babies if not from man. I was proud of him.

It was Luke who first got news and brought it back to us, running into the house and calling, wild-eyed and urgent with the knowledge. 'Mother! Mother! He's alive! He's still alive!' he cried breathlessly, half laughing and half crying and so crazed with the news that he bumped into all the furniture. The boy had caught sight of an old acquaintance of ours outside the government house when he was on his way home from medical school. I had insisted he kept attending for the fees for that term had been paid and he had every right to the knowledge available. The man he met was Constanzia's husband who recognised him and had the kindness to stop and talk with him. He was able to tell him quietly that Apollonius was well and being sent to Rome the following morning to Caligula's own judgement for predicting the Emperor's death.

Luke was ecstatic with the joy of any child with hope; I, on the other hand, heard the death sentence proclaimed.

'What do I do now?' I asked my friend Philo, that kindly and indefatigable philosopher. 'I can't think straight. All I want to do is to go with him, just to be with him but I can't.'

'No, you can't,' said Philo. 'You must stay here and pray and wait. One thing: you can write, now, to Herod Agrippa in Rome and ask him to intercede for your husband. He is your friend and his daughter is married to my son. He does have influence. If we act fast we can get that letter onto the same boat as the one carrying Apollonius. It's the best we can do for now. I, too, will send to Rome for the best and fastest information. There are ways and means.'

'Should I not go to Herod Agrippa myself?'

'No,' said Philo firmly. 'Deborah, use your head. You are not strong enough; you do not have the resources. In any case, he may not be in Rome. Even with the swiftest ship and the fastest recovery, you could not get there in time. Don't forget too that you could put yourself in danger by returning to Rome. Luke and his sister do not need to lose you too.'

He spoke sense and I knew it. I controlled myself and wrote an impassioned plea to Agrippa and another to Cypres, his wife, asking for their intercession. I had saved the life of their daughter Mariamne and they had fond feelings towards me. If they received my letter—and Philo's missive too—and if they *could* act, I knew that they would. But they were not all-powerful and Caligula was incredibly dangerous. Even his favourites trod warily for his wrath was legendary and lethal.

Some terrible fatalistic feeling kept coming over me that perhaps Apollonius's life was forfeit in return for either mine or his daughter's. I knew in my heart that that thought must be ridiculous but there is a deeper source than the heart of such fears and they hold fast to the soul.

That night I railed against God and my husband. Why had Apollonius allowed his curiosity to lead him into looking into the rumours? If only he had not, he would still be safe and we would be happy together in our small but comfortable home.

'Why?' I asked again and again. I listened in meditation for the answer. The only one I got clearly was *'so that the works of God can be manifest in the world.'* That made me want to spit.

I also heard *'patience.'* But I am not patient. I know it.

And there was also *'There is a wider plan. Time is not the same to us as it is to you. All things work together for good.'*

I took all three answers to Philo and he reproved me for my doubts. 'You have good clear answers there, Deborah,' he said. 'And we *don't* know the higher plan.'

Philo and his wife were so kind. They let me grieve and concentrated on strengthening me and turning my mind away from blame.

'You don't know that Apollonius would not have been taken even if he had not investigated Caligula's stars,' said Philo. 'This may just be an excuse. He is a good and honest man and such are not liked in government circles. He did not compromise on his beliefs although he did all he could to help others. He gave judgments for and against the rioters; he tried to keep the peace in this city and that alone would make him enemies. It is entirely possible that a plot was laid against him by the Greeks, the Egyptians, a Roman he has offended or even, dear Heaven forbid, a Jew.

'What is important is that he remembers you as strong and brave and that he has that image to call on as well as his faith in the Lord. You and your children must be at the quayside tomorrow morning before dawn, dressed in your best and showing him that you are unharmed and strong and will wait for his return. He may not know if you and Luke are even alive.'

His words made sense. I had not thought of Apollonius's worries about us. Somehow Luke and I managed to snatch some uneasy rest and we were waiting at the wharf before sunrise, standing as near as we dared to the great troop ship.

Philo was with us and he had bribed several of the guard-house servants and the boy porters to try and get a message to a tall, dark Roman in chains. These children were skilled at darting in and out, almost between the legs of the merchants and soldiers, and they loved such a dare as to speak to a prisoner or to call insults to the Romans.

'Please let him see us and know we are safe,' I prayed, standing as tall as I could with Sarah wrapped in my shawl and with one hand on my son's shoulder for mutual support. Luke stood tall and dignified and I had never felt so proud of him as I did that day.

The men came out of the prison block by the harbour's edge. Apollonius was chained but, as his tall figure came in sight, it was obvious that he had not been beaten or tortured. He stood straight and although he seemed dazed by the light he was obviously looking for something in the few moments he had before they took him below.

I waved. Luke waved. Philo waved. He did not see us. Then Sarah took breath and wailed with all the force of a hungry child and he heard her. Amazed, he turned and saw us. He saw that the wife that he loved had survived childbirth; that he had a daughter and that his son stood tall and true.

The love that flooded between our eyes would have to be enough, perhaps forever. I knew from his stance that tears came to his eyes, too, but they would have been tears of joy as well as sadness for he now knew that we were safe, that we would be taken care of and that we loved him.

Philo offered us room in his home for as long as we wanted and I allowed myself another month to recover enough of my senses to be presentable and to think straight. I was lucky in my friends for, although there had been no official contact with anyone back at our home villa, Giacinta had been to see Constanzia and had returned with herbs, potions and strict instructions for a new mother, her baby and the effects of grief and shock. None of Apollonius's own relatives even sought us out. Anyone in disfavour with the Emperor was dead to them too—for their own sake. And their cousin's unconventional Jewish wife had never made friends easily.

I knew I must now, somehow, earn a living for myself and for Luke so that he could finish school and so that I did not go crazy with the waiting for news that could only break my heart.

On the twenty-eighth day I took my courage in both hands, took a litter to the villa and asked to see Constanzia. She was out but expected back quite soon and one of the slaves who knew me was persuaded by a drachma slipped into her willing hand to allow me to wait in the garden which Constanzia and I had shared and nurtured and where we had consulted over potions and remedies.

At first sight of this place where I had been so happy, the ever-present tears of the last weeks threatened to choke me but I kept my mind busy in pretending to show Sarah the plants and identifying their uses to a plainly bored baby.

Constanzia, when she came, greeted me stiffly but kindly and made no reference to the bundle of life in my arms. Walls have ears and, according to the rest of the family, I was dead. She had the grace to hide her curiosity at my temerity in turning up in the place where my husband and I had brought such disgrace until she had offered refreshment and all the slaves had been sent back to their business.

Apollonius's arrest changed Constanzia's rank towards me; she did not have to see me at all. Soldiers and their wives were used to people vanishing from their lives and, even if the ties of friendship were strong, the disgraced were not expected to visit.

Once we had been served with a tisane on the terrace between the house and the garden, I came straight to the point. I knew that my presence there would not be welcome, I said—and Constanzia had the honesty not to contradict me—but I was there to ask her if I might continue to use of the herbs and flowers from the garden to support me in work I would need to seek. She knew that was fair for I had grown them myself and taught her much of what she knew but even so, she did not have to agree for I owned nothing in law.

Constanzia heard me through thoughtfully and drank her tisane. 'Hmmm,' she said. 'Let me hold the baby.'

I passed Sarah over and Constanzia's heart melted as she looked down into the serene blue eyes of the miracle child.

'Beautiful,' she said, my friend returning through the frost.

'Deborah, I'm so relieved, I can't tell you. I thought you were dead. They said you'd been taken and I never thought you would survive in jail without the herbs.'

'It was an easy birth,' I said. 'I was blessed.'

'You were indeed. I will sacrifice to Juno. She is a miracle. I didn't tell you but even with the herbs, I did have doubts that either of you would live—without all this ... Are you nursing her yourself?'

'Yes, no problem with that.'

'Two sacrifices,' said Constanzia, thoughtfully.

I stayed silent as she looked down into the little girl's serene face. Sarah was a peaceful child, undemanding and very still. But, like most babies, she had the ability to charm. And I knew, from her insistence over her name, that she had a will as strong as a princess.

Constanzia and Sarah chatted in baby language while I waited as patiently as I could. My pride was always my weakest point and I found it hard to be a supplicant where I had once been a teacher. I concentrated on keeping fresh tears from my eyes and letting the regular waves of panic that had assailed me since Apollonius had been taken wash away without reacting to them. Holding Sarah always calmed me and, without her in my arms, the difficult feelings threatened to flood me.

'Well,' said Constanzia. 'I think we can help, don't you, baby? What were you thinking of doing, Deborah?'

I reminded her of my past work in the Mikvahs and said I could probably get work in the Jewish quarter and as an apothecary to the wives those who used the library.

'You could work here,' said Constanzia as Sarah's hand curled round her index finger.

'I could?' I was wary but encouraged.

'Yes, I don't see why not,' said Constanzia thoughtfully. 'I shall still do some work for my friends but I don't have the time or the inclination to do more than that and there's certainly a demand. I haven't your energy and I certainly never had your talent or your abilities. I've never had to ask for payment of course but there is no reason why you should not and I can certainly recommend you.'

'What would the others living here now think?'

'That you are my servant.'

I blanched but said nothing. It was true; I would be her servant.

Constanzia went on: 'There's no one but myself and you who uses this garden. The others prefer the atrium for its shade. They probably won't even notice. And even if they do, they will keep their mouths shut if I tell them to do so. All this may be hard for you, Deborah, but for others it is just a nine-day wonder. No one will even remember by the end of the month.'

Hard words. One always thinks that personal tragedies are big but they are not important to the world. I bowed my head.

'I'll have to check with my husband,' Constanzia continued. 'And I'll idly tell a few of the others I have somebody working here but this has always been our own private garden and I don't see there being a problem. The woman who lives in your old apartment—she's called Pulsamilla and her husband is Tertius— is always feeling faint and spoiling dinner parties to get attention, so you should do well from her at least.

'You can charge her but I think it would only be fair for you not to charge anyone else from this house and there may be others I'll ask you to treat for free as well,' she added.

I nodded in agreement, keeping my head down so that the resenting pride did not show. Constanzia was being fair and I knew I could trust her not to abuse that agreement. She stood up. It was time for me to leave.

'I'll tell the servants that you are working for me now and that will be that,' she said. 'It won't be a problem, Deborah. I'm glad to help.'

As I left I hugged her and she returned the embrace with affection. However we both knew that this was the last time we could appear as friends. From now on I was officially a lesser creature and, if she spoke to me at all, I would be wise to call her 'Madam.'

Four weeks later, Sarah died. We had no warning; no presentiment, no idea. She suckled happily that last evening and was sleeping peacefully when I went to bed.

In the morning when I woke, surprised to have achieved a whole night's sleep without her calls for nourishment, I leant over to touch her. The tiny body was still and cold. In the air, there was no echo of the soul that had shone so brightly for such a very short time.

I will write no more of the days that followed but I will write of the exercise that Philo, Luke and I did together that helped to keep us sane enough to live some semblance of a life.

A week after Sarah's burial, after I had sat shivah with Giancola and her family, the three of us met in a small annexe room upstairs in the great library; a room which had been set aside for private ceremonies and which had glass in the windows of different colours so that beautiful light would shine across the walls and floor when the Sun was in the West.

I brought Sarah's swaddling clothes and dressed in my best as if for a party. Luke was resistant to doing the ceremony—he was still so young then—but I insisted and I will always be grateful that I did.

Together, Philo and I sat in silence and then in prayer. Then the three of us, separately, recited the Kaddish, the prayer for the dead. I spoke it in Aramaic, as was traditional, Philo spoke it in Greek as is now customary and Luke recited the half-Kaddish, also known as the orphan's Kaddish, in Hebrew.

The Kaddish is not a prayer of sadness, more a reminder of the glory of God and one of its purposes is said to be to banish feelings of anger or bitterness. These are the words that we used: words I had said for Yeshua, for Judah, both grown men cut down early. But at least they had more than thirty years of life. My daughter had sixty days.

Magnified and sanctified be His great name in the world which He hath created according to His will. May He establish His kingdom during your life and during your days, and during the life of all the house of Israel, even speedily and at a near time, and say ye, Amen. Let His great name be blessed for ever and to all eternity. Blessed, praised and glorified, exalted, extolled and honoured, magnified and lauded be the name of the Holy One, blessed be He; though He be high above all the blessings and hymns, praises and consolations which are uttered in the world; and say ye, Amen. May there be abundant peace from heaven, and life for us and for all Israel; and say ye, Amen. He who maketh peace in his high places, may He make peace for us and for all Israel; and say ye, Amen.

*

There is wisdom in the words for they remind us of eternal life and the grace of God in times when both seem sadly lacking.

Then Philo led us through a guided meditation for the whole of the life that we could have imagined for Sarah. He spoke spontaneously, asking for guidance from angels as to how that life might have been. Luke and I wept unashamedly when he told of her growth from baby to little girl with red hair like mine. How she loved to watch the ships in the harbour and to play with puppies and kittens that she found in the street. How she found a floppy-eared tricolour puppy and made us adopt it for our own.

He spoke of how much Apollonius loved her, when he returned safe from Rome after three years, and how she grew strong and spirited. How Luke would look after her and chide her for her adventurous spirit that got them both into trouble.

He talked us through Sarah's love for an artisan of mixed race called Corinius and how we opposed their marriage until it became apparent that our strong-willed daughter would have her way.

He told us how Apollonius and I helped the young couple to prosper so that they could set up their own home and of the birth of Sarah's daughters Philomena and Ruth.

He took us through a hazier time after Apollonius's and my deaths when Sarah herself grew old and wise and taught the mysteries of the Merkabah herself—strangely he saw her in Judaea and described the place where Joseph Barsabbas, Magdalene and I had lived when Luke was born, although he had never seen it himself. And he told us of her husband's death and her own death at the age of fifty-nine with her daughters and grandchildren around her.

And then he blessed her at her funeral in that distant land and wished her soul well and committed her into the hands of Shekhinah for her return to the higher worlds for the next stage of her journey.

'Sarah Miriam Apollonia, we understand that your life was full in potential in the weeks of your physical existence,' he said. 'We honour your decision to come to us in this world and we honour your decision to leave.

'We hope that we will see you again, in another body, in this world in our lifetime but we accept that you and only you know the perfect passage for your lives.

'We ask you now, as our sister, whole and perfect, if you have a message for any of us, to tell us now what you wish us to know.'

We sat in silence, breathing deeply and waiting for some sign.

I have had many signs in my life; words from the great messenger, Gabriel, insights and knowings. But never had I hoped more for an answer than at that moment.

'Be still,' I told my mind, for I knew that my thoughts would block any words that might come.

Then I saw her, inside my mind. Full-grown and beautiful, I saw my mother, Miriam. '*A life for a life and given in love*,' she said. That was all.

After a few more moments, while I wrestled with what that might mean, Philo spoke again, inviting us to say anything we might wish to say.

'I didn't want her to come,' said Luke. 'I didn't want her. Is that why she died?'

I resisted the mother's urge to deny and comfort and looked to Philo instead. He was the father figure now and his words would be what a young man needed to hear.

'You did not want a rival,' said Philo. 'But you did not want anything bad to happen either. Without knowledge of who Sarah would be, you could not see good in her coming. But it was never Sarah that you did not want; it was the idea of another child.

'When your sister came, you were as much a part of her birth as your mother was. You will be a superb apothecary because of Sarah. And when she was here, you loved her. Some part of you will always love her.

'None of your thoughts, great and powerful though they are, are powerful enough to have taken the life from another human being. Sarah died because she had work to do elsewhere. It was not because of anything that you or your mother may have done wrong.'

There was silence. Then Luke nodded and wiped his eyes. He sat up straighter and took my hand. We exchanged slightly watery smiles.

'Did you receive anything?' Philo asked me. I wanted to hold my tongue but I thought it better to speak and own up to the fears in my mind.

I told them in very few words what I had sensed and added: 'Was it my life that was given instead of Sarah's? That is hard to know, if so.'

'Perhaps,' said Philo. 'But Sarah can return and grow again. If we lost you now then it would take many years before you too could return to do your work in the world. If Sarah had to give her life to save yours, why come at all? That is not logical, Deborah, and the Lord is apt to be quite logical.'

I wasn't sure I agreed with that but it turned the corner of my mouth in a smile and broke the energy.

We ended the little service with a few words expressing our love for Sarah and our hopes that we would see her again—and added prayers for Apollonius's safety.

Only as Luke and I left the annexe to walk home together, leaving Philo to attend a meeting of Platonists, did my son venture to mention the other, obvious link.

'It could be Father's life,' he said. 'I didn't want to lose Sarah, but oh, Mother, imagine if it were Father's life!'

'Well let's hope that it is,' I said.

Never have I forgotten to bless and pray for Constanzia even in the years after Luke and I left Alexandria. She spread the word as only those wonderfully deceptively lazy women can. She looked languid and bored with life—and she was!—but when she wanted something done, it would be done and she wanted me to succeed. I am quite sure the first clients only came because she coerced them but my skills were good and the healing power I had learnt so many years ago now was still there and clients returned in their dozens.

Work was the only thing that kept me vaguely sane in those dark days.

Within two months I was able to rent a small but respectable apartment for Luke and myself with a tiny stove which meant I could cook and save money by not always having to buy from the street stalls. Achmed made a point of over-feeding me every time I managed to get to a meeting at the library—and he would look after Luke for me too if I was working late and he needed a meal. I was so blessed with my friends.

After pressure from Philo, the college even agreed to allow me to pay them in instalments for Luke's tuition so that he could continue with his studies. Had he not been such a bright and sensible boy they might not have wanted him to continue but Luke was always popular and, although he had developed a healthy self-esteem and a fairly emphatic temper, he was a good student and respected those who had something to teach.

We needed that solid foundation for, four months later, news came in. Not the news we had been dreading but tidings that turned the world upside-down nonetheless. Caligula was dead. He had been assassinated by members of the Praetorian Guard on his way back from a play. His uncle Claudius was now Emperor of Rome and we must wait to see what his plans for the Empire might be.

At first the news gave us hope. Perhaps the ship carrying Apollonius had been delayed and not reached Italia before the Emperor died. Perhaps it had arrived but there had not been enough time for Apollonius to appear before Caligula. If he were in prison, perhaps Claudius would free him as part of an amnesty.

Slowly but surely news continued to filter through. Names of some of the conspirators became known though the fate of most of them was uncertain. Most people said that they must be executed or it would look as though Claudius supported people who killed Emperors—a most dangerous stance. One name struck us to the bone, although it was hard to realise that there was room for more grief. Lucius Norbanus of the Praetorian Guard, one of the conspirators, had been struck down and killed during the melée following Caligula's death. Lucius Norbanus? But Rizpah and Lucius were in Gallia! Why would they be in Rome? Surely it must be some other Tribune?

I heard nothing from Herod Agrippa and neither did Philo. We could only assume that either he had decided not to write or that he and Cypres had returned to Judaea. It was possible that the letter had got lost between the ship and the city itself; no one would ever know. But news did come in, eventually. One of Philo's contacts sent word to us three months after Caligula's death. The message was short and to the point. Apollonius had been taken to Caligula for his judgment on the morning of the very day that the Emperor met his fate. My husband had been sentenced to death and there was no reason to suppose anything other than that his life had been ended even as Caligula's was. Our correspondent considered the matter to be closed.

So, there it was; the end of all hope, they said. And yet I did not give up hope. I did not have ultimate confirmation of his death and I wanted so much for the words from Imma to make sense. But time passed and continued to pass and there was no word from Apollonius. Luke stopped believing and I retreated into a kind of numbness.

I had raised my son into the knowledge of the circle of life and the laws that govern our souls. Sarah's death had shaken him; but he had hardly known her. Apollonius, he worshipped. He knew that his father was still alive in spirit and that death was only the end of a stage in our evolution and I know that did comfort him; but he was also a child who had been bereaved and who needed love more than he ever had done before. We went about our business as best we could and, sometimes, at night Luke would climb into bed with me so that I could hold him while he wept the tears he needed to shed. Then, he would get up and go back to his own mattress and deal with his own demons alone as a man would. Many, many times we talked long into the night for we both needed to let out our anger and regrets. I allowed him to be angry with me and also with Apollonius's studies and his investigation into Caligula's destiny. He needed to be angry about something and he wanted to hate the people who had taught his father the esoteric knowledge that had led to his death. Philo, too, allowed Luke to argue with him and with his philosophy and I debated with him, over and over again, all that Yeshua had taught me about life and death and sacrifice. Eventually, Luke came to the best personal understanding he could have at that time and he seemed to relax a little and even to smile again.

A year passed and that is all I can say about it. We survived.

One cool and windy morning, just as Luke was about to leave for school, there was a knock at our door. We opened it to a strange woman, lean and stringy and with harsh lines of suffering on her face. Luke did not recognise her at all and it was not until she smiled at me and spoke a greeting in Aramaic that we realised that it was Rizpah.

Three

She was alone. Before we even considered the fact that her children were not with her, we could see that Rizpah was not well. The strain of her husband's death and months of travel had taken their toll; she had only managed to get a passage on a very inferior vessel and now that she was safe and home, reaction could set in.

She stumbled into my arms and we both wept, holding onto each other so tightly that it would have hurt if we had been sensible to what we were doing. Then, when we drew away from each other, Rizpah sank down onto the floor. 'I'm so tired,' she said. 'So very tired.'

Luke grabbed hold of some cushions for her to rest on and I rubbed her hands. 'I'll make you a tisane,' I said. 'Don't worry about talking. We have all the time there is.'

Rizpah smiled weakly as Luke wrapped her in a blanket and stood awkwardly on one leg wondering whether to stay and hear her story or go to school.

'She needs rest,' I said to him. 'The story will still be here when you get back.' Luke smiled and nodded and was gone within seconds, his quicksilver mind jumping to the day ahead. Rizpah and I were alone. We just sat and looked at each other for a while and then she began to speak.

As the day unfolded and Rizpah drank her herbal teas and ate enough to give her strength, she told me her story in fits and starts which I was able to put together later. She began with the voyage back to us in Alexandria and then went back in time to happier days. It was obviously too hard for her to talk about the circumstances surrounding Lucius's death and I could understand that.

Her ship had arrived only that morning and she had gone straight to Philo's house in order to find out where we were living.

'No one was there but luckily there was someone in the street who knew you,' she said. 'They told me where to go but I couldn't believe it. Why such a poor area of town? And they said you were on your own. I thought you would still be wealthy. Where is Apollonius? Why are you living here?' Then she broke down and began to sob as she realised that no vestige of her old life was left and even the safety of the home she had once known was no more. I comforted her as best I could but I did not tell her then what had happened to us for she had enough to deal with in finding my circumstances so changed. I told her that all would be well but it was hard at that moment to sound confident for it seemed, from what little she had already told me, that Rizpah owed money and had been relying on us to help her pay it.

We sat and hugged and she managed to sleep a little in my arms, comforted by the familiar touch and so tired that she had to leave the questions behind for a while. When she awoke I drew out a little more of her story.

She had not been in Rome. As I thought, she was living in southern Gallia where Lucius's family had a villa. But her husband had taken the first opportunity to return to the capital with his brother and uncle.

'He was talking dangerously even when we were together in Rome,' I remembered. 'Did he go back to take part in the plot?'

'I don't know,' she said. 'I don't know anything. He didn't confide in me. I didn't mind; I didn't think. I knew I would miss him but I was happy with the children.'

From there, her story was horribly similar to ours. Rumour, gossip, fear and uncertainty.

Lucius's name was on the lips of a hundred people in Rome.

Some said he had tried to save Caligula; some said he was the killer. Some acclaimed him a hero and some a villain—but nobody knew for sure.

Rizpah and the children lived unreal lives of waiting and grieving with Lucius's family until the attitudes of the others began to crystallise into open hostility. Once the news was out that Lucius was confirmed as one of the gang of killers she became a marked woman, the wife of an assassin, and it was no longer safe to acknowledge her within the tribe.

The family told Rizpah that she could stay in the compound but that her children would be adopted by Lucius's cousin so that their names would not be tainted by their father's action. From then on she was treated as a slave for, like me, she was a foreigner and an inconvenience—and someone had to be to blame for the downfall of a favoured son.

'These were the people who hated Caligula!' she wept. 'They approved of what Lucius had done in secret—which is more than I do!—but they were more concerned for their good name than for anything else. When I protested about the way I was treated they said they would keep the children and I could just leave. Then I would have no rights at all and nowhere to live.'

She had very little choice but to obey; the grief and shock were paralysing. Timothy and Sophia were too young to understand and it soon became apparent that the children were being kept away from their mother as much as possible and life became so lonely and harsh that Rizpah was in despair.

'To my husband's family I was a foreigner and a heathen,' she said. 'It was one thing when I was the adopted daughter of a Senator and Lucius was in the Praetorian Guard. Everything was wonderful then. But when Lucius was disgraced it was felt that it was my influence which had corrupted him and which had even caused him to follow Mithras instead of the Roman gods. At the family's house, I was not allowed to worship in my own way or even suffered to eat with them—although the children did. It was as if they needed someone to blame and I was the perfect scapegoat. I coped; I didn't know what else to do but it just got harder. Then, when my son was corrected when he called me

'Mother' and told to refer to me as 'Woman' instead, something in me just snapped.'

She had made plans to get the children away and find a ship to Alexandria but when she went to the chest where she and Lucius had kept their money, it had gone. She knew he had not taken it for he had shown it to her before he left, in case she needed it for any crisis.

'I confronted my father-in-law,' she said. 'He admitted that they had taken the money but said it was their due as Lucius's parents and with me and his two half-bred children to raise at their expense.

'I didn't know what to do. I prayed and thought and prayed again and, for a while, I thought an answer had come. Lucius's other cousin, Archelaus, started to be kind to me and I thought he would take my side. I even wondered if he would marry me because then I would, at least, be a Roman wife again, with some say in my children's life, but he only wanted to sleep with me. When I mentioned marriage, he laughed at me and told me to be grateful for what I could get.'

Rizpah broke down and it took all the comfort and love I could offer before she was ready to go on with her story. She had stolen some money from her parents-in-law and run away alone, without Timothy and Sophia. When she talked of leaving her children, her already tear-stained and painfully pale face blanched with horror. 'But I couldn't do anything else,' she said. 'I left because staying with them would have meant destroying myself without even keeping them. They were beginning to realise that to come to me meant that they would be punished and they didn't understand. I couldn't bear to see them so hurt and confused. They were being taught that they should hate me so by leaving I have at least made that easier for them. They have to fit in to the family to survive. That's the way of the tribe and they are too young to fight it.

'I hope I can get them back one day but, even if I don't, they will be better off in a family which will take care of them without me than with a mother present who is dying inside and whom they are taught to deny and despise.'

She squared her shoulders and looked me in the eyes. I could see the grief there and the determination. I admired her, though I knew that many others would think her wicked or even insane.

'I must pay the money back,' she said. 'And there is an even greater debt which I must pay.'

She had not been able to pay the full fare from Rome to Alexandria, even for herself alone, but had found a ship that was travelling to Alexandria via Kreta and paid for the first part of the journey, sharing a cabin with three other families. In Kreta she had managed to stow away on a ship to Alexandria by going on board with a group of prostitutes and hiding in a cupboard for two days, cramped and uncomfortable and creeping out to take care of bodily needs when she dared. The captain of that particular ship looked like a fine man and not one who would throw a stowaway overboard when she was found or she would not have dared.

'But I was so unhappy I don't think I would have cared if he had thrown me over,' she said sadly. 'Deborah, will the pain of what I've done ever leave me?'

'You get used to it,' I said, thinking of Sarah. I took Rizpah's hands in mine. 'You are incredibly brave,' I said. 'No Greek woman could be so resourceful or independent as to find her way here without a man and I don't believe any Roman woman would dare either. You had already been sacrificed for your children by Lucius's family. You could not have run away with them but you were brave enough to know that your life is of value too. I don't think I could be as brave as you.'

'Of course you could!' said Rizpah. 'You're the bravest woman in the world.'

'Wouldn't it be good not to have to be brave?' I said with a sigh.

Once the ship was two days into the voyage, Rizpah went of her own free will to find the captain and offered to cook and clean in return for her fare. It was not a pleasant interview; although she wore no make-up she still had henna tattooed on her eyes as any wealthy Roman wife did and she looked more like a prostitute than a servant. She glossed over the interview as well as she could but I could feel the embarrassment and fear seeping through as she spoke.

'I was lucky,' she said. 'Or I had chosen well. He did not abuse me and once I'd told him that my husband was dead; the family unkind and that I was trying to get home, he allowed me to act as a servant in return for—well, some obvious favours. I won't go in to that but, as it was, I was taken care of before anything actually happened.'

There was one other woman aboard the boat, a Cypriot travelling to Alexandria with her merchant husband, and they were first intrigued and then horrified by the idea of a Roman girl acting as a servant on a ship. Swiftly they took Rizpah under their wing and, when they found she was travelling to respectable friends in Alexandria and could give the name of the Alabarch's brother as security, they removed her from the Captain's cabin and lent her the remaining fare.

This couple were staying in a lodging house near the harbour for six weeks while the merchant did his business and Rizpah had promised to take them the money to repay their kindness within a few days.

She sighed and settled back on the cushions, staring into the feeble flames of the fire. I got up and went to look out of the tiny window of our apartment, trying to choose the words to tell her what had happened to me. There was a long, deep silence. I looked back at my friend. She was sitting, curled up on cushions, and was fiddling with her long, brown hair, plaiting and unplaiting it. Her eyes were sparkling with unshed tears and her face was drained and prematurely lined with sorrow. I felt my own eyes well up in sympathy and empathy. It seemed so very long ago that we had found each other on the road to Qumran; she a runaway and I so recently a widow. Time had moved on and we were older but the situation we had to face now was not so very different. Life had repeated itself and this time felt even more painful.

I crossed the room, sat down and put my arms around her and, in a shaking and uncertain voice, I told her what had happened to Apollonius and to me; that she and I were in exactly the same position and that we would have to start again together, alone.

*

We spent the rest of that day talking, praying and crying, filling each other in with excerpts from our stories and wondering what would become of us. Once Rizpah had eaten some bread and soup and taken some herbal tinctures for dehydration and grief, she gained strength visibly. Often, over the years we had known each other, I had marvelled at the depth of her faith. She, who had only met Yeshua once and who had learnt all she knew from me and from Joseph and Magdalene, was stronger than I ever had been. She had never faltered once she had understood a point and, even now, she rallied herself and could even begin to laugh.

'Whenever anything looks hopeless,' she said. 'It must simply mean that God is going to handle it for us. I have to believe that. There is nothing else to believe. We have always been taken care of. It may not look like it right now, and we have more grieving to do than I ever imagined could exist, but I know you have done it before and, with you and with God, I can do it now.'

Such words of strength helped me for I was aghast at how both our lives had been slashed to the core. It was tempting to lash out at God again—and His shoulders would have been broad enough to take it—but what would be the purpose? Both our husbands had fallen by their own hand, through actions consciously taken. We are all responsible for the decisions we take; there is no point in blaming God.

'I am glad we do not know ahead what life has to show us,' said Rizpah. 'I remember that I almost turned against you and the teaching once I had met Lucius. I spent time with him and his friends instead of following what I knew to be the path I was destined to follow. It is so easy when you are in love to turn away from everything else. I almost did not take my copy of Magdalene's scroll with me but I was so glad that I did. Once the first delights of marriage had become more commonplace and I ran out of enthusiasm for my husband's beliefs it was still there for me to return to and remember all that had sustained me before.'

'Was it a good marriage apart from that?' I asked.

'There is no good marriage without a common faith,' said

Rizpah bluntly. 'There is the illusion of a good marriage but Yeshua taught us that real marriages were made in heaven. For an earthly marriage, Lucius and I did well but there was a lack and a distance that I never saw between you and Apollonius. I would talk to women friends in Massalia and they felt the same and we all took comfort from the ideas that Yeshua had taught.'

Oh, it was a joy to talk with Rizpah again! On the other hand, I could not see how we were going to pay back her debts. I was earning, and not badly, but not to the extent that I could spare enough to cover a sea voyage.

'Over to you, Lord,' I said once she had settled into a healing sleep. 'Of ourselves we are nothing but with you we can do anything.' And I thought that if the Lord could show me how to change Caligula's mind when I was in Rome, He could show me what to do now. All I had to do was trust and wait. As usual, it was a hard lesson.

It must have taken us both the best part of a week to tell our stories to the point where we were up to date. Luke, too, wanted to hear everything over and over and it was heart-warming to see how pleased he was to see Rizpah again. He was too grown up now to cry in front of her but at least he had someone else to talk to about his father and I know that helped him.

She talked a great deal about Gallia which fascinated him, for Constanzia's husband was half-French and used to tell Luke stories of northern heroes and gods. Rizpah had been content in Gallia 'though it was yet another new language!' she said ruefully. I smiled for she was a natural linguist and had learnt to chat away in colloquial Greek and Latin quite happily when I was still getting grammatical constructions comically wrong.

But she found it hard to realise that the man she had loved and married was an assassin. 'Why did he do it?' she said. 'He knew it was wrong to commit murder and, whatever Caligula had done, it was murder to kill him like that.'

We tried to comfort her, saying that he might not have been involved in the plot after all; but just been on duty that day with the ringleader, Cassius Cherea, and killed as part of the melée.

'No,' she said. 'He knew. He was a part of it. I can feel that.

You do know if your husband has other things on his mind but most of us choose to ignore them. I had a friend whose husband had a kept woman. She knew something was wrong but she ignored it, hoping it would go away. When she found out she was angry with the woman who told her because she couldn't go on pretending. She didn't want to face up to it. It was easier just to pretend.'

She dashed a tear away from her eye as she spoke. 'This is anger,' she said. 'Anger at myself. I don't know if I could have insisted on going to Rome with him but I should have tried. If it was Caligula's destiny to be killed—and the Lord knows it could have been the only way of making our people safe—then so be it. But you don't have to be a part of it. The Lord could just as easily get him to have a fall from his horse or crack his head open while drunk. You don't have to be the agent.'

She sighed and started kneading the dough for bread we were making with a furious hand. I made a mental note to tell Luke not to be surprised if the bread were heavy and hard to eat that day!

'Could you have stopped him even if you had been there?' I said.

'I don't know.' Rizpah rested for a while, her face crinkled in thought. 'All I do know is that he knew the commandments. He wasn't a Jew but he knew them. And he did believe in a Higher Power. He believed in good and he was an honest man. I keep wondering if perhaps he linked Yeshua's death with Mithras's and decided that he too should face death for the sake of mankind.'

The bread continued to be pounded. 'One of the greatest mistakes is to do something for the wrong reason,' she went on. 'You may think that it is your task to save someone but that could just be your ego talking. Only God can decide the destiny for each of us and, unless we are certain that we are doing his will, we should always consider the basic commandments. To love God first and our fellow man as our self. You can't love someone as yourself and plot to kill them.'

Another tear trickled down Rizpah's face and into the dough. 'I want to find excuses for him—and for me—but I can't. I took more notice of the children than I did of him. I hardly bothered with him some of the time. His work did not interest me and I was often too tired to give him anything like the attention he deserved.'

'If I had a drachma for every woman who has ever said that…' I said wryly and Rizpah gave a bitter laugh.

'What fools we are,' she said.

We talked to Philo, of course, and he was wise and sweet and philosophical. From him came a temporary respite from the debts of honour that Rizpah held. He was able to lend us enough money to repay the Cypriot couple although he said that earning the money to repay the amount she took from Lucius's family was up to her. Rizpah quite understood that and said with a grimace that she hoped that the fates would give her enough time to raise it before exacting their price.

She did not come to work with me in Constanzia's garden for healing and herbs had never been her forte. Instead, Philo—the man who so disapproved of women outside of the home—found her work and allowed her to use one of the anterooms of the library. She became a scribe like the men who had stalls outside the library. When people needed a letter written they would go to a scribe but, up until then, there had only been men available to write. A woman who would take a letter was a novelty that Alexandria had never seen before and Rizpah wrote a beautiful hand in five languages. Slowly, over more than a year—and secretly at first—women from all over the city began to use her services to write to family and friends both locally and abroad. They could talk about their children and ailments and gossip on paper for the first time, for no one had ever dared ask one of the learned male scribes to write such things. The men from whom she took some work were indignant for they disapproved of women writers and, even more, of anyone who took money out of their pockets and Rizpah was grateful that she did not have to work on their pitch. Luke acted as a kind of bodyguard for her, when he was not in school, as the men shouted insults at her as she passed on her way to her desk and he, too, wrote letters when she was busy and he had the time.

We used to laugh together at the reaction in other towns and cities when the letters' recipients took their missives to another scribe to have the written word translated into speech. The details of babies' births or family situations must have caused a few raised eyebrows all round. 'If there are any women sensible enough, they'll set up shop their end and get business reading those letters and replying to them,' said Rizpah and, surely enough, as time passed it did seem as though that might be happening for Rizpah received more and more clients wanting return letters to decipher.

I began to help her out when I could for her work grew increasingly popular. We paid off all her debts in two years, including sending money back to Lucius's family though, of course, we never knew if it had got there safely. Eventually we even had the money to move to a better apartment.

Hard work also helps the time to pass and, although for many months I haunted the harbour mouth hoping against hope that every ship arriving would bring Apollonius home to me, I grew used to his absence and could begin to admit to myself that he was not coming back.

Rizpah, Luke and I continued to study and to go to Philo's groups. We even started a small women's group of our own—all Jewish women—to study the Torah and the Merkabah tradition. I even began to teach the rudiments of the Tree of Life, the sacred diagram based on the Menorah in the heart of the Jewish Temple. Luke grew tall and gangly and left school and began to work as a medical apprentice to a respected doctor in the city. We began to hope that he would find a suitable and lovely wife—and he was certainly beginning to look!

It was into this world of peace and learning, if not of total contentment, that Paul of Tarsus finally arrived with his powerful oratory, hypnotic voice and passion for change.

Four

I was poring over a scroll in the library when he came. You would always hope that such a meeting would come when there was time to be prepared but how rarely it does! As it was, I was dressed in faded, old clothes; my palla had fallen away from my face and my hair was breaking free from its plaits as it so often did. There would have been ink on my fingers and probably on my face as well for I had been making notes on papyrus and I was an untidy penman at the best of times.

Whenever I had leisure time I was likely to be found in the research rooms of the great library. Ever since Yeshua had taught me to read Greek and Hebrew so many years before, I had loved to lose myself in the history of the faith of my birth and its stories.

On that particular day, I was studying the Greek version of *The Book of Esther* for the Hebrew and the Greek versions are quite different—the Greek edition having much in the way of added text which did not make much sense to me.

I had been trying to work out whether it was just prejudice on my part or if there was a good reason for the additions by a later author which made Esther seem a very Jewish but ungracious wife who spoke openly of her distaste for sex with her husband.

'Why agree to marry someone of a different religion if you don't want to understand the differences? How can you become a saviour of your people if you bemoan the path you have been given by God and hold onto the letter of the Law instead of the Spirit?' I muttered to myself as I scribbled and pondered and wiped ink over my nose.

Those who loved me would certainly have recognised such a Deborah, tussling with language and religion, frown lines on her forehead and her hair in disarray.

He had to say my name twice before I heard him. Then, as I looked up, the shock I felt must have drained all the colour from my face. There was no doubt who it was, even if more than a decade had passed from our last meeting and, although I had half been expecting him for almost as long as I had lived in Alexandria, it had become an unspecified event which would happen someday. Not now. Not here. Not standing in front of me when I looked such a mess.

Paul of Tarsus was never a handsome man but no one who had had cause to fear that face or that manner could forget him. He had a presence; the Greeks called it *Charis*. I felt as though I were hallucinating for I thought, just for a second, I saw a smouldering sensuality in those dark eyes. I shook my head, mentally. Mesmerism and delusion had often followed this man and I must be very wary.

He offered a formal bow. He was always dignified; always correct and always dangerous.

In hindsight I can see how hard it must have been for Paul to meet his saviour's sister; a living person who had intimate knowledge of the man to whom he had devoted his life. I was the only woman alive in the world who would be able to contradict him if he spoke erroneously of Yeshua's early days when he and I had lived and travelled together in Galilee. A living relic is not helpful when you are starting a new religion, particularly if she has her own opinions and, when the last time you saw her, you had threatened her with a beating for heresy.

But, of course, I did not think that at the time. Instead, I felt strangely young and defenceless and frightened at the sight of this man who had been such an implacable enemy and who now, it was said, was Yeshua's representative on Earth.

I remember standing up and smoothing my hair, covering it

correctly and bowing back to him without speaking. I was surprised to see that I was as tall as he, for memory had made him larger in my mind. My face wanted to put on a mask of coolness and hide but I managed to resist that and smiled instead, offering the traditional Hebrew words of welcome and blessing to a friend.

Paul regarded me gravely, his dark brown eyes mysterious. It was that half-remembered magic of his; the one that looked into your soul and laid you unconsciously open to his charm. As he replied to my greeting, walked forward and kissed me as a sister in Christ, I found my heart pounding and my brain racing with questions and warnings both about him and about my need to be so suspicious. 'Sister in Christ?' That was obviously now a well-used term but it sounded strange to a woman who had had no part in the forming of a new religion and no wish to be involved in it.

I smiled and shook my head. 'I'm sorry,' I said. 'I am very out of date with all the practices and terms which you must have developed and I do not recognise that term. You will have to explain many things to me. I did not know that you were coming to Alexandria so soon so I am unprepared for you. But for now, may I invite you—and our mutual friend Joseph if he is with you—to dine with us tomorrow or at your earliest convenience? The food will be acceptable to you; we do not eat flesh that is sacrificed to the Roman gods or anything you would find profane.'

'It wouldn't matter if you did,' said Paul, smoothly. 'As the Lord Jesus Christ said, nothing can defile the body if the soul is cleansed. Barnabas, whom you called Joseph, is indeed here with me and will be with us very soon. I just wished to come and greet you myself for I need to apologise to you for my behaviour so many years ago when we met in the Temple of Jerusalem. I had not yet seen the error of my ways and believed you to be my enemy.'

I made a gesture of negation and was about to speak but he continued.

'I can already see that you have followed the Lord's teaching and have forgiven me, as is right, and for that, I thank you. I would have expected nothing less from his sister. We would be pleased to dine with you and your husband whenever is most convenient to you. And perhaps with my wife as well? I trust she is in good health?'

Not even the honey-deep, thrilling voice could prevent both outrage and disbelief from flooding through me. To have this man tell me the teachings of my own brother when, not knowing his level of orthodoxy, I had tried to be courteous! And was he really assuming that the woman he had divorced when he still counted himself as a Pharisaic Jew was still his wife or was I mistaking things?

'Joseph has not had my letters,' I said bluntly. There was no question. No one who had knowledge of me would have been so tactless as to speak in such a way.

'There is much that we must discuss,' I continued rather stiffly. It seemed so unfair that having written so long and painstakingly to keep my old friend Joseph up to date with developments in Alexandria, I had to go through it all again. 'Many things have changed in the years since we last met and you need to know about them before we can talk.'

'I know that you are married to a Roman,' said Paul. 'I know that he is not a Jew but a gentile who knew and admired our Saviour. I know that you had to flee your homeland because of those who persecuted you; both myself and those who were disciples of your own brother-cousin. Neither of us understood you at the time—and that was our fault more than yours.

'I know that you have a son and that you are a friend of the Jewish philosopher, Philo. Is there more?'

'Oh yes,' I thought. 'There is more.' But I said nothing. That I was perplexed must have shown on my face for Paul took a pace forward, looking concerned and reached out to take my hands.

I wanted to run away; it was too much to have to recount everything yet again and I was still frightened. As he caught my fingers in his I took a step back. Something dynamic, sensual and frightening raced through me, making me shiver. I remembered that I had not eaten that day and felt my head begin to swim.

At that moment, the door opened again and in came someone else. I saw the much-missed face of Joseph Barsabbas, my friend and teacher from Emmaus, and it was all too much. There was a buzzing behind my eyes and my limbs felt like liquid. Joseph just managed to catch me before I fainted.

When a woman faints it is left to other women to take care of her—or, in the most serious of cases, an apothecary would be called. Although there were doctors a-plenty at the library, there were no other women and neither Paul nor Joseph knew of Achmed or any other servant who was my friend. They must have supported me themselves and fetched water for me to drink.

I remember keeping my eyes closed for a little longer than necessary, once I felt recovered, so that I would have time to think. I had known for years that this moment would come but, even so, I was completely unprepared for it.

And when I did open my eyes and drink the water held for me by my old friend Joseph, I found myself concerned more at his aged and shrunken appearance than at the pleasure of seeing him again and I found it hard to remember that he had changed his identity and had been Barnabas for many years now.

First, we had to establish what letters each of us had received and what news we had not heard. As we spoke, Paul stood at the arched window, looking out over the harbour. He seemed very patient.

'I last heard from you five years ago,' I said to Joseph. 'Before Apollonius was arrested and taken to Rome. I wrote twice, once before and once when we knew the worst.'

'What worst?' asked Joseph gently and I told him, time having made it possible to talk of such tragedy with calmness.

Joseph did look distressed. 'I'm so sorry,' he said. 'Apollonius was a good man.' He took my hand and squeezed it and we were silent for a moment.

'And what of your son?' he said, after a while. 'And Rizpah. What happened to her?'

This was the moment I had dreaded. I had taken great care to broach the subject of Rizpah's marriage in my letters—and had told them that she was no longer living in the same city. How ironic that, now, she was here and the subject had to be faced openly.

'Rizpah is here,' I said. 'She married a Tribune and had two children. Her husband was killed at the time of Caligula's assassination and her children live in Gallia with their grandparents.'

Before either of us could say more, Paul stepped in.

'She married again? But marriage is indissoluble under Christ,' he said. 'You know that!'

Anger raced through me. How dared he respond to such a story with his own opinions without even acknowledging what Rizpah had been through! I wanted to snap at him for his discourtesy but I managed to make a gesture of conciliation. He had had a shock. His extreme presumption and my own pain I must put aside for the moment.

'Marriage is not indissoluble under Jewish Law,' I said. 'When you divorced Rizpah when she was barely a child, you both considered yourself bound by Jewish law. A divorced woman had no redress and she was cast out to our mercy. She was living in Roman society where divorcées may re-marry and, believe me, she had no expectation of your returning to her. How could she have? You made your feelings very clear at the time and we have never heard from you in more than ten years! Even if we had been party to your beliefs on marriage, we would have expected to have heard from you a long time before now if you had wished to restore it. I hardly think you can be surprised that she has created a new and fulfilling life for herself.'

'Mary Magdalene was divorced and she did not marry again,' said Paul. 'A divorcée who marries again is an adulteress.'

'*Not* in Alexandria,' I said patiently, but with emphasis. '*Not* under Roman law *nor* under Judaic law which was the law under which *you* instigated a divorce.'

I stopped and heaved a great sigh. Paul was pacing up and down the room, his face flushed with anger. Somehow I had to smooth over these ruffled waters.

'This is not the best way to get acquainted, is it?' I said.

'Rizpah's story is her own to disclose, not mine. Suffice it to say, for the moment, that I am quite satisfied that she has followed the Lord's will for her.

'Now, I'm sure you have had a great shock but, believe me, things have been fairly difficult for us here too. I did write to inform you of Rizpah's marriage and I was not expecting to be challenged like this on first meeting.'

There was silence for a moment. Then Joseph spoke and I could hardly believe his words.

'I am sorry to find you still so argumentative, Deborah,' he said. And it felt as though the world fell apart beneath me.

'I won't cry,' I told myself fiercely. 'I *won't*.' Anger curled in my throat like red fire. If I let it go now—either in words or tears—I would never be able to retrench what was likely to be done.

'Help me!' I said, silently, instead. 'Help me. I don't know what to do.'

There was silence. I sat down and folded my hands in my lap. I had asked for help; it would come. I would do nothing else until it came.

It is quite easy to have faith when you have nothing else; if only *because* there is nothing else. I was so confused that there was no more I could offer but hate and I was disciplined enough—thank the Lord—to resist at least the open expression of that.

Into the silence came the sound of someone clearing his throat. Achmed was standing in the doorway with a polite look on his face. 'Madam,' he said. 'Your friend Philo is waiting in the lobby, hoping to meet with you and your colleagues. Perhaps you would be so kind as to bring them through as soon as you are ready.'

Dear Achmed! Dear Philo! They had been standing by to help me in case of trouble. I threw Achmed a look of gratitude and, inviting both Paul and Joseph to follow me, I stood, smoothed down my dress and walked, stiff-backed, out of the room.

Philo was waiting for us and greeted me with a kiss. For a man of such small stature, he had dignity and power. He bowed to Paul and Joseph—no, Barnabas—and invited them to sit. They obeyed (for it was, in truth, a command).

In the bustle of small-talk and with Achmed's offering of

refreshments and cool drinks, the difficult moment passed. Philo was as charming and chatty as always, putting both men at their ease and enquiring about their journey and accommodation. As I listened to him I realised that I should have behaved more elegantly, avoiding the difficult questions for the moment and leaving them to be resolved later. If I had been less hasty and done my part in welcoming them to the city, all might still have been well. Could I reverse the damage which had been done—and more to the point, could I release my anger at this upstart's arrogance? Even thinking that, I knew, showed how much pride I was holding.

Seeing clearly! Surely I was not seeing clearly as I looked at Joseph Barsabbas, that pillar of strength who had always been so quietly supportive and true to himself? He did look different but I had assumed that was the passing of time. But his features seemed set and harsher than just the passing of years would bestow. What had made him change his allegiance and, more importantly, why was it necessary to have sides between people who were trying to work for the same good?

As I wondered, he spoke to me directly.

'Deborah, I noticed that you introduced me as Joseph Barsabbas,' he said. 'I certainly wrote to you by that name for that is how you knew me, but I am now renamed in Christ as Barnabas.'

'Yes,' I said. 'I am sorry. I did know that. I forgot. You are still Joseph to me but I will try to remember.'

Paul looked up.

'It is a better name,' he said. 'It means "The Encourager." ' Again, I had to school myself not to react. I knew perfectly well what Barnabas meant!

'Barnabas has been the greatest help and support to me since I came to realise the truth,' Paul continued, gathering our attention towards him with his own indisputable magic. 'In the days after I had received my correction and revelation from Christ himself, I was in great need of a friend and supporter. I had much to re-think and to learn and Barnabas was the greatest of help to me.

'Again, when I came to Jerusalem and wished to be known to

the disciples of the Lord Jesus, Barnabas supported me against their initial doubt. How could they not be doubtful? I had been a persecutor of theirs and it was hard for them to realise that the Lord Jesus had spoken directly to me and chosen me as his vessel for the teaching of the Gentiles. Even with my Lord's blessing and guidance my mission would still have been far harder without my Encouragement here.' He smiled at us all and placed his hand on Barnabas's shoulder.

'Oh!' I said again. There was not much else I could say.

'So,' said Philo, sitting back and holding his drink in both hands so that he appeared to be looking over the rim of his chalice. 'I gather that things have progressed somewhat in the East. We, in Alexandria, have been going along in our own little way, studying and writing and striving to understand the secrets of life while you, it would appear, have been out in the action.'

'Yes indeed,' said Paul keenly. 'But my mission is hardly started and it was to increase my knowledge of the mysteries and to spread the word that I am here. My friend Barnabas assures me that I will find much of interest and many people willing to listen to us in Alexandria.'

'Undoubtedly,' said Philo, nodding wisely. 'While my own inspiration and encouragement—this talented and beautiful woman you see before you—has been helping those of us interested in the inner wisdom, there is still much need to take the news to the people themselves. I'm sure you are just the people to do that. We, on the other hand, are the kind who stay in the background. If there is anything we can do to assist you, you must, of course, allow us to do it.

'I thought, however, that you were a student of Gamaliel, who himself was a student of Hillel? Surely that should have given you a solid enough grounding in the Torah and the mysteries for any man?'

If my eyes did not deceive me, I saw the vestige of a blush on Paul's neck. 'Indeed I was,' he said. 'How well informed you are, Sir. However, my family's tent-making business took me away from my studies on the death of my father. I had to support the family. I was needed.'

' "If not myself, then who is for me, and if not now, when?" ' Philo quoted the great Rabbi Hillel in an absent-minded manner. 'And how are your family now?'

'I believe that they are well, Sir, thank you,' said Paul.

'You did not marry again, I gather?' said Philo and I caught my breath.

'No,' said Paul. 'One marriage only, so taught the Lord Jesus.'

'Did he indeed?' said Philo. 'Well, it makes sense, of course when a marriage is made in Heaven. Shame you hadn't learnt that when you *were* married, eh? You could have spared that excellent lady a certain amount of grief and she could have been of great help to you. If I remember correctly—not that she has ever spoken a single word against you, you understand—your former wife was a believer in the Lord Jesus long before you were and wishing to improve upon her knowledge of his teaching. Was that not why you divorced her? I believe that you wrote her a bill of divorcement as dictated in Torah for I remember seeing it myself.'

Paul's face, now, was bright scarlet. I kept my eyes low and sat as still as I could. Had Philo overheard our conversation in the book room or was this just a coincidence?

'I was mistaken' said Paul, humbly, and I looked up at him in surprise. His arrogance had not given any indication that he could capitulate so thoroughly.

'I did not know any better,' he said. 'I had hoped … in fact, I had strongly hoped … that she would take me back now that I do know better and we could be as man and wife again.'

'Well, I'm sure she would have done if you had contacted her a little earlier,' said Philo, cheerfully and mendaciously. 'But that will have to be your eternal loss, I'm afraid. The Lord is merciful but he is also just and if he decided that the lady was to be best taken care of elsewhere, having been abandoned previously, then who are we to judge?'

'The Lord Jesus said no divorce,' interrupted Paul but Philo spoke out again, at once.

'The Lord God is greater than the Lord Jesus,' he said sternly and with authority. 'The Lord Jesus is the servant of the Lord God as well as His son.'

There was silence. Then Philo went on, very quietly. 'Up until now we, here, have been content with the Holy One's recommendations,' he said. 'Messianic Judaism has not arrived in Alexandria and we live in the old ways. If you know more than we, it is up to you to teach us. We are very willing to listen and learn. What I think you may find is that we all, like you, Sirs, may have to wipe our slate clean from the moment that we understand this religion of yours. To condemn others for what they have done when they were acting in the belief that they were doing their best in the sight of the Holy One is, let us say, *unwise*. Especially if we, the ones who condemn, may not have been entirely skilful ourselves in the past. It will not encourage people to want to listen to the truth if we are open to the accusations of hypocrisy or uncharitable behaviour, you know.'

The old man and the two younger ones looked at each other for some moments. Philo's face was gentle but intractable. Never had I admired him more.

'You are right,' said Paul meekly. 'Rizpah's remarriage is part of my punishment. I was presumptuous.'

Even as I acknowledged this climb-down from so proud a man I pondered, inside, how he still assumed ownership of everything. Rizpah had her own life; she did not exist only in relation to him. Then I shook myself; I was judging again. Where was my own mercy and loving kindness? I turned to Barnabas.

'You must have been through many trials,' I said. 'I would love to hear your story when you have time to tell it. You know your strength and wisdom have always inspired me. Without your support and kindness I would have fallen by the wayside many times.'

As I finished speaking, the old, dear Joseph looked back at me and reached out to touch my hand. 'You look well,' he said. 'I am glad to see you and I am sorry I spoke to you as though you were a child earlier. I think we are more tired than we thought. It was only yesterday that we arrived and we have been so eager to meet you and your family that we did not rest. Your news shocked us and perhaps we concentrated on the part which could make us angry rather than counselling you through the great grief which you must have experienced alone.'

I thanked him but still something rang a little untrue. I would have given much to have had my old friend Joseph's support when Apollonius was taken but I did not need him to tell me that now.

We parted some little time later after agreeing that Barnabas and Paul should come for supper at my home the following night. As they left, Paul turned to me and took my hands with a smile that transformed his apparently plain features. It felt as though the Sun began to shine and that old feeling of being mesmerised returned to me. This man was so strange; one moment so hostile and the next so enchanting. This was danger indeed. To my relief Philo also accepted an invitation for the same evening for himself and his wife. I could hardly wait until the two other men had gone to thank him from the bottom of my heart for what he had said to them.

'It was my pleasure,' he said. 'I did overhear what was going on when you met. You are a little hasty, now and again, my dear, but I am sure you know that. However,' he continued. 'I regret to say that I do disagree with you on one important point. One very important point.'

'Yes?' I was prepared to be criticised by Philo, if necessary, but I need not have worried.

'You once told me that you thought that your friend Joseph, I mean Barnabas, was the Axis of the Age to follow your brother. I'm afraid I do not believe that at all.'

'But nor do I!' I burst out. 'I must have been mistaken! I agree with you. He doesn't have that light any longer. This is not the man who taught Yeshua and me at the Essenes, who followed with the other disciples, who stood by me when the others turned against me and who approved my marrying Apollonius. I know he's still there, somewhere, but there really is something very different about him.'

'Hmmm,' Philo looked worried. 'So you think he has changed, do you?'

'Yes, of course! He was—how can I explain it?'

'You don't have to. I remember how warmly you spoke of him and, up until now, I have never had cause to doubt your assessment of a character. Now I know that you think he has changed, I fear the worst.'

'The worst?'

'Yes. Perhaps he has failed in his mission. Perhaps you are right and he was the chosen one. Perhaps he has lost the light.'

I looked at my little friend, a cold shiver running down my back.

'Can that happen?'

'Of course. You know it does! It happened to Solomon and to many others.'

'But not to Joseph! Not to that most wonderful of men!'

'My dear, you never know. Now don't worry yourself unduly. I could be completely wrong and you could have mistaken the light you saw around him all those years ago. You were young, pregnant, frightened. He was your saviour. All I do know is that we must be incredibly watchful. It is not lies that are dangerous. Outright lies are easy to deal with. It is distortions of the truth which are the hardest to counter—and even to see. Doing the right thing for the wrong reasons; telling ninety-nine per cent of the truth and missing out the final part—or adding a little for its own sake. Those are the greatest temptations. We must be alert for them in ourselves and we must look out for them in others.

'I have a theory,' he continued. 'That is all it is but you know how these things can come into your mind while you are praying or meditating and they make perfect sense.'

'Yes?' I was always interested in any of Philo's theories. On a good day we would debate them for hours but I had always found there to be sound good sense behind the reasoning for even his most outrageous thoughts.

'We are agreed, are we not, that there is always a Messiah alive in the world?' said Philo.

'Yes,' I agreed. 'My memory seems to tell me that Yeshua was the Messiah from the very first days when I met him. I could be wrong but he had that light even as a child. And if there is always a Messiah then there should have been someone to carry the mantle for him until he was full-grown.'

'Great souls will shine even before they receive the mantle,' said Philo. 'And from what you told me, your brother received the Teaching from the Lord when he was twelve years old—officially a man. So, he may have received it then.'

'Yes, that's quite possible.'

'Well, the point is this,' said Philo. 'Because, as usual, we are in danger of getting off it—there is so much of interest to discuss whenever we meet. The point is, that I believe there are greater and lesser Messiahs.'

'Well, some branches of the Essenes do believe in two,' I said. 'One for the physical world, a leader to release us from the yoke of oppression—whether it's Roman or Persian or whatever—and another for spiritual enlightenment.'

'Oh that's just a load of horse dung,' said Philo dismissively. 'What's the point of a Messiah for the physical world? You have Kings and rebel leaders and ordinary people like us for all that. I do wish people would learn some philosophy and a bit of sense before they declaim that kind of rubbish.'

Despite myself, I smiled. Philo was such a breath of fresh air. People with an interest in the Higher Worlds were so often over-serious and reverential.

'Anyway, what I believe is,' said Philo. 'That there are always three people set aside for any job.'

'Yes, Yeshua used to say that.'

'Maybe he did, but what do you think?'

'I agree.'

'Yes, but do you think so yourself or are you just using Yeshua's knowledge?'

It was a good point. 'I'm not sure,' I said. 'Well, yes, I am, because I know everyone is given choices and turning points in their lives and they always have the free will to take on a task or refuse it. The task still has to be done. Yeshua said to me that the first disciple who was chosen to have handed him to the Romans was not strong enough to do it; Judah was the second and I, the third.'

'How very interesting,' said Philo. 'Now who was the first one, I wonder—no, don't tell me (not that I believe you would). I'm getting off the point again.'

We smiled at each other and Philo continued.

'It follows that there must be three contenders for the Messiah also,' said Philo. 'Only one being the true Anointed; the others being stop-gaps if you like. Souls who are nearly worthy and who would be able to hold the spirit of the world steady even if they were not strong enough to enhance and improve the Teaching.'

'So there is only one of what is called 'The Only Begotten One' in every generation?' I said. 'The others are there in case he—or she—fails?'

'Yes indeed,' said Philo. 'However, I was thinking more, in this particular situation, of that person's holding the mantle for the true Messiah while he—or, you are quite correct, much as it pains me to admit it, it can indeed be a woman, look at the story of Esther!—while he, or she, was growing up or even during the new soul's gestation in his mother's womb.'

'So, are you saying that Joseph could have been a kind of intermediate Anointed One while the new, great Messiah is born and grows up,' I said, excited at this new idea.

'Yes. That means he does not have to be a great leader or a teacher, rather someone who just quietly gets on with fulfilling the Work without expanding it.'

'Surely most Messiahs do that. After all, we don't hear of many of them.'

'We, that is you and I,' said Philo. 'Only hear about the Jewish ones. The world is a very large place, my dear, and there may well be many good and strong religions in it apart from the ones we already know. The Messiah probably goes to some of them as well.'

'But they don't have the Torah.'

'Torah just means the Teaching. All religions have the Teaching in one form or another.'

I nodded for I did believe that to be true. 'Love for one's own people dies hard,' I said with a smile. 'But even the Romans and the Egyptians have Torah—for all their gods fit onto the Tree of Life and together, make up the sum of the Holy One.'

'Exactly,' said Philo. 'So, there is nothing in particular to worry about with your friend Joseph-Barnabas. And even if there is, as I told you on the very first day that we met, then it is your task to right it. Is it not?'

Would that I could have. In retrospect things always seem so clear but those first days with Paul and Barnabas were more confusing than I could have imagined.

It soon became clear that it would be hard for any woman not to fall in love with the transformed Paul of Tarsus. I found it hard not to be enchanted by him once he began to give me his full attention. That was the trouble; he was addictive. His approval was so warm and his disapproval so like the turning out of a lamp of light and peace that you felt that your behaviour had mortally wounded someone who loved you deeply. If you were not careful, you could easily begin to crave his approval and act only to please him—or his Jesus.

It was not that Paul was young or handsome or strong—he was none of those things. Instead he had that strange magnetic appeal which began with the look in his deep, brown eyes and was confirmed by the alluring velvet tones of his incredible voice.

I had remembered it from the time we had first met but it had grown as Paul himself had diminished. The man I had seen in the Temple had carried some physical attraction. This one was bowed by a repetitive illness and a stoop but you forgot both of those the moment he looked and spoke directly to you

As he began to meet people and teach in Alexandria I could see that both men and women were swayed by this power. Paul could make you feel as though you were the most important person in the world to him—and then turn to the next man or woman in such a way that you knew that he was reluctant to do so and that he waited only to return to you.

Then he would do exactly the same to them.

His appeal was sexual, sensual, powerful, hypnotic. He was clever too. Although he never gave women any power within the religion he created he did make them feel special and loved. Even better, he targeted the wives and families of men who worshipped

Mithras—a cult of human sacrifice with parallels to Yeshua's own story. Mithraism excluded women totally so they had no place to turn and no god to worship. Paul's faith opened its arms to them, valuing and cherishing their work behind the scenes. I never knew if he realised why he had such an effect but I suspect he believed it all to be the work of Jesus the Messiah.

He was devoted to this image, so much so that he owned it. Often, I remembered my original, inner conviction, formed in the Temple in Jerusalem as we first met, that whatever Paul was given he would improve on and turn it into being his. This was exactly what he had done with Yeshua and his teaching. Whatever it was it was magnificent; but I did not recognise very much of it and that, alone, was terrifying.

Let me say now that what Paul did in those following years was a miracle. He did take Yeshua-Jesus's teaching to people who could never have heard it before and he started a monotheistic movement that I believe will gather in strength as the years and even the centuries last. Even in the depth of his fights with Peter and James I knew he was right about the need for the faith to be accessible to the people. He taught that the *form* of the Law was outdated; that circumcision, food laws and even women's impurity laws were not necessary if you lifted your heart and soul and cleansed yourself from above.

No wonder he was loved by women! He made our lives so much easier. No more worrying what to buy, what to cook, whether your presence would make someone else impure. No fears about taking care of the sick or the dead and being tainted until you could get to a Mikvah. Those who came from Judaism found their everyday work transformed.

Those who came from other faiths were hardly less empowered. Here was a God who did *not* require physical sacrifice; did *not* reward those who could spend the most on priestly blessings; did *not* care if you were rich or poor or what your background and breeding were. Here was a God who had sent his only son into the physical world to die for you and your sins so that you might start again, anew, now! And without all the half-understood regulations which had cluttered your life. This was a God with a prophet now living and vibrant who loved you and who told you how his saviour, your saviour, Jesus Christ, loved you even more, You! Yes, you! You the one sitting there. *Your* life is special to God. *You* are unique. *You* are welcome in the Kingdom of God!

Even better than that was Paul's and Barnabas's complete conviction that the end of the world was coming; that Jesus would return in less than a handful of years and all who believed in him would be saved while the rest of the world fell away. Powerful stuff—and who does not want to be on such a winning side?

It did not happen all at once of course. In fact, Paul did not begin his ministry proper for another year or so. Some of that time he spent with us but, when he found me just too difficult and Philo and the followers of the Way too exacting, he would set off again for the East where he could have an easier time of it and, as he would say, be able to listen to Jesus' voice in peace.

Paul's first meeting with Rizpah passed surprisingly well. Now the expected crisis had arrived she, at least, was calm and assured. I was still feeling ragged from the encounter in the library and by Paul's indubitable ability to swing my senses one way or the other and it was she who comforted me. We prepared a special dinner with Luke's help for he was looking forward to meeting visitors from a foreign land he had learnt so much about from me. He intended to press Joseph—I mean Barnabas—for more stories about Yeshua or for a different angle on the old ones which had coloured his entire childhood.

Philo arrived before the other two men, bringing gifts of flowers and apologising that he had not brought his wife but instead, was accompanied by his son, Philip, and daughter-in-law Clarissa. The old fox knew perfectly well that we would have plenty of food to spare and that Philip's and Clarissa's sturdy good sense would help defuse any possibly difficult situations. Philip was a confirmed Jew but a tolerant one. He respected his father's opinions but differed from them in most respects. He regarded Rizpah and me as rather strange but basically harmless and although he was interested in the idea of a Messiah, or even Messiahs, he was entirely convinced that none had arrived yet.

Together with his wife, who cared little for religion at all, he was the perfect chaperone. Philo had to take great care when he visited us for rumours could easily start and he was courteously careful of our virtue.

Paul and Barnabas brought flowers too. This was an Alexandrian custom and I was pleased that they had been so thoughtful as to realise that. Paul, especially, was charming and my strange dichotomy of feelings about Joseph was dispelled in seeing his and Rizpah's obvious interest in seeing each other again. I wondered, cynically, whether Lucius's death had helped the situation; for it would be hard to imagine Paul and Barnabas being so comfortable with a Roman Tribune who was married to the little Jewish girl they remembered.

Paul said all that was appropriate to Rizpah and was able to give her much-wanted news about her family. Her parents were still alive, though frail; Jairus particularly was crippled with arthritis and had long handed over the administration of the synagogue in Tiberius to others. Chloë, her sister, once raised from the dead by Yeshua, had, however, died from a recurrence of the same disease some two years after we left. Rizpah shed a tear for the sister who had all but faded in her memory, but later she told me that she was not surprised. 'We have learned more and more that you have to change and grow to survive,' she said. 'Chloë never wanted to change. She would not look at any reason for altering the way she lived before she became sick the first time. I suspected that she would become ill again and perhaps that she would die.' She was particularly remembering similar cases where we had watched the miracle healings of the disciples in Jerusalem before Luke was born. So often the people who had received the miracles were well for a week, a month or perhaps longer but then, slowly began to return to their former state, re-infecting themselves in a way by not changing their thoughts and ideas to suit their new and healthier bodies.

I had to admire Paul for the way he had recovered from his shock and anger over the news of Rizpah's marriage. One of the things I was to learn about him was his complete ability to set a problem to one side if it could not be dealt with at that time. It was a tremendous strength and an example to me for I was prone to going over and over an incident in my mind even if it were over.

That evening, he set out to charm his former wife and he encouraged her to talk about all her experiences, her love for Lucius and the great pain of the loss of her children. He said that he was planning to go to Gallia at some stage and that he would be sure to look them up and, if there was any possibility of their returning to their mother, he would do what he could to arrange it.

I had a job not to snort with derision at that. It was such a hair-brained scheme and one that he could never carry out. Rizpah, however, thanked him with genuine feeling and I could see that she was impressed by the changes she saw in him. However, she did not speak of her own abilities in writing and translating for those might not have pleased him and already she did not want to do that.

Again and again, I warned myself against being too cynical. I had to admit that I, too, was affected by the stardust which hung around this man and disorientated by the way his manner had me swinging from admiration to derision in a way which was, frankly, exhausting. I had to admit that, had he told me that he would go to Rome to look for proof of Apollonius's death, I too would probably have been as glad and grateful as Rizpah.

The one who got the most out of the evening was Luke. His manners were always excellent and he waited until the visitors spoke directly to him before beginning to question them about their travels and experiences. His knowledge of Yeshua and the teaching were bound to seem impressive in one so young and I could see that both men took to him greatly. Over the evening Paul and Barnabas took great pains to draw him out and Barnabas complimented me on such an accomplished and knowledgeable young man. I cited Apollonius as the greatest influence but I was pleased nonetheless.

I could see that Luke took to Paul particularly and I could understand that. Even without that great charm that enveloped all to whom he spoke, an older man with Roman attitudes but similar interests was bound to be attractive to a fatherless boy. I felt a tug at my heart as the two heads grew closer together as they talked and talked and I supposed that I was jealous. I had hoped that Paul would only be transient in our lives but if Luke should come to love him, that would probably not be so.

I think that first evening was a success. There was no sign whatsoever of the discord of the meeting in the library and I wondered how much of that had been sparked by my fear and suspicion. I made a mental note always to be watchful of Paul— and of Barnabas too—but it was very pleasant to feel their admiration and their encouragement.

I met with Philo and Philip a few days later, anxious to talk about the evening. 'Dangerous man!' said Philip matter-of-factly, as soon as the subject turned to Paul. 'Evangelist! So sure of what he's talking of that he has to be incredibly ignorant. Very credible of course. Always are, evangelists. Don't believe he studied with Gamaliel for a minute.'

I found myself laughing at this but I was amazed too. I had never yet met anyone who did not react strongly to Paul of Tarsus; whether it was to like him or hate him. This man was an enigma and, as such, he would go far. Whether or not I and my friends wanted to travel with him, was another question.

Five

In the spring when the air was fresh and mild, I used to love to sit at the far edge of the harbour, the other side of the Pharos, looking out to the open sea as though Apollonius might still come home on the next ship. I knew that it was a foolish thing to do; even Luke had fully accepted by now that his father was dead but I could not. Perhaps it was some kind of a reaction from losing two husbands, both good men, in such similar situations. Both had meant well and been misunderstood. Both took with them a part of me; a piece that had to be rebuilt both from my own reserves and from new experiences. The loss of Apollonius had also brought back, in full measure, the loss of Judah and I realised just how much my second marriage had helped to paste over the wound of previous losses. As I sat on the harbour edge, my mind would go back again and again to Yeshua's death; to Magdalene's and even to my own dear Abba, my adopted father, Joseph. The sea winds and the flying spray would be hardly less salt than my cheeks as the tears flowed to open and heal the old wounds from within.

Then I would think of Imma; and thinking of her always calmed and comforted me as though her spirit wrapped itself around me in just the way that she would always provide comfort and friendship when I was a child. Even when she was angry, Imma always showed that she loved you still and that it was the behaviour which was wrong, not the child.

At the harbour I could think and ponder and pray and allow the griefs to be felt and to pass so that I could continue with the life ahead of me. At other times when I was not at my best I would count blessings—perhaps fifty or a hundred at a time—and just doing that would help immeasurably. Sometimes it was all too easy to forget how lucky I was, with a healthy body, good sight and hearing, a face unmarked by pox, a good mind and plenty of friends. Many women did not live as long as I already had done and they had had the advantage of health all their childhoods. My body was a complete miracle. It was hard even to remember that I had once been twisted and crippled and in constant pain. Yeshua's love had healed me and it was the love I felt for God and the Earth that kept me well. When we lived in Rome I had begun, temporarily, to stiffen again and, whenever I was unhappy and allowed that feeling to rule me, I could still feel some distant root of disease within, but it left me as soon as I remembered how lucky and blessed I was and got on with creating new life.

Oddly, the grief for Apollonius did not affect my body—which was another reason for thinking that there was still something unfinished between us in this life. I had known that Judah was dead even before I was told; I did not know that with Apollonius.

I was not helped by both Paul's and, to a lesser extent, Barnabas's opinions that Apollonius had asked for what he had received. Of course, with the law of cause and effect, they were correct. But it was not tactful to say it both to my face and to others.

The two men were both Greeks in clothing, social attitudes, appearance and language but they thought that the Greeks themselves, with their knowledge of the stars, were generally heathens whose opinions were worth nothing. I had learned enough of Apollonius's passion to know that it was valid—if limited. The study of the stars and planets belonged to Yezirah, the world of forms and the psyche. At all points it could be overruled by Beriah, the world of spirit or Azilut, the world of Divinity, but it was a useful system for most human beings who did not aim so high and which could help them develop valuable insight into themselves and their fate—if that was the path they chose.

In vain did I suggest to Paul and Barnabas that the Zoroastrian priests who had visited Yeshua as a baby had been the first to recognise a Messiah—all Zoroastrians were astrologers—or that Yeshua himself had a healthy respect for other customs and beliefs.

'He would tell us a story about a good Samaritan to show people that those of other cultures and beliefs might be as good as—if not better than—holy men of our own faith,' I said. 'In Alexandria I have learnt that all the faiths are valid. They all fit onto the Tree of Life which itself is not a faith but a system. It's just that some regard the different aspects of God shown on the Tree as being different gods. The Greek and Roman Gods have the same names as the planets but true astrologers don't see the planets as gods but as indications of God's plans for us in the skies. Yes, much of everyday belief in astrology *is* blind belief and superstition because people don't want to think for themselves and look for a system that will do it for them but that is exactly the same as the way most Jews use Jewish lore. Half of our own faith is used to condemn and destroy others rather than setting examples of love and compassion. Look at the orthodox Jews who won't even touch a sick or dying person because it would defile them. Look at those of us who call good men evil because they use a different system from ours. You cannot use Yeshua's teaching to condemn other people and their faiths. That is exactly the opposite of everything he came to tell us.

'How can we set ourselves up as better than others when just the action of doing that shows that we are so arrogant that we cannot possibly be better?

'As for the stars, it's well known that the Essenes at Qumran study them and their effects on humanity and you're not condemning them. They did the same at Emmaus—and that's where Barnabas trained!'

'I don't like prophecy,' said Paul in that dull tone of his—like a stone coated with velvet—which meant that he would brook no argument.

'That's good coming from you!' I said, my temper rising. 'Half your Christians in Rome are prophesying in the name of Jesus! I've heard them!'

'That's different,' said Paul. 'I don't like those who think they can predict the future for individuals.'

'Well I don't like market-place seers either,' I said. 'I'm not talking about people who give cheap answers to cheap questions though maybe even they have their place. I'm talking about those who have studied the beauty and magnificence of God's Universe. I know that my husband fell because he was tempted to predict the death of a King and that the lives of Kings are beyond star-gazing. He should not have done it and he—we—have paid in full for such a mistake. But he was not all wrong. He used the stars to help him to worship God and what greater use could there be for them? Why are the stars there if they are irrelevant? The Holy One does not waste time or space or anything. It is all of use even if we don't know how to handle it. Even in the Torah it says that they are there in order to be signs for us.'

'Well, that may have been true in the past,' said Paul. 'I don't think so but I will let that go. However, it is not true now. All anyone needs to know is that the Messiah has come in the form of Jesus the Christos. God Himself came to us to show us the correct way. Nothing else matters.'

As he said that, Yeshua's own last words to me in the Temple came back to me. 'Tell Paul I am not God,' he had said and I had wondered whom he had meant. I had never met Paul then—though Saul was known to me as an enemy. Only now did those words make sense. But how to put them tactfully to someone like Paul? Perhaps I should have held my tongue but I was so incensed by the debate that I could not.

'Yeshua is not God,' I said bluntly. There did not seem to be any point in saying anything else to dull the blow.

'Yes he is,' said Paul.

'No,' I said. 'Yeshua was Messiah. That, on the Tree of Life, is at the place of Adonai—the Lord—in the world of Azilut. It is not God Itself but a place of pathway towards God. Being at the crown of Yezirah, it is the pathway through to worlds where forms mean nothing; where pure spirit exists, not divisions or religions. Even Azilut, the world of light, beyond the place of the Messiah, is not God. God is beyond even that. Beyond existence. Even beyond Ayn Sof, the never-ending. Beyond so far that we cannot even perceive of It. And It is not male, nor female. Being beyond form, it is way beyond sex. It is Absolute. Yeshua—Jesus—was not Absolute. He was—is—a great soul, possibly even the greatest who has lived so far, and he represented Divinity—but he is not God and he must not be claimed to be God. Doing that only blocks the way to God instead of opening it. He told me to tell you that himself.'

'When?' Paul challenged me.

'He gave me the message in the Temple after he died,' I said. 'He brought me several messages and one of them was, "Tell Paul that I am not God."'

'Paul, I know you find it difficult to listen to me because I am a woman, because I am his sister and because I have a quick temper—and because I have studied longer than you have—but please do take care of what you say. It is true to say that Jesus is Lord because Lord is Adonai, the place of the Messiah and the lowest sephira of Azilut but that does not mean that he is God. There is a huge difference and the average person, who does not know any of the inner teaching, will not be able to see that difference.

'You know that no Jew pronounces the name of God. Even when it is written it is still pronounced "Adonai." If you say that Jesus is Lord they will misunderstand you and believe that he is God Itself. That is so dangerous!'

'Jesus is part of God,' said Paul, bristling.

'Of course, but only those who know the structure of the teaching will realise that he is a *part* of God.'

'They don't need to,' said Paul. 'The teaching is far too hard for the everyday person. They need interpretation. That's what I'm here for.

'Yes, exactly. But please watch your words.'

'I don't need to be dictated to by a woman,' said Paul. 'You may think you know a lot—and too much learning in a woman is not an attractive thing, I can tell you—but Jesus the Christos spoke to me directly *after* he had spoken to you. He spoke to me from the Heavens where he had access to more knowledge than he had on the Earth. I don't have to listen to you. I have his voice in my own ears. I have his authority.'

What could I answer to that? I had passed on my message and that was all I could do. But of course we bickered for days afterwards with Paul going back again and again to the idea that other faiths and ideas and methods of divination were no longer necessary with the knowledge of Jesus's love for us. That was his favourite angle; that Jesus had loved humanity so much that he had died for us and it was up to us to be grateful and to behave better.'

'But that means that his love was conditional!' I would cry. 'It wasn't; it isn't! The idea of following his teaching because someone tells you that he died for you and because you ought to is no better than rejecting it outright! That's not what he would want. He didn't do what he did so that people would be forced into being grateful!'

And on we would go, round and round again until the others despaired at us. I have to say that Paul did not generally press his point that if Apollonius had only believed in Jesus's teaching and not meddled with the stars, he would be here with us now but it hovered unspoken in the air between us.

Barnabas and Rizpah stayed out of the quarrel. In fact whenever Paul and I began to throw sparks at each other, they would both back away and leave us to it. Neither of them wanted to be drawn into the debate and neither would take sides if pressed afterwards. I knew they were being sensible and that it was foolish to keep arguing but it was so hard not to!

The irony of it all was that one of the reasons that Paul said that they had come to Alexandria was to learn more of the background of Yeshua-Jesus's beliefs. If what he said was true, he would not need to know any more. With the break-up of our community at Emmaus he had to rely on Barnabas's reports of what Yeshua had learnt instead of being able to visit and find out for himself.

If I talked of those days, another unspoken accusation would hover in the air above Paul's head. He could not have studied at Emmaus if he had wanted to—because of me. I was responsible for the break-up of that group. I had begun to teach as Yeshua did instead of keeping quiet and earning my keep like the other women on the outskirts of the community. Such behaviour from a woman was not tolerated at Emmaus but neither was the action of stoning the transgressor universally approved of either. The debate over what had been, and what should have been, done with me was the reason for the community's death.

Other Essene groups were fairly similar but almost all were harsher than the regime at Emmaus. The Essenes at Qumran were, without a doubt, the most severe of all. They were adamant that the last days were coming and that everyone alive was either a creature of darkness or a creature of light. Whichever we were was pre-ordained and there was no escape. Very different from what we had believed at Emmaus! Paul's Messianic teaching took some of that fierceness from the settlement at Qumran but added Yeshua's life and death to it, saying that those old days were finished; that the resurrection of the Messiah changed all the rules and that those who had previously been damned could now be saved. 'Even you!' was the unspoken addendum.

Paul was certain that Yeshua would return within three of four years to judge us all as the world ended. 'Those who believe in him will be saved,' he would declaim. 'This is our chance to repent and see the light. All past evils will be forgotten.'

I could see what he was getting at but I did not believe that the last days were here. In vain did I remind him that the cornerstone of the Teaching was that we were all aspects of God and that our task was to perfect ourselves. This could take thousands of years and the state of the world (as I saw it!) showed that we were a long way from our goal. There might be thousands of years to come and even then, we might not have got it right.

But no, Paul was sure that God was hurrying the plan up. The Messiah would come at the End of Days and we were close to the End of Days. I could see that he had a burning desire to see Yeshua in the flesh, coming to us again and thanking us for our belief and fidelity. That made me nervous. Paul's love was ecstatic and all-embracing and that was what was needed for an inspirational preacher but not what was needed to spread the whole truth.

That day, on the sea-front at Alexandria, I was not so concerned with Paul's beliefs but with another sore that marked my heart. Once, long ago, I had owned some land in En Gedi; the place where Luke had been born. It was land that Judah bought with the thirty pieces of silver that were traditional payment for information passed to the Sanhedrin. It was a matter of honour for us Jews that exchange was made for valuable information; it was not, as the Romans thought, a bribe. Judah and Yeshua had both agreed the rôle my husband had to play in the unfolding of the miracle and Judah knew that his own death too also result from his actions. He had used that money to buy land to keep his wife safe in the after-days.

When I left Jerusalem as Apollonius's wife, I had put the care of the deeds of the land into the hands of Joseph Barsabbas for safe-keeping. And he had sold it to raise money for the disciples before he began to work with Paul.

He told me, quietly, while we were walking together through the Egyptian part of town. Joseph had been born in Alexandria and, although he left the city when he was still young and none of his family remained, he still wished to tour the city to see the old sites that he remembered from childhood. I had offered to be his guide on a day of re-discovery, hoping that spending time together would have brought us back to our former ease. I began the day with the best of hopes but I must admit that I finished it with gritted teeth. Whether Barnabas (for it was not Joseph) felt the same about me I don't know but we were never more than polite to each other. There seemed to be no place to re-discover intimacy and, even when I referred back to the old days, he seemed distant and inaccessible.

I know he had enjoyed the old sights and he commented on all the new innovations and I know that he was uncertain of how I would take the news of the sale. He wanted not to be disappointed by me; wanted me to tell him that I was glad but I had to admit to wishing it had been otherwise and that the land was still in my name. I did my best not to over-react and to understand that he had done what he thought was right but it did not help.

I sighed and bowed my head as the fair wind carrying salt and adventure across the Mare Nostrum lifted and danced with the edges of my palla. The sale of some land in a far country would not have mattered to the wife of a Roman Senator. But now, as a widow maintaining herself, it would have been good to have known that I had that small piece of security in this uncertain world. I was angry that it had been sold even though I knew I had little right to be. Greek women, Roman women were not even allowed to own land; it was only my status as a Jew which had made it possible at all.

As I searched within for the root of the anger I realised that it was not truly about the land; it was the old story; the one that I had discovered in Rome; the need to make Judah the villain; the contagious heresy that he was an evil, jealous man; the very fact that the new non-Jewish Christians could not see those pieces of silver as honourable and, therefore, would not think the land that it bought anything but cursed. Better to get rid of it and expunge the memory of the man and his awkward wife and move on.

The pain of the slander against Judah would probably never leave me. Perhaps it was the cross that I had to bear, alone. No one else still living had been at the meeting where Yeshua and Judah made their decision. My word was all there was. And as Christianity began to find its feet in Alexandria, I knew my word would not be good enough.

But such thoughts are not productive and there was work to do in the garden; shopping for supper to be done on the way home and a vibrant boy coming home to be listened to, loved and fed. Far distant lands and long-dead husbands were not the priority today. I stood up, rubbing the gravel from the harbour edge from my hands and flexing them to remove the stiffness. They were strong working hands. Once, they had been pampered and oiled and the nails shaped and painted as befitted a good Senator's wife but now they had returned to the Galilean peasant's hands they were before. I smiled; they were good hands and I had much to be grateful for.

I sang an old Galilean song as I made my way back towards the town and thanked the Lord for a life where I could take the time to reflect and, if not heal the wounds, certainly apply the warming salve of contemplation.

Paul began his ministry of Christianity by teaching in the streets and, although at first I was embarrassed and kept away, thinking he would fail dismally, I was wrong. His method worked. I think it worked more through his incredible tenacity than anything else but there was no doubt that he had a great power of oratory as well. Much of the time I thought that he was wrong but even I found his talks fascinating. It was partly the mesmerism but it was also his incredible depth of belief and assurance that he really did have the answer which would save the world.

That, of course, is irresistible. We all want to save the world! Especially when we can do it by proving that we are the ones who are right.

As he began to become better known in Alexandria I could see that both men and women were swayed by this power.

Within weeks, people were beginning to turn up at planned meetings for prayer, discussion and healing and they came back for more. Slowly but surely, both Paul and Barnabas were becoming the talk of underground Alexandria. At first all other religions discounted them but people began turning up out of curiosity and many stayed on to listen and to be baptised and before we knew it, there was a Church.

Then the real troubles began.

Paul attracted four basic types of people. Firstly the intelligentsia of all faiths, interested in new ideas who wanted to know more about the links between different faiths and to discuss and argue salient points. Then there were the Jews who were interested in the supposition that the Messiah had finally arrived. They knew the Torah and followed the Law—each one slightly differently, as was normal within the Jewish faith—but their background knowledge of Yeshua's teachings was both helpful and challenging to Paul's theories. Half of being Jewish seemed to be about arguing with your family or your neighbour about how *they* did things wrong and *you* did things right and a new preacher teaching something different was a wonderful opportunity for new and better arguments!

Thirdly, he attracted women who saw an opportunity to believe in one God rather than many and who had often felt excluded within their own faith. Many of them, I'm afraid to say, fell half in love with the idea of Yeshua and wholly in love with Paul.

Finally, as Philo had put it so bluntly, he drew the worst of society. Rejected people, social misfits, outcasts, even perverts. People who came because nobody else would have them. These were not necessarily people who looked like trouble from the start; they were enthusiastic, helpful, friendly and, most importantly, they came in their droves. Some of them flourished for there was much for them in Paul's message, but many brought just too much inner pain to be able (or willing) to let go of it or to follow any kind of discipline.

Paul was teaching 'liberty in the Law through Christ' which was bound to attract people without discernment and who followed their own ideas about which laws could be broken and which should be kept. At first they were enthusiastic. Then they began to quarrel among themselves and to complain when others got more attention than they did. Many of them started claiming that they were receiving visions of Yeshua which told them different things from what Paul was saying.

'The Lord Jesus told me that I should have as many sexual partners as I want' was a fairly easy one to deal with, as it was so patently unlikely, but those who passed on more subtle messages were more difficult. I remembered what Philo had said about the dangers of twisted truth—and I was sure he was right.

The Christians would meet in people's homes by prior arrangement until the group got too large for that. Then they hired a small hall in one of the city's many clubs and asked members for donations. Some gave generously and brought food to share with the others but some never gave a thing and, of course, some of those who did give began to get resentful.

Within weeks there was trouble within the group and the dissenters got Paul a bad name without. The priests and Rabbis who had lost members of their own groups were angry and resentful. People who got visions of Yeshua began to preach themselves and soon even we had the 'official' teaching and the 'unofficial' teaching. Christians were unpopular with the conventional people from day one. And they were an easy target for the prejudiced or the orthodox.

I just watched. I was not allowed to do anything much else as Paul was adamant that women might not teach. You might be tempted to think that I, being quarrelsome by nature, would have fought him over that but I did not. I knew how dangerous it was in Greek society for a woman to step out of line and, even more, I remembered my time of teaching with Yeshua when I had learnt to wait and watch. If I were meant to do any teaching within this new system, then my opportunity would come. I understood Paul's point of view—the cult of the Magna Mater in Rome had given many people a disgust for 'women' teachers which could spill over into violence and it simply was not safe for a woman to expose herself by teaching in the streets. To compete with that was foolish and I just had to trust that in future, more sensible years, our time would come.

In any case, it was not exactly my faith which Paul was promoting so why should I want to teach it? My job was to hold the knowledge which formed the structure behind this belief and I was content to do that.

Barnabas taught as well as Paul but he did not draw crowds in the way that his friend could. His role was more to tease out those who genuinely believed and who had potential to learn and to understand and deal with those who just wanted attention or who were trying to cause trouble. As soon as he and Paul had found a central group of people to help them and to co-ordinate talks and worship, those on the outside would begin to complain that there was an 'inner group' and that they were being excluded and this was supposed to be a religion where no one was excluded.

When one woman appeared, ecstatic, at one of the services, claiming that Yeshua had come to her in spirit and made love to her and now she was pregnant with his child, I saw even Paul's shoulders droop and his strength, momentarily, fail him. He did not expel her from the group as deluded, rather allowed her to leave in her own time by his passive resistance to her claims. I rather admired the way he did it—but even that only started a rumour that the (very real and certainly illegitimate) child was his.

In the midst of this chaos I began to develop a reluctant respect for Paul himself. Again and again he was confounded by the very people he was trying to help. Again and again they let him down. He became the laughing stock of much of the Alexandrian intelligentsia within months for he had no proven knowledge to back up his claims. Philo's group of students of metaphysics were doubly scathing of his tactics. I did not like much of what he did either but I could think of no other way he could act if he wanted to bring this teaching to those who needed it.

Eventually, things settled down. Rizpah and I did our best to help behind the scenes where the women had questions which were not appropriate for a man to hear. Most of the women, though, were not interested in us; the men were the exciting people and the attractive ones.

The most difficult thing that Paul had to deal with was the Law. Not only the Jewish law but the rules and regulations that the others knew from the Roman and Greek gods and the deities of Egypt and Syria. No matter that he did not follow the food laws or the cleanliness laws, he still followed the Ten Commandments and many of the people who came to him had no idea what those were. So, he had to teach people the law while preaching that Yeshua released them from laws. This was rather hard for some people to understand!

The idea of getting our band of Christians to sit down together to eat, for example, was almost impossible. Some were screaming that you should not commit murder and that killing any animal was murder. Others were refusing to eat any meat sacrificed to any god whatsoever while their companions would not eat meat which had *not* been sacrificed! Some said that a particular animal was impure; others would not eat something grown by someone of a different race, even if they were of the same religion. In those cases, Paul was superb. He taught that nothing could profane the physical body, just as Yeshua had taught, but that it was the mind that was important. Shouting at someone else for being 'wrong' profaned you far more than eating or doing the 'wrong' thing yourself. He ate things which his personal inclination would refuse, including meat sacrificed to gods. He dealt with those who had abandoned all laws and who mocked others for keeping hold of some and he dealt sternly with those who believed that no laws meant that you could sleep with another man's wife or hurt or even kill another human being.

Slowly this new religion staggered into some kind of shape. Paul said that it had been just the same in Antioch and Rome and it would be the same anywhere. You just had to have patience. And he had patience!

One more issue dogged him, particularly within the Jewish contingent of his new religion (and make no doubt that it was Paul's religion, not anything which had formed of itself) and that was the question of his marriage.

As the weeks and then months went by I started wondering whether the idea that he had come to Alexandria to learn was the whole story. His initial eagerness to reclaim Rizpah as his wife appeared to me in a different light when I saw just how opposed the Jewish contingent of our Christians were to an unmarried teacher. And quite rightly in my view! For if you have a religion where the men teach and the women are kept apart, then there must be a Rebbitzen to take care of the women's needs. Just one male teacher leaves half your congregation unaccounted for.

I could see how wonderful it would have been for Paul to have found a ready-made wife waiting for him in Alexandria. A woman with whom he could have a friendly relationship, perhaps even a celibate one, so that he could both emulate his Master and provide for the community. Just how much he needed this became more apparent every day despite Rizpah's and my best efforts behind the scenes.

Apart from anything else, everyone knows that it is the law in the Roman Empire that citizens should marry. The Emperor

Augustus decreed it in the first days of the Empire and although widowhood is permitted marriage, at some stage, is the required state for anyone. Oh, and parenthood of course. That goes without saying. Most Jews are not citizens of the Empire but we too have our customs and to marry is one of them. The only major difference between the two cultures in that respect is that Roman divorcées remarry and Jewish divorcées rarely do.

I began to watch for signs that Paul was trying to fix his interest again with Rizpah. After all, she was widowed and they *could* marry again by any of the local laws. It would not be as ideal as Rizpah's having not been married again between times but it could have worked. I had very mixed feelings about it because I feared that Rizpah could become overwhelmed by Paul's version of Christianity. I think that I was jealous: I wanted to be the greatest of her influences just as much as he did but I knew that it was important to let her go and make her own decisions. Self knowledge is not always comfortable, just as spiritual growth is rarely convenient.

Paul and Barnabas were often with us socially and I began to try to make special efforts to be less quarrelsome and to allow Paul and Rizpah more time to talk together and get to know each other. Paul and I had, so often, run the evenings ourselves with our constant debates and ideas and conflicts that no one else got much of a say. As I backed away, I could see Rizpah coming out of her shell a little more and it was good to see the two of them laughing together and talking about everyday things. Eventually they were also able to talk about the past and debate their strange, failed marriage and that, in itself, earned my admiration. It was obvious that Paul was genuinely contrite and Rizpah truly forgiving and able to accept her own part in its downfall.

Barnabas and I would talk together, too, on these evenings and I would encourage Luke to join us rather than to interrupt the others. He was slightly put out by this as he hero-worshipped Paul but when I told him my thoughts he understood and watched with as great an interest as I did. I would have told Barnabas too but, despite his great love and kindness, there was a closed-off part of him nowadays which did not encourage such confidences. I was beginning to understand why that was and it gave me compassion for him.

On the Tree of Life, the place to stand is the central column. We are meant to balance our lives out so that we have the perfect mixture of thought and action, discernment and mercy, understanding and inspiration. If one of us is filled with the right-hand pillar of loving kindness and action but has no balancing left-hand pillar of discernment and the ability to communicate clearly, he or she will burn out—be unbalanced and unable to maintain consciousness or make careful judgments about their life. In the days when I knew Barnabas as Joseph Barsabbas he had had the perfect balance. Just to be with him was to feel peaceful and secure and right. Now he spent his time balancing Paul.

At first glance you would think Paul was the right-hand column of action and Barnabas the left-hand of stability and that would have made more sense than the way it truly was. In fact Paul was the clever communicator and the voice of fire and brimstone; it was Barnabas that added the little, all-important kindnesses and actions that helped people to understand.

He did all of the organising too and, without that, Paul could not have been half as effective. He had become Paul's counter-weight and without him, Paul would have fallen.

What sacrifice it must have meant for my old friend. He was no longer the man he had been—literally as well as in name. Once I tried to talk to him directly of what I perceived but he stopped me dead with a look of steel. Oh, he knew the truth and he knew that I could see it too but he saw it as his duty and he intended to fulfil it. Without Paul Barnabas could, perhaps, have held the place of the Messiah himself but had chosen to promote another instead.

I thought it was a great mistake. I thought he had thrown his life away and that his action in refusing to be the one who led and taught could have catastrophic effects on this new and blossoming faith. But what did I know? I could see also that Barnabas's own way of teaching would bring slow results and, if the two of them genuinely believed that the end of the world was at hand, they must also believe that there was no time for that slower path. It was obvious, at times when Barnabas did follow Paul's teaching with some of his own or when Paul was too tired and his friend had to take over, that there was still a quiet greatness in Barnabas which Paul simply did not have. Paul had charisma and style but Barnabas had the whole of the truth within him. He just chose not to use it for what he saw was the good of the world.

I heard, many years later, that they were once teaching together in Antioch and the crowds mistook Paul for Mercury and Barnabas for Jupiter. Those who told the tale saw nothing odd in this—Mercury being the god of communication seemed most appropriate for Paul. But Jupiter is the King of the gods so, in their hearts, people had seen who was the greater. On the Tree of Life Mercury, the communicator, the Trickster, is much lower than Jupiter and, if you extend the Tree into the Great Tree on the centre of Jacob's Ladder, you see that Hesed, the place of Jupiter, is also the place of the Messiah.

I had been right all those years ago; Joseph Barsabbas could have been the Anointed of the Age after Yeshua's death. But he held that place only until he met Paul of Tarsus and then became Barnabas, the Encourager, surrendering his power to help this showman to create a religion.

How judgmental that sounds! And of course it is. This is only my opinion and I cannot see the outcome. Only future generations will be able to say whether Barnabas's sacrifice was worthwhile. But, of course, they don't believe that there will be future generations.

It is so easy to look at others and ignore what you, yourself, are doing. After all, there was I backing away to promote Rizpah with Paul in case they should choose to make a match of it. That was just as much a way of trying to manipulate. If it were meant, it would happen without my interference!

She did like him; you could see that. He made her laugh and, as her thin body began to fill out again, she rediscovered that bloom of youth which is so attractive to men. Paul would compliment her and they began to smile at each other in a way that seemed, to me, to mean more than just friendship.

He would compliment me too, of course, but I was a tall and angular woman and, although I could look imposing and dramatic, I had never been beautiful as Rizpah was beautiful and I knew that his compliments were just courtesy.

The trouble was that, as time went on, he did not cease to have that uncomfortable ability to make my body react to him. I had to admit that even though I did not like him, he affected me just as he affected most of the other women in the group. 'Stop it, you're like a bitch on heat,' I would tell myself, disgustedly when I felt the now familiar swimming feeling inside when he came over to me, took my hands in that intimate way he had and devoted his whole life to me in the few moments that I held his attention. After he had turned to the next person, I would feel an overwhelming sense of confusion and guilt and loss. For a while, each time, I would find that Paul dominated my thoughts but, as I calmed myself and got on with everyday tasks, he retreated back into his proper place and, instead of the urgency of (yes, I admit it) desire for him, the deeper, calmer, hole-in-my-heart ache I felt for Apollonius would return. No matter how much time passed it was my soul-mate I truly wanted in myself but I had a woman's body and it had been used to the arts of love. It made its needs known as loudly as it could whenever the opportunity was shown to it.

'Vegetable soul, animal soul, human soul,' I would say to myself severely. 'Your vegetable soul wants food and sex and sunlight just like any plant. Your animal soul wants to be the leader of the pack—the woman most admired and looked to. But your human soul knows that these are just desires of the world. In the rest of your time after your body dies, it is the human soul you will keep and that is the one you need to develop, not the others. Have patience.'

But it was hard. Apollonius was dead (no, he is not dead, I know he is not dead). And, for all my friends and business and faith, I still missed the love of a man, the holding of him; the scent of him, the familiar domestic squabbles, the catching of eyes across a room and the knowledge of a thought shared. Sex was a part of that but not all by far.

Rizpah began to talk to me of Paul in a way that showed me that she could begin to care for him. I encouraged her although we were friends enough for me to be open about the problems such a re-marriage might bring.

'He might be able to help me get my children back,' she said wistfully but we both knew how unlikely that was. Roman law puts a child directly in the care of its father (even after adulthood and marriage, unless a 'manus' is obtained to release that law) and after the father, then the grandfather is in control. Rizpah was as unlikely to regain her children with a new husband as she was without one.

That she missed them and grieved and was angered about the situation was obvious to anyone who knew and loved her but she had an essential dignity which hid her loss from prying eyes; and very few outside people knew of the existence of Thomas and Sophia at all.

Having more children would not have taken away Rizpah's grief but she was a natural mother and re-marriage with Paul might have given her the opportunity to exercise her natural instincts again.

The one thorn in the flesh that was obvious between them was Paul's consistent disapproval of Rizpah's work as a scribe. She defended it as a necessary way of earning money but she did not do as much work as she had before and I could see that her enthusiasm was waning. Instead, he encouraged her to help me in the garden which was more appropriate woman's work. Despite the fact that she did not enjoy it as much, she would have done so had I not told her, in no uncertain terms, that she should stick at what she was good at and not allow other people to rule her life!

One day, when Paul, Luke, Rizpah, myself and a small group of the Christians had been out for the day visiting some people in the Egyptian quarter of the town, another of Alexandria's periodic riots flared up. We were in the wrong place at the wrong time and such events were still frightening. It was in just such a riot that Magdalene had died, so many years before, so I knew how quickly death could strike. I still remembered Yeshua's teaching of how to stay calm and detach from situations which did not involve you (and that teaching would have saved Magdalene, too, had it not been for Luke's baby cries) but Barnabas was not with us on this particular day and it was impossible to get the idea through to the others. Paul was all for bravery and walking through the crowds, trusting in the Lord to protect him and the others, while I was for standing still and waiting for the flood to pass us by. He won, of course, and everyone began walking together in the middle of the street, singing a psalm of worship and, in my view, drawing attention to themselves.

I'm stubborn by nature and, rightly or wrongly, I just did not go with them. I stood, in a doorway, making myself as invisible as I could with my thoughts and waited for the furore to pass me by. Which it did. And the rioters ignored Paul and the others too, so I have to record that they were perfectly right in what they did and, knowing now what I did not know then, I wish with all my heart that I had not been so determined to go my own way.

After everything died down, I was alone in a relatively unknown part of town and I had to make my way back home without guidance or company but that was no problem. To start with, I rather enjoyed myself. I knew that I could take a litter whenever I wanted and I would be carried straight home, but instead I wandered in and out of a few market-places enjoying the Egyptian wares and haggling cheerfully with a few merchants. It was a relief after a rather intense morning. After a while, however, I realised how selfish I was being. The others would certainly have missed me and, if so, they would be worried. I had seen them walk to safety through the rioters so I had no worries about them but they might not realise the same about me. It was time I went home.

I looked around for a litter but just where I was at that time there were none. I walked up and down a few streets and asked what people I saw but it was already coming up to dusk and there must have been some Egyptian festival beginning for people were vanishing. Very soon I was alone and rather too near the rough end of that district for comfort.

Carefully, I looked for the direction of the Sun and calculated how far south of west it must be at this time of year. Then I walked towards the harbour. From there I would know my way.

Even so, I was beginning to grow footsore and angry with myself for my stubbornness before long and, by the time I made the shoreline, I was feeling genuinely sorry for myself.

I'd just turned a corner into a road that I knew and had spotted several litters for hire when Paul found me. He was angry and upset and after the first cry of 'Deborah!' where anyone could have heard the relief in his voice, he berated me loudly and vigorously. I was tired and angry too and gave as good as I got and, within moments, we were squabbling like children. Paul always had an irritating habit of touching people and, this time, he took my shoulders as if to shake me. I tried to strike both his hands away but he just held me tighter and the close proximity of his body and his attempt at controlling me infuriated me further. I hit at his chest with my fists and he had to hold me closer to stop me. Then we were really fighting (in the street!) and then something happened, something unwanted and unplanned for, that changed everything.

My palla had slipped and Paul took hold of my hair, the most beautiful part of me. Perhaps its oiled softness in contrast with the raging lioness before him made him pause; perhaps the feeling of his hand at the back of my head calmed me. We stopped and just looked at each other, eye to eye, suspicious and confused but still. And the worlds shifted so that we could see through all the anger into what lay behind it and beyond and we knew both that we lusted for each other and that there was also something deeper; some possibility that we could work together and even be happy. That the sister of Yeshua and the preacher of Jesus could find a synthesis which would work.

Paul spoke. Probably all he said was 'Deborah,' but it was not all I heard. There had been a moment of second sight or shifting worlds on the day that I had returned from Rome and been reunited with Apollonius. Then, I had seen Paul's face in his face and heard Paul's voice in his, reiterating his love for me, even though the only Paul I knew then was Saul, my implacable enemy. What I heard now was, 'Deborah, my love, my life. Now we will be together forever,' and what I saw was two faces at once; that of Paul and that of Apollonius.

For a moment it was as though there were two futures laid out before me and I could see them both clearly. I had to choose between them. 'Paul is here, in front of you,' said my body and my emotions. 'And you like the fight and the challenge. Your whole life has been about fighting. Here, now, is a future that will excite you. Travel, influence. The chance to clear your first husband's name for good. A chance to be loved and appreciated and admired and well-known. A chance to find a father for your son who loves him. He is young; he will protect Luke for many years. And how flattering that he finds you, the older woman, attractive!'

'No!' I said as the two faces danced before me. 'Yes,' said the face of Paul before me and Apollonius faded away. 'No,' I said again but weakly, as the vision of fame and passion became stronger and I felt the heat and strength of Paul's body against mine. This was my chance to be heard; to change the world as well as to have the physical joy I missed so much. Paul would come to understand me and to teach the truth as it really was; I was strong enough to ensure that. Rizpah was not. And after all, Rizpah did not really love him. It was better that I should have him; Rizpah would understand.

Then, far away, almost inaudible, I heard an echo of Yeshua's voice. 'Take the untrodden path,' it said. 'Don't need to be understood; don't need to be loved.' But it was so hard to walk alone and on a path where there were no smooth, familiar ways. And Apollonius was dead.

'No!' I must have cried out, aloud. 'I won't love you, I won't!' And I pulled away from Paul to run, shaking and crying, down to the sea shore.

Six

Paul proposed to Rizpah less than a week later and she accepted him.

He and I had talked before he spoke to her—we had to, for to leave such an wound open and bleeding would have been even more destructive. His pride was desperately hurt for he had opened his heart to me—even if just for a moment—and I had rejected him. I never actually found out whether he had spoken the words that I had heard but his demeanour afterwards implied that he might well have done. He was embarrassed and angry but determined to keep himself under control when we spoke the day after the riot and he said, with great dignity, that he hoped that I would believe him in his assurances that he would not trouble me with unwanted attentions. He had not wanted to have feelings for me, he said, and indeed had been unaware that he was in danger of experiencing anything for me at all apart from brotherly affection.

By then I had had time to calm down and regret most of my actions of the day before. Like Paul, I was hideously embarrassed and I was sorry, too, that I had obviously hurt him. Unfortunately, to start with I tried to lighten the atmosphere by being playful, thinking that it would make it easier for us, but it only offended him more. The only thing to do was to apologise and start again.

'I am so sorry for my behaviour,' I said. 'Whatever happened yesterday was at least partly caused by my stubbornness and pride. Like you, I find it uncomfortable to admit that I do have feelings for you. We have quarrelled so much and so often that it is hard for us to admit that there is an attraction too. I… I do care about you—in many ways—and I am honoured that you care for me. But you must know that I cannot marry again—I have no proof that Apollonius is dead and I cannot legally remarry without that certificate even if I wanted to. You know that.'

Then, of course, Paul had me at the perfect disadvantage; and he used it.

'Marriage?' he said. 'I couldn't marry you. I'm already married. One marriage only. Don't you remember? *You* might be free to marry again if you took the trouble to find out. I am not.'

'Well what else were you offering?' I flashed at him, bitten to the quick.

'I wasn't offering anything,' he said. 'I lost control for a moment and let my animal self rule me. It won't happen again. But as for marriage, Deborah, you are deluding yourself. Nothing like that was mentioned and never could have been. How could it possibly have even been contemplated between us?'

He left me then, filled with that anguish of humiliation that eats you up and makes you want to throw yourself around the room in anger and lamentation.

Paul and Rizpah's betrothal was not announced to anyone for it was not a formal arrangement. Just how the situation would be resolved when it came to the marriage itself was open to question for many Rabbis might have baulked at it, the law on remarriage to the same partner being uncertain. However, Paul considered himself above the law and knew that all would be well and he was probably right.

I had not told Rizpah about what had occurred between Paul and me but she was not stupid. She knew that something had happened but she also knew, as well as I did, how totally incompatible we were. She also understood that if Paul wanted a wife, the only possible one available to him was her.

'I do love him,' she said, shyly. 'Not in the way I loved Lucius but perhaps in the way that a wife loves a husband after many years of marriage. It's more of a friendship and a partnership. I do deserve something like that after so much tragedy and perhaps there will be children. They can't replace Timothy and Sophia but it would be nice…'

I kissed her and wished her every happiness in the world and that wish was completely genuine. I thought too that she might provide an essential respectability and stability that would benefit Paul—and perhaps give Barnabas the freedom to become more himself again.

Even so, my relationship with Paul did not improve. How could it? We were coolly courteous to each other for a while but, all too soon, the niggles and arguments began again and this time they had a sharper edge to them. Rizpah would calm us down and look at us both gravely with her beautiful clear eyes and we would subside like scolded children … for a while.

It soon became very apparent that the community was not happy with the idea of Paul's intended marriage. There are no secrets among women who are vying for a man and a look, a touch or even a thought will be observed and built upon. The first signs came in a spate of intensely bitchy remarks aimed at Rizpah but made behind her back. Other people made sure that she became aware of them nevertheless and, before we knew it, there was a small but malicious campaign to slander her to everyone.

How anyone knew about her children I cannot tell but rumour was soon out and being debated fiercely. Was a woman who had wilfully abandoned two children a suitable wife for a prophet of Christ? No matter how her story was told, the truth was that she had left the children behind. That she could not have taken them with her or that they were not even, legally, hers to take was not the point.

After that it was only a matter of time before someone discovered the identity of her second husband—an assassin!

The back-stabbing went on for more than a month, poisoning everything that the little group had aimed to achieve. Where there was love, they sowed discord. Where there was peace they stirred poison. The worst thing was, they hardly even knew they were doing it and when Paul addressed them on the importance of unconditional love they all looked wise and accepting and truly believed that it was everyone else who was causing the problem.

I thought that Rizpah behaved with impeccable dignity. I would not have done; rather I would have fought back but she ignored the rumours and kept her head held high. She did not even criticise the fact that people who were supposed to be following Christ and teaching salvation and forgiveness were choosing, instead, to condemn one of their own.

'It's jealously, of course,' said Philo when I told him about it. Our dear friend had been less in evidence of late for his health was beginning to fail. We still met for our meditations and talks as before in the traditional upper room but instead of walking he was now forced to take a litter or, at the very least, lean upon the arm of a servant or friend. 'You've told me yourself—and I've seen it with my own eyes—that half the women in the group are in love with our friend Paul.'

I hung my head. I had not told Philo about my own shaming experience. He was not a supporter of the passions of life and I felt rather small when I considered how much I had studied and tried to raise myself to be familiar with the higher worlds instead of ruled by my vegetable and animal senses.

'There's not much she can do about it,' Philo went on, 'apart from seeing whether it dies down of its own accord. If you are going to rise high in this world you must have a past as white as bleached linen for the faithful will be the first to judge you.

'What does Paul think of it?' he asked. 'I would have thought he would have considered the matter and realised what might happen beforehand.'

'He is acting with great dignity,' I said, which was true. What I did not say was that he was incredibly angry—although it was hard to tell whether the brunt of his fury was with himself or with the Church. However, I did not have to say any more for Philo knew Paul well enough.

'Did he ever ask *you* to marry him?' he said, suddenly. I jumped. My friend's perception was often uncomfortable.

'No,' I said.

'I'm surprised,' said Philo. 'I realise that he wanted to stay married to the original wife for form's sake; but when it comes to founding a new Church I would have thought that his Saviour's sister as his wife would have made a far more attractive package.'

'We fight like cat and dog,' I said, cautiously.

'Many couples do,' said my friend. 'Some marriages can work on that.'

'I'm older than him.'

'But how convenient that would be,' said Philo airily. 'No one would assume that you had a sexual relationship and it would lessen the jealousy. It would just be a very sensible, political marriage.'

That stung a little and I acknowledged that with a wry wave of my hand. Philo beamed at me and shook his head until I laughed with him.

'Well you, of all people, know that we don't think in the same way,' I said. 'It would be a hopeless arrangement.'

'Possibly.' Philo nodded. 'But, all the same, don't be surprised if he changes his mind and asks you instead of Rizpah.'

'He couldn't do that!' I was genuinely shocked.

'It's amazing what people can do for the good of a much-loved project,' said Philo.

I thought of him the next week when Paul asked Rizpah, Luke and I to meet him at the building where the congregation met. It was a strangely formal request for someone who was betrothed to one of us and who often simply called in, either to see us or to take Luke out. We went, of course, and Rizpah was nervous, fearing that it was some kind of conference on the situation within the Church. 'It amazes me that people think that I am some kind of monster without even considering what it cost me to leave my two children,' she said. 'I suppose they think I didn't care about them— that I couldn't have done it if I had. Have they never considered that love means letting your children go? Letting them stay in a situation where they will be better off without you? Taking care of them by taking yourself away when you are the cause of the dissent and anger in the house? It would not have been love but possession to have taken them with me and put them through the agonies of probable starvation, let alone being chased and dragged back by Lucius's parents. That would have happened, you know. They would have imprisoned me, if they had not killed me.'

I gave her a wordless hug. We had been over this a hundred times and there was nothing I could say. I had tried to argue the tongue-waggers down myself but their self-righteousness angered and then frightened me. It was so rigid that they had no ability, let alone willingness, to see any point of view than the one that served their ends.

Paul met us alone. Barnabas and the rest of the Christians would be arriving at dusk, he said, and he hoped that, after this meeting with us, he would be able to make an important announcement to them.

He had a proposition to put before us, he said. It would be hard for him to suggest it but it was for the good of the community and the good of the Teaching. Rizpah went white—I am sure she knew what was coming. I put my hand out to reassure her but, in a gesture very unlike her, she dashed my hand away. She stood very straight and still.

Paul addressed her first. He said that he regretted saying what he had to say but that the community was being torn apart by his plans to marry her again and the community was his first priority. Rizpah said nothing. She was not going to give him the satisfaction of agreeing and condemning herself.

'Your past is not one which can inspire others,' said Paul. 'You ran away from home; you would not obey your parents. You married a man who became a murderer and you left your children behind.'

'And would the children of a murderer been acceptable if they were here?' she asked with a strange twist to her beautiful mouth.

Paul ignored this interruption. He had a speech prepared. To my surprise, I began to feel slightly sorry for him as well as for Rizpah. He was trying his best. He probably *was* thinking of the community's good.

Paul went on and on, talking about the greater good of all and, perhaps to my relief, my compassion changed into irritation at his sanctimoniousness. Paul always over-did it in my opinion. He ended up inviting Rizpah to terminate their agreement so that he could tell the congregation that she had acted out of strength and with regard for their feelings.

'I won't,' she said, with her chin held high.

What happened next surprised both of us women because Paul said nothing; it was Luke who spoke next. 'You must,' he said. 'There is no shame in it. It is the only thing to do. Paul cannot refuse to marry you because his honour is at stake.'

'And what about my honour,' Rizpah flashed at him. 'You don't think about that do you? No one is standing up for me or for what I have been through.'

'Mother has,' said Luke.

'But *you* haven't,' said Rizpah, dangerously. 'You are old enough and wise enough now to make your own decisions; but you won't. You will only follow your friend Paul! Listen to me, Luke. This is none of your business. None, do you hear me?'

It was the first time my friend had ever chastised my son and I was taken aback. What she said was right but it was surprising nonetheless.

Luke walked over to where Paul was standing and looked at me. 'Mother,' he said. 'It's up to you. She won't listen to us.'

'Up to me?' I said in genuine surprise. 'What do you expect me to do?'

'Tell her that it's you that Paul should marry,' said my son. 'That you are the one who could make him happy—and serve the community—and that he would be a good father to me.'

'I knew it,' said Rizpah, viciously.

'Hold on!' I put my hand on her arm again. 'What did you know?'

'That they've been planning this,' said my friend. 'You didn't know, I excuse you for that—though you do want him, I know that you do for you've told me yourself.

'It would be so neat wouldn't it? After a reasonable time, for Paul to marry you—Yeshua's sister. Just a neat, political alliance for the good of the cause! Perfect! But don't delude yourself, Deborah, that they are going to allow you to be your real self in any convenient marriage with Paul!'

'It couldn't happen,' I said, wildly, ignoring Paul and Luke. 'Paul only believes in one marriage. I've had two! He doesn't want to marry me; believe me, I know!'

'So you've discussed it!'

'Yes. Once. It was quite definitely a "no" on both sides—but it had to be discussed, Rizpah, *because* of the politics of it all.'

'Well the people want it.'

'That's their problem—anyway, they wouldn't want it if it happened. They'd find more ammunition against me than they ever had with you. It's ridiculous.

'Let's go home—the three of us—and just start again.'

Rizpah gave that same, twisted smile again.

'Would that we could,' she said. 'But it's not just about us any more. I don't think that "no" you are talking about was final at all. Paul will cast the same spell of magic on you as he has to me. It's so easy to think his way; I've been thinking his way, myself, these last few weeks; blinded by the beauty and excitement of it all. But it's not *real*, it's a fantasy. '

'Rizpah, I can make my own decisions,' I said, although my heart was sinking. 'But what is this to do with whether or not *you* will agree not to marry Paul? It doesn't look to me as if you want to any more, so why refuse to back down? It's not you who's supposed to be full of pride, it's me!'

'Oh!' Rizpah sat down and put her head in her hands. 'You're right. I'm just maddened by it. Why should I not be furious? I had a future and now it's been taken away by other people's judgement.'

'I don't think you would have been happy,' I said, gently, kneeling down and putting my arms around her. Rizpah leant her head on mine without speaking. The two men stood silently, watching. With a jump I realised that Luke *was* becoming a man. He was taller than Paul already.

'Very well,' said Rizpah, lifting her head. 'Paul, I release you from our betrothal and I wish you luck with your next proposal.' Saying this, she gently pushed me away and walked out of the door.

I stood up and looked at the men before me. They looked back and I saw the relief in both sets of eyes. They did look similar with their dark colouring, though Luke was by far the better looking of the two, even taking into account his excellent health and his youth. A part of me still felt drawn to Paul but the events of the last few weeks had made me a wiser woman. In fact, I could not believe that anyone could seriously think of asking me to marry them when they had made it so clear, so very recently, that it was an impossibility.

And, if this were really going to happen, did Paul really think I could just forget the embarrassment I had felt? Or the humiliation that he had just handed out to my friend? Of course he could. He would expect me to rise higher than any sordid little moment. After all, I was his Saviour's sister and I should know better.

Paul began to speak but, strange though it may seem, his words seemed to pass me by completely. I heard them in some far distant way but a new thought had come into my mind with a clarity which stunned me and, I'm afraid, made me want to burst into laughter.

I could not possibly marry Paul! I had been the wife of the man whom, legend said, had betrayed his Saviour! He must have forgotten that for it was a powerful argument. If people did not want him to marry a woman who had left her children then how would they feel about a woman widowed by the man they believed had caused the crucifixion of their Lord!

'So, Deborah, what is your view on this?' said Paul and I came back to myself. I had not heard a word.

'I'm sorry,' I said. 'Would you repeat it?'

Then Luke, impatient, quicksilver Luke burst into words. We could all travel together, he said. We could go to Ephesus and Antioch and Jerusalem and life would be wonderful.

'I would go ahead,' said Paul. 'You and Luke could come later. We could be married in Antioch. It would be for the good of the Work. People would accept it once it was done; no one would be threatened by it. We would be an invincible team for the Work.

'I know…' he said as I made a gesture of perplexed astonishment. 'I led you to believe I could not marry you but I was mistaken. I learn more every day in my meditation and I know now it is better to marry than to live with unfulfilled desire. And if a marriage is made by God it is indissoluble but not if it is made by man. My marriage to Rizpah was a social marriage, not made by the Lord and I am grateful that I have realised that in time. A marriage to you would be a marriage in Spirit—two people brought together for the highest good.'

I could hardly believe it; he was repeating my own words back to me as if he had invented them himself. And the callousness of it! He truly believed that I would do such a thing to my friend.

But I also saw that he had no idea that anything he was saying was inappropriate. His mind had changed and therefore what he believed now was correct. Any previous thought was discounted; not even overturned—it had never happened at all.

He truly believed that I would marry him and that it was the right thing for us to do. And I knew, with a feeling of true, physical pain in my heart, that if I did not see it his way, I would be judged as wanting.

Never had Paul been more dangerous than this.

I thought quickly and sat, raising one hand to ask for time to consider. In that moment of silence, an answer came through me, not of me.

'Forgive me,' I said. 'I hear all your reasoned arguments and I understand their validity. But I am a woman, an emotional creature, and my best friend and sister has a broken heart. I cannot now consider a proposal that would cause her such additional pain when she is in need of my friendship.'

Both Paul and Luke took a step towards me, their eyes alight. I held up my hand to stop them.

'What is more,' I said, firmly. 'I am afraid that, in any case, I am not free to accept your kind offer. I have no proof that my husband is dead and I believe in my heart that he lives. Therefore I am not free to marry.

'I will, of course, endeavour to find out the true situation about Apollonius but, until then, my answer must be a negative one.'

Luke turned away, making a sound of derision but Paul laid a hand on his arm, stopping him. Only then did I see how much power he had over my son.

'Your sentiments do you all the credit I would expect,' he said. 'We will, of course, put into effect everything appropriate to discern your husband's fate. And until we know, then we will consider the matter closed.'

And then, of course, I saw the truth. This was all because he was afraid to marry Rizpah; afraid to be a lover; afraid to be a father; afraid to lose himself in another's heart and soul. He knew I would never accept him but that to have a tenuous hold on me would be the safest answer. No query would go to Rome for Apollonius just as no query would have gone to Massalia for Rizpah's children.

But in the meantime, he was becoming father to my son—and my son loved him more each day.

I bowed wearily. Nothing could be said. There was nothing to be done.

'Luke I'm going home now,' I said. 'You stay for the meeting if you like; I'll see you later.'

'I'm staying,' said Luke, flicking his heavy hair back with one hand and standing tall, with a touch of defiance. I nodded to them both and let myself out.

Rizpah and I sat down together by the hearth and talked it through with some tears and more anger. But we went to bed friends and that was the only important thing. Luke and I had a tremendous argument where he accused me of ruining his life and then subsided into misery over his father's memory and forgave me. He was at that kind of age.

Then we all picked up the pieces and got on with our lives. We even attended Paul's meetings when we could. Rizpah and I knew that we could never trust Paul again but we also knew that we had work to do in Alexandria.

Life for the Christians settled back into a pattern as soon as it was known that Paul was a single man again. Several women even apologised to Rizpah for the other women's ignorant views, emphasising that they, themselves, would have been happy to overlook the obstacles to such a marriage had it been right for both parties. Rizpah got quite a lot of illicit fun in imitating these women after we got home and I'm afraid I laughed with her at their ridiculousness.

Time passed in the relative peace that was Alexandria. Riots were the norm; religious intolerance flared, threatened and died down again. There is nothing new under Tiferet and those of us who attempted to live around and beyond our Selves, waited and watched.

Then, just as the whole group of Christians was working together; when the drop-outs had dropped out and the curious had gone on to some newer and more exciting venture, Paul seemed to lose interest. About twenty five people now came regularly, worked hard, learnt and taught and lived their lives according to the principles of Christ—and Paul considered his work done for the moment. He and Barnabas began making plans to travel to Ephesus, to visit John and see how the teaching was going there. Both Rizpah and I debated whether or not we would be asked to go with them. Nothing more had been said between Paul and me; whether he knew I understood or not, I couldn't tell but I was glad to leave the matter lying fallow. I knew that letters were regularly sent to Rome by Paul and I must admit that I was slightly nervous whenever a reply arrived for him; but nothing came back about Apollonius or, if it did, it was not revealed to me. I did not further any enquiries myself; all lines of communication had been tried before to no avail and a brief word to Philo had elicited no more hope.

I was curious as to how Paul would get on in Ephesus, the city of the great Temple of Artemis where women were priestesses, but I would never know. However, when the money gathered up from the faithful to pay for Paul and Barnabas's trip was not enough, they asked Rizpah and me to raise the extra. Paul had this wonderful attitude that all monies belonging to any of us were to be pooled. Of course, this is what we had done when Yeshua was alive but that was because we all went home in the winter and earned and everyone took their own part. I did not mind paying for Yeshua's teaching. I did object to paying for Paul!

Just before they were due to leave, Luke qualified as a

physician. I was relieved for, as he had become more and more involved in Paul's and Barnabas's teaching, I had seen less of him. Every available moment he had free from his studies, he had spent with the Christians. That I did not mind but he was beginning to question some of the things I had taught him, preferring to see them from Paul's perspective. Part of that was the need of a young man to rebel against his mother and I always took care not to contradict him but to say that it was important that he found his own answers to things for it was as dangerous to take what I said for granted as it was to assume that Paul was automatically right too. However, for Luke the Sun shone from Paul's eyes and he now preferred to spend Shabbat Eve with the two men and their followers rather than at home with us. He thought our way of invoking the Four Worlds was old-fashioned and boring and preferred Paul's service which was very similar but only involved bread and wine, based on what he had heard that Yeshua had said during his last meal with the disciples.

It surprised me that they were only working with two worlds—wine representing Beriah, the world of spirit and bread representing Assiyah—but when I asked the men about it they said that Yeshua had shown that understanding those two was all that was important. He himself represented the world of the Divine and the person carrying out the service represented the world of the Psyche. If you pushed it, they had a point, but it worried me that Paul still insisted on referring to Yeshua as if he were God.

My argument sounded weak for Paul had removed the woman's role of lighting the candles and it looked as though I was campaigning for my own sex again.

'Though why I shouldn't campaign for women, I don't know!' I said to myself irritably and tried again.

'I am not excluding you,' said Paul, blithely ignoring that he had ceased the only part of the service with a rôle for women (and what a rôle!) and replaced it with nothing. 'You can have your own teaching group for the women when we're gone. You can light lights in that if you like.'

'It's not that *I* need to light the lights,' I said. 'It's that they are an integral part of the service. They are the invocation of the Shekhinah, the Daughter of the Voice; without the drawing down of Azilut, the service is not complete. Without that, women find it hard to understand why they don't need to take part in the rest of the service. I don't want women to feel excluded.'

'Ah,' said Paul in that silky way of his. 'But what you want doesn't matter, does it Deborah? It's what the Lord Jesus wants.'

'It's what God wants!' I said, exasperated, realising that I had argued myself into a corner.

'Well what the Lord Jesus wants and what God wants are the same,' said Paul. 'And they are Azilut. There is no need for the lights. You and I will just have to differ, won't we? After all, I was made Jesus' envoy, not you. You have not created this religion, I have. You have your job to do and I have mine. Let's leave it at that and not quarrel.'

It was just after that argument that Luke told me that he too wanted to go to Ephesus.

'But what about your physician's work?' I asked, knowing again that I was saying the wrong thing.

'I can practise in Ephesus,' said Luke—and I knew that was true. 'Oh Mother, don't oppose me. I'm an adult and I can do what I want to. I do so want to go with Paul and Barnabas. I really do!'

As he spoke I knew that he was right: I had no choice but to let him go and that it would be the right path for him. I could see him with Paul, many years in the future, even better friends than they were now. I could not stand in his way.

I gave him my blessing—and, yes, I did give him money for his fare, so Paul got my money anyway!—but I cried for three full days. Luke was only living the child of my body and my soul and it hurt desperately to see him choosing a different life and teaching from the one that Apollonius and I had given him. Rizpah was wonderful to me; we had both lost two children now…

Paul had done all he could to keep my husband Judah's memory pure while he was in Alexandria. This was another great confusion about Paul! On one matter he could be so harsh and on another, so kind. When I had first talked to him about Judah and about my experience in Rome with the Christians who had condemned him as evil, he had put his hand on mine and promised me that he would never speak a word that would promote such a story. I wondered whether he liked the idea of being a step higher than the disciples and having a different story to tell but he was so kind and so steadfast about his promise that I berated myself for being unjust. However, the rumour had spread, even without Paul's help, for few people could understand the story of Yeshua's crucifixion as it was and the need for a villain was deeper than the urge to understand.

I had told Luke the truth when he was six; that I did not know who his father was. He knew that I had been assaulted by Roman soldiers and that I did not know whether he was their son or child of my first husband. He had never worried about it, regarding himself as truly Apollonius's son and loving his adopted father so deeply that no other father was needed. Once he knew that Apollonius's physical son Vintillius had been one of the men who had lain with me and that we hoped that Luke might have sprung from his seed, he took that as whatever truth he needed. In any case, an adopted son in Roman society was a true son and Luke was legally and emotionally Apollonius's child. Even more, I had taught him that children were sent into their families for particular reasons. Luke's birth had been a miracle, to a mother believed to be infertile, just as Yochanan the Baptist's birth had been to Elisheva, his mother. If the identity of Luke's father was uncertain, then that was not so very different from so many of the heroes and heroines of our traditional stories. God was able to make the barren fertile and bring children to those who needed them in whatever way He wished. Blood lines are only important to those who do not understand spiritual lines.

Most of these explanations were irrelevant to Luke. He was a Roman, son of Apollonius. The doings of some strange Jewish man who might or might not be his father were of no real interest to him. Had he heard the cries of the mob in Jerusalem, calling for vengeance on the family of the betrayer, he might have thought differently but, so far, he had never heard that side of the story.

Barnabas took it for granted that Luke was Judah's son for I had never told him of the possibility of any other father. From Luke's own words he gathered that the boy regarded himself as Apollonius's son which was only right in his eyes. Paul, on the other hand, had probably never even considered Luke's siring, assuming it to be as it appeared to be. For that I was very grateful.

However, over the last year, I had come to know the truth. Luke had grown into Judah's son. Despite the almost impossible timing of his birth, it was unmistakable. His hair grew in the same way and was of the same thickness. Luke had exactly the same habit of flicking it back with one hand and there were other tell-tale signs as well. He would whistle through his teeth just as Judah had—and it irritated me in exactly the same way! He could also write with both hands and play games with either just as well. Judah had been able to do the same. Of course I had no idea what talents or otherwise Luke's other possible fathers might have had but Luke had the same tilt of the head as his natural father and the same explosive but swift temper.

I had said nothing to Luke. I thought that was best. But now my son was leaving to a country were there was no one to defend his father's memory—but there might be many who would see the similarities. How could I not worry?

'It will be all right,' said Rizpah, for I had told her everything. 'He does not know and he doesn't need to know.'

'Maybe he does need to know,' I said. 'I am withholding a truth from him.'

'Well try telling him then!' said Rizpah. 'I don't suppose he will listen to you but at least you will know that you did your best. I don't think he will even hear you!'

She was right. One afternoon, two days before the men were due to sail, I began to talk to Luke about Judah and how the two of them had the same little habits.

'Oh that's rubbish!' said my grown-up son. 'You're imagining it. Anyway, how can you remember that far back?'

'I'm not imagining it,' I said. 'Listen, this is important.' But Luke would have none of it.

'Mother, I'm not the son of a Jew,' he said (and that alone made me blanch!). 'I'm a Roman though and through. I *know* I am. Anyway, you're always telling me that blood lines don't matter so why are you trying to tell me that they do?' I had no answer to that and could not help laughing at my son's logic. We embraced. 'I shall miss you,' I said. 'But I hope that you will be very happy.'

'Oh, I'm sure I will!' he said, his eyes lighting up with pleasure at the thought of the journey. 'I shall learn so much. Anyway, I'll be back one day.'

'I hope so.' I said, but my heart sank. Was he coming back? Would I ever see him again? I pushed the doubts down and smiled at him. I did not raise the issue of his parenting again.

That night, I crept into Luke's room while he was sleeping. I knew that I had to let go of him but I wanted just once more to look on him as my child.

As I looked down at his gangly limbs and the rounded face of youth I thanked God for this miraculous life. Who his father had been really did not matter. Luke was Luke. His life had saved mine through the link to Apollonius—I still shuddered to think what would have happened to me abandoned and condemned in Jerusalem without that blessed child.

It was then, as I watched my son sleeping, that the angels came again and told me what Luke was destined to do. I saw people in a far distant land wearing strange, outlandish and heathen clothing and with extraordinary hairstyles, reading Luke's words from bound volumes of writing. Men and women! Both were reading about Yeshua's life—and about Magdalene my friend and Yeshua's disciple who had given her life to save me and my child from the Roman soldiers when Apollonius and I met. They were reading about Paul as well and his travels. 'You won't be there, Deborah,' said the angel. 'You will not be in these writings. But remember what your brother told you: you do not need to be loved; you do not need to be understood. You have your work and others have theirs.' The image faded as the words echoed in my mind. My task was not to be at the forefront but to hold the value of the Teaching behind the scenes. Luke, on the other hand, was to be remembered forever. A mother can be comforted by knowledge such as that.

It was to be many years, if ever, before any of us were to meet up again and it was yet another hard parting as Paul, Barnabas and Luke embarked on the sturdy little ship bound for Ephesus. They planned to be gone for a year, maybe two, and they left the Alexandrian Christians to take care of themselves. They even had the nerve to tell Rizpah and myself not to interfere and said that they would be writing regularly in case there were any problems. We were both cross and relieved at such a stricture. We mere women would not be able to disentangle the mess that erupted once the group's leader had gone.

Seven

Life went on in Alexandria much as it had before Paul and Barnabas erupted into our lives. And although it was lonelier, we had quite enough to keep us busy to dissolve the pain more quickly than if we had been bored or idle. Years seem to pass more quickly as we age and nothing of much note happened while four summers blossomed, fruited and waned.

Rizpah continued with her letter-writing and also did some translation and copy work for the library. It made us laugh to think that she was a scribe and to imagine the reaction that people in Jerusalem would have to that idea.

I continued working in Constanzia's garden and treating women of all ages. One aspect did trouble me: the amount of unwanted pregnancies in the city. Children were seen as the primary reason for marriage here just as much as at home in Judaea. Having as many children as you could was insurance against losing them—and it was all too common for the young to die from all the childhood ailments in both the cities and the countryside. However, giving birth continuously weakened women greatly and death in childbirth was a common as losing a child in its first years. It did not surprise me that this should be so; the spirit of the child came from the heavens but the body was built entirely from the woman's own flesh and blood. Her bones created the child's bones and her strength dictated the child's strength. It was very obvious that the weaker the woman, the weaker the child and nature is savage. It will side at all points with the new life so if the child needed more to sustain it than the woman could provide, it would still be taken—but her life would be forfeit.

I had long been of the opinion that two or three strong children with a healthy mother was a better idea than seven increasingly frail children and an exhausted woman who wept at the idea of yet another pregnancy instead of greeting it with joy.

Sarah's presence in my womb and my life had taught me more than I ever thought possible. It was not apparent until I began to work in the garden again but from somewhere—from her—I had inherited knowledge. Not information but knowledge. Just like Rosa, my first-ever teacher in Nazara had, I now understood the secrets of life and death within a woman's womb.

It became fairly well known throughout the underground of the city that a woman could come to the garden and, in return for a little work of weeding and cultivating, she could learn how to prevent constant pregnancy without harming herself. She could be taught what plants to use and how; and take away seeds in the autumn to start her own little plot. But sometimes the flowers would fail as I knew only too well myself (or the woman had not been as careful as she thought). There were also many women after a feast day or a festival who took a chance and lost. Even more common were girls just past puberty who, in the first excitement of first love, hardly knew what was happening to them but who found, two or three weeks later, that they and their life were ruined. In either case there would be a woman, white-faced and desperate, waiting for me in the early morning, fearing that I might be a witch but so frightened that they would go to almost anyone. They would beg me to help them and I would weep with them for their pain was so stark, so sharp and so guilty.

'Why?' I thought. 'Why does the Lord give children to those who do not want them and none to so many women who are desperate to conceive?' In my heart I knew the answer. Our lives were woven in the Pargod, the great tapestry of creation, and everybody's story was uniquely his or her own; there was no overall answer which could not offend or upset. Some were simply destined not to conceive—this time. There were other matters or other people's children for them to care for.

The first option I would look at, when there was a woman with an unwanted pregnancy, was whether this imbalance could be redressed. Could she, with the aid of herbs and teaching, change her mind or, more accurately, get in touch with true feelings of motherhood? Sometimes this worked but more often it did not. The fear was too deep. The next option was whether she could carry the baby and give it to another woman who had none of her own to rear? Rarely but, in a few very valuable cases, this could be done. If there were a husband in the case it was not often possible; if there were no acknowledging father, with care and subterfuge it might be. There was still pain and grief involved, of course, and my herbs and remedies for the resentment that women suffered while men appeared to go unscathed (this life!) were much needed and, fortunately, very effective.

To very few of them could I say that each life was part of a pattern and that one uncaring father in one generation could, possibly, come back to learn how it felt to be so unloved.

There were abortionists of all kinds in Alexandria, just as there are in any city. For every young woman like Mariamne, the daughter of Herod Agrippa in Rome who nearly died from clumsy handling of herbs, many more escaped and continued their lives, often wiser but frequently infertile from that moment because of the remedy they had taken. Perhaps that was a punishment; perhaps it was a blessing; it depended on the woman and what she wanted in her life. For those who regretted their decision later, there could be the understanding that to adopt the child of another unhappily pregnant woman would repay whatever cosmic debt there might be. Often—so often that it could not be coincidence—once another woman's child had been taken in and cared for and loved, the first woman's womb would respond again and new life would come for her as well.

If you could understand that all children came from God and that the raising of that child as your own was as important as its blood, there was no problem. Luke and Apollonius were a wonderful example of a child coming to Earth to be the son of a particular man. No matter who had sired him, Luke was Apollonius's son.

For those who came to me asking for help to end their pregnancy, we tried a different tack from the traditional herbalists. Yes, the plants which could release the tiny temple within the woman's body were there and, if the woman wished, she could arrange to see Constanzia, take her dose and leave with no further contact. But for those who chose to work with me it was a different matter. We worked together with prayer, ritual and love to solve the problem with the soul of the child itself.

It can be done. Not easy, perhaps, but it can be done. If contact is made and the soul understands, its temple can be dissolved with no damage to it or to its mother. If the soul needs that particular mother it may (and often does) decide to wait in the heavens and come again later when the time is right. Souls are filled with love for their mothers before they incarnate. They do not suffer if they are consulted. If their temple is destroyed in fear or anger they may well feel shock at the termination of their tenuous hold on the physical world. They may also grieve and their future lives might perhaps be affected—but they do not die. Until the soul is firmly attached to its body it exists only in the world of Yezirah and neither birth nor death on the Earth can touch it. Miscarriage or abortion simply mean that the child will come to Earth later, perhaps into the same family, perhaps not.

No one knows when a soul actually slides between the worlds and becomes firmly attached to its body. I have studied this whenever I can but there is very little written for this is women's knowledge and that is carried from mother to daughter or held in the heavens until someone is willing to listen.

My own belief is that the souls flit in and out of their temple, checking on it now and again and getting used to being there. They are often to be found around the mother and the father and others of the family, observing them from outside and sometimes they take a decision not to incarnate. Perhaps they realise that their choice was inappropriate; perhaps they are too frightened to come; perhaps a fellow soul whom they love takes another path which would make their life less worthwhile. It is a matter that can be debated for years. We forget that souls are not children. They, too, have a say in their incarnation.

Only the mother of the child can know when the soul is fixed inside her for it is her choice and the soul's—and its father's—and nobody else's. Sometimes the father is important for the soul's link may be with the man and not with the woman; sometimes a woman would be brave enough to bear a child but her husband would take it and expose it so that it died as soon as it was born. This happened far more often than we admitted in Alexandria. We pretended that it was a barbarian practice but any doubt over a child's parentage usually meant that that child did not survive to cause embarrassment.

With that in mind, how can you blame a woman who has made a mistake or acted stupidly for wanting to ensure her baby is sent home to the heavens in peace rather than pain?

One thing is sure; at birth the soul is joined fully to the body. That is why babies cry. It must be so hard to be an infinite being of such might and power and to be enclosed in such a helpless body for so long. I don't remember my own first years but I have watched many children, including my own, and I have seen the frustration and even anger of a soul feeling so compressed. You can speak to them without your voice but with your eyes and your knowledge and they will often acknowledge you and know that they are understood.

Once a woman has learnt to communicate with the soul of her unborn child, more often than not they will make an agreement between them and either the woman will become content or the soul will withdraw until a better time. No herbs may be needed at all. Sometimes help is needed to shift the temple even if the spirit has agreed to leave it. It depends.

I would also help those women who had acted before they thought, had aborted their baby and were upset and guilty at their decision. Then, if they were willing, I would teach them the art of stillness within and we would enact a small ceremony of repentance and a request for forgiveness. The emphasis on 'repentance' being that it means 'to think again' and the emphasis on 'forgiveness' being 'to let go what went before.' I used a service

I devised myself based on the structure of the Tree of Life and often, in fact nearly always, the woman felt the soul's love and forgiveness rush in over her in a wave of emotion. Perhaps that was the greatest work I ever did: the teaching of women that a soul has its own life; that it can, and will, work with its mother and that conscious choice is better for all concerned.

The little group of Paul's followers continued their meetings and their teaching of the coming of Christ and his anticipated return at the end of days but Rizpah and I had less to do with them once Paul had gone. We were friendly and courteous and attended perhaps one in four or five meetings when there was a separate women's group that we were asked to oversee—and some of the Jewish converts sometimes asked us on a point of law which we answered to the best of our ability.

None of them whatsoever was interested in the inner teaching or the Tree of Life, even though that was what Yeshua had taught himself. They said that it was unnecessary once you knew Christ and I was torn between admiring the simplicity of such a faith which needed no structure and irritation that they rejected Yeshua's own beliefs in his name!

Rows boiled over from time to time and the little group had a loud voice. It made its presence known throughout the city. Matters between the Greeks and the Jews were still simmeringly uncertain at times and a new, volatile religion did not help matters by condemning both sides. I did try to suggest tact and discretion but the impulse of the faith was so great that people found that hard. The Christians were so proud of their knowledge that they were prone to throwing it in other people's faces or to try and convert them from their 'false' way of thinking.

Sometimes, indeed often, they did convince people to join them but then the old arguments about food laws and what was right and what was wrong would break out again. Without the structure of the Tree of Life to look at and understand it was hard to decide what was practical and sensible and what was prejudice and the squabbles took up valuable time which could have been used in much better ways.

One bright autumnal morning, when Paul, Barnabas and Luke had been gone for nearly a year, I was talking with Philo and members of our study group in the library when a great cry went up in the street outside.

'Oh my goodness, what now?' said Philo wearily as the rest of us jumped up and rushed to the window. As we did, a stone smashed though the beautiful coloured glass, sending shards of sharp, flashing light crashing into the room.

Several of us yelped and backed away.

'Another riot,' said Philo heavily without getting up himself to look. His ailing strength galled him but he was wise enough not to over-exert himself. The rest of us shook our heads in irritation and concentrated on clearing up the mess. Outside, the noise continued although it was hard to tell exactly what was going on.

'There'll be real trouble if they don't stop soon,' said Roshan, the Egyptian who was one of our most regular attendees. 'The army will be here before we know it with that kind of row going on.'

I pricked up my ears. 'Isn't that "Jesus" being shouted?"' I asked and we all stood silently for a moment. Philo heaved a big sigh. 'I'm afraid so,' he said. 'Too much enthusiasm and no balancing discernment as usual. Faiths are best left to grow quietly, not thrown at everyone in the street.'

'But surely the Christians know not to fight back or to attack,' I said doubtfully. 'They must have been provoked severely.' Carefully, I peeped out of the shattered window at the crowd below. From my vantage point it was obvious that not even those who were shouting and fighting below were entirely sure what was going on and, as usual, there seemed to be a few who had joined in for no good reason apart from enjoying a good fight, whatever the issue might be. I did recognise four or five of the Christians including two women but, even more importantly, I could see a Roman cohort running down a nearby road towards us.

'Run!' I shouted to those below, waving to try and attract their attention but Roshan pulled me sharply back into the room. 'Never, *never* do that!' both he and Philo said in unison. Then

Philo went on: 'If anyone in authority saw you trying to help rioters escape you will be in as much trouble as they will—and so will we. Honestly, Deborah, show a little sense!'

I shrugged my shoulders and licked the back of my hand where a sliver of glass had drawn blood. 'I had to try and do something,' I said. 'I don't think anyone heard but at least I tried.'

'Humph,' said Philo. 'Well, I think we should all retire to a back room away from all the trouble and, if we are asked, say we know nothing. That may sound harsh but if we get involved it will only exacerbate the situation. We can do what we can to pick up the pieces afterwards.'

'The pieces' included two Christians dead, four more in prison and a shattered community in danger of losing its faith. And, which was worse, one where several people threatened to turn actively and publicly against what they had formerly believed.

I went to their next meeting, two days later. I must admit I was wary but I was also curious and anxious to see if there was anything I could do to help. Rizpah, always more sensible than I, tried to dissuade me from going then sighed deeply, threw her shawl over her shoulders and stomped along beside me muttering until we both began to laugh at ourselves.

'If this is the right religion and Jesus loves us, why did he allow those men to attack us?' asked one of the most faithful of the group, whose heart was more broken than his head.

'It is because the last days are coming and those men were the messengers of the evil one,' said another. 'We must resist them and stay close to our Lord.'

'But why didn't he protect us? Two of us are dead! If he loved us he would protect us.'

'He did protect those of us who are here. The others must have been secret sinners who had to be removed.'

I winced at this. Such talk could never lead to reconciliation within the group—or without, for that matter.

Both Rizpah and I tried to talk to them about the dangers of too much enthusiasm and the importance of balance in all things. 'Not even the Christ can protect you if you are out of balance,' I said. 'You have to be in the place of truth within yourself before you can contact the higher worlds. If you are not still and clear inside then you are prey to illusion and illusion is very tempting.' But they were not going to listen to a woman. I tried to tell the story of the Good Samaritan, the parable which was meant to show that a man's or a woman's race or religion was irrelevant, that it was the love in their hearts which counted, but that, too, fell on stony ground. I tried as well to tell them of Yeshua's and my visit to Jerusalem on the day when riots broke out and how he had guided me to be still within, to hold the point of Tiferet within me so that I was not involved in the wave of fear and hostility which broke out. But they did not have the discipline or the understanding of the inner worlds and what I said made no sense to them.

For all that, when more of the group were rounded up and arrested as troublemakers, the group's leader Philip came to me to ask me to intercede for them.

'How would I do that?' I asked in genuine surprise. ' Nobody knows me and I have no influence with the governor.'

'But your friend Philo does, through his brother the Alabarch,' said Philip. 'If you ask him, he will speak for us.'

'If you had troubled to get to know Philo or the deeper teaching behind your belief, you would not have to come to me now,' I snapped, exasperated—and then softened. I knew only too well the fear of imprisonment and judgement from those who did not begin to understand another's way of thinking. 'I will do what I can,' I said. 'But I can't promise anything. Just tell me one thing; why do you disregard the words of your Saviour's sister who was there with him and learnt from him? Do you think that I am making it all up or something? Do you think everything I say about learning to know yourself is just rubbish that I have made up?'

Philip looked at me blankly. 'All you need is Christ,' he said. 'The Risen Christ, not anything which went before that.'

I sighed heavily and left him. There was no point of contact between us. Although he was devoted to Christianity he had no interest in letting anything else in his life change. He still did not understand the difference between the ego and the Self or any of the hard work it took to lead the life that Yeshua had taught. 'Oh Paul!' I said to myself. 'I hope you know what you are doing.'

I did speak to Philo but there was no need. He had already spoken to his brother, the leader of the Jewish people, and he did intercede even though the Christians were nothing to do with him. They were released but not before they had been whipped and cautioned to keep the peace.

That year, several letters arrived from Luke. He wrote that the mission in Ephesus was going well (although both Rizpah and I read between the lines and wondered). The letters were long and affectionate and it was obvious that Luke was growing steadily more sure of himself. His strengths as a physician were often needed and he enjoyed combining spiritual teaching with medicine. 'People recover so much better when they realise that there is something they can do to help themselves,' he wrote.

The third letter from Ephesus carried news of Salome, my sister. I had had no idea she was living there with her children nor that her husband had died some years before. 'They are a lively and happy group,' wrote Luke 'I have missed having a mother and Salome reminds me a little of you. I like her very much and she has told me many stories, of you and your childhood and of Jesus too. It makes the stories come alive when you hear them afresh from someone who was there. I think we should weave all the stories together into an account of those times so I have decided to keep a record of all the things I hear and perhaps of our travels as well.

'John, Jesus' disciple has sons of his own and one of them, also called John, is only a couple of years younger than me. He is a real mystic! He has told us about some amazing visions he has had about the last days which are approaching. Jesus is coming back to us very soon and then it will be the judgement time! John wants to write as much as I do and I think it would be wonderful if a group of us wrote four different accounts of Jesus' time with each one reflecting a different world. One could be about the physical ministry, the second about the soul and the images of life and the third about humanity and how it can rise above the animal (I'd like to do that one!). John would write the fourth one, Azilut, of course. He and his father have such a way of speaking that it makes me feel as though I am on fire with excitement.

'These accounts could be stored and taught from so that everyone can learn the truth and then they can be given to Jesus when he comes. I wish I knew when and where that will be. I would so love it to be in my lifetime.'

When I read that, my heart sang. So Luke had not forgotten the teachings he had learnt as a child at all! Even if the Christians believed a structure did not matter, those who were closer to Yeshua still did.

'This writing sounds a good idea,' said Rizpah when she read the letter. 'They're all a bit enthusiastic about the end of the world, though, aren't they? Do you think they're right?'

'No,' I said. 'Not about that. But, of course, I could be wrong. I think it's very natural when you have had a tremendous mystical experience to have a desire that things should be coming to an end soon. Everyone likes to think they have had an important part in matters and how much more important could you be than to be there at the End of Days?'

There was much to think of and discuss in the letter but, the next day, Rizpah came home with a sore throat and, despite my patent remedies, by late evening she had a raging fever.

There were always sicknesses such as typhus circulating in a sea-port like Alexandria and I was concerned for her. I sat up into the night with her, bathing her brow and trying to make her restless body as comfortable as I could for I was sure that sickness was alleviated by cleanliness. Then, having done all I physically could, I sat and prayed and watched until dawn. This was a long dark night of the soul for if Rizpah did not recover I would truly be alone. Philo, of course, remained but without Luke, without Apollonius, without Rizpah—without even Paul and Barnabas—I would an orphan indeed.

As my friend and sister cried out in delirium a soft, hazy rain fell over the city. I walked up and down, up and down the apartment, thinking. I prayed fervently for her recovery for both our sakes. She had endured so much in her life with so little complaint that she deserved a blessing. '*But life is better in the higher worlds*' was the answer I received and I had to admit that I could not quarrel with that. If Rizpah were to be taken it would mean rest and light for her but only additional pain for me.

'Please,' I said. 'I do my best; you know I do. I'm not perfect; I'm not even good but I try. I really need her here with me and, if it's not too horribly selfish, please let her live. Please don't let it be typhus.'

It was not typhus. By first light, Rizpah had come through the worst and, although she was still very sick, I felt far more confident that she would recover. I managed to persuade her to drink some soup and she slept in my arms almost as peacefully as a little child. Within three days she was well on the way to recovery and I could relax.

That was the last I remembered for some days for the fever took its turn with me. It was nearly a week before I could think, speak or make myself understood again and in that time I believed myself to be back in Jerusalem after Yeshua's crucifixion. Again, I overhead the disciples discussing Judah. 'It's lucky he's dead,' said one voice echoing around my head. Was it Thomas or Andrew or Nathaniel? Then I was at En Gedi at the time of Luke's birth. Strange images raced in and out of my mind and the faces of Joseph, Magdalene and others I did not recognise swam in and out of my consciousness. 'Will she die?' I heard—Rizpah's voice sounding young and small—but then she had been so very young then. 'She has died,' came the answer. Was that Imma? Was I really dead? Then would I see Apollonius again? Or Judah? Which one was my husband? Perhaps it was all a dream and none of us were dead? Not even Yeshua.

Another time I was back in the dim, scented room at the brothel in Jerusalem with Magdalene bathing my face and snapping at me as she had when she thought that I was an ascetic holy woman who wanted to judge her. My body ached again from the stones which had been thrown at me. 'You're lucky you're not dead,' she said. 'One of the children died. You should have died instead.'

Then I was in Rome, nursing Caligula who was tossing and

turning in his bed, foaming at the mouth. I took the ailing Emperor of Rome by the shoulders and shook him, shouting: 'Where is he? Where is he? Did you kill my husband? Did you kill Apollonius?' Then the air shivered around me and I saw a strange man before me with Apollonius standing behind him in a haze of silvery light. I spoke to him but the words echoed strangely and I could not hear them.

'The answer to your question,' said the man in the foreground but at once, he began to fade away. 'The answer to your question is…' I strained to hear, desperately I strained and, as the image and the voice disappeared, I heard clearly, like the tone of a bell, 'Yes.'

I cried out and woke.

It was Rizpah, not Magdalene who was bathing my brow. Still hazy, I could see how similar they were with their dark beauty and kohl-ringed eyes. I smiled at my friend gratefully and held on to her arm.

'So you're back,' she said with a welcoming smile. 'We have been so worried.'

'Have I been raving?' I asked, feeling slightly embarrassed for enough of my dreams and delusions had stuck in my memory to make me hope that I had not shouted out loud.

'Oh yes,' said Rizpah. 'But don't worry. Very little of it made any sense. Look. I have brought you some fresh oranges. Could you swallow a little juice?'

I said yes and lay back, exhausted, on the pillows while she cut and squashed the fruit. My mind was still wandering, full of that confusing last dream. What was the question I had asked? And who had that man been—the one who was answering it?

The thought nagged at me for several days while I was slowly recovering my strength. Those were good days; Rizpah and I were both silly like children, playing and talking and enjoying living again. On the fourth morning I awoke with a jump. The man in the dream had been Tacitus, Apollonius's teacher at the library. I had only seen him once but now I could remember his face. Tacitus studied the stars and was able to answer questions for people with information from the Heavens. So, what was the question that I had asked in my dream? Surely it must have been about Apollonius? Perhaps Tacitus could tell me if he were alive or dead?

From that moment on, you would have thought I was impatient to get up and go out to the library. But I was frightened at taking such a step. I talked it over and over with Rizpah while I recovered my strength and, bless her, she listened as she always had. I had defended the astrologers against Paul's judgement but did he not have a point? After all he had said about knowledge of Yeshua being the Messiah being all that we needed, why did I need a star-gazer to tell me the truth. Surely the angels would have told me themselves if there was anything I needed to know. I, of all people, who knew from experience of angels, should not need an intermediary.

'Well, the dream may have been the angels telling you to go to Tacitus,' said Rizpah.

'Or it could just be an illusion—or even a temptation,' I said. 'If Apollonius had not studied the stars he would not have been taken. Isn't that enough of a lesson?'

'You don't know that,' said Rizpah. 'Apollonius was a good man. He put God first in all things and he was not dabbling or messing about with something he just thought was amusing. He was trying to increase his knowledge of God's existence and power and using that knowledge in worship. You told me yourself—and Philo has said the same—that an honest man has many enemies and this might have been an excuse. There were plenty of other people predicting Caligula's death who got away with it. There's really only one way to tell.'

'Which is?'

'To follow your heart and go and find out. But take care, keep your wits about you and, if you get any inkling that what you are doing is wrong, turn round and come straight home.'

Even so, it took me two whole weeks to make up my mind. I battled with myself constantly until I realised that my whole argument was an illusion. I knew that using different techniques to approach God was perfectly acceptable if you used them carefully and consciously. Even the Tree of Life was only a technique for approaching God; it was my fear over the answer which was stopping me from going. That set up a whole new argument and, this time, I did not know the answer. The dream said that the answer to my question was 'yes' but what had the question been? What if the question asked in the dream was 'is Apollonius dead?' Could I really face knowing once and for all that he was? Surely I could, it was more than ten years since he had been gone and I had grieved my fill. No, it was not so much that for if Apollonius were dead then there was nothing for me to do but to continue living my life. Did I really have the courage to find out that Apollonius was still alive? If the answer were yes, then what would I do? Go to Rome? Stay here and wait? And if he were still alive, where was he? In prison? Or had he, for some reason, decided not to come home? No, I shook my head. He would not do that. But what if he could not get back? I shook my head again. I knew he would send me some message even if he could not come home. But what if he had sent one and it had been lost or misdirected? He might think I had simply not replied. And round and round again went the argument until I was in danger of worrying myself so much that I might sicken again.

Rizpah pointed out that I had to do something, anything, to end the *impasse*. In fact, she as good as ordered me down into the town to face up to my fears once and for all. I went into the library deliberately at the time when the astronomers and star-calculators met for their weekly discussion group. I had often met the other men who had studied with Apollonius but, since my husband's arrest, I had avoided all his former companions. It was illogical to blame them for what had happened but it was still difficult not to do so.

To my surprise, I did not have to ask for Tacitus. He came into the lobby within moments of my arrival and, even more amazingly as we had only met once, he recognised me. He nodded and signed for me to wait while he talked to a group of men also waiting in the lobby. Had he known I was coming? Nerves fluttered in my stomach. I didn't like that.

I waited, impatiently, but once the meeting was over Tacitus walked back across the lobby to speak to me. He was a tall, thin man in his late fifties—a fine age for an ascetic for they rarely took care of themselves and often died young. His face was lined and pale and his eyes a deep, cold blue. You could be very afraid of Tacitus even if you could not see that his eyes were filled with the Glory of God as well as the mysteries of the Universe. Just one look at those eyes reassured me. This was a man who plied his craft for the sake of enlightenment. Apollonius had once said that Tacitus believed that the stars were the servants of the Creator; each one a perfected being like a god; each with its own character and effect on our worldly affairs. Tacitus would not say such things to people who would not listen or understand nor, being Greek, would he say them to a woman. I knew that I was honoured when he come across to me without my having to ask for an appointment.

His voice was surprisingly thin and reedy but it had authority and I found myself shaking at the knees when I voiced my request. Was there any way of knowing, I asked, whether Apollonius were truly dead or whether he might be in prison, alive but still lost to me?

Tacitus looked down at me thoughtfully. I was tall for a woman and it was rare for me to have to look up into anyone's face. 'Do you really want to know?' he said. 'Sometimes it is better not to know the answers to questions such as these.'

I thought of my weeks of turmoil. 'Yes I do,' I said, stoutly. 'I have thought long and hard. I feel that there is no proper ending to our marriage. If he is still alive that would make sense to me but if he is dead, I have to learn to let go, finally, and move on. I have held onto a vague dream for much too long.'

'And if he were alive but imprisoned and you were never to meet again,' asked Tacitus. 'What then?'

'The stars could tell you that much?'

'Yes.'

I swallowed but took my courage in both hands. 'It would be hard but at least I would know the truth,' I said. 'I would know what to pray for. It is the uncertainty which is the worst thing. I feel inside that he is alive but I cannot trust my judgement because it is what I want to feel. Everyone else tells me that he is dead but, over ten long years, I have not managed to accept that. I had a dream about you so perhaps you are the path to the answer that I need.'

'Again, I ask you, are you sure?' said Tacitus. He was going to test me as long and as hard as he could. Strangely, that only gave me confidence. He could be no charlatan if he were trying to put me off so thoroughly.

'I'm sure,' I said. 'If Apollonius is alive I can at least write to people I knew in Rome or I could even go there to see if I could do anything. Even if we were never to be together again I would be willing to do anything I could to free him. If there is a reason why he cannot return to Alexandria, well, I will just have to accept that.' As I spoke, I realised just how hard that would be but I was not the kind to turn back and I was driven to find out the truth. If it was painful I would just have to cope with it. I had done just as much before and I was still strong.

'What if there isn't an answer?' said Tacitus.

'What do you mean?' I was confused.

'Sometimes the Great Ones know that it is better for someone not to have an answer,' he said. 'Often the answer is not in the fate of a person but in the actions still to come. Then, the stars cannot foretell what will happen. It is up to the individual. Apollonius may be alive today but dead within a month. Then, it is no use for the stars to give you false hope.'

'Look,' I said. 'I have to believe that I am here for a good reason and that I will get an answer. If you don't want to ask the stars for me, then just say so. But I want to ask.'

Tacitus looked at me long and hard. 'Very well,' he said. 'Come with me.'

He led me first into the great centre courtyard of the library where the sundial stood.

'Ask your question,' he said. 'Form it simply so that the Great Ones can answer you directly. Just one question. Take your time to get it right.'

I thought hard. There were several questions. 'I don't know which one to ask,' I said. 'If I ask if he is alive and he is then there are so many others to follow that. What should I do; where should I go; will we ever meet again?'

'Just ask the main one and the others should also be apparent,' said Tacitus kindly.

'Then the question is this: "Is my husband Apollonius still alive?"' I said. Tacitus checked the exact markings on the sundial. 'Come back tomorrow at the same time and I will tell you the answer—if there is one,' he said.

He nodded, turned and left me, standing abandoned in the great courtyard, torn between hope and a sudden, fierce desire to turn back time and to run away and hide.

One whole day to wait. Not much. And I have faced harder days. But I did not sleep; I could not concentrate. I could not think straight; I could barely eat. I was back at the library far too early the next day, pacing up and down like a caged animal.

Tacitus did not come to me himself, this time. Instead he sent a young man to fetch me to his rooms at the back of the building—a singular honour had I but realised it. As it was, I followed the youth irritably, stumbling in the dim, winding passages and up flights of stone stairs. Tacitus's study was on the second floor in a part of the building where I had never been before. It was empty when I entered and the young man mumbled something about waiting for a few moments. Nervously, I began to pace but then the glory of the surroundings began to work its way through to me and I became interested, despite my impatience. The study was a great, high-ceilinged room draped with all kinds of exotic wall-coverings—mostly diagrams and charts of what seemed to be great complexity. The floor and the tables were covered with papyrus and instruments of calculation and the atmosphere was both hallowed and slightly chaotic. He obviously had an area for teaching—as Philo had—for there was a clutter of seats and cushions around a chalking board and there was one great desk where Tacitus himself obviously studied. Everywhere there were pictures and calculations of the planets and the stars and, to my amazement, among the beautiful and strange pictures and charts pinned to the wall was a diagram of something very like a cross between the menorah and the

Lightning Flash image of the Tree of Life I had first seen in my fifteenth year.

I was standing before it, on tiptoe with my hands behind my back, peering up and trying to decipher the letterings that were inscribed on the Sefirot, when Tacitus came into the room behind me. I felt his presence before I heard it but I did not turn round.

'Yes,' your husband liked that too,' he said without bothering to greet me. 'We often talked about your Tree of Life. Your system is very clear.'

'Thank you,' I said. 'Where did you get this? Did you draw it yourself?'

'No,' said Tacitus. 'It comes from Sidon. There are astronomers there with whom I trained. They use that system to great effect. Look, you can see where all the planets fit onto the structure.'

'And the gods too,' I said. 'My brother Yeshua taught me about the planets and Apollonius and I placed them on our own diagrams and discussed them and the gods they represent. We have … I have … quite a few such diagrams. Perhaps a little more refined but essentially the same.'

'Hmm,' said Tacitus, looking at me curiously. 'You are a most unusual woman.'

I could tell that he was not sure whether he approved of me or not. His Greek background and training would have given him a less free attitude towards women than Apollonius's traditional Roman one. I looked back at him without expression. His opinion of me did not matter—as long as it did not affect the answer to the question I had come to hear.

'Sit down,' said Tacitus. 'There is much to tell you.'

I obeyed. Suddenly my mouth was dry.

Tacitus unrolled a chart on his desk and began to talk. 'The answer to your question is very clear,' he said. 'One of the clearest charts I have seen in a long time. Your husband is alive, my dear. He was not executed. He is in prison, possibly in Rome—certainly under Roman jurisdiction.'

The room lit up around me. 'Alive?' I breathed. 'Are you sure?'

'Quite sure,' said Tacitus. 'And you will meet again. How, it does not tell me, nor can I be certain when. The love you have for each other is shown and it is lasting and there is a desire on both your parts to be reunited. It will not be here in Alexandria; that much is plain. It could be in three months or three years. It is hard to be precise. But you will meet again and you will have many more years together.'

I sat, silently, seeing only my hands folded in my lap. The sudden knowledge was too much to take in all at once. All logic revolted against it but, deep inside, I knew that it was true. Had I not always, secretly, felt differently about Apollonius from how I had felt about Judah? I had *known* inside that Judah was dead before anyone told me. With Apollonius I had never felt that.

I was silent, marshalling a hundred clamouring thoughts.

Tacitus waited with impressive patience.

'Does it have to happen exactly as the chart tells?' I asked eventually. 'Is it set in stone or can my—or his—actions affect this outcome even now?'

Tacitus looked at me appraisingly. 'A very intelligent question,' he said. 'And one which I cannot answer. This science is still quite young.'

I looked puzzled for I had thought that astronomers had been following the stars for all time. 'We learn more every day,' Tacitus went on. 'But the more we learn, the less we know.'

I laughed, despite myself. 'I can understand that,' I said. 'I too study ancient knowledge and the more I learn the more I realise there is to learn. Do you have an opinion based on what you *do* know?'

'I would imagine that the outcome is set,' said Tacitus. 'The indications are very clear and there are signs of destiny there. Do not make the assumption that a chart is always easy to read. Often, in fact very often, the question cannot be answered at all or the signs are very vague. Then it generally does mean that all the actions depend on human free will and not everything is in place which can make a certain outcome.'

'Does it say what I should do?' I asked hopefully.

'No.'

'Nothing?'

Tacitus looked at me with one eyebrow raised and then looked down at the chart again.

I waited. My patience did not match his.

'No,' he said again. 'Only that you will not meet in Alexandria. It will be north of Alexandria. But more than that I cannot tell.'

'And you can tell all of this from the placing of the stars at the time that the question is asked?' I said. 'It is extraordinary.'

'It would appear so,' agreed Tacitus. 'But it is always interesting to see when someone chooses to ask a question. It is very rare that they think of a question and can contact someone who can help them without a certain amount of time passing. It is as though the higher powers arrange for the question to be delayed until the stars will be able to answer it.'

'I have been thinking of coming to you for some weeks,' I said. 'Would the answer have been different if I had come even the day before yesterday.'

'Completely different,' said Tacitus. 'Even earlier or later on the same day would have given another answer. That is what makes each moment of our lives unique and shows how we are guided, even without our knowledge. You knew, inside yourself, when to come and no other time would have been appropriate.'

'I still find it extraordinary,' I said. 'To think that the stars which circle us can tell us so much!'

'Ah, but they don't circle us,' said Tacitus with a twinkle in his eye. 'The Earth is a planet like Mars or Jupiter. It is a sphere just like them. It, like them, circles the Sun. The stars don't move at all. It is the Earth which moves.'

'No!' I could not believe him. It was too ridiculous. Everyone knew that the Sun, the Moon and the stars moved around our Earth. And the idea that we lived on a circular planet was ludicrous. Why, we would all fall off if it were not flat!

'Look at your diagram,' said Tacitus. 'The Sun is at the centre. You call it Tiferet do you not? The place of stillness and truth.'

'Yes, yes, that's right.' I began to feel slightly dizzy. 'But that can't mean …'

'Of course it does,' said Tacitus. 'Why would your diagram lie? But you don't have to believe me. Perhaps it is better if you don't.

Frankly, I wouldn't recommend you to try and tell the people in the street.'

'No, no of course not.' I was totally bemused. My mind had been stretched too far and a fog of uncertainty was threatening to cloud it. All this had been rather too much for me. I had enough to think about with the news about Apollonius. What should I do now?'

Somewhat dizzily, I got up and turned to go, then stopped. 'I must pay you,' I said. 'I am sorry; I never even thanked you. It's all such a shock. I am grateful; very grateful indeed. I never asked what you charge. I may have to pay you in instalments if it is very expensive.'

'There is no direct charge,' said Tacitus. 'Usually there is but there is something I need more than money.'

'Which is?' I asked, slightly nervously.

'I will ask for some of your knowledge in return,' said Tacitus. 'For my daughter. She has long been sick with a wasting illness and I have been unable to find a cure for her. I know that you are a herbalist and your abilities are well spoken of. Also that your brother was a miraculous healer. If you will treat my daughter for me, she will recover and I will consider myself fully repaid.

'Of course I will,' I said. 'You daughter will soon be well.' I stopped, surprised at the words which had come from my mouth. They sounded so arrogant. And yet, this time I *knew* it was true. And so, I could see, did Tacitus.

'Thank you,' I said again. 'I hope we will meet again.'

He nodded and then bowed. I bowed back and left the room; my body felt a different weight from when I entered and I knew I was walking taller.

I hardly remember how I made my way back home. I think I danced. Rizpah was out and I reorganised most of the apartment and cleaned it from top to bottom before I could stop. Then, I made myself a tisane and sat on the floor, hugging a cushion to me and rocking backwards and forwards and trying to think straight. Apollonius was alive! Apollonius was alive (and the land we lived on was spherical!). Apollonius was alive! (and we lived on a planet!). Apollonius was alive! (and the Earth moved around the Sun!) My mind, went round in circles, just like the Earth. Now what would I do?

Before all the doubts could start up again, I heard that Tacitus's daughter had been healed of her malady. Within hours of my visiting her father, she became hungry again for the first time in many months and her strength and health were miraculously returned practically overnight. I never even had to visit her. That, alone, told me that I had done the right thing, no matter what anyone else might think. The Lord would never have done such a miracle had I gone in the wrong direction.

I did not trouble others with my new knowledge but hugged it to myself in a kind of secret delight. I did not even tell Philo to start with, for he was sick with an ague, but Rizpah and I talked it over and over trying to work out what was best for us to do. Should we sell up and travel to Rome to join Apollonius? Was there something I could do to hasten his release? Would Rizpah want to come with me, even? And what about Luke?

'You can't leave,' said Rizpah, sensibly. 'Your income is here; your home is here. What if Luke were to return here with the others and find you gone? He was upset enough last time you took a decision like that and stayed behind in Rome to deal with Caligula and he and his father came on to Alexandria.'

'I can't be dictated to by my child,' I said. 'Yes, he is important to me but so is Apollonius. Luke chose to go with Paul and Barnabas and I'm not going to let my own life go by in waiting for him to come back.'

'But you hate Rome,' said Rizpah.

'Yes, I hated Rome. But maybe there is something I need to be doing in Rome. Anyway, Tacitus said Apollonius and I would not meet again here, so there is no point in staying here, is there?'

'There's no point in going to the wrong place, either!' said Rizpah. 'That would be even worse.' Wisely, she did not try to impose her will on me suggesting, instead, that we let a week go by before even trying to make a decision. 'That will give us a chance to be rational instead of emotional,' she said. 'Though how you can achieve that in this case, I don't know—having to risk missing your son if you go to your husband and risking not seeing your husband if you wait for your son.

'Ask the Lord what to do, Deborah. He sent you to Tacitus, surely he'll tell you whether to go to Rome.'

Although I knew that half her motives for saying that were to preserve the status quo—for Rizpah had travelled enough in her life to want, and deserve, a settled home—I knew what she said made sense.

'I will wait,' I said. 'When Philo is well I will talk with him. And I will look for signs.'

But Philo did not get well again. He died four days later, at seventy years, peacefully and at home. He had been failing for months but, even so, it seemed impossible that he should slip away without more warning. I did not see him again to say my farewells and I wish so much that I could have asked his advice and enjoyed our jokes and squabbles just one more time.

Six days after his sons buried him, after we had visited the family to sit *shivah* and mourn with them, a letter arrived from the travellers. This time, for once, it was not from Luke but from Barnabas. There is a special feeling that you get when you know that a letter contains bad news; it's hard to describe but the timbre of the writer's words permeates the air around such a missive. This one was delivered to me at the library (which was the safest address for all correspondence). I was sorting out some of Philo's unfinished charts and writings with his son Philip and still seeing my dear and much-loved friend sitting at his desk, arguing or teaching in his own inimitable way.

I paid the messenger and broke the seal, feeling my bruised heart sinking. The letter started with news of the men's work and their travels. They were all well, as was my sister Salome, and the work was progressing. I skimmed the letter anxiously until I came to the part which explained why it was Barnabas who was writing. As I read the tears of an old, old pain ran down my cheeks. In its way, the letter was a confession. Barnabas had allowed himself to be over-ruled and two of the others (un-named) who had known Yeshua, and known me, had recognised Luke's features and told him that he was the son of an evil and greedy man who had betrayed his master for money.

My poor child! As I blamed those blind people who had blighted a young man's life I wept both for myself and for him. Barnabas said that Luke had left the little community to spend some time alone to struggle with this new knowledge. That he now believed his new friends rather than the story that I had told him was implicit in Luke's not writing to me himself.

Barnabas set out clearly and concisely why he had allowed the slander against Judah—a man he had known and trusted—to go unchecked. Why he had not stood up for an innocent man so that the others would not fall into the temptation of having a convenient scapegoat and a better story to tell.

'You must understand, Deborah,' he wrote. 'The story of the 'betrayal' is important in the story of Christ. People can relate to it. It makes sense and it shows us that we, all, turned against the light. Judah's name stands for the people of Judaea and they did refuse to release the Messiah when Pilate offered them the chance to spare him or to spare a known robber. This faith and this impulse are more important than one man's reputation. Judah, himself, is dead and safe; to him, his reputation does not matter. In fact, I am sure he would sacrifice it gladly to help our cause.'

I breathed deeply and sat, lost in thought for a while before I read further. In a strange way, Barnabas was right. Yeshua's teaching was far more important than the life or the reputation of any one of us. However, I had been there when Yeshua and Judah discussed their plan. I knew the truth. I could not teach that Judah was a betrayer—and his son should not do so either. Luke had known that Judah was not what he was said to be; I had told him that from the very beginning. And it was Luke who had named my first husband 'Iscariot'—the Deliverer. Surely he would not believe John's or anyone else's word over mine. The pain that was welling up in me was more to do with Luke's own pain. I read on.

'I know that Luke regarded Apollonius as his father but, as time has gone past, I have seen more and more his physical resemblance to his Earthly father,' Barnabas wrote. 'John and the others could not but see it too. Anyway, they knew that you had given birth to a child. Once they realised that Luke was your son and not just some young man who had joined us on our travels, the truth had to come out. Luke could not but be hurt by it.

'There was little I could do,' he went on. 'What happened has happened. Luke is shaken and angry and, at the moment, does not wish to be in contact with you.'

Inadvertently, I crumpled the papyrus with anger as I read. Of course I could see the logic in this but it was so hurtful that the nephew of the very man who had founded this new tradition, a young man who, if anything, should be fêted for his blood and his connection to Yeshua was, instead, told that he had the mark of Cain. It was the very last line of Barnabas's writing concerning the matter which stabbed the deepest. 'After all,' he wrote. 'I only have your word for it that Judah was innocent.'

He only had my word for it! What else was there to say?

Six weeks later, Rizpah and I left for Rome.

Eight

It would be wonderful if we had the ability to view our actions from hindsight before we embarked on a project or adventure.

But then it would need to be the kind of hindsight that could see the good in the trials that we passed through before the desired outcome was achieved instead of thinking the road had been unnecessarily hard. And it would need to be the kind of hindsight that was satisfied with a completely unexpected outcome and which saw that outcome as good.

That may be why we cannot see into the future; because we would be too tied up in the good we want that we could not possibly see clearly any other good that might emerge.

At times of great crisis it is rarely easy to see the positive outcome in many a situation. It is hard, too, not to blame yourself for any decision that led to the crisis itself. It was only in years to come that I could see how right it had been to decide to sail for Rome at that time. But despite my certainty before we left, during the journey itself I was nagged by every doubt I could muster—and I knew that if things went wrong, there would only be myself to blame.

And they did go wrong; desperately, totally wrong. But the ultimate outcome was so different and so good that it is hard to know how else it could have been achieved.

Both Rizpah and I had sufficient savings and enough items to sell to ensure that we could buy a comfortable passage to Rome and, if we were careful, to be able to look after ourselves (and, hopefully, Apollonius) for some little time once we got there. Dear Philo had left me some of his possessions, including scrolls and books that the library was delighted to purchase from me— and which would be much safer with them anyway. Did the dear old cynic know that and want to prosper me? I think he must have done.

Of course, Rizpah and I made copies of the ones that we wanted to keep...

Before we left, I was able to write both to Barnabas and to Luke. At least Barnabas had had the courage to write and to tell me the truth and I could honour him for that. I had to realise that if Judah's memory were to remain tarnished, it would be for some good reason that I did not have to know about. I was very angry but I knew that feeling would fade in time, if I let it. Barnabas had been so good to me over the years that I did not want to throw away all aspects of our friendship for one mistake, no matter how much it hurt.

My letter was stilted but I was still able to wish Barnabas well and say that I hoped that we would meet again in happier times. I did add however that whatever the others chose to say or to believe I could not live with myself if I condoned what I knew to be lies about my husband's actions.

'I cannot be a part of a ministry which, in my opinion, would be founded on a lie,' I wrote. 'I can understand your reasoning but, to me, some of the teaching is tainted by this. It seems to me that the disciples are choosing to sleep again, just as they did in the Garden of Gethsemane and there is obviously friction between the different groups.

'I ask you with all my heart to watch over Luke and protect him.'

To Luke I wrote a similar, but shorter, letter. I told him that I loved him; that Apollonius loved him and that whatever his opinion of his physical father might be, he should remember that the physical world was the weakest and most fragile of all. 'You yourself told me that blood lines were unimportant,' I wrote. 'What you have heard and what you now believe about your own blood line is a heavy weight on your heart but, even if all of it were true, it affects nothing in you. You were a gift from God, not from man.

'If you cannot believe my words about the innocence of your father, so be it; but do not take on yourself any of the blame handed to him. You are Yeshua's kin as much as Judah's and mine and, if blood line is to become important in your life, that is the most important blood of all.

'I love you and will always love you. You do not have to believe that Judah is innocent in order for me to continue loving you.

'Even if you do believe that Judah was evil, the most important thing that Yeshua taught was forgiveness. Not only for them but for you. Keeping hatred in your heart will hurt only you. Yeshua said "If thy brother offends you, forgive him seventy times seven times." Remember that. Your task now is to forgive whatever you perceive Judah to have done, just as mine is to forgive those who have hurt you with their beliefs. I wish you well and hope to see you again one day.'

I did not tell him about Tacitus and my new belief about Apollonius, it would not have been appropriate. He had enough to deal with without the knowledge that his mother was off on what would be seen as a wild goose chase started by a charlatan...

Rizpah and I packed up and said our goodbyes to everyone. It was sad but not as sad as if we had been leaving Philo behind. Part of him would be in my heart forever.

'We're not coming back are we?' said Rizpah astutely. 'No one else knows that; but I know it.'

'No,' I said. 'We're not coming back. Even when we do find Apollonius, we're not coming back. I don't know why.'

We had the option of two ships and were able to look both of those over in the company of Philo's son Philip. Having the nephew of the Alabarch to help us book our passage helped to smooth our way; two women travelling alone were not a favoured cargo. We were fussy, seasick and worrisome to most sea captains.

We decided to choose the smaller ship; the captain seemed pleasant and knowledgeable and the ship felt friendly even though it was sailing six weeks later than the bigger one and we were already coming close to the end of the safe sailing season on the Mare Nostrum. We couldn't explain the feeling about *Oleanna* to Philip and expected him to try and over-rule us. Shipwrecks are too common to add any extra risk and, as a norm, a bigger ship would seem to be safer.

But Philip surprised us by agreeing. He thought the *Oleanna* was a tight little ship where the *Colossus* was just a little too battle-scarred for comfort. There was a private cabin available on both but the *Oleanna's* was snug and pretty whereas the one on the *Colossus* was stark. On such silly things do women place much importance. But it was the right choice. News of the wreck of *Colossus* reached Alexandria the day before we left. There were six survivors.

Goodbyes were hard. Constanzia and all my patients were upset that I was going. Most of them chose to believe that I would be back and I let them rest in that illusion. After all, maybe I would be; my gut feeling might well be wrong. But they all knew that I was expecting to be gone for at least a year.

I didn't inform Apollonius's family of my errand; he had been dead to them since his arrest and I was not recognised by any of the cousins and other relations I passed in the street nowadays. The group at the library was the hardest to leave; they had been my spiritual life-line for so long and we were all suffering from the loss of Philo. But I told them laughingly that they could return to being an all-male group and I knew that they would enjoy that. Having a woman in a group changes the dynamic radically.

Our friends in the Christian community and our own group of women who studied were confident that they could handle their work perfectly well without us. That was good. And if it were not true, they would certainly learn from finding that out.

The one thing I could never leave behind me on any journey was a small olive-wood chest, rounded on the top, stained and worn but small enough to tuck under one arm and carry without difficulty. Inside, it had wooden compartments, lined with fleece, and in those I kept my herbal medicines. In there, too, were strange personal mementos that would make me smile or bring happy tears to my eyes as they took me back to far distant times when the world seemed to be a very different place.

There was a ring—Judah's ring; a crystal stone from Emmaus, a dried flower Luke had given me when he was four, a pair of jade earrings—the first that Apollonius gave me—and for which I had to have my ears pierced. The holes weren't level and I remember worrying that people would notice that!

Everything in that box was special; it even contained pure rose oil; a regular gift from Apollonius which I adored. It was hugely expensive and my greatest luxury. I used it as a perfume and a calming remedy and even one sniff of the beautiful scent would make me smile. Right now the box was stuffed with every dried medicinal herb I could think of; such things were expensive in Rome and carrying my own healing remedies brought great comfort.

The chest itself was special too. In its lid were carved two words in Aramaic: *Talitha Cumi*, 'Maiden, awake.' Yeshua made it for me on his last visit to Judah's and my home; the last time I saw him alive. It reminded me to change levels of consciousness whenever I saw it; not to look at life from the everyday point of view but to wake up to the wider picture. Yes, we were leaving our home and everything familiar—but from the wider viewpoint, our life had already left *us*. Luke had gone, Philo had gone, Paul and Barnabas had gone, Apollonius was long gone and although we had friends and clients they, too, had begun to come less frequently as if to give us a sign that we were no longer needed in Alexandria.

Neither of us loved Rome but Rome was the logical place to go. At least we both knew the city.

On board ship we found ourselves looking back over the stern at the Pharos disappearing over the horizon and making slightly tearful jokes about Lot's wife. But there was also a sense of adventure and, once the *Oleanna* was on the open sea, we remembered our first ever sea voyage from Judaea to Alexandria and how we had watched dolphins and sea birds and become lost in a sense of wonder.

Two families were travelling on the same ship so we had

company but curiosity from others did not appeal to two women with such an unsubstantiated reason for travel as ours. When asked, we said we were travelling to join my husband in Rome and we knew nothing of where we would live or what we would do. That was enough.

The Coreanos family was native Alexandrian so they all wanted to chat about possible shared friends and patterns of worship. They were, however, most put out when we said we were Jews and didn't go to those kinds of places but, as the days passed and partners for games of chance and dice were the only way to stave off the gnawing boredom of life in an enclosed space, you could see the fact that we were friends with the Alabarch's brother managed to outweigh our religion.

'Though if Philo was a Jew, then surely Alexander must also be a Jew!' wondered Rizpah, shaking her head.

'You're never a Jew if you're in a position of influence,' I said. 'Just Jew*ish!*

We laughed and played cards and bones with the family—elderly mother and father and middle-aged son and his wife. The other, younger, couple kept to themselves and had a cabin lower down in the bowels of the ship. Both husband and wife were desperately sea-sick and refused to believe the sailors' and the Coreanos family's exhortations that they would feel better on deck. Their six-year-old son, however, did not feel a single twinge and was full of life. They couldn't possibly cope with his bounce and verve so he spent most of his time on deck harassing the sailors and everyone else who would talk to him. His name was Tobias but we didn't discover the name of his parents—apart from 'Mater' and 'Pater' or of his baby sister as he called her 'Little Horror' and didn't see why he had to have had a sister at all. 'She's no use,' he said. 'She just lies there like a sausage. Or she cries which is worse. Hades, she can bellow fit to deafen you.'

'It's what babies do,' said Rizpah. 'They grow out of it. You did.'

'I wasn't a baby!' said Tobias scornfully. 'I was a gift from the gods.'

'As are all sons—or so they are led to believe,' said Rizpah laughingly but she would look after the boy with a yearning in her eyes. He reminded her of her own Timothy. 'Though, of course, Timothy's grown by now,' she said wistfully. 'He was Tobias's age when I left.'

The two of them made a wonderful team, playing and talking and you could see that Tobias was happy just to hang around with Rizpah; she had a knack with children, never talking down to them or assuming that they wouldn't understand.

Four days out from Alexandria, the weather became brisk, the sea grew choppy and the wind rose alarmingly. We were sent below; our value as passengers required us not to be thrown overboard as some of the cargo might have to be but our uselessness as passengers required us to stay out of the way of busy sailors.

Then we were all ill, trapped in the dark, lurching cabins where no candlelight could be maintained without endangering everyone's safety. Even Tobias became pale and unenthusiastic in the claustrophobic dusky light with no sight of the waves for orientation. For twenty four hours the wind and the seas rose until it became a true storm and, apart from staggering out to follow nature and to fetch mostly unwanted rations of biscuits and dried fruit, we were left to our own miserable devices.

Fear grew slowly but steadily in everyone's mind and when, on the second day of the storm, the sailors caught sight of the wreckage of another ship, we all began to pray to whatever deity we held dear.

The *Oleanna's* forward mast broke on the second night and took her figurehead with it. The ship lurched and rolled as the sea roared and the sky hailed. You could believe in Neptune's rages now. More than one sailor was lost.

What is the point of writing of terror? You can perfectly imagine the fear of people who are lost in the bowels of a plunging ship. Even the sailors were white-faced and drawn when we saw them, barely pausing to shout to us to get back down below when we had braved the rage of man and sea in order to get a precious breath of air. Looking out at a raging sea with no visibility in the louring cloud to offer any hope of sanctuary was no heart-lifting experience.

We huddled together, the Coreanos family, Rizpah and I, in their larger cabin. The others too, finally came out of their tiny cell to draw what comfort there was from the group.

The captain did not have anything to say to help us; when Claudius Coreanos approached him he was sent away with curses. Nothing more could be done for the ship or for us than what the crew were attempting already.

Strangely, now the danger was clear most of the sickness dissipated. Tobias's mother was the only exception and it was clear, too, from the baby's fitful crying that she was very distressed. I didn't take much interest in her except to offer some dry bread we had brought with us from Alexandria for her to suck on for her mother was too ill to feed her.

At last, the driving rain stopped and the wind abated slightly. A member of the crew came down to our cabins and told us to stay put despite the falling wind. We could come up in the morning, he said, but now they still needed all hands on deck— bar us. We agreed and settled down fitfully but with renewed hope to pass a less frightened night.

I woke at the first light conscious immediately of unease. The boat was still rocking but not as wildly and I was surprised that I didn't feel relieved. A warning note inside that was trying to catch my attention.

'Let's get on deck,' I said quietly to Rizpah as she too awoke. 'They said we could, come morning and the stench of our fear and sickness will be cleared if we open the hatch to let the light in.'

She nodded and we pulled ourselves up the roped steps to the deck. The trap-door was incredibly hard to open for there was rigging draped right across it. 'Odd,' said Rizpah, pushing it with her foot after we had pushed and shoved and, eventually, clambered out. 'You'd think…'

We gaped. There was not a sailor in sight. What *was* in sight was land.

'They've gone,' said Rizpah, running forward and slipping on the still-damp deck. She caught herself on a fallen spar and gasped with the knock. I helped her up, staring around me at the crippled ship. She had no masts, no sails, the great rudder was smashed. Rizpah was right. The sailors had all gone; as had the life-boat.

'They've left us?' I couldn't believe it. But the sight of clear skies—and land—were balm to my soul. 'But we're saved—look!'

'Saved?' said Rizpah bitterly. 'Oh yes—saved until the ship hits the rocks. This is a wrecking coast. Look!'

You could see the great shards of rock all around us, poking up through the surface of the water. The ship lurched steadily in the brisk wind, every moment getting closer.

'We go down with the ship—or we swim before she hits,' said Rizpah.

'Swim? You're mad. Of course we're safer on the ship! She may run aground but that will make her stable and we can get off then…' I thought I was using logic but Rizpah would have none of it.

'And be thrown overboard in a place we do not choose,' she said. 'And be crushed by the ship coming apart. No. There's a current across those rocks—look at the change of colour in the water over there. The ship will be dragged along it. There's not much hope anyway but getting out now is the only hope there is.'

We looked at each other with blank faces. Sensation stopped because there was no point in feeling; it could be of no help. We either jumped or stayed; either way we were probably dead.

'But you will meet Apollonius again,' said my heart, remembering. 'Tacitus told you so.'

Would that be in Heaven?

'What about the others?' I said.

'Tobias!' said Rizpah, catching her breath. 'We must tell them—but we don't delay, Deborah, we mustn't delay if they don't understand. There isn't the time to argue.'

Back we clambered, into the stench of the ship's guts to wake the men and tell them the news.

They came back up with us to see. Rizpah showed them the current and told them we must jump. They disagreed.

It was then that Rizpah's stubbornness showed. 'You can do what you want,' she said. 'We're going. Tobias!'

'Yes?' The boy was clambering out of the hatch after his father, loath to be left out of anything interesting.

'Fetch your sister,'

'How dare you!' said Tobias's father. 'Tobias, take no notice of the woman.'

'Why?' said Tobias, jumping up and down with all the pent-up energy of a six-year old but looking at Rizpah for her answer.

'Because we need to get off this ship. Now,' said Rizpah. 'And you're both coming with us.'

'I'll do it,' I said hastily. I'd remembered my precious olive-wood chest which was down below. 'I'll tell the women.'

'You will not!' said both men.

'Why not?' asked Rizpah. 'They're going to have to know very soon.'

They stood, nonplussed; their natural instincts to protect their wives and children thwarted. What could they do but jump or wait?

I slid down the rope into the ship, barely touching the steps, and went to fetch the box. All three of the women were waiting anxiously at the cabin doors. The baby grizzled miserably in her mother's arms.

'The crew have taken the lifeboat,' I said brutally. 'We're alone on the ship and it's heading for rocks. But it's in sight of land. There's a chance if we swim.'

'Swim?' Panic showed on already lined, drained faces.

'You can hold onto a packing case or a piece of wood from the ship,' I said, hardly knowing what I was saying. 'But you must all come up—now.'

I turned from them to pick up my precious chest and held it to me as tightly as the baby's mother held her child.

She held my eyes with hers. 'I can't swim,' she whispered. 'Neither can my husband. Can you?'

For a second, a patchwork of early childhood years of living by the harbour at Bethsaida flooded through me—and I remembered the times I had wallowed in the Pool of Siloam. I could swim a little but not enough for that sea.

'Yes,' I said. There was no point in saying anything else. 'Come.'

'Take my baby,' she said. 'She'll be safer with you.'

'No.' I knew I was cruel but I knew too that I didn't have time to debate. 'You come. She's your daughter. She's better with you.'

I turned away and she spoke again.

'Take her,' she said. 'Please. Take her. Take my Sarah and save her.'

The connection in my stomach and soul was immediate; I had no choice.

'Give me your shawl,' I said, pulling it from her head and emptying the precious contents of Yeshua's chest into it on the floor. I slid Judah's ring back on my finger, pushed the jade earrings into my ears—half of me appalled at my selfishness and the other half screaming at me to save all I could that was familiar. I pulled out the box's carefully-crafted partitions and tipped the herbs and spices together into in the bottom, giving a soft bed of sorts. Then I took the baby from her mother's arms and with the automatic 'shush shush' of the comforter laid her twisting, crying body in the makeshift wooden cradle. Sarah was silent at once. She looked up at me and smiled.

I could just manage to carry the box with her in it and climb the steps.

At the top, Rizpah was waiting for me. I handed up my burden and she took it with a hiss of indrawn breath.

'What's your name,' I called back to the woman as I scrambled out. I would need to tell her child one day.

'Marguerite,' she said, trembling.

Of course.

There would be enough air for the baby in the chest for the five minutes it would take us to live or to die in the waters so I closed Yeshua's carefully carved lid on those round, deep blue eyes and tied the box to me with the shawl. And then, as the women climbed out of the hold, crying to their husbands and distracting them, Rizpah held out her hand to Tobias, who ran to her. We clambered over the wooden railings at the stern of the ship and slid into the cold, black water.

Nine

Cold, cold to the bone; breathless, hideous, numbing, paralysing cold. Salt water choking ears, eyes, throat, water slapping, flaying, destroying. Muscles screaming. Sinking, gasping. Alone.

The chest would be torn from my arms at the end; with Sarah locked inside it, dying differently, also alone. Nothing would make me let go until I lost the power to decide but that would happen; there was no escape, no redress. Now, in the midst of the pain, I sang to her wordlessly as I locked out the screaming voices, bombarded muscles, severing nerves, freezing bones and the final terror of no way out.

As I began to lose the last strength, I felt a gentle light growing inside me and for one, beautiful moment I was in the Mikvah at the temple in Jerusalem, held tightly in Imma's arms and sinking into delicious, cleansing coolness. 'A good death then,' I thought gratefully and was gone.

Oh my Lord, I have not been who I could have been; I have not done what I could have done. I have not spoken when I should have spoken and I have not been silent when I should have been silent. I have not learned and I have not understood. I have not succeeded and I have not loved as I could have loved.

This grace; this light; this love; this beauty; this glory; this blinding truth; this acceptance of all that I am hurts more than your judgement could ever have done for I could have recognised that and understood it. That I am perfect and whole and loved makes me weep tears of golden light—and even they do not sting but soothe, even though I cannot bear to see the love that shines everywhere.

I cannot resist your giving much longer … I cannot resist your joy much longer … but I cannot survive this. I cannot allow it not to matter that I am not worthy; I cannot understand that all is well at all times and with all thoughts and all beliefs.

I didn't know; I didn't know. I had no idea…

I am that I am. I am the way, the truth, the life. I am One.

They hauled me up into the coracle by an arm that was already broken, dislocating it in the process. They said they had to; my other arm was clamped around the chest, the magical chest that gave them a goddess from the sea. For when they left the dead woman face-down in the sand, prised the treasure from me and levered it open (for it had swollen in the waters) a dry, conscious baby looked up at them, took one great breath and yelled the glory of life.

They had already saved Rizpah and Tobias and she, her face scarlet with blood from the shattered cheekbone, had shouted and screamed at them from another of their tiny boats, ignoring her pain; ignoring the boy who was coughing but alive. 'Go back, go back! Find the red-haired woman. Find her!' she yelled and the terror of this banshee streaming blood, who should not even be able to speak and whose words were roared in such a strange accent, was so immediate that they obeyed.

She saved me herself, inadvertently, after they dragged me ashore, by trying to pick me up from the rough, grey-stoned beach with her hands knotted around my stomach. With superhuman strength she pulled and hauled until she had me half lifted and then lost her balance and fell forwards. The weight of her and the cracking of her fingers on stone beneath us knocked the sea out of my lungs and left me choking and gasping as vanquished death flooded over the grey shale and sand beneath us.

And Sarah smiled and gurgled and won our rescuers' hearts so that the mothers of the tribe nurtured and fed her, swathed her in bright-coloured clothes and pierced her ears for stones of coral set in gold. The leader's wife had given birth to a still-born daughter only one day before Sarah burst into her life and the miracle child was suckled and nurtured as if she were that lost child itself.

The sons of the tribe barracked for the right to hold or carry the goddess and to bring her gifts of shells and fragments of treasure from the hungry sea. She took some offerings and discarded others. She wept when she saw the pain and fever of her two Sea-Mothers and held her hands out to them, so they too were precious to the tribe. She was a princess and a holy woman before she cut her first tooth.

They had no daughters in the tribe of Alethis of the Rose Island. Their wise people thought it was the sea-food that they ate but girl-children were rarely born alive and there had been none which survived babyhood for twelve years or more. So women, here, were cherished, not reviled. And this was the only place we could have landed where that was so and our baby goddess would be worshipped at first sight. Even her brother was welcomed for the sea had brought them three women and they were in need of us.

Rizpah's face was never perfect again. Although the bones knitted, there were always scars across her cheek and jaw. Tobias called them 'Mother's sea lines' and she loved that. The grin which I had always loved was very lopsided now but that had its own attraction. Less classically beautiful but far more mischievous. Her lovely nature and strength endeared her to everyone in the village and within a month of our arrival she had had three offers of marriage.

People were more wary of me. They had seen witchcraft close at hand and although it was good magic its perpetrator—or at least the owner of the box which had brought the miracle child—was someone to be respected rather than loved.

The head man of the village set my arm for me and re-located the bone into my shoulder. I cannot even think of that now without a hiss of remembered pain but he did an excellent job even though he got no credit for it. It was no doing of mine that at the moment he completed his healing work two rainbows spread across the sky in glorious spectrum. Rizpah, who had been holding my less-bruised hand, looked up and, in spite of her own pain, pointed in joyful wonder and recognition.

'The sign to Noah!' she said. 'The Covenant! One for each of us!' What we did not know was that the villagers had never seen a double rainbow before.

The fact that my arm healed so well was attributed to my great powers in creating the rainbow—and the fact that I was also priestess to the goddess from the mysterious box, not to Alethis' prowess. Even he thought that it had not been him, despite my assurances to the contrary.

It was a long time before Rizpah and I could thank the people of the village properly for their bravery, kindness and hospitality. They housed us and fed us, gave us clothes and tended to our every need while our broken bones mended and the swellings, bruises and cuts healed from the inside. They took care of the children for us for we were both very weak and sick for some time and, by the time we were fully ourselves again, they had totally blended into the life of the village.

The villagers told us that there had been no more survivors from the ship although three bodies had been washed up on the shore, including one of a young woman. Of the crew there was no word but if they had got to safety they would have found a harbour and be further up the coast were there were larger settlements.

The little boy was too young to be able to grieve in a way that he could understand. He knew that his mother and father had gone and would cry and be sad; but a few minutes later he was distracted by something new and interesting. I compared him with myself at the same age, also losing parents so suddenly. I had to admit, he adapted better than I.

Rizpah and I spent hours talking to him and asking about his family so that we would be able to remind him in years to come but he knew very little about them; not even his father's family name.

He was tolerantly proud of Sarah, now he saw that she was popular and not just an irritation. The little girl thought she was everybody's daughter, not just the child of Thorakis who suckled her, and she smiled only for each individual, holding her arms out with gurgles of glee as if they and they alone were the light of her life. She was nearly old enough to crawl and sufficiently weaned to be able to suck on the plain but wholesome diet of the villagers supplemented with Thorakis's gladly-given milk.

Day after day, as we recovered our strength, we would look out from the tiny settlement across the bleak, wind-driven dunes of grey sand towards the dark and hostile sea. It was hard to believe we had survived and yet all of life before this seemed to be cut away by the Divine surgeon's knife. Without understanding why, we were totally content to be exactly where we were, even on this bleak and barren landscape.

'Perhaps it's a normal reaction to cheating death,' said Rizpah as I bathed her purple, swollen face and fingers with a tincture made more with prayer than with accuracy. I had saved most of my dried herbs—though they were sadly adulterated—and ground up what I could to make salves and tinctures to help the two of us to heal. Apollonius's jade earrings and Judah's ring, however, had vanished.

The one thing neither of us had thought about at the time— our money—presumably lay at the bottom of the ocean. There was nothing we could do about it—and very little that we could do without it either.

We weren't alone in lacking finances. The tribe lived in a very poor settlement by our pampered Graeco-Roman standards. There were nine families living in wooden or mud huts with goats, pigs and chickens—about seventy people in all. The men were fishermen as well as farmers, spearing their prey in waist-deep lagoons created by the rocky coastline. Sometimes when it was very calm they used the tiny skin-lined boats they called coracles and very rough nets and ventured out to the open sea but it was nearly always windy and such expeditions were dangerous.

Nobody had anything as luxurious as a donkey or a cart and, apart from a little trade with other villages half a day away, no one had ever travelled to the other parts of the island.

They knew that it was an island from their folklore and they knew that there were Romans there because they had to pay a tax every year. There were thought to be two or three really big towns elsewhere on the island but when I asked what they were like I got nothing but shaken heads. No one had ever had any call to go there.

Their other income came from the debris of a hundred wrecked ships. Not a week went by without flotsam and jetsam turning up on their shores, tossed into the lagoons by the reckless sea. The villagers pointed out cheerfully that there was nothing they could do to stop the continual tragedies at sea so they might as well benefit! Our ship in particular had been a source of great wealth to them; they collected rolls of beautiful cloth, several full barrels of grain and some strong wooden staves for building houses, all of which were washed up on the shore. It was also the only ship in living memory to produce survivors. There was a cemetery at a suitable distance inland from the settlement with a separate ossuary for the bodies washed up on the shore where the bones were picked dry by animals and birds.

This coastline was well-known for its wrecks and too far from any other settlement and too barren to invite many inhabitants. But the villagers disposed of the treasures without travelling to the towns quite easily; many pedlars and merchants were willing to travel to their little settlement, and no doubt to others, after any noticeable storm to trade for the goods that they had salvaged. That the villagers never got a fair price for their wares was certain but they did not know that, so they did not mind.

Slowly but surely, we got to know our new friends. Alcon, Vettias, Hiero Thalpius, the councillors who supported Alethis as leader. Melas, the village shepherd, not that he had any more than a few goats to his name, Ocealus, appropriately named as the chief fisherman and Kopris—whose name meant dung—who dealt with the village's night-soil. The women's leaders were

Thorakis and Stratippe, wives of Alethis and Thalpius, and Arete the medicine woman.

Arete could have seen us as a threat but she was wise enough to see that we could be a gift from the gods for she was afraid of her rôle. Her mother, the previous herbalist, had trained her elder sister who died at fifteen and the mother herself had died before Arete felt confident to take over. So instead of hating us she adopted us, hoping to learn more. She was married despite the fact that her face was scarred by pox and her teeth poor and crooked for, whatever their appearance, women were at a premium in the settlement. I write 'married' with a laugh because there were no ceremonies here. But it worked for them and, despite their obvious poverty, these people were rich in family.

They built us a house of our own and the women, hustled by Stratippe, brought us food until we were well enough to join the communal fire and the cooking area in the centre of the circle of huts. Everything was shared out completely fairly and the women took it in turns to cook for everyone. When Rizpah asked Thorakis and Alethis why they had been so generous to us she was told that much of the village's food and livelihood came from the sea so they made a point of welcoming everything that Poseidon, the sea god, sent them. As he had sent us to them, they reckoned there must be a good reason. Besides, they had no girl children and the little goddess was a gift from the sea. She was passed around among the women like an amulet, each one spoiling her and loving her. But each night, as we went to bed in our little house, whoever was caring for the baby would bring her back to us and tell us of the miracles that her sacred presence had wrought that day. It is a good thing that Keera-Sarah did not understand how powerful she was. The villagers also thought it wise to keep on the good side of the miracle child's priestesses who did magic and owned the mysterious cradle-chest. If they pleased us, they thought that we might help them in difficult times. I was not sure whether to laugh or to fret at their attitude but we both began to repay our debt to these proud people, as soon as the bruises had faded enough, by taking care of the children while the other women worked.

No one in the village could read but they did know what writing was. When part of a ship's name was washed up, the youngsters who had found it ran into the centre of the circle of huts and called to everyone there to look. It was beautiful name-board which still shone in green and red but it was not the *Oleanna*. This was part of the mast-head of the *Muses of Greece*, a great and beautiful Alexandrian ship which had been due to set sail for Antioch two weeks after we left. She too must have sank— and out of reach of any land for survivors. When I saw the sodden wood already coated with a few barnacles my blood ran cold.

The village children roused me. They wanted to know what the words said so I traced out the letters in the dust and showed them how they had been put together. From there it was an easy stage to show them the Greek alphabet and the sound for each letter. This was a wonderful new game! Before the day was out nearly all the villagers had come to look at the marks in the dirt and to discuss the sounds they made.

'So that's how we repay them,' said Rizpah. 'We teach them to read.'

And that was what my clever friend did. She was such a talented teacher that she made it an adventure for them. I did my own part by showing Arete, Thorakis and Stratippe everything I could about herbs and medicine. Together we scoured the countryside for every edible, effective plant we could find, both to flavour food and to salve the villagers' prevalent wind and salt-irritated skin rashes and blemishes. Over the next two months we also taught them our own beliefs about one God, omnipotent and about Yeshua and the rudiments of the Tree of Life. I hasten to add that we imposed nothing on them—only answering questions they asked as they saw how Rizpah and I lived. They had their own local goddess, like Ceres, the Greek Earth Mother and they worshipped Poseidon, the Greek God of the sea but the idea of one God encompassing all others did not repulse them at all. I don't know why they took it so well but nearly every evening we ended up sitting around the fire and talking, outlining good and evil, temptation and love in parables and they listened and enjoyed the stories that my mother had told me when I was a child. As Thorakis told me, theirs was a culture based on stories; there had been no new ideas for many years and their storytellers' tales were stale to all. Our thoughts were like fresh water. In fact, we were telling them nothing that they did not know instinctively anyway. They were so close to nature and so in tune with the land and the sea and the sky. These were a holy people for all that most of the civilised world would have called them primitive heathens.

We were very happy there. Strangely so. But before that peace descended, I went through oceans of guilt over whether we should have left Alexandria and I fretted over Apollonius. Simple and restful as this ordinary bare life was, it was not what I had set out to do. I should be in Rome, looking for him. What if he were on his way to Alexandria to look for me? Even though I had Tacitus's word that we would meet again, it was hard to hold on to words from a different world. Free will stood higher on the Tree of Life than astrology and if Apollonius had changed his fate and was on his way home he would never find me now.

I would walk across the dark, rough stony ground until I reached the sand dunes that gave the village a barrier against the sharp winds from the sea. Carefully, for the stones were sharp, I would climb them, slipping here and there on the loose earth, until I found my favourite hiding place, a little nook with sea-grass surrounding it and a tiny wall of wood made from a spar of some long-dead ship. There I sat and, looking out to the sea shore, talked to God as though He were my friend and brother— just as Yeshua had taught me.

'I should know better,' I said. 'But I don't understand any of this and I want to. I can't just let it be and trust you, can I? I never could. I should know better than to doubt You by now but I don't. You must have sent us here to this island. Sent us on that particular ship to save the children. Perhaps getting me to believe that Apollonius is still alive was the only way to link Rizpah and me with these children. I suppose that the ship was destined to go down anyway—and we might have saved the children's parents too if they had listened earlier.

'But how *can* we understand? How can we see that wider picture? Can't you see how cruel this can seem to us at times?

Your plans seem to be so much bigger than we can comprehend and so unkind when we are here in the middle of it all. You seem to be able to use our mistakes just as well as our virtues. To you our lives have a specific purpose and when we have fulfilled them we can come home to you; to peace and beauty. We, this end, misunderstand that and think of early death as a catastrophe, a failure even, instead of a success. But this, Lord! A life in a village on an island? Is that my destiny?

'And what of Apollonius Lord? Was this journey all an illusion? I believed Tacitus because he is so obviously a servant of yours. Or am I wrong about that too? Please help me to see this clearly. Am I supposed to stay here or am I supposed to try and leave again? If so, you will have to take care of how. I've lost all my possessions and my money—I might just as well have given it all to Paul! I'm also far too afraid to take another ship for a very long time. Do you want us to stay here and continue teaching? What shall I do? Please show me in a way that I can understand.

'Do You think we will ever learn to work it out ourselves? I suppose we must if we are all sparks of light in your great plan. It's not easy, Lord. You must realise that.

'Give me a sign. A clear and obvious sign to tell me what I need to do now.'

The thing about God is that when you talk to Him with emphasis, He answers you with emphasis. I used to avoid talking to him in my youth because any answers I got were usually not ones that I wanted or that I wanted to understand. If (or rather when) I didn't listen I would receive visions instead because I was more likely take notice of them. This time, however, the answer came directly but it was a pretty obscure one for all that.

I got up and wandered down towards the sea shore to bathe my feet in the waters. As I walked along, thinking, looking up and not minding my feet, I tripped on something in the sand and sprawled headlong into the shallow surf.

Oh it hurt! My poor shoulder and arm shrieked but they were strong enough not to crack again. I sat up, spitting both sand and fury and trying to steady myself with my good arm in the sodden, shifting sand.

Then my eye was caught by a flash of metal in the water. I looked again and saw a Roman coin. Then I scrabbled about a little and found two more denarii. Fascinated, I began to dig in the sand and soon I found a half-rotted little bag with twelve more coins inside it. How on earth had it got there? Coins did not float. Then I looked at the bag more carefully. It had been lined with a sheep's stomach. Air must have got in and enabled it to float for a while at least. I shook my head in wonder.

Once I had finished searching the area I had seventeen silver denarii. I recognised them although they were older versions than those in current use, appearing to be heavier with more silver, and tried to calculate how much they were worth. One thing was sure. There was not enough to pay for a passage for two adults and two children to Rome. Once I worked that out, I felt a surge of relief—and then guilt that my fear of the sea was greater than my wish to find my husband. What was I supposed to do with them? At once a voice, clear and silvery in my head said: 'build a cart and buy a donkey.' I think I must have burst into laughter but fortunately you can't offend angels. 'What?' I said out loud. 'Buy a donkey? What for? What are you on about?'

No other answer came. After a moment or two I clambered up and brushed down my sodden clothes. There was enough of the bag left to carry the coins safely and I clambered back up the beach and through the trees and shrubs to the village. Rizpah was waiting for me with Keera-Sarah in her arms.

First we built the cart. More accurately, we showed the boys of the village how to build a cart. They had seen one or two but no one had even thought of trying to build one without a donkey to pull it. For all our experience of carriages, Rizpah and I could not work out exactly how they worked either. We could show the boys how to make wheels and axles and the cart itself but how the axles fitted to the body and still managed to turn was a complete mystery to us.

One evening we were almost hysterical with laughter at our efforts to work out what went where and how. 'Come on, we must be able to do it!' said Rizpah. 'There must be someone up in the heavens who can remember how to build a cart. Come on angels! We need some help here!'

In the end it wasn't us but two of the boys, Aristos and Peisandros, who worked it out although whether that was anything like how any other cart worked I could not tell. He made a tube for the axle to go through and attached it to the bottom of the cart. Then he greased the insides with chicken fat so that the axle would turn and the cart worked.

We let the pedlars and itinerants who passed by the village know that we were looking for a donkey to buy and some harness and within two weeks a man turned up on the back of a rather old and shabby beast with a one-year old colt he was willing to sell. He was delighted with the price of four silver coins and left with a great smile stretching across his toothless face.

'You were done,' said Rizpah accusingly but I laughed. 'Who cares?' I said. 'I'm happy, he's happy. What else can you do here with silver coins? Wear them in your hair?'

We made the harness ourselves with ship's rope and strips of leather—and then we had to teach the colt to accept it and to obey simple commands. It was as infuriating as it was funny but everyone in the village joined in and we managed a basic training that worked well enough. Of course I called the donkey Zoresh, after the kind Samaritan who had given me my very first own donkey nearly forty years before.

'Now every donkey in this village until the end of days will be called Zoresh,' teased Rizpah. 'Do you really think that is how that kind man would wish to be remembered?'

'Yes I do!' I said with spirit. 'His legacy shall be donkeys for a thousand years!'

As we had worked and laughed and chafed our hands and had our feet trodden on and our fingers bitten we felt so at home with these strange-accented, simple people even though we were living in the most primitive of conditions.

'It's as if the air is clearer here,' said Rizpah. 'There is less of the frantic life of the city and there is more space in the air. I loved Alexandria and there is much that I miss but now I know how the Israelites felt when they left Egypt. If this is the wilderness, it is a very happy place and I would not want to go back into bondage for all the comforts that I miss.'

I thought long and hard about her words. The story of the Exodus was one that Jews learnt with their mother's milk. It was Joseph, our ancestor, who had first gone down into Egypt and the power he achieved there had saved the lives of the rest of his family when famine came. But later, when the Jews were reduced to slavery, it was Moses who showed them the way out of what had become a land of bondage to other people's rules and beliefs and into the place where they could find their own laws and identity.

Perhaps our life had mirrored that. I chose to go into Egypt when I was rejected by my own people and for a time that had been greatly beneficial. Now, though, it was time to leave and to start yet again. But if I had not been meant to go to Rome why had I believed that I was?

The answer to that was simple; I would never have thought of coming to this island and perhaps the Lord had to get us here somehow. I shook my head for it was getting too confusing; all I could do was trust and know that, for the moment, I was doing what I was meant to do, even if it did not make sense to me.

Once the donkey was used to the cart and the cart itself was modified, Rizpah and I formally presented it to the villagers as our thanks for their hospitality and kindness to us. To them it meant unheard-of riches and it was very touching to see their delight that what they thought was something they were doing for us turned out to be something for them

That evening when we were all sitting round the great fire, sharing out a fish stew with dark bread and olives, the elders got together in a cluster. It was considered polite to ignore groups which were talking animatedly together so the rest of us continued eating normally. After a while Alethis called his eldest son and sent him back to their hut. When he returned carrying a sealed pot, Alethis gestured toward to me and the boy came on over to the two of us.

'This is for you,' he said. 'To thank you for the donkey and cart.'

I smiled and thanked him and took the pot. The seal had been stained and dented by its passage through the waters from some long-forgotten ship but it was still watertight. I pierced it gently with a knife and withdrew the tip coated with a dark, clouded oil. I sniffed cautiously—black pepper! One of the most valuable oils there was! It was so valuable that the Romans would even accept it instead of money for tax. If it were still pure it would be wonderful for treating fevers, breathing difficulties and even sexual diseases but even more valuable to sell.

I thanked the men profusely and took my treasure back to our hut. And, as is so often the way, I took so much extra care that I overdid it. After placing the pot on our little wooden table, I backed away instead of turning; trod on one of the children's sandals and, in losing my balance, knocked the table over, throwing the pot to the floor.

It smashed. Not into one but into a dozen pieces and the oil went everywhere.

'Oh Lord! Oh Lord!' I intoned to myself in horror, trying desperately to scrape up what I could and pour it into an earthenware bowl. It was a pointless task but I tried so hard! At last, I had salvaged all I could; it could still be used to treat people here but it couldn't now be sold. Defeated and cursing myself I began to pick up the oily shards of pot. One piece seemed to be covered in material—in fact cloth was wrapped around it and tied with twine. Distracted and puzzled, I turned it over and over. The strange object was circular and heavy. I pulled at the cloth that covered it; the fabric dissolved into pieces—and a coin fell into my hand.

It was solid gold, so pure that it was slightly soft and my teeth left a tiny mark where I bit it cautiously as a test. The remains of a man's head was just visible on it wreathed in laurels. It was old, very old and probably not even Roman.

I looked more closely. The wording around the man's head was worn but just still decipherable. 'Apollo' it said, in Greek. I had no idea whether the coin itself was legal tender but the gold itself must be worth something. As I looked at it the strange swimming feeling came into my head which meant contact with the higher worlds. In front of my eyes the word 'Apollo' changed to 'Apollonius' and I saw the two us again, older, still older and standing by a harbour side. It was neither Alexandria nor Rome. This time the image was so short and brief that it was gone before I could comprehend it but my heart leaped with joy because never, once in my life had such images proved to be wrong.

Apollonius and I would still be together again even if it were years from now. All I had to do was follow each inch of the path I was shown and trust and all would be well. The first thing I knew I had to do was to take this coin and travel to the nearest town, many miles away to the north. Maybe there I would find information about my husband or find someone who was willing to travel to Rome to find him for me. Perhaps the golden coin would pay one passage and a return but no more than that. I would not go on my own—even now some nights were filled with dreams of panic and fear of a sinking ship. It would be a long time before I wanted to travel by sea again but I knew with great relief that that was not being asked of me.

No one in the village was the slightest bit surprised that I seemed to have been given a message from the god Apollo via the pepper oil. All things magical or spiritual made sense to them. Once, when I had tried to explain about the stars in the skies showing us the patterns in our lives, I had been amazed that the village elders knew far more than I. They called the stars by different names and had different ideas of how they worked but they knew that they were the handiwork of the gods and that there were lessons to be learnt from them.

I travelled to Lindos with the fisherman Aruth and his eleven-year-old son Alephus. There was huge interest in the idea of such an expedition to go so far and everyone bustled around for days collecting provisions for us and seeing if there might be anything the villagers had that we could sell or exchange for food. We rode in the donkey cart and the goods that we took weighed it down considerably. They included bales of cloth which had been washed up from Rizpah's and my ship and which had been washed in fresh water and dried carefully out of the bleaching Sun. It was not a cloth I recognised—some kind of mix of threads—but it was beautiful and coloured in reds and yellows. It was not the kind of cloth which was useful to the villagers and it had not been wanted by the passing pedlars but they would certainly be able to get a good price for it in the city. Then, I told them, they could buy some seeds of spices or vegetables which would benefit everyone. I still had some silver spare, and I gladly offered to donate that for the price of accommodation while we were in the city, but it was returned with laughter. We would sleep in the fields outside the city gate, said Aruth. How strange to think of resting inside a city's walls! No villager liked the idea or being cramped inside a fortress let alone a stone building. 'You could never breathe in a city,' they said in all seriousness and I bit my lip. Maybe they had a point.

It was four days' journey to Lindos over land that was brown and dry. We saw other settlements but avoided them for the most part and nobody bothered us. Sleeping under the stars was easier for them than for me and I found the nights slightly scary. It feels as though the stars watch you when you lie down beneath them; I swear they have spirits or angels of their own.

Lindos is a pretty town—much smaller than Jerusalem and nothing compared to Alexandria—but it looked enormous to Aruth and Alephus's virgin eyes, mounted as it was on a hillside with a Parthenon at its summit. They stared at the distant outline warily and grew increasingly quieter as we approached. But a town of any sort was a joy to my eyes and I found myself almost salivating at the thought of the luxuries there would be within. Perhaps I could find a bathing house and wash the salt of the sea out of my hair or use up some of my silver coins on new salves for my precious medicine box. There might be a Jewish community too—although as I thought that I laughed for no self-respecting Jew would want to be associated with a southern village woman with no relatives and who was so out of touch with the dates and the festivals that she was no better than a heathen!

We slept outside the city walls, rather too near to a number of goat enclosures for my comfort. I say 'we slept' but we each took a turn to watch over our cart of precious goods. Aruth was adamant that someone might steal our wares in this den of iniquity if we simply trusted and slept.

In the morning we went our separate ways, agreeing to meet up at the main gate at dusk. I dawdled as I entered through the gate, enjoying the feeling of a real city around me again. The streets were narrow but colourful, alive with shops and merchants, and I found myself yearning for many of their wares. So much for enjoying the simple life of the wilderness! Given the chance I would return to Egypt as soon as I could. Once I had resisted the temptations of the market place, I found myself at the harbour and spent the rest of the morning looking around and marvelling at the bustle of life and feeling myself tugged towards the ships that were moored in the deeper water.

I asked around about ships going to Rome but there appeared to be none. However, my questions to the sailors and merchants did elicit one answer which gave me hope. Apparently berthed a little further along the harbour wall was a ship from Rome which had been planning to sail to some other, unknown destination via Athens and had diverted here because of bad weather. It was carrying livestock which, it was thought, might not survive the rest of the trip and so were being offered for sale at good prices here. If the captain had found a good market for his wares he would very likely give up the second half of his voyage and turn back for home.

I hurried along the harbour-side towards the great ship, dodging all the porters and cargo-carriers and what seemed to be a hundred or so baby pigs. If the captain were a kind man and if he were going back to Rome he might help or at least take a message for me.

As I did so I found my heart sinking. I had been so full of the idea of just getting here after finding the golden coin that I had not thought through what I would actually have to do. I had assumed that God would take care of that; that I would meet the perfect person to help. So far, so good, but the Lord helps those who help themselves and what was my part in this? It was synchronicity that the ship had come in on the very day so presumably this was the right place to be. But how do you ask someone to go to the Emperor's prisons in Rome and ask whether there is a prisoner there who predicted the death of Caligula? How do you ask him to take your money and use it as best he can to bribe others if needed and to bring that prisoner back to his wife in Lindos? It was impossible. I muttered an anxious prayer under my breath and, for probably the thousandth time, berated myself for not asking for God's help when I woke that morning and for not directing my prayers to asking His angels to help me.

But as I came up to the side of the ship I forgot my troubles as I heard two voices arguing on board. They were men quarrelling over money. The first man seemed to have promised payment for his passage on arrival but was protesting that they were not at the correct destination

'How can I pay you? He asked. 'You have my fare as far as Athens and I told you that you would be paid the rest when I arrived back home. I gave you everything else I possessed as down-payment for a journey to Alexandria. This, as you undoubtedly know, is not Alexandria! And now you tell me that you are going back to Rome! I can't possibly pay you any more.'

'Then you will go straight back with me and into jail as a debtor,' said the second voice. 'Right back where you came from.'

'Don't be ridiculous,' said the first man, whose voice was cultured and lyrical. 'At least let me off the ship now. Perhaps I can earn the rest of my passage. I am certainly not going back to Rome with you.'

'I'm not letting you off this ship until I'm paid,' said the captain. 'You are in my debt and it's not my fault that we had to divert here because of the weather.'

'You are contracted to go to Alexandria!' The cultured man sounded increasingly exasperated. 'What about your cargo?'

'There's plenty here who are already buying my goods and I'm not being told what to do by a jailbird!' was the answer and the argument continued, growing increasingly more heated. I slumped, leaning against a barrel of wine, and wept. I could no more have moved or spoken that I could have flown to the Moon. After what seemed like a lifetime the cultured man stopped trying to press his point and paused to listen.

'Listen. There's someone crying,' he said.

'What do I care?' said the captain angrily but his passenger leant over the side of the ship and looked down at me. 'What is it, my good woman?' he said. 'Why do you weep?' Of course he did not know who I was; he was not looking for me here. I was so much older than he would remember and shabbily dressed as a Greek peasant, not as a Roman noblewoman. My whole body shuddered with joy but I could not speak.

Oh, he was changed! The years in prison had all but destroyed him physically. His hair was thin and white and his face pale and lined. But his voice was the same and the kindliness and concern for others was still there.

Dumbly I held up the gold coin and he looked at it in curiosity. I made a gesture that it was for him and sobbed out almost indecipherably: 'For you. For your passage.'

'But I'm not from here,' he said kindly. 'I come from Alexandria. My wife will pay my passage when I get home.'

'I am your wife,' I said stupidly, looking up at him. 'Here. In Lindos.'

Apollonius's face changed from kindness, to disbelief and shock.

'Deborah?' he said.

Yes, it was Deborah standing there on the harbour side, looking up at him with love and holding up the golden coin that secured his release. Thanks be to God the Great, the Almighty, the Merciful.

Great tears began to form in his eyes and he stared at me as if I were the most precious thing in the world. I saw his body begin to shake at the realisation that he *was* home, not in Alexandria but on Rhodos. He was home and the great ordeal was over.

<h1 style="text-align:center">Ten</h1>

For the first months of our life together on Rhodos we lived with the villagers on the southern coast of the island. Not surprisingly, Apollonius had been weakened by the years in prison and it took time for his emaciated body to fill out and gain strength.

At first I was uncertain about taking him back south to the village. Could he bear four days in a rickety cart when what he truly needed was rest and relaxation? But he assured me that it would be nothing compared with the long sea journey and I did not have enough money to rent us any accommodation in town. I need not have worried, the joy of being reunited and the hours of questions and explanations filled the time so swiftly that we hardly noticed the journey. Apollonius might be weaker than he had been but he was still a soldier and his powers of endurance were phenomenal. As we talked and talked and exchanged our stories, our only sadness was that Luke could not be there to see his father again. I left the full story until later, simply saying that Luke was an adult now and he had chosen to go with Paul and Barnabas.

Apollonius said that it was enough to know that he was safe but I could tell that it was a great disappointment for him not to see his son.

Of Sarah's death, he was more stoical.

'I am sorry, Deborah,' he said. 'It must have made it even harder for you. I never knew her so I cannot grieve as you do.

169

Though I did enjoy imagining her growing up while I was in prison. I wondered what colour her hair might be and whether she was inquisitive or quiet; healthy or difficult. I thought perhaps she was God's gift to you to replace me.

'I thought of all of you; of Luke growing stronger and of you finding ways to survive and take care of yourself.

'I thought you might marry again; I had been condemned to death and, to all intents and purposes, I was dead. I was never to be released again.'

'I knew you were alive,' I said, holding on to his arm tightly; I found it hard not to touch him every moment. 'I just knew.'

'So you had offers!' said my husband, half teasingly and half jealously.

'It's a bit more complicated than that,' I said and told him something of Paul's visit to Alexandria.

Afterwards, he held me closely for a few moments in a softer way from the exuberant hugs and kisses of reunion.

'I am so sorry, Deborah,' he said. 'I was so foolish and I destroyed your life along with my own.'

I said nothing, just rested my face against his chest. Yes, it was true; he had. But it was not meant. It was all so long ago and all that mattered now was that he was home and that I still loved him, and he me. After so many years there might have been awkwardness or even disdain over how we had aged and grown differently but there was only the peaceful remembrance of the scent of his body; recognition of the texture of the skin on his face, neck, arms and hands; the touch of his hands, so well remembered; the mole on his forearm, forgotten but recalled with ridiculous joy; the weight of his body leaning against mine as we embraced.

Aruth and Alephus took my husband's unannounced arrival perfectly naturally. Most things I did seemed strange to them but they accepted them as they would of any foreigner, especially anyone they believed to be a holy man or woman. The villagers thought that those who spoke to the gods, whether it was the great Lord or to any of the minor ones, were all slightly mad: they had to be in order to be in touch with divinity. As long as you allowed them their strangeness and were nice to them they were very rarely any real bother and they could be a positive asset in times of sickness, uncertainty or when any particular god's intervention was needed.

In any case, the two men were so delighted with the prices they had been given for their cloth and with the purchases they had made that they felt incredibly prosperous. They were certain that the village could afford another mouth to feed. As Aruth said, without the shipwreck which bought Rizpah, me and the children, to them they would not have had this prosperity. Never before had they done so well from a wreck.

We trudged our way back to the southern coast with Alephus herding a small group of newly purchased sheep and goats behind us. The cart was piled up with chickens in coops, grain and tanned skins for weatherproof roofs. Apollonius had to sit on the top of the great pile; he walked when he could but he grew tired easily. I worried that I was taking him to such a basic place as our village without sanitation or comfort but when I voiced my fears my husband roared with laughter.

'I've lived in army camps for years' he said. 'And do you really think that it would not be better than a prison cell or the hold of a ship? Just having the sea and the land, a fire, good food and freedom to move is all I want. And you, of course, my love.'

The last of my silver coins had enabled me to buy some good and nourishing food for the journey and some basic cloth for clothing us all but we were both eager to arrive home so that Apollonius could begin to recuperate in earnest.

It is wonderful to meet again someone that you love but it is just as good to see the expression on another's face when they too are reunited. Some of the village children had alerted all the others that we were on our way and everyone ran out to meet us, including Rizpah and the children. My friend's scarred and sunburnt face was a joy to behold as she recognised the stooped but smiling man who walked proudly at my side. The three of us embraced and wept and gave thanks for so long and with such verve that Tobias came up and tugged at Rizpah's dress, concerned that so much attention was being given elsewhere.

Apollonius had already told me some of his story but Rizpah needed to hear it too and, as the evenings after we had eaten the communal meal and were sitting by the fire were traditionally the time for teaching and telling stories, he was automatically viewed as great entertainment by everyone. A real Roman senator in their village! They knew that strangers always had an interesting tale to tell.

Apollonius took three nights to describe his life and travels for he started at the very beginning before I was even born. I already knew how he had escaped and was able to fill Rizpah in so that she could listen without feeling frustrated. But this was the very best way to hear the story; in a homely atmosphere sitting in the light of the fire where people could ask questions to fill in any gaps.

Apollonius had undergone many trials and endured so much so that his story was quite the most exciting thing that the villagers had ever heard. Rizpah's and my travels paled into insignificance and I could tell that, despite the customary dislike of having an occupying force on your home country, having a real live Roman soldier, centurion and Senator living with you and telling stories of battles and other worlds was very impressive. Apollonius was very matter-of-fact and accepting of all that had happened to him and he spoke well in a voice which commanded attention without intimidating.

At last he reached the point where he had been arrested in Alexandria and I could see the villagers' eyes widen at the realisation that this stranger was a wizard as well as an important man. Had he not predicted the death of an Emperor? Even here, in a place almost totally cut off from the Roman world, they heard of great events; of wars and deaths.

'And we knew of this crazy Emperor,' said Aran. 'He made a nobleman of his horse!'

'No!' we laughed. It had not been quite like that but the legend was already stronger than denial could be.

The ship which took Apollonius to Rome for Caligula's judgement had been no worse than many a troop-carrier although he admitted that he had realised that he had become rather more used than he had thought to the comfortable life.

'But it was not a bad journey,' he said. 'I was allowed on deck very day to wash and exercise and that is more than many paying passengers are allowed to do. I was strengthened, too, by seeing my wife and children by the harbour side before I left. I was afraid that the soldiers had taken them too. Deborah is quite hot-headed enough to have done something reckless and to see her and Luke, both looking so dignified and standing with our friend Philo who would take care of them, was the best memory of Alexandria that I could have had. And I knew our daughter was born and my wife had survived her birth.

'I always knew that they were safe and that, if I ever got back, that I would find them again.'

He had arrived in Rome during a great festival of plays and it took Caligula more than a week to find time to see him. Instead he was kept in isolation in an earth jail with only bread and water to eat and drink. On the morning that he went before Caligula he was allowed to cleanse himself of the worst with a wet rag; the Emperor was very fastidious about smells, he said wryly.

'When I went before him, he was not interested in who I was or how I came to be there,' said Apollonius. 'I don't think he even recognised one of his own Senators. He was quite mad, ranting and raving at me for daring to assume that he was anything other than immortal. He was a god, he said. A god! I was nothing; a worm to be trodden under foot.

'I knew it was death. I'd known that all along. We'd been told just that on the streets of Alexandria, of course, but what you hear is not always the case. With Caligula, though, it was always best to assume the worst. But no other sentence would have been possible. As far as he was concerned, it was just irritating that he couldn't strike me dead on the spot with a thunderbolt.

'He wanted me thrown to the lions but even he couldn't do that—a nobleman has to have a nobleman's death. If he had not been so interested in the plays I might have been hacked to death in front of him there and then but his current favourite, one of the actors, was with him and obviously impatient to get back to the stadium so I was sentenced to die the following day.

'I spent the night in a cell with six others who were condemned for this and for that. One of them was a Jew convicted of some dishonesty. I never knew if he had done what he was accused of but he was a saviour to me that night for he was sitting apart from the others praying calmly. Thanks to Deborah I knew some of the Hebrew words so I began to speak them with him and then asked if I could sit with him and join in. He wasn't at all sure if he should let me but one of the others—they were all frenzied with fear and who could blame them?—overheard and tried to attack him for being a foreigner and a Jew. I beat them off and after that he became more friendly. We talked through much of the night about our beliefs and our families and our lives. I liked him. We decided that we would try to stick together the next day and, if it was possible, to die singing the praises of the one God. He taught me the Kaddish and that kept my mind occupied when he fell asleep.

'He had such faith, that man, that he could sleep on the night before his death. I spent every moment not in prayer remembering my wives and children.' Here he stopped and took my hand. I smiled at him and squeezed it. Of course he would have thought of his first wife and first children, all of whom were long dead now.

Morning dawned but no one arrived to take the prisoners to the place where sentence was to be carried out. 'That was a terrible time,' said Apollonius. 'If you are going to die you don't want a delay! You prepare yourself for a certain time and if that time passes your preparations begin to erode. We were all hungry and thirsty, too, and several fights broke out. I got a black eye and two bloodied fists but I managed to save my Jewish friend from any major hurt. He was the one who said that perhaps the delay was the will of the Lord and we had all been saved. I thought that he was being rather over-optimistic but that sliver of hope stayed with me. I'm not sure whether that was worse!'

Midway through the afternoon the jailer had come and told the men that Caligula was dead and everything was in chaos. No one was sure who the new emperor was—or even if there would be one. The Praetorian guard was in disarray and what was going to happen was anyone's business.

Apollonius took matters into his own hands and risked telling the guard that he was a friend of Claudius, Caligula's uncle and the heir apparent. 'If you give us food and water I will speak for you,' he said.

The guard had snorted; he did not need favour from would-be emperors, he said, but nonetheless he did bring victuals and the men were able to slake some of their hunger and thirst.

It was in the guard's own interest to do so. Death comes easily in the Roman world whatever your rank and position. Should some new ruler have decided to rescind Caligula's order, it would not bode well for a guard to have killed prisoners who were now wanted alive. Should it turn out that they were meant to be dead, it would be quite simple to dispatch them at any time.

It was six more weeks before Apollonius and the others were to know their fate. Claudius, the new Emperor, eventually granted an amnesty to wrongdoers, as was the custom, and Jacob was set free.

But some crimes were exempt. Just as Claudius could not let the killers of Emperors go, he could not set free a man who had predicted the death of a King.

'Eventually I was taken before him,' said Apollonius. 'After so long in one room I must have been a sorry sight. We fought every day over the allotment of food and I was covered in bruises. Some days I won; others I lost. My friend the Jew was a hopeless fighter and he would have starved or been killed, without a doubt, had I not been there. But I was glad to fight for him. He kept me sane. He was orthodox enough to protest about the sacrilegious impurity of the food for three whole days until I, and his stomach, reminded him that the commandment to preserve life was more important than all the others. Apart from that, I told him that I wasn't going to fight to get him food if he was going to be picky about it!

'We had some good talks. He was quite interested in Deborah's brother Yeshua—she's told you about him, of course? Anyway, I told Jacob about how the Pharisees had been angry with Yeshua and his followers for picking corn to eat on the Sabbath day and that Yeshua had reminded them of King David who ate from the holy place in the Temple when he was in need. He argued about it for a while but then he agreed that it might be a valid point. He told me some other laws and who kept them and who didn't and why. It was all quite interesting. Jacob talked a lot of sense when he used his brain. A lot of the time he just recited dogma but he stopped that when he realised that I too knew something of what I was talking about. I told him that my wife was Jewish and that our son was too and he had a real battle with himself not to disapprove; but he managed it in the end.'

Claudius, always a fastidious man, sent Apollonius off to be washed and shaved before interviewing him, 'I took that as a good sign,' said Apollonius. 'Who would bother washing someone if you simply intended to condemn them to death again? And I was right but Claudius was a wily old fox and I had to do some pretty clever juggling with words to let him have what he wanted all along.'

'What did he want?' asked Rizpah, agog, as was everyone. Apollonius's strength and bravery amazed us all.

'He wanted his own fortune-teller,' said Apollonius with a grin. 'He remembered the Emperor Tiberius's astrologer—who, apparently, had told Claudius that he would become Emperor—but he wasn't sure if he dared have someone who had predicted his own predecessor's death. I was obviously good at what I did—but was it politic to keep me?

'I managed to persuade him that I had not wished for Caligula's death but had simply been investigating the rumours which were already spreading though Alexandria. I said that I knew a system of checking such rumours but it was not one which, generally, could be used to predict things outright.

'He was a cunning one, that Claudius. He really only wanted to know if I could foretell his own death. For all his cleverness he was a nervous man and he had every right to be. All his family had been against him at one time or another and he wasn't a beautiful young man like Caligula whom the people could love, to start with at least.

'I took a risk, once I knew what he was looking for, and told him that although I could not predict events as such, if I had my own equipment and access to the stars, I could confirm or deny rumours or answer specific questions.'

'I didn't know you were that skilled,' I said in surprise.

'I'm not!' said Apollonius. 'But I wanted to live.'

We all laughed. It was safe to be amused now, sitting in the cool of the evening on the island of Rhodos.

Claudius had sent Apollonius to another cell on his own while he considered what to do with him and, for the next year, Apollonius was kept in the palace prisons, taken care of and allowed exercise and access to the courtyard at night to study the stars. He was also given books to read and write in. But officially he was dead.

'I knew what Claudius was doing,' he said. 'I asked if I could write to my wife but I was told to contact no one. I tried to get others to smuggle letters out to you,' he turned to me. 'I spent hours writing to you but I don't suppose a single one got through.' I shook my head. How I would have loved to have received one of those letters!

'What was Claudius doing?' asked Rizpah.

'Waiting for me to predict his death,' said Apollonius

''But you had told him that you didn't do predictions.'

'But he didn't believe me. I had never intended him to believe me—though I told him nothing but the truth. He would send messages down with specific questions, most of which I couldn't answer for the life of me, even with the entire night sky to tell me. Most of them referred to his own health or his family and I used to send back the vaguest answers I could—mostly the answers that I suspected he wanted to hear. I knew that I was on borrowed time and one day I overheard the guard talking about me to a colleague. He said that he had specific orders: as soon as I told the Emperor of any plot against him, or gave a date of his death, I was to be killed. That way no one else would find out but Claudius would be able to avoid the plot or the poison.

'Sometimes Claudius even came to see me in secret but, of course, I would disappoint him every time. It's not a good idea to bore an Emperor—and I knew for sure that he would never set me free so I decided to invent a prophecy to ensure that I would stay alive as long as he did. Maybe the next Emperor would free me!

'So, I sent him a message that implied that I had found what he wanted. He arrived in person as soon as he could, half out of his mind with terror but excited, too. I told him that I did not know the actual date of his death but that it would be a natural one of old age. But I added that I knew the date of mine.' Apollonius began to chuckle.

'Why's that so funny?' asked Rizpah.

'Because I told him that I would die the day before he did!' said Apollonius. 'And he believed me! After that I was kept in secure prison quarters near to the palace so that the Emperor could send every day to see how I did for all the days of his life.'

'So Claudius is dead?' I asked. The news had not yet reached our village and I had not thought to ask when we visited Lindos.

'Oh yes, he's dead. He ruled for just under ten years. I was freed when Nero came to power. He gave an amnesty like everyone else and although everyone knew why Claudius *kept* me in prison, no one could remember the original crime. When they asked me I said that I had cheated someone—that was the safest crime to be imprisoned for because most people do that sometime in their life and they don't hate you for it. People came and went and time passed, as it always does. I used to read the books Claudius had allowed me and think and daydream and I realised that it could have been worse. I tried to remember everything I had ever learnt and more. It was good to get out.'

'What did you do? You had no money. How did you get here?' Rizpah asked.

'I went to Jacob's family,' said Apollonius simply. 'It might have been ten years later but he had been released and he owed me his life; the others in the jail would have killed him without me. As soon as I was released I made my way to the first synagogue I could find in the Jewish quarter and sat on the doorstep reciting the Kaddish until they found the Rabbi. He took me in, for want of anything else to do—he thought I must be an Alexandrian Jew—and he found Jacob for me.

'To tell the truth, they all wanted to get rid of me as soon as they possibly could, especially when they realised who I was, but luckily Jacob was still alive and he remembered me. He gave me some money and got some of the others to give me some too and he organised some clothes for me and some decent food. Then I went to the harbour and waited for the next available ship. I hadn't got the whole fare but I could get a little further than Athens and I just had to trust that my wife would be able to pay the rest when I got home.'

Apollonius hugged me and I snuggled up to him. It was tempting to think how very easily we could never have met again, but for the will of God and the forces of nature, but all things work together for good in the end and I was sure that all of this had been planned in the heavens to be exactly as it was.

'Why didn't you go to your cousins in Rome?' I asked later when we had gone back to our little hut.

'I have no family except you,' said Apollonius fiercely. From that I suspected that he had been too proud to return to his family as a felon and beg for their help and I could not judge him for that.

To the general view, from a place in the Senate to a tiny primitive village on a rather backward part of an island was a great slide of misfortune. In fact this was the perfect place for resting and growing strong and Apollonius thrived. He remembered many of his skills from living in military camps and was soon able to show the villagers new ways of building their huts which meant they could be bigger and have individual fires inside each one. He also helped to build a stockade for the animals so that they did not have to be watched all night and all day and he trained some of the dogs which lived among us to guard the stockade against wild beasts.

He was tactful, too, for it would have been easy to have antagonised Alethis and Thorakis, or the councillors or even have challenged them for their position, but he managed to let them know that he was only passing through with Rizpah and I and that we were doing what we did in return for their hospitality.

The children took to him easily; Keera particularly loved him on sight and held out her arms to be picked up. She was just beginning to form words and her first clear uttering was 'Papa.'

He called her 'Sarah' so many times, by accident, that we stopped correcting him and let it be. Keera was Sarah and Apollonius was her father.

'It's just like Luke again,' I said, amazed. 'He has a magic with children; something I've never had. But look how happy she makes him. Do you mind?' This to Rizpah who had been referring to Keera-Sarah as her daughter.

She threw her hands up in the air in mock exasperation. 'This God of ours!' she said. 'So complicated! So what is the truth? Should we believe Keera-Sarah is my daughter; your daughter; his long-dead daughter from the fire that killed his first wife? His first wife herself? His mother? None of the above? I give up.

'Let's all just be one happy family. Everyone here already thinks Apollonius has two wives—not me, Deborah! And not him! We don't think that!' This to me as I made an involuntary movement of protest. 'You've nothing to worry about. You *know* that!'

In the end, we decided that now was the only important time and, to clarify matters, Sarah became Apollonius's and my daughter and Tobias, Rizpah's son. But even so, Tobias was soon asking Apollonius if he would be his father. Everyone else had a father and Tobias thought that he should have one too.

'No, I'm not your father, I am your Uncle,' said Apollonius kindly and he took great pains with the boy, teaching him Roman etiquette and Latin. I knew that he was grieving for Luke but living with Sarah and Tobias did soothe that hurt a little. My husband knew the trials and tribulations of life even better than I and, if he knew that his son were safe and doing what he wished to do, then he could only trust that, if necessary, they would meet again.

We talked about Luke often and I confessed that I could and should have done better with him. I explained about Paul and Barnabas and how they confused and captivated and repulsed all at the same time.

'You did your best,' he said. 'You can't do more. Just consider; most women would have done nothing—would have handed him over to the extended family. Both you and I are outsiders; we don't do that kind of thing. But there is no precedent for a single woman raising children in a foreign country with no support, is there?'

'There was Philo,' I said, with a tear, for I still missed my old friend.

'And thank God,' said Apollonius. 'So much might have been destroyed if it had not been for Philo.'

We smiled at each other. Yes, Philo had saved us—and the Jewish world. It had been his determination that had persuaded me to help him in stopping Caligula from raising his statue in the Temple in Jerusalem. He had, so many times, calmed the Jewish riots in Alexandria and his quiet stoicism had influenced so many people whose lives were important that he had to have had a much greater effect than anyone could ever know.

'We should have no complaints,' said my husband. 'After all, we have each other. Most people would say that our meeting again was more than impossible. But I have given up doubting that miracles exist—or even that they happen in any way or any time that I could possibly understand. It is not God who makes mistakes or who is impatient. It is only us.'

We were quite certain that at some time we would move on from the village. For the moment the nearby stream was enough for washing; the huts enough to live in and simple food was enough to eat. We had basic clothes and skins to wear in the cold weather and our minds were kept supple by the rituals we followed and by teaching the villagers whatever we could. We brought good things to them in return for their hospitality and, to everyone's joy, two healthy girl babies were born nine months after Apollonius returned. I thought it was to do with the herbs and greenery that we had insisted on their eating or maybe even the medical properties of the pepper oil. Whatever it was, it was Sarah—or us—or the soldier—and we were praised for it and honoured. But the three of us missed being able to read or to discuss matters with our peers and, when it was right and the opportunity came, we knew we would go.

'Though I do hope it doesn't mean taking a ship,' said Rizpah. She was still as nervous of travelling on the sea as I was. 'I suppose it may have to be, one day, but please God, not yet.' We assumed that we would, somehow, be able to move to one of the towns but it was a question of how and when. We could all work as scribes of course but whether the people of Rhodos were ready for women scribes or to trust three complete strangers was bound to be in doubt.

At the tail end of the winter, there was another wreck on the shoreline where we lived. Wind and rain had been squalling around us for some days and we were all feeling irritable and cramped inside the huts, especially the children. Going outside meant getting cold and wet and it was hard enough to get a good fire burning with damp wood and rain seeping in without having people steaming their damp clothes all over the inside. We did what chores were necessary and hurried back home where we told stories and made honey cakes but we were still struggling with bad tempers and irritability. It was late afternoon when we heard the shout go up and then everyone tumbled outside to see what was going on.

This time the ship was clearly in sight and close to the shore for she had already been scored by the fatal rocks that took the *Oleanna* down. She was listing and tossing, taking on water and groaning with the tearing of her timber.

Two of the village boys had lit torches and run down to the beach to wave them in warning but, even if it were not already far too late, the spitting rain extinguished the lights. Two masts were still standing but what sails were still up were torn to shreds and she was helpless in front of the wind, failing and torn, broadside to the coast.

Rizpah and I shook in horror when we saw her and heard the groaning as she broke, our own experience flooding back into our minds. The slashing rain made us shiver and Rizpah called out sharply to Tobias to stop him from trying to run down the beach with the other boys.

'Can you see anyone on board?' I asked Apollonius who, as the tallest, had the best view.

'I think so,' he said, squinting against the wind and rain. 'I can just make out a couple of what look like crew members hurrying around but I don't know what they are doing. There is nothing we can do at the moment. Why don't you go back inside; you'll get wet enough when the worst has happened if there is anyone or anything to save. You can probably do more good by staying warm and praying for the poor souls on board than you can standing here and freezing.'

We took his advice, Rizpah gathering up the children like a broody hen.

It was not long before we heard the ship's death screams as the heart of her was torn apart by the rocks. It is an eerie, living sound, which echoes in shudders through your body. It was hard to tell if there were any cries from survivors among the ship's own screams or if it was the whistling of the wind.

'It sounds like souls in torment,' said Rizpah, covering her ears and shivering.

We waited, banking up the fire and collecting together every possible medical supply until Alephus banged on our door to tell us that the villagers on the beach were calling for help. I wrapped Sarah in a shawl around my neck and Rizpah tied Tobias to her waist by a rope so that he could not stray far, despite his protests. 'It's no use expecting him to stay here with all the excitement,' she said sensibly.

We squelched our way back down to the beach. The rain had stopped but the wind was still strong enough to knock the words from your mouth. The ship was still afloat, looming huge and menacing in the first evening shadows and rocking uncertainly on the ring of rocks that had finally impaled her. She looked like a living being; as though she could still break free and throw herself at the shore itself, chasing these puny people waiting on the beach for any signs of human life.

The young men of the village were wearing ropes around their waists, larger and tougher ones than Tobias's but of the same design. We knew that they were a safety device so that anyone who lost their balance or was swept off their feet in the water could be pulled to safety. For many years our villagers had pillaged cargoes from the great sea and they understood the best way to do it.

As the men waited in the shallows, looking for cargo, four coracles were launched from the beach and headed out towards the ship, each one with two strong men paddling. They would get as close as they could for rescue purposes—but they knew not to get too near to the danger areas. After all, why sacrifice your own life in vain?

Apollonius, Rizpah, the children and I hovered at the steep end of the beach looking for anything significant so that we could help in any way possible. Around us our women friends stood, waiting excitedly. They rarely found human survivors and were not expecting to; it was shipwrecked treasure they were looking for; not money but wood and stores and maybe even a drowned animal or two which they could roast for a feast of a meal. One such was legendary among them. It sounded as though it must have been a prize bull for it fed the village for more than a week.

An hour passed and slowly and, finally, the great ship sank. She screamed again and again as she went down but there was nothing we could do to help.

The coracles bobbed back through the dark waters towards the fires we had lit on the beach.

No survivors. Just three, pathetic, half-naked bodies towed behind them. All young men; probably the crew. Apollonius said it looked as though they had been dead before they hit the water. Rizpah and I snivelled a little over their cold, broken bodies as they were dragged ashore. We could do nothing else; the Kaddish would not come to our lips. Apollonius seemed strangely interested in them and seemed to be thinking deeply but he said nothing and I assumed that he was regretting their short life and violent end.

Then, it was just a matter of beachcombing. The hoard did not seem so exciting at first sight. So far, whatever cargo the ship was carrying had either sunk or stayed inside her. Three chests appeared, tossing on the foaming waters and they were eagerly seized and carried back to dry land to be chiselled open and examined. It was hard not to feel revolted by the image of people being delighted by the results of tragedy but the fascination of wanting to know what the boxes contained was contagious. Had we not wanted even more to look for anyone still alive who might be saved, we too would have joined in with eager men and women searching through the possessions of someone who, now, would probably never need them again. What we did see told us that there had been one woman, at least, on board.

'Shall we go back?' suggested Rizpah, holding a bored and sleepy Tobias in her arms.

'Not yet,' said Apollonius.

'Praise be to Poseidon!' A roar of delight echoed across the beach. The final chest had been opened and it contained a cache of jewellery, gold, silver and copper. The villagers swooped on the glittering prizes with delight, each festooning themselves with pretty bangles, just like children.

'Do they know the value of those things?' asked Apollonius.

'Probably not,' I said. 'But they are getting more joy than any Greek or Roman matron ever did.'

Apollonius looked out at where the hull of the ship was still visible. She had turned as she sank and nearly a quarter of her bulk was still visible, captured on the underwater rocks.

'I'll stay a little longer,' he said. 'You two go back.'

The rain had stopped. I stayed with him but Rizpah took Sarah from me and went home to put both the children to bed: Tobias insisting on wearing a copper and lapis necklace that he had been given by Alephus.

I felt exhausted but I wanted to stay on the beach. Probably foolishly, I hoped that if I stayed I might still see the woman whose possessions had been stored in that first chest struggling in the water and be able to save her as Rizpah and I had been saved. To my surprise, Apollonius agreed with me, suggesting that we sat in vigil together in the shelter of one of the overhanging rocks at the edge of the beach. He went back to the village to fetch us some blankets and, when he had returned, he was carrying a knife and great staff as well.

'In case we can use it to reach someone in the water, and in case we need to cut someone free from ropes,' he said in answer to my unspoken query.

Around us, the last few people were still scavenging on the

beach. Aruth came to say goodnight and said we were to call him if survivors did appear for he and Alephus could swim for them. He shook his head while making the offer and reminded us that very few people had ever survived such a wreck. We thanked him and settled against the great rock to watch and wait.

The night passed. The wind dropped and the sky cleared slowly above us. The Moon was in its third quarter and it shone brightly over the inky water, casting a jagged silver light which shimmered across the bay. I cuddled up, close to Apollonius, feeling the echoes of the ghosts of the wreck around us. Together we recited the Kaddish again and again both to comfort ourselves and to inform those spirits around us that they were dead and that it was time that they moved through to the levels of paradise.

It was hard not to doze off and I did so, several times but every time I woke Apollonius was still watching. After years of training he could rest in any position and be alert at the slightest sound or sight. I tried to keep awake with him but it was so warm and comfortable in his arms that I dozed again.

Just before dawn, I woke with a start feeling strangely cold. The Moon had moved overhead and the rocks cast long shadows down the beach. I was cramped and my cheek felt sore from resting on the sand. Apollonius was not there. Blearily I rubbed my eyes and looked around for him and, as I did, the sound of swift footsteps alerted me that something was wrong.

Apollonius slithered down the rocks by my side, his arms filled with what looked like blankets. I only had time to see the steely look in his eyes before he laid the two children in my arms, put his fingers to his lips to indicate silence and vanished up the beach again. Sickness grabbed my stomach and I found myself holding my breath. Every hair on my head was prickling with the sense of danger. In my arms the children stirred and muttered and, more to give myself something to do than anything else, I wrapped the blankets more tightly around them. I could see nothing but the sea ahead of me and hear nothing but the lapping of the waves and the pounding of my own heart.

The sound of footsteps again—hurrying but trying to be quiet—and Apollonius swooped down again, this time half carrying, half dragging a tousled Rizpah. He as good as dropped her by my side and whispered urgently, 'Stay here. Do not move an inch. Do not say a word. That's an order.' Then he was gone again.

Silently I handed Sarah to Rizpah and we rocked the children gently, looking at each other in terror. Rizpah shook her head in return to my anxious, unspoken query—did she know what was happening? She gestured that we should curl up as small as we could so that we were completely in the shadow of the rock so we rearranged ourselves as quietly as we could, trying to calm our harsh breathing and keep each other warm.

Almost at once there was a flash of light behind us, a roar of sound and then more lights all around. Flames leapt up behind us sharpening the shadow of the rock and lighting up the sea. Shouts, grunts, screams echoed all around together with the clash of swords and sticks. Our village was being attacked! Rizpah and I stared at each other in horror. 'What do we do?' she mouthed— perhaps she spoke but the noise now was too great to hear. 'Obey' I said fiercely and covered Tobias's ears as best I could with my skirt and hands to lessen the impact of the noise. He awoke and opened his mouth to scream but both Rizpah's and my fierce commands to be quiet and the terrible sounds above were enough to keep him mute although the terror in his eyes was heartbreaking to see. Rizpah held the waking Sarah tightly to her breast to muffle her waking cries and rocked her to try and comfort her too. But how could she succeed when she too was as frightened as the children?

After what seemed an age there was the sound of running feet above us. We cringed back and an involuntary cry broke from my lips as a figure leapt down beside us and seized my arm.

'Come now! Swiftly' It was Apollonius, panting and daubed with what looked like blood. 'This way. Run!' He pulled Tobias from my arms and half-led, half-pushed us out of the precious shelter of the rocks and further along the beach, away from the flame-filled sky of the village. Once we were under the next rocks—so high they were almost cliffs—we stopped and Apollonius put Tobias down on the sand where I grabbed him and held him tightly to me. Both he and his sister were crying loudly now but there was nothing we could do to reassure or calm them.

Apollonius issued orders in a harsh voice. 'I'm going back,' he said. 'You must run—or at least go as far as you can. Always keep to the beach and the rocks; I don't know how many there are but there may be watchers posted. On the beach with the light behind you should be safe. Go as far as you possibly can—further. Don't stop until the pain is so great that you see red in front of your eyes—and then try again. I'll find you in the morning. Now go!'

I saw his teeth flash in the grin of a soldier in battle and I knew that he was eager to return to the fight.'

Rizpah began to run but I did not.

'You must come with us!' I said, savagely. 'I'm not going without you and you are not going back there to be killed!' Apollonius glared at me but I caught his arm. 'Please!' I said. 'You've done what you can. We need you too. Don't leave us now! Don't sacrifice your life!'

He hesitated for a long moment; then took Tobias from my arms. Then, grabbing hold of my hand, he pulled me after Rizpah's fleeing figure.

We ran until there was no breath left in our bodies. In our arms the children were now frozen with fear, hardly even crying when we slipped or slid or lost our hold on the slippery rocks and fell. Every one of us was grazed and bruised and both Rizpah and I were weeping with the pain of forcing our tired muscles to go on moving.

We kept moving until dawn and then rested nervously for an hour while Apollonius kept watch. The day was dry and the Sun was sending its first rays across the horizon; hopefully they would soon warm our aching bodies. We were no place that I had ever seen, a bleak and unwelcoming area with only a little shelter— but hopefully far enough away from the village to be safe.

'There is no reason to think that they would follow us,' said Apollonius. 'They shouldn't know that you even exist and they may think that I am dead—until they count the bodies. Even then, I don't think they will be interested in pursuing one man. They'll be more interested in getting away themselves.

'Who are they?' we asked. Fresh tears forming at the thought of the fate of all our friends.

'Wreckers,' said Apollonius. 'Pirates if you like. That storm was not enough to wreck a ship like that so close to the shore. She was driven.'

'Driven?'

'Yes. I wondered at the time but I could not be sure. Those men who were washed up had been killed and thrown overboard. Pirates or wreckers have small, fleet vessels and they often draw their ship alongside the merchant ships and force them into dangerous waters—or they just chase them onto hidden rocks. There may have been some kind of a fight. If they actually boarded the ship they would disable the crew and leave the others to their fate below decks. They couldn't just take over the ship; she was too big for them. I was certain when I saw the lights of their own ship dropping anchor out in the bay and the boats which came to loot the crippled ship once the waters had subsided.'

'She was boarded in the night? And you didn't wake me?'

'What for?' he asked. 'I hoped that they would just raid the ship and leave. The last thing I wanted them to do was see a movement on the shore and know that they were being watched.'

'But they came anyway.'

'Yes. They must have seen the village from the sea or had people who landed further up the coast who realised that there was a settlement and that its people had been able to rescue some of the cargo themselves.'

'But didn't they have enough treasure?'

'Obviously not.'

'Did you manage to warn the villagers in time?' I asked in a small voice. I was very aware that more people might have died because I had made him come away with us. 'I presume that they intended to kill them...'

'Oh yes,' said Apollonius. 'They intended to kill them all right. They would have killed the men first and then taken the women.

They were all young men and I expect they wanted some sport as well as their treasure.'

Rizpah and I shuddered. 'How many of them?'

'About thirty. Quite enough to destroy a whole village for fun. But they didn't have it all their own way.'

'What did you do?' asked Rizpah. 'You saved me and the children first and I can never thank you enough. But what else did you do?'

'I woke the men,' said Apollonius. 'Once it was obvious that the wreckers were getting back into their boats and coming ashore I knew that they were looking for the chest the villagers found and, once they found it, that they would take the village too. The men knew what kind of a raid it would be; that's the way it is. Anyway, apparently it had happened once before about twenty years ago. In fact one or two of them are the sons of the women who survived.

'Those who could fight went out to fight and those who couldn't gathered the women together so that they could kill them as a last resort.'

'Kill the women!' Rizpah choked. 'Did they? Did they have to?'

'I don't know,' said Apollonius. 'I killed as many of the wreckers as I could and then I ran back to you. I would have gone back, but you were right, Deborah. You are my first duty and I couldn't let you—or myself—be lost just because of my anger and my need to fight.' He looked at me with a kind of appeal in his eyes and I knew that his decision to stay had hurt his pride.

I put my hand to his cheek and kissed him. 'Thank you,' I said. 'If you had gone back you might have saved more but you might also have died. We will never know and we will always wonder. I am very grateful to you for listening and staying with us.'

'What happens now?' said Rizpah unhappily. 'We are lost, hungry and thirsty and the children must be fed soon even if we aren't.'

'We are alive at least,' I said. 'Had we all gone to bed last night, we would all be dead—and such a death that...' I shuddered, the night so long ago in the Roman jail could still turn my flesh cold after all these years and I remembered Apollonius telling me that he had often seen women die, horribly, from such treatment.

My husband put both his arms around me. 'You're quite safe,' he said. 'Safe with me. Always.' He patted my back clumsily and rocked me like a little child.

'We'll stay here until the Sun has warmed us through and there is enough light to see clearly,' he said. 'Then we will follow the sea again until we find a stream and can drink. Upstream from there we may be able to find food or another village.'

As he spoke, we could feel the golden, warming rays seeping through our tattered and dirty clothes and onto our skins. I rested my head against my husband's chest appreciating the warmth of his body and the heat of the Sun and thanking God for our deliverance. The children woke again and began to whine and fret so, reluctantly, I stepped back, smiled up at Apollonius and began to look around for signs of water or habitation.

There was a palm tree just a few yards away and, although it bore no fruit, there were some still dates on the ground which were just edible. Rizpah gave them to the children to chew on while we looked further afield. Although we had eaten the previous evening I was beginning to feel faint with hunger and thirst but there was still enough strength in me to laugh when Apollonius came back up from the beach with a handful of mussels for our breakfast.

'Not kosher!' I said with a giggle reaching out to take my share. 'Ah, you're as bad as Jacob!' said Apollonius, breaking one open with a stone and eating it with relish. Rizpah and I wrinkled up our noses and ate anyway and then fed the children. We had both eaten shellfish and pork regularly since we came to the island but neither would ever be a food of choice if there were an alternative. Tobias had always scavenged on the beach with the other boys and had no trouble with the familiar food but Sarah was not very keen.

Next we found a dribble of water running down to the sea and, after digging a pool, were able to drink and be satisfied. Then we all lay down in the sunshine and slept until the Sun was high in the sky. My last waking thoughts were for Yeshua's wooden chest. Perhaps this time I had truly lost it and I guiltily shed a tear. In comparison with the loss of life of our friends it was such a little thing but it had been such a comfort to me for so many years.

In the afternoon we found another settlement. It was larger than our own but similar, with fishing as the main occupation of the men and the women farming chickens and goats. They lived in an area where the sea was calmer—almost a lagoon—and were able to keep their boats in the water without fear of their being tossed by the wind and cracked from beneath. The people were wary of us strangers but once they had understood what had happened, they allowed us to join in with their evening meal and to sleep by their fire. Four of the men offered to travel back with Apollonius to see what had happened to our friends. I was permitted to go, too, when my husband explained that I was a physician, but Rizpah was glad to stay behind with the children who were unsettled and fretful and needed her there.

We started at first light and it took us until nearly midday to find the charred remains of our little town. The fighting must have been terrible but there were already people starting to rebuild the ruins and, to our delight, we discovered that more than half our friends had survived the attack. The men, having been warned by Apollonius, had all been armed when the wreckers arrived and gave as good as they got. Their homes had been fired and much of the livestock scattered and seventeen villagers were dead including our friends Alcon, Ocealus, Stratippe and eight of the children but Arete, Vettias, Hiero, Aran, Thalpius, Alethis and Thorakis, Melas and Kopris had survived and the women and I hugged and wept while the men looked on. We exchanged news, including Rizpah's and the children's safety—they had thought us all dead—and it was Arete who brought to me the charred but still serviceable little chest that Yeshua had made for me so many years before. I squeaked with delight to see it for its own sake, but even more because of the salves it contained which could be used for burns and cuts on the survivors.

Of the treasures they had amassed from the wreckage there was no sign. Perhaps they had saved some, perhaps not, but in the company of the strangers who had travelled with us this day, no one was going to mention any possible valuables.

It was less than twenty-four hours since the attack but the dead had already been buried and the bodies of the wreckers who had not fled lay dismembered and burnt in an ancient ceremony of revenge which left their charred flesh and bones still red-hot and stinking. From the evidence around, I suspected that our friends had eaten part of their foes and my stomach churned at the thought. Apollonius smiled at me when I pointed it out. 'It happens, my love,' he said. 'It's important to some cultures. Some think it gives them the bravery of their opponents; others do it to humiliate them. The men are dead; it can't affect them.'

'It's just that I was raised to believe that our bodies are resurrected at the end of time,' I said, apologetically. 'I know that all happens in a higher world than this physical one but it's still rather a shock even to see bodies burnt, let alone eaten!'

'My poor lamb,' said my husband, affectionately. 'What an innocent you are! I forget that you have not travelled with soldiers nor seen war.'

There was much to do in that short visit. And visit was all it was. Somehow it seemed right that we should move on instead of helping to rebuild with the others. They had some booty, for the wreckers had had to leave one of their boats on the shore to make their escape. That they had gone was obvious for there was no sign of a mother-ship in the bay. Apollonius advised Alethis to move on and rebuild in a different place in case they came back for revenge—or the same thing happened again—but neither he nor any of the others understood what he was saying.

'This is our home. We live and die here!' Alethis said proudly. 'As our ancestors did before us. It was our ancestors who brought these women with the miracle child and their great God to us and because of them, you came. And because you came we were warned in time to defend ourselves. Our ancestors and your great God will continue to protect us as long as we stay here.'

Although their attitude seemed strange it had an inherent dignity to it that few races have. When attacked and murdered, most people understandably seethe with a resentment which calls for revenge. Our villagers took their revenge on the bodies of those who had attacked them, buried their own dead and accepted he laws of nature. They did not blame the great God of the heavens or their own earth gods—why should they? Death was a part of life and it was a matter for them and for the ancestors. Rizpah and I had taught them a little more about the worlds after death where people are happy and learn different things and could wait for those they loved—and they had merged those beliefs with their own. Their dead were safe and the fact that the crisis was not worse was due to their own hospitality. We should be repaid, they said. Such is life. What you put out, you get back. If we thank you, we will be taken care of. Simple! Such is life. We will worship your heavenly God and our earthly gods and go on as before. Such basic belief but very moving. As Yeshua had once said of Apollonius: 'I have not found faith like this in all of Israel.'

Alethis drew Apollonius to one side, away from the strangers, who were being offered olives and bread by women who had only just buried those that they loved. I looked at my husband, he gestured towards me and Alethis inclined his head.

We went into Alethis's damaged but still habitable hut and he lifted the rug from the floor with a grin. Underneath it was a hole in the earth containing one of the chests rescued last night; still half-full of gold and jewels. I felt my jaw drop; of course I had assumed that the wreckers had taken it all.

'Take,' said Alethis. 'As much as you can hide on your bodies. It is your right.'

I felt repulsed, it seemed tainted to me and I stepped back. But Apollonius was firm. 'This is ours as much as theirs,' he said. 'It is spoils of war. That is the law throughout the Roman world. Don't be squeamish, Deborah. We need money if we are to prosper in this land. Here is the wherewithal to move to the town. It comes from God as much as from man and it may be the best way for God to send it to us.'

He switched from Greek to Latin seamlessly, and continued: 'It would be foolish to refuse. Its original owners have no need of it now and these people have no idea of its true value. They may get cheated—or even attacked again for it. If we don't take our share, who knows whose hands it will go to.'

I nodded weakly. 'But I don't know what to take,' I said.

'Oh I do!' said my husband with a strange smile. 'Take some trinkets for you, Rizpah and the children and leave the rest to me.'

Hesitantly, I picked out two gold necklaces and two silver bangles and slid them over my head and onto my arms, covering them with my clothes.

Then Apollonius picked out just one object from the pile—a bag containing what looked like grey stones. None of them glittered or looked particularly valuable.

Alethis was pleased with his choice; he could see no value in things which did not glitter but I suspected that my husband knew what he was doing. Like Alethis, I preferred the brighter and more ornate golden pieces. That ship had certainly been loaded down with treasure.

Apollonius lectured the village leader, briefly, about keeping the gold hidden and selling it piece by piece but, as he told me on the way back, he knew that he was wasting his breath. 'They live the life they have lived for a thousands of years,' he said.

'Basically, they are still children and children they will remain until the good Lord wills it otherwise.'

We took one more thing: a long-legged lop-eared puppy who was thrust into our arms by Melas. His dog had been a favourite of Tobias's and when she had puppies the little boy was in ecstasies over them. We accepted the wriggling little bitch, knowing that the children would be very happy to have her to play with and cuddle in their uprooted lives, and I was glad to hold her for I felt such sadness; we would never see these people again and they had loved us as their own.

Our farewells from the women were affectionate and emotional; the men saluted us and wished us well. We left them already turning to the rebuilding of their life and the surviving children, resilient as only they can be, were running down to the beach to look for anything else which might have been brought in by the sea.

Apollonius and I travelled back with our new friends, reaching their village at dusk. There, they offered us food and left us in peace in a hastily-erected tent of skins.

There, we uncovered our booty to Rizpah's wide-eyed wonder while Tobias cuddled the puppy with joy and she wriggled and squeaked in his arms. It was hard to know who was licking whom but, for the moment, we let that go.

'But these are huge riches!' said Rizpah. 'More than I've ever seen.'

She wasn't looking at the lovely filigree of the necklaces or the bright stones in the pretty bangles but at the dull rocks from the leather bag.

'Diamonds?' she said.

'Diamonds,' said Apollonius. 'A gift from God so that we can start again.'

We stayed with the farming community for a month before we could arrange how to get to Lindos. We paid them for their hospitality with one of the silver bangles which pleased them greatly.

Our new friends had a solemnity which our former companions did not have and we could see that they thought that they were a stronger and better people than the group we had left behind. The two groups were certainly different but neither was better or worse than the other. Even in such small places, between tribes divided by just a day's walk, the signs of division already existed. How could humans ever hope to keep nations together?

Apollonius did all the talking and negotiating and worked out how to locate a cart and a horse to transport us and Rizpah took care of the children. There was no one here who wanted to associate with us in any way other than as paying guests and they had a medicine man who did not approve of women, so I had leisure time to myself and took it gladly for I wanted to be solitary for much of that time. So much had happened that I needed to take stock and reflect.

I would sit at the edge of a cliff on the lee side of the bay, in the shade of a great palm tree, just thinking. After a while I began again to practise the inner journeys that Yeshua had taught us, so many years ago. I had continued with them until we left Alexandria but the simple village life of Rhodos had seemed enough and I had lapsed in the discipline I had set myself.

It was in those meditations that Yeshua came to me again and sat with me, every day, mostly in silence but with thoughts shared and understood. It was as though he brought a gossamer covering of light to soothe and heal the scars and misunderstandings of my life and sometimes, when he was there, I hardly felt as though I lived on the Earth at all.

I seemed to spend hours, days even, in different celestial dimensions, meeting loved ones remembered and forgotten. It was with Yeshua that I spoke again with Imma and my earthly body wept with grief as my spiritual body rejoiced with her for her happiness. Another time, I saw Joseph, my adopted father, and then my birth father who died in Bethsaida more than fifty years before. And, in yet another world, I saw my blood-mother, the glorious red-headed Petran, and she recognised me and smiled. I knew at last that both she and I were on the pathway to peace.

I learnt many things under the great palm. I learnt of past and present; of why I was in Rhodos and what else I had to do. Most of these dreams were half-forgotten within days, if not moments, but their essence remained. Yeshua reminded me that I had one message still to give, to Cephas, and that time was close at hand.

He knew that I had failed with Paul and he was severe with me then for, with less pride and more womanliness, I might have done better.

'But then I would have fallen for him and lost myself,' I said and Yeshua looked at me with his warming, softening, visionary eyes.

'No,' he said. 'You might not have fallen. You could have risen.' He smiled and I felt the echo of his touch on my cheek. 'You see, it would not have been so very bad!'

And then I knew that I had always loved Yeshua far more deeply than I had ever known. What I felt did not take away from the love I had for Judah nor for Apollonius for this was a love across centuries; one which did not need a physical expression but which could have yearned for one had it been uncovered before its time.

'I didn't know,' I said.

'No,' said Yeshua. 'But now you do. Perhaps you can understand Paul a little better, for he knows. He knows his love and he knew it too early; he looked too deeply into the other worlds before he was ready.'

'It must be hell,' I said. 'To know and not to understand.'

'It is,' said Yeshua. 'He does suffer greatly. However, he will do his job, for better or for worse and, through that, he will change the world.'

'I won't,' I said sadly.

'Oh yes you will,' Yeshua said. 'That is, as long as you stop wanting to. Remember, Deborah, you don't need to be loved and you don't need to be understood. You don't even need to be remembered.'

I looked at him doubtfully. 'I don't?'

'You don't!' he said, smiling and then, as I saw him surrounded in light, his image faded away.

Eleven

We lived on the edge of the walled harbour town of Lindos for nearly twelve years. The home we could buy with just three of those rough, dull-looking stones was comfortable and spacious and we women sank into it with tears of joy and relief, spending wonderful feminine weeks furnishing, decorating and creating a nest of peace and tranquillity.

He had no need to work again but Apollonius had had enough of the idle life and, when he found that he had once fought alongside Quintinus, the commander of the Roman garrison nearby, he arranged a meeting as soon as he could. Ex-soldiers of the Senatorial caste were few and far between and Quintinus snapped up the offer of help. Apollonius could be assured of enough work to keep him happy and busy.

Three or four days a week he would help out with the administration or the justice system of the little city and Quintinus and he became friends which was even more pleasing for us all. The jail sentence under Claudius's rule was disregarded as 'just one of those things' and, so far, Nero's rule had not brought any problems to a distant garrison such as Lindos.

There was a greater city—Rhodos Town—where most of the country's intelligentsia lived and Lindos, although it was a thriving port, was regarded as somewhat of a backwater. Many commanders might have felt that sorely. But Quintinus was not an ambitious man. He had fought enough and quarrelled enough, he said and, just like me, all he really wanted was a little peace and quiet and the company of friends. He was a widower and, in the first four years, he proposed repeatedly to Rizpah. She liked him and was happy to accompany him to events as part of a foursome with us but she preferred her single status more.

Besides, she was a mother again. Sarah and Tobias were as dear to her as her own children had been and she devoted herself to their lives; teaching them both all the talents of aristocratic children. They learnt how to read and write before they knew that they were being taught, so talented was she in the way she embraced life and education together. They called her 'Matera,' me 'Theia' (aunt) and Apollonius 'Theis' (Uncle) and, with the extraordinary elasticity of youth, soon forgot everything before. In the day that is; sometimes Tobias had nightmares and Rizpah would sit with him, the room lit with candles, talking and singing until he slept again.

We settled and the years passed peacefully. It was almost like being back in Alexandria except, of course, for the lack of a spiritual centre such as the great library. The Jews of Rhodos were a very self-concerned bunch and, try as I might, I could not find any trace of the esoteric teaching there, even when we went to Rhodos Town to see the remains of the great colossus and attend a festival dinner.

In fact I was as good as hounded out of a synagogue when they discovered I was married to a Roman and elsewhere my discreet enquiries met a hostile wall of silence. There were Christians here—and their group was based in Lindos. Paul and Barnabas had travelled to Rhodos many years before. We approached them and were made cautiously welcome (they were a very secretive group) but they were all Greeks with no Jewish background and we found them quite alien to our beliefs and without any esoteric knowledge that we could assess. I didn't tell them who I was; it would have sounded made-up anyway to turn up out of the blue and say 'I'm Jesus' sister' but we said that we had known and worked with Paul in Alexandria. Even so, they thought us rather strange and arrogant and were adamant that, as women, we would not take an active part in the group.

So, as we had done before, we did without others in the Work. There was a small library in Lindos and a larger one in Rhodos and books between the two could be traded. Although I admit it was rather high-handed of me, through Apollonius's influence I was able to persuade the men who ran the local library that copies of the Torah and the Prophets should be included as well as their Greek philosophy. The Jewish community, extremely reluctantly, surrendered their scrolls for copying and Rizpah and I occupied ourselves in the evenings by writing out each chapter and verse and translating them from Hebrew into Greek. It was a very satisfying exercise for both of us as it gave us much cause for speculation and debate. In Hebrew writing there are no vowels whereas Greek is, on the face of it, far more complicated. However, the consonants of Hebrew are like the structure of a teaching, whole and pure, and the interpretation of which vowels should be added to create each full word can change as appropriate according to the times. I thought this was a wonderful system, as opposed to the Greek where one view was crystallised with each word fully defined.

The Torah is the word of God. It is believed to have been dictated by Him and to be infallible. Yeshua had come to fulfil it, not to destroy it and his message was that all of us could do exactly the same as he did. But given his free attitude to the food laws and other matters, it was hard for orthodox Jews to understand his message. He was looking at the Torah from a different dimension and he taught us that it is a structure rather than a form. Rizpah and I did two different Greek versions over the years, one based on my interpretation and one on hers. They were fascinatingly different in form but both entirely faithful to the structure.

We could not be expected to make many friends among the local women when that was the kind of occupation we most enjoyed doing at our leisure but the children, as always, broke the ice and stopped us from being totally isolated from our peers. Apollonius and I were also invited to dine at a few eminent people's houses now and again and I was tolerantly regarded as being rather eccentric but basically harmless. With age had come some mellowing so I could talk quite peaceably about everyday nothings.

Apollonius enjoyed his work and even began to advise on military strategy whenever that was needed and many a night he chatted to me about things which blanked my mind over with boredom. But it was the least repayment I could make for the joy of having him back with me to have to listen to his enthusiasm for things that went right over my head. Sometimes he realised that I had lost track of what he was talking about and would put in a ridiculous sentence that made no sense at all. After a minute or so, I would frown and raise my hand, having finally worked out that this was ridiculous and we would laugh. 'Bless you,' he would say and give me a kiss, both of us knowing that I did not mind his talking and that it was more important to him to have a listening ear than it was for me to understand. He had all the male company he needed but he also enjoyed debating and discussing with us at home. Rizpah understood him far better than I did and would often challenge some of his views—which they both enjoyed. In a Greek country, that was eccentric indeed.

Although there were many different temples in Rhodos we did not need to do much but pay lip service to them and, as long as Apollonius approved, Rizpah and I were regarded as amusing for practising our own rituals and services at home. Sometimes others who were interested in the exotic would even come and join us but never once did a Jew step willingly over our threshold.

The children learnt about the Jewish festivals, just as I had taught Luke in his childhood and Rizpah had taught her natural children Timothy and Sophia. We re-enacted the Exodus from Egypt through our own version of the Passover service, based on the sefirot of the Tree of Life and our memories (for we had not managed to inveigle any prayer books from the Jewish community); we encouraged the children to live in a bower at the time of the Succot, just as Rosa had encouraged me when I was a child back in Nazara. We fasted for the day of Atonement (although we allowed ourselves water) and contemplated our mistakes of the last year, owning up to them and being absolved as we absolved each other. Apollonius made us a *hanukkia*, a kind of model of the menorah in the Temple for the festival of Hanukkah and, in fact, we were more observant than we had been in Alexandria where we could have done it all so much more easily.

'It means more like this,' said Rizpah. 'We have to improvise and rebuild the services ourselves and we can make them fit more easily.'

She was right but we were always careful not to bend the structure even when it seemed tempting to do so. Even if there was something we remembered but did not understand we would do it, thoughtfully, and think and talk until we had made sense of every word and every action. Worshipping in that way required discipline but it was satisfying.

'You know, Paul was right to ban us from carrying out services,' I said one day when we had decided to put together our own ritual of mourning. 'We know that it is the structure of the services which is important, not the form. The form of all the services we do traditionally was written by men, for men. It's not for us to steal those and do them in an identical way; we should build our own. We can make our own for childbirth, menstruation, miscarriage or whatever. We have all the knowledge we need and it would help the feminine in God to be reflected back. That doesn't happen very much nowadays, at least not in our tradition.'

'I prefer the traditional,' said Rizpah stoutly. 'I agree that we can create services for women only but for worship itself I want to work with what already is.'

Now she was truly her own priestess, with no Jewish men to rule her, we had began to differ more in how we interpreted our faith; but it did not really matter. Perhaps I grew a little lonely inside myself but I did not regard it; there was too much happiness in Apollonius's company and the luxuries of life in Lindos to have regrets.

Because Rhodos was a small and quiet community and the adherents to each of its religions were, for the most part, tolerant of others, it was easy to go to the Temples of Apollo or Artemis or any of the other gods and goddesses to see how and why their services had been created. In Alexandria or Rome I had been shy of doing so and had gone as little as I dared for the priests and priestesses and many from the gathering itself would want to involve you; to convince you that this was the right religion for you. In Lindos people did not mind if you just called in for a little while and did not want to join in. It was very restful that way.

And it was because of this that I finally found something I had been searching for unconsciously since I left Judaea: a woman deeply versed in spiritual tradition who could teach and inspire me.

Her name was Prokne, priestess of Athena, and she ruled over the Acropolis that watched over the little city with its winding streets and colourful markets.

Most people did not know her even if they worshipped regularly at Athena's shrine, laying gifts at the feet of the ancient, much-loved wooden statue of the goddess or offering sacrifices. They *saw* her, sitting on her priestess throne meditating or, at new and full moons, they could petition her much as the famous Oracle of Delphi was petitioned to know what the future held. But the woman herself was a mystery. She lived, celibate and alone, within the Temple and never left it without a retinue of acolytes.

I became curious about her when I overheard two women in the marketplace complaining about a prediction one of them had received.

'She wasn't definite. She said it was down to me,' said one. 'I don't want vague predictions for my money; I want yes or no!'

'What did she mean "down to you"? You can't make Aristides leave you his money.'

'Well she said that. But she said prosperity would come from my own belief and that to be prosperous my belief needed to be stronger. Now what were the words she used…? Oh yes. "If you believe it to be true with all your heart and soul, it will be true. If you doubt, then it will fade away from you." What kind of answer is that?'

It was just the kind of answer that Yeshua would have given.

The day that I finally went to the temple (without taking a

sacrifice) was a time of the dark Moon. I loved those nights for, if the sky were clear, the stars that were hidden by moonlight raced across the sky in their thousands.

This time was the rising of the Pleiades and I knew from my years in Alexandria that, at the temples of Athena, it was the year's end; the Cleansing Festival known as Plynteria.

First thing in the morning, the goddess's statue was stripped of its clothes and jewels and taken, reverently veiled, down to the sea to be washed. It would be accompanied by women carrying offering-baskets of fig pastries or a fig cake, representing purification and the dissolution of negative energies. While she was away, the temple was scrubbed inch by inch.

In Lindos we had slaves and servants (and were lambasted as being ridiculously indulgent masters in insisting that they all took a day off a week for the Sabbath) so I was, again, a lady of leisure and had no need to cook, clean or do anything but supervise the work of others, smooth my work-roughened hands with sweet-smelling unguents and please my husband. Even with the copying of the scrolls, life had the potential to become very boring. Greek women were less free than Romans who, in turn, were less free than Jews. There was not much that I could do to thrive here. For Rizpah, it was a little different; she relished her role as a mother and teacher of children and her studies were more fulfilling to her than to me.

Something told me very loudly—and much against my natural inclination—that I would enjoy helping to scrub Athena's temple so, that morning, I got up early, just before sunrise, left a vague message that I would be back in the late afternoon, and made my way up the winding streets to the top of the little city where the temple loomed in the first light. At the foot of the steps leading to the Acropolis I let my fingers trace the lines of the great ship carved into the rock at the foot of the steps to the Acropolis itself. It was a Rhodian trireme, an ancient war galley with three rows of oars each side, and it guarded a marble staircase leading to a D-shaped courtyard of colonnades and five door openings to different parts of the temple.

As with all spiritual disciplines, the ritual of taking the goddess to the sea appeared to be the most popular of the options available for the festival and the temple appeared to be completely empty. I hesitated then walked quietly, aware that I was on holy ground, through the main doorway and towards the inner sanctum.

There was the empty space where the goddess normally stood—and one woman, roughly dressed in brown, knelt on the floor cleaning around its base.

I bowed to her; made the appropriate greetings and requested that I should be permitted to help.

'Hmm,' said the woman, kneeling back to take a look at me. 'I've never seen you before in my life. You're certainly not an acolyte.'

I shook my head, smiling. 'I'm afraid not.'

'Oh well. You must be sent from Olympus,' said the woman in a gruff, irritated tone. 'There is more work here than I can do alone. You are welcome but don't tarry and don't be idle. You can start with the floor over there. Here's a bucket and brush. Sacred water in the trough. Work from the end backwards. Can you sing?'

The question surprised me.

'Not particularly well,' I said.

'Singing helps get the work done and cleanses the air,' said the woman. 'With two voices we should make enough sound. Listen and join in.'

I raised a spoilt lady's eyebrow for a moment and then laughed. For years I had worked with my hands but now I was a lady again I expected to be appreciated for lowering myself to clean, not ordered about! So I picked up the bucket, filled it and walked to my spot. There I sat down, twisted my silvering hair into a tighter knot and, winding my veil around it as securely as possible, rolled up my sleeves and reached for the scrubbing brush.

The gruff voiced woman began to sing a rhythmic, old-Greek language folk song about *Helena Dendrites,* the legendary woman whose relationships with men caused the fall of the great North Eastern city of Troy.

I listened to the words, fascinated by the sensuality in the tone

206

and hearing again the old story of how Helen visited Athena's sanctuary here, offering a cup made in the measure of her own breast which, apparently, miraculously provided milk for orphaned children. Legend said that this cup had got lost or been stolen sometime in the last few hundred years—and it probably never existed at all. But the song was lovely and the tune familiar for I'd heard it many times on the streets of the city. I had also read the long inscription on a marble tablet on the temple's outer wall that listed ancient treasures dedicated to Athena and included Menelaus' helmet, a pair of bracelets, inscribed *Helen to Athena* and the steering oars belonging to Kanopos, helmsman of Menelaus. And the song was enticing and rhythmical; good to work to. After I'd heard it through twice I could join in and the two of us had the floor of the inner court dealt with before the Sun rose to the height of the hillside.

The woman had already dusted and wiped the walls around the statue's plinth so we were free to move out to the next area but she held up her hand in a motion that meant 'be still,' and listened.

I could hear nothing, apart from the distant sounds of city life on the hillside below us, but the woman either had sharper ears than I or she heard something on a level which did not speak to me.

'The others are coming,' she said. 'They will cleanse the outer rooms. But you and I must talk. You are a holy woman sent for a reason and, more, you have a daughter—one born twice in the last decade—a special child. We must discuss these things.'

'Who speaks to you?' I said stone-faced because I felt a huge resistance to her words and, yes, even anger. She turned to me a great, wide smile expanding to light up a broad-boned, lined but beautiful face.

'Yes,' she said. 'You know them. You do not listen half the time that they speak, you even place walls against them; but you can hear them when you want to. I've never learnt to block them out. We can learn from each other, you and I!'

'I don't hear Athena,' I said cautiously.

'Oh you do,' said the woman. 'You may call her something else or you may think her a man—but you hear the spirit that I hear.

Or at least, she speaks to you. And others too. Others whose voices I do not know.

'My name is Prokne,' she added. 'Wait here, I pray of you. I will greet the late-comers, the cleaners and slaves who come at convenient hours to suit themselves, and then we can break our fast together perhaps?'

Prokne? The priestess of Athena herself? 'Don't you have to be here for the re-robing of the statue—the goddess?' I said.

'Of course I do,' she replied, with a grin. 'But if I am not, no one will notice.'

I felt my brow furrow in confused thought but it was none of my business so I stood, leaning slightly against the stone wall, stretching my stiff, now work-shy arms in the sunlight that played through the open window behind me onto my shoulders while Prokne went to speak to her acolytes.

I resisted the light as it touched me from Beriah, the world of the heavens, because I was prejudiced and I did not want the energy of a—still alien—goddess to enter my consciousness. But the higher realms can choose whatever form they wish in Yezirah, the world of the psyche, dreams and illusion. Where Prokne saw and heard Athena, I sensed the essence of the great angel Samael, the messenger of the Silence; of justice and of judgement. I knew of him from my studies with Philo and, of course, I believed that I was making it all up as I felt the sight of his red-robed figure in my head. You don't 'see' these angels; at least I don't. I sense and feel them but there is an image too. It's hard to explain…

'*Agapetos*,' I said, the traditional greeting and bowed; just in case there actually were an angel there.

It laughed. 'You are afraid of war,' it said—though of course it said nothing but the words ran across my forehead and into my eyes.

'I am.'

'I am Mars,' it said. 'Mars the patient, the strong, the passive, the wise.'

'Aren't you meant to be Athena?'

'I am her too,' I sensed laughter in the depth of the voice.

'You wish to speak to me?'

Again, the amusement. Most humans in sacred work want to prolong contact with the angelics and often seek it. It makes me acutely uncomfortable. I can't work out what's real and what's my imagination.

'Agree with the priestess,' I heard. 'Give her your daughter. She will return to you strong and wise and all will be as it needs to be.'

'Well I'm glad you told me,' I said out loud, with deep sarcasm. 'I might have objected. Actually, I do object. I don't have a daughter. And I'm making this up myself. You don't exist.'

'We only don't exist when we tell you things you do not wish to hear,' it said.

'*Aposkorakizō*' I said rudely. If I'd been ten I'd have stamped my foot.

'Your accent's appalling,' said the angel with great satisfaction and the energy dissolved.

I turned to find Prokne standing in the doorway, shaking with laughter.

'What?' I said.

'Well I've never heard her insulted quite like that,' she said. 'But of course, you don't see her the way I do. It's not your job.'

'She was a he,' I said, torn between irritation that she had seen and heard me and deeper irritation that what had happened had probably been true.

'To you,' said Prokne. 'I agree. The gods and goddesses can be most annoying.'

'Oh it's insupportable!' I spat. 'I hate it.' As I spoke I was amazed at what I was saying.

'Me too,' said Prokne. 'But we are stuck with it, I believe!'

She held out her hand and, somewhat shyly, like a little girl, I took it.

We sat and ate white bread, honey and figs together, this outspoken soul-mate friend and I, perched on some fallen stones at the back of the temple. Inside the acolytes and slaves finished the work that we had begun and re-installed the goddess in her niche, re-clothed and garlanded in flowers and gifts. They did not notice Prokne's absence.

'So, will you bring her?' said Prokne, at last.

'She's not mine to give,' I said.

'Well ask her.'

'There is someone else involved,' I said. 'Two people in fact.' My heart shrank, realising what a fight I might have on my hands with Rizpah. 'We are Jews. We are monotheists. Well, we women are. My husband is Roman.'

'And I believe Roman husbands have the say in these matters,' said Prokne, gently.

'But she is not his child and…'

'And your friend believes she is hers…?'

'Well…'

Prokne took my hand and turned it over, looking at my palm and running her fingers along the lines. 'Such a life,' she said. 'No, don't worry; I'm not a fortune-teller but people's hands fascinate me. They do tell the story of life. You are a survivor. If you knew how strong you are…'

For no reason, I felt tears spring into my eyes. Since Philo died I had had no teacher and, even with him, I had often felt isolated as a woman in a man's world. Perhaps now I would be able to learn more and find my way closer to the Lord.

It was Apollonius I talked to first which meant holding my tongue until he came back from his day at the garrison headquarters.

'May I speak to you alone?' I asked when he greeted me in the atrium. Servants took his scrolls and offered him wine; our life now was rarely spent alone except when everyone else had gone to bed.

'Of course,' he said, looking at me quizzically. 'Would now be convenient?'

When he offered that exaggerated courtesy it was a joke between us and a moment of deep contentment; he knew so well how impatient I was and never, if he could help it, made me wait if I were bursting with news. Once or twice he had done it out of a wish to tease me and he would watch me fidget and lose focus but he preferred to please me—as I did him. I never failed to thank God for our love each night as we lay down together.

We retired to our room and closed the door. After I had described my day, my husband was thoughtful.

'I don't mind,' he said. 'I think I can trust your instinct by now and, as a Roman, I'm not going to object if the child learns the ways of Athena—or Mars. She could do a lot worse than become a priestess herself.'

'But Rizpah won't like it and Sarah is more hers than yours. Rizpah is a lot more orthodox than you, my dear.'

'I can face Rizpah if you are agreed,' I said. 'If you did not agree, then I wouldn't go ahead.'

'Oh yes you would!' said my husband affectionately, giving me a playful cuff on my backside. 'You would just wriggle your way around me.'

'I can't always do that,' I said, smiling up into his eyes.

'No, not always,' he replied. 'But on this occasion, you can. In fact, I think it's a very wise thing to do. Sarah is too much the little Jewess already to assimilate easily into Rhodian life when you, I and Rizpah are gone.'

It was the first time that he had spoken of our deaths and I caught his hand swiftly.

'Not yet,' I said. 'Not yet.'

'No, not yet,' he said, sitting down beside me and putting his arm around me. 'But I am feeling my age these days.' We held each other tightly without words for a few minutes.

I had suspected opposition but not jealousy. Rizpah exploded into sudden anger when I told her the day's story and that both Samael and Prokne had asked for Sarah to go and study at the temple. In vain I tried to explain that it was not my idea.

'Oh of course, your wonderful angels!' she said, bitterly. 'They told you, so I can't tell you you're wrong!'

'Rizpah,' I said. 'Don't … it's not as if we'd lose her. It would just be like sending her to school each day. She would still sleep here and be your daughter.'

'My daughter,' Rizpah said bitterly. 'Oh yes, my daughter until you want something. My daughter to nurse when she is sick and teach good manners to—and then your child when you have an inspiration that she should be taken away from me.'

'I'm not trying to take her away from you.'

'Oh,' Rizpah sat down abruptly. 'No, probably you are not.

But that is what is going to happen. You'll get your way and I'll give in. Just like coming here.'

'Oh Rizpah…' She was right but it was hard to hear it just like that. 'Do you really feel that? Do you regret it?'

'No. I chose to follow you all those years ago,' she said. 'I went my own way when I married Lucius but, in times of trouble, back I came. I know you don't mean anything by it but I don't want Sarah to go to the Temple.'

'Then she doesn't go,' I said.

'Oh don't be so ridiculous,' said Rizpah. 'In a Greek house where the man rules even more than in Rome—and you will already have spoken to Apollonius before you spoke to me—of course she's going. I don't have any say in the matter at all.'

'You think we'd send her against her will?'

'No, it's worse than that,' said Rizpah. 'You will bend my will to yours—or Sarah will ask to go.'

'What can I do?' I asked helplessly. 'What do you want me to say? What resolution is there then?'

'Just ask the child,' said Rizpah heavily. 'No, I'll ask her.'

She clapped her hands and Cassandra, her attendant, appeared in moments.

'Send Sarah to us,' said Rizpah. 'She doesn't have to have her hair brushed; just as she is.'

We waited in silence. I could feel that some deep unacknowledged rivalry within us was trying to lift itself out to be faced and resolved. I had known it was there but never given it any thought. I had always been the one with the last word in everything; had I been wrong?

Sarah walked in; she was nine now and had developed a young lady's elegance. She wore a simple dress in green that complemented her brown, slightly golden hair and grey eyes. She had freckles which would fade as she grew but she would never be beautiful. She had something more; an ability to be loved and a talent for giving people her full attention. Just to be in a room with her calmed people. She would be chosen for her character not her face or figure and, already, she knew that.

'Sarah,' said Rizpah. I saw that she was trembling slightly.

'Mother?'

'Sarah, have you ever been to the temple of Athena?'

'Yes, Mother,' the girl's voice was expressionless. She was waiting to find out whether that was a good thing or not.

'What have I taught you about Athena?' asked Rizpah.

'She is a goddess of wisdom and of just war. But she is like the other gods; a vessel not the truth,' said Sarah.

Rizpah nodded. 'Would you want to be a priestess of Athena?' she said.

Sarah looked puzzled. 'I don't understand,' she said.

Then we both saw it; the air changed around her and Sarah was wrapped in light. She looked scared and then radiant.

I bit my impatient lip and held back my words, waiting for Rizpah to ask what she saw. But Rizpah said nothing. Her face had gone white and a tear slipped from her eye.

The moment—an hour—vanished.

'Yes, I would like that,' said Sarah. 'I would like that very much.'

Rizpah married Quintinus three months later and they took Tobias into their home, just a few streets away from us. Sarah divided her time between the two houses but, as the weeks passed, she preferred to stay with us when she was not with Prokne. It was closer to the Acropolis, she said. And her mother's house was always full of boys talking about being soldiers.

It would be wrong to say that nothing was ever the same again because, once a few months of adjustment had been allowed to soothe our scars, Rizpah and I still met and talked and worshipped and laughed and squabbled. We went shopping together and I know she forgave me; she had that kind of a heart. But I was scarred and I felt that there was some deeper division. Perhaps that was guilt for, in truth, I wanted to spend more time with Prokne than I did with Rizpah. It worked out wonderfully for me…

I tried to talk to Rizpah about it but, from her heart, she said there was nothing wrong and, if there were, it could only be in me. She did not love me one iota less.

Marriage suited her; she bloomed and became agreeably bossy as the ruler of her home. She had not been matriarch for too long and the role suited her. Quintinus adored her and, in less than two years, after the birth of their son, Alexander, she came to love him too.

'And Isaac married Rebekah and loved her,' Apollonius said to me. 'Just like Rizpah and Quintinus. Just like us.'

Alexander's birth healed whatever rift there might have been within our deep sister-friendship. Rizpah was far too old to bear a child again and the baby had come despite her best efforts at keeping herself safe. But he was so deeply wanted that we worked together to build her health throughout the pregnancy and I, with riches again, had no problems finding all the herbs and spices that would strengthen her both through the pregnancy and birth.

We had a Rhodean doctor on standby for the birth itself but Rizpah, Sarah and I were the three who welcomed Alexander to the world. He tried to spite us, turning inside Rizpah's womb to present himself as a breech birth, but I was wise to that trick. When he finally came, with Rizpah's last exhausted push, he shot into the world, large and sturdy and screaming from the moment I freed his windpipe from a potentially fatal twist of the umbilical cord and forced him to breathe at once instead of allowing him to learn gently while the placenta freed itself from the mother.

'He's a fighter,' I said, as I laid him, wriggling and gasping, on his mother's breast. 'You'll have your work cut out with this one.'

'I know.' Rizpah took my hand and smiled weakly. Sarah bathed her legs and thighs and we wrapped both her and the baby in clean, fresh linen. 'It all begins again now.'

'Yes it does.' I smiled at her and across to the young woman who was tidying away all the stained linen and the by-products of a birth. 'The world is new again.'

Two weeks later, Sarah took part in a sacred ceremony at the temple to mark her womanhood. At that moment, an intelligent and excitable little girl with a huge capacity for love became a prophetess; a voice of the Divine; someone who would be a worthy successor to Prokne.

Though both Prokne and I knew that she would never take up that role.

'All religion is lies for the masses,' said my friend one day as we ate our midday meal just outside the temple. 'Athena, Moses, Jupiter. All lies.'

'Whoa!' I said, pausing in my enjoyment of a luscious fig sprinkled with honey, lemon juice and nuts. 'That's a little excessive!'

'There is a Truth,' said Prokne. 'There are energies and angels and man-made gods. There are nature spirits and personifications of principle. But to hold to any one lesser god is to close your mind to truth.'

'Born Jewish were you?' I asked with a tinge of sarcasm.

'Just as bad,' said Prokne. 'Your god is vengeful; destroys thousands of people on a whim; demands total obedience and inflicts—how many is it?—a thousand laws.'

'Six hundred and thirteen,' I said. 'But that's not what my brother, the Anointed, taught.'

'Ah,' said Prokne, with satisfaction. 'Here we are. Tell me about your brother, the Anointed.'

We spoke then, on and off, for six days, comparing notes, knowledge and discussing Yeshua's interpretation of God, God the Highest, I Am That I Am and how this revelation had changed and opened my life. About how I had learnt to see that God reflected what we thought He was—if we expected judgement and pain, we would see only judgement and pain; but if we saw the beauty and the good in life then it would be reflected back. I told her of my life and travels and my beliefs and my losses and gains. Oh it was marvellous! Prokne was such a clear outside voice with no Jewish prejudices. She ripped open my lost and lonely corners and applied astringent to my prejudices and lazy thoughts. She challenged all the teaching that Yeshua had brought and put Paul and his beliefs into perspective. She honed my soul and, in return, I gave her a whole new perspective to clear her own mind.

We discussed sacrifice—Athena received the blood of lambs and calves as did so many of the other gods. I had not been comfortable with it in my youth and still preferred to make gifts of grain, vegetables or fruits. But I was not one of those people who did not eat meat and I had seen over the long years that animals sacrificed to a god (or *the* God) were often killed more peaceably and swiftly than those simply butchered for their flesh with no ceremony or sacred prayer for their afterlife or rebirth.

Prokne had never thought of sacrifice as anything 'wrong' or to be considered but, to give her due, she thought through my views without decrying them. And it was this conversation that led to the most important discussion we ever had: blood.

Sarah was a priestess; there was no doubt about that. Like Prokne, she did not regard Athena as the only god; she knew there was a greater truth. But she served the goddess with a passion and a discipline which both amazed and slightly unnerved me. There was not a morning when Sarah did not rise early for her prayers; not a day when she did not study and not a night when she did not count her blessings and pray for healing for all those she knew in need.

'She reminds me of Yeshua,' I said. 'Even her face has a touch of his elfin looks; her ears are tiny and so delicately shaped—a woman's version of his. And the way she moves her arms is the same as he did. And she has a grace…'

'But she is not your daughter; there is none of his blood in her veins,' finished Prokne.

'No none. I did—I have—wondered if she is my daughter reincarnated.'

'Well she is that, I am sure,' said Prokne. 'Remember, Athena told us she had been born again. But even if she is not, the important thing is to remember that spiritual heritage does not follow by blood. In fact, the last place to look for the successor to a great priest or priestess is through their blood.'

'But people do.'

'Always. Perhaps that is why so many great ones choose not to have children—so they do not pass that burden on to generations who could never carry it. Spirit will not travel through blood.'

'But if Sarah is my daughter—even though born from different parents—isn't that a kind of spiritual blood?'

'She, you, I and all the people in this city have been born a dozen times, perhaps a hundred times, perhaps more,' said Prokne. 'Just once, for a few months, she shared your blood. It doesn't count for much, you know!

'But what is important is that she chose to come and live in your line of teaching.'

'And yours.'

'Yes, there will be something here that she needs—and she seeks it, just watch her!'

'I do. Every day. She amazes me.'

'Remind me of what Athena represents in your—sefirot is it?'

'Yes, sefirot. Discipline, discernment, justice, judgement, strength. And on the other side, ruthlessness, cruelty, narrow-mindedness and lack of joy.'

'War?'

'Yes. War. But war comes from the attributes of Gevurah—that's what it's called—rather than being an aspect of it. War is either terrible and ruthless or wise and necessary; it depends on whether the attributes are used well or badly.'

'So we can hope that she is learning discernment and justice. Those are rare. In which case, maybe she is an Anointed One,' said Prokne. 'Or, of course, we could be seeing the genesis of a despot. A priestess of Athena who will rule this city with a rod of iron.'

'You see her as your successor?' I didn't like the idea but I could see the sense in it. I still had to learn a great deal about religious tolerance.'

'Actually, no,' said Prokne. 'She will travel with you.'

'Me? I'm not going anywhere. And even if I did, Sarah is of Greek birth and heritage; why would she travel with me?'

'You who are of Jewish birth and heritage? Because blood and heritage are not important. That's why she will travel with you.'

Twelve

Cephas arrived in Lindos on one fresh spring morning. Together with three men whom I had never met, he was travelling to Rome to visit the Messianic Jewish Community—as opposed to Paul's Christians.

Apollonius always kept an eye on the dossier of arrivals and departures to our bustling little port and he broke habit to come home directly to tell me as soon as he knew that Cephas had arrived. Although the two men had never met, he knew all about my burly friend and the name 'Simon Peter of Jerusalem' struck him immediately when he saw it. We went together to greet him at the harbour side inn where the four were putting up and I sent my name up to their room with trepidation.

Cephas, I was sure, would be the same, only older. Of the attitudes of the three men with him to the wife of the betrayer, I was less sure. But I need not have worried; Cephas gave out a roar of surprise and delight which must have shaken the rafters of the house when he read my note. I could hear it through the floor. Then he bounded down the stairs to the atrium where we stood waiting. 'By all that's holy!' he shouted. 'It's his sister! Deborah! What are you doing here? And here's your Centurion too! What a joy to find you both!' He engulfed me in his old bear hug and greeted Apollonius with just as much enthusiasm. Both of us were a little taken aback. Apollonius knew full well the reaction of the disciples in Jerusalem when I had chosen Rome over

Judaea but it looked as if times had changed—or that Cephas had not been of the same mind as the others. It was both. Cephas, Matthew, Lukas and Judah (how those names made my heart jump) were perfectly comfortable in the company of philistines.

'If the good Lord Himself hadn't shown us that this is the way it should be, we would still have been having problems,' said Cephas. 'But nowadays we meet so many Gentiles that it would be almost impossible to keep all the food and social laws without a heavenly dispensation.'

That meant that the four were happy to come and stay in our home for the month they planned to spend in Rhodos and we were delighted to offer them our hospitality. Money was a little tight so they were as pleased as we were to be able to accept the invitation. Cephas told us about a vision he had had of animals in a tarpaulin and how that was the sign to him that all animals were good to eat. I couldn't quite work out the significance but it had worked for him and that was all that mattered.

'It's hard to make the orthodox see it,' he said. 'It's a big change—the Law is the Law so it's not easy to acknowledge that it *can* be changed. Perhaps they never will see but the Lord God is capable of changing his Laws for us as we grow and the world gets smaller. It may well be that the law of everyday living needs to be revised every hundred years or so.'

'But Yeshua said that not one jot of the Law should pass away,' said Rizpah, who had met Cephas again with as much trepidation as I had but who had been greeted in return with great civility. She was only trying him out for she had eaten 'forbidden' foods for a lot longer than Cephas had.

'Yes, the Law, the Great Law,' said Cephas. 'Not the everyday laws of how we eat and drink and who we talk to. There's no change in the Ten Commandments and they are the greatest of laws. I don't eat a pig if I possibly can and I don't make myself unclean on purpose but loving kindness is greater than truth and if it is an unkindness to a good host to refuse his food and lodging then a greater sin has been committed than transgressing one of the food laws.'

Time had certainly mellowed the great giant with whom I had

so many quarrels and so many happy resolutions but his spirit was just the same. He was rather stooped now and his hair almost white. Once the enthusiasm of going over old times was complete, he was cautiously friendly with Apollonius just as he had always been slightly cautious with me. A Roman soldier or an intelligent woman would never make Cephas entirely comfortable and he was the first to admit that. He was as tactless as always, pointing out how much Rizpah and I had aged, myself particularly, although he acknowledged that Roman unguents and paint had probably postponed the worst!

We told him cheerfully that we thought we had done very well considering shipwreck, bereavement and life in a tiny, primitive village and did not mind his bluffness.

The four men were just as prone as Paul was not to take women seriously and so, if they wanted evening conversation on the days they were not visiting the Jewish quarter, they had no choice but to talk to Apollonius. His courtesy and wisdom impressed them, I think, for he was careful never to let his superior education show or to contradict them other than in heated philosophical debate. Rizpah and I were able to catch up with as much news from Judaea as we could possibly want and the first news was as shocking as it was unexpected. My brother James had been stoned to death on the orders of a new high priest called Ananus.

Ananus himself had been shorn of his job for his actions, Herod Agrippa and the procurator, Albinus, both having ruled that he had no right to assemble a Sanhedrin to pass the death sentence without Roman permission.

Whatever the rights or wrongs of the situation, James was dead. Rachel, his widow, who had never thought much of we Messianic people, had been distraught and furious. She had vanished into a tribe of children, grandchildren and great-grandchildren and discouraged any of her offspring to have any more to do with Cephas or the others.

'I am so sorry Deborah,' said Cephas and I smiled wanly. In fact, it was so long since I had seen James that the blow was not harsh. I was deeply sorry for the manner of his death and I asked

Cephas and the others to visit the synagogue in Lindos to say a Kaddish for him on my behalf but I shed only a few tears for the brother of my childhood.

There was plenty of other news, once the shock had worn off, but Rizpah knew very little of the names Cephas spoke of and I, myself, could hardly remember the names of those who had been born to disciples and followers of Yeshua while we were in Judaea, let alone relate to those souls who had flooded in since.

We were able to watch the men take what they called 'The Good News' of Jesus the Messiah to the Jews of Lindos and compare their manner of teaching with Paul's. The thrust of their message was Jewish and aimed at those born and raised in the same religion as they. They taught in the synagogues and in the streets and, if Gentiles heard and came to them, then they taught those strangers just as courteously and diligently. However as they based their teaching on the Torah it was hard for Gentiles to follow all that they said. Some listened and went away saying 'It's about a Messiah for the Jews' and disregarded the rest of the message but others heard more deeply and said, 'It's a Messiah for all of us; he just came as a Jew.'

The Christians would have nothing to do with them. The difference in Cephas's teaching, as compared with Paul's, was that following the Christ was hard work. It meant observing the Ten Commandments diligently, throwing out all other gods and their images and loving your neighbour as yourself. He did not present Christ as the panacea of all ills; yes, prayer to God through Jesus would be enhanced by the understanding of the Christos but you had to do your part too. The Christians didn't like that at all and the two parties formed an uneasy truce and ignored each other as much as possible.

'John teaches a kind of ecstatic Christianity, a bit like theirs,' Cephas said one evening over supper. 'All feelings and visions and airy fairy stuff. But I teach it at ground level. I let people know what they are really in for. Rather one serious convert who's going to make a good go of it than twenty who think it's all rather fun and won't stick it out at the first temptation.'

I liked Cephas's way of teaching. He was a little too harsh for my tastes but then Paul was too liberal. I could join in with Cephas's services and listen to him speak and hear the words that Yeshua had spoken. With Paul I had felt as though I was listening to the ideas of someone else completely. Cephas and I had long conversations about Paul, about Barnabas and about God's will for this new branch of faith and he was amazed that my son had left with 'that Evangelist.' I couldn't explain it to him without going into all the history and, somehow, I couldn't do it so skirted around the issue. Nevertheless, Luke's reaction to the stories about Judah gnawed at me and I knew I would have to talk about it to Cephas some time.

'I can't say I like Paul,' said Cephas. 'He is impetuous, fanatical and has no reason. He's an excellent orator but he does let his mouth run away with him. We've had a fair few scuffles with Paul of Tarsus and he doesn't give way easily.'

I smiled. Cephas would not give way easily either.

'It's not just me,' he said when I told him that. 'We have a council; there are still many people around who remember your brother alive and what the feeling with him was. Without the memory of who he was and how he spoke and what his beliefs were it is almost impossible to represent him truthfully.'

'But Paul says Yeshua speaks from the heavens,' I said.

Cephas snorted. 'Many souls speak to us from the heavens,' he said. 'The Lord speaks to everyone all the time; you only have to stop and cock an ear and there are the voices of angels everywhere. It's not so special to be able to hear them. He may hear Yeshua but so do I. So do the others. I expect you do, too, but the thing is that Yeshua seems to be telling Paul different things from what the tells us. We can't both be right.'

'Well maybe you can,' I said thoughtfully. Cephas made a face at me. 'What Graeco-Roman philosophical rubbish is that?' he said bluntly. 'If one's right then the other's wrong. It's as plain as the nose on your face.'

'No, it's not,' I said. 'You know as well as I do that it is only Yesod, the ego, that thinks that. And it's only in this world that duality exists. God is not masculine or feminine, Jewish or Christian, left-handed or right-handed, black or white, tall or short. God just is. 'He may speak and Yeshua may speak from those higher levels and their words may not be words at all but feelings; impulses if you like. We can only hear them according to our personalities and our psyches. If we are balanced and strong we will hear them clearly but if we are not perfect in ourselves (and who of us is?) then we may hear them in a slightly distorted way.

'Paul is all about the joy of the information; he wants to spread it far and wide. Without Barnabas to balance him, he cannot hear Yeshua from a balanced perspective.

'You, on the other hand are more Gevuric—further up the Tree of Life and able to discriminate. And you are in touch with Hesed, the principle of Mercy. You think things through (when you are not exploding!) and you will pick up the more rigorous aspect of Yeshua or even of God.'

'Hmmm,' said Cephas, not quite convinced. I had not expected him to be.

'It's thinking that something is either right or wrong which creates half the problems we have,' I continued, warming to my theme. 'What's right for one person is often wrong for another. To ninety-nine out of a hundred Jews the idea of marrying a Roman is outrageous, but it was right for me.'

'Ninety nine thousand nine hundred and ninety nine out of a hundred thousand Jews, more like,' said Cephas and I laughed, agreeing with him. 'But wait,' he went on, his brow furrowed. 'That's like saying it's allowable for one person to kill and not another.' 'Well that's probably true!' I said. 'We have laws to prevent us from doing anything stupid and we should do all we can not to kill but, every now and then, people have to kill if you or your family are threatened and it's the only way out; that's what you have to do. The commandment is not to commit murder, not "Thou shalt not kill." It's a question of balance. Everybody's destiny is different. It was right for you to follow Yeshua, leaving Leah and your family at home, but someone else might be on Earth specifically to take care of their family and their task might be about *not* being tempted to follow an itinerant teacher.'

Cephas snorted. 'That's just an excuse,' he said. 'If the Messiah comes, you should follow him.'

I sighed. 'Well of course I agree,' I said. 'After all, I did just that (and you didn't like that or think that I should at the time!) but there are people who have different destinies. Many, many people will never even come to hear of Yeshua but that doesn't make them wrong. The Lord won't turn his back on them because they weren't destined to hear the news.'

The evening wore on as we argued amicably. We both knew that we were on the same side, we just had different perspectives. Cephas, unlike Paul, was quite happy for Rizpah and I to act as Rebbitzen for the women who heard them and wanted to know more. There were very few for the Jews of Rhodos were very orthodox and even those who were interested in what the four Judaeans had to say were not sure that their wives should hear it too. However, we spoke with those who did want to hear and that in itself gave us more contacts with the others in the Jewish quarter and, at long last, there would be a few nods and smiles as we walked down the street.

I remembered that I had a message to give Cephas, a message given to me by Yeshua more than thirty years before, but I wanted to wait until the time was right to give it instead of leaping in with both feet as I had done with Paul. In fact it was just two evenings before their ship was due to leave that the right time came. We were alone together in the atrium and I knew it was my last chance to ask about Judah and the stories about him. It was hard to open the subject but I was glad that I did, for it meant that Cephas and I were able to part the greater friends than either of us could have hoped.

I told him, at last, what had happened to Luke and how Paul and Barnabas had allowed the story of betrayal to spread, even though they had not perpetrated it themselves. I added that I had discovered for myself, in Jerusalem, how hard it was to try and persuade a crowd who needed a villain that there might be another alternative.

I knew that I had to realise once and for all that the story of betrayal would be the one remembered but I needed to talk it over with someone who had been there at the time. 'We do try not to blame Judah,' said my gruff old friend. 'Even now, we try. Myself more than others particularly; the good Lord knows he was never close as a friend but he was one of us and I am one of the few remaining who actually does remember.

'I remember the Master telling us not to fall asleep, to keep our eyes open so that we would see the truth when he came with the soldiers. Whenever we tell the story, people assume that we slumbered and snored while he was praying but it wasn't like that. We prayed, too, but our eyes were looking only for what they wanted to see. We wanted to see betrayal and so that is what we saw. We did not choose to look at it from the point of view that the Master and Judah saw it, so how could we understand them?'

He was silent for a moment and, to my surprise, tears formed in his eyes. One brimmed over and slid down his ruddy cheek into the snow-white beard.

'It should have been me, you know, not Judah,' he said.

I waited carefully, not looking at him and saying nothing, for I knew that this was an important moment and I did not want to rush in and damage it.

'If I had done it, maybe my name would not have been damned as Judah's is,' said Cephas. 'It was his calmness which fooled us all. As if he really didn't care. Everyone knows how I can go off at the deep end. I'd have made it quite clear that it was Yeshua's orders and not my will. I wasn't brave enough to do it. But it should have been me.'

'How do you know?' I asked quietly.

'He tested me once,' Cephas said sadly. 'He asked me to do something for him which I disapproved of and I didn't do it and he looked at me—you know how he used to look at you when you had not understood something and you should have?'

I nodded.

'Well, he didn't say anything then but he told me at the last supper we had, the Passover supper, the night he was taken, that I would betray him.'

'That *you* would?'

'Oh yes. It's told now as if it was Judah he was talking to, and that's what will be remembered, but you and I know perfectly well it wasn't him. It was me. He said I would deny him three times before the morning and I was outraged. But he was right. Good Lord, you were there for one of the denials. You remember!

'I could have killed myself when I'd done it. I'd just proved again that I wasn't brave enough or strong enough to serve him.

'I couldn't have done it, you see; handed him over. I would have struck out at the soldiers myself—well, I did when they came for him. Anyway I couldn't have carried it though.'

'Why didn't you tell me this at the Temple?' I asked, my mind spinning back to the day he had found me in the courtyard, exhausted and frightened after seeing Pilate myself.

'I didn't dare,' Cephas said sadly. 'It was such a surprise to see you. I did try. I did tell you some of it but I couldn't face it all.'

I put my hand on his arm reassuringly. At last, it was the moment to pass on Yeshua's message. Had Cephas told me the whole story that day in the Temple then perhaps I could have told him then and spared him many years of regret. The temptation for me not to tell him was very strong for it still hurt that Judah had been unjustly accused.

I savoured the irony that the woman whose husband had been slandered should be the one to tell him that his saviour did still believe in him and that he was as brave as strong as he needed to be.

I told him simply what Yeshua had said to me that morning in the Temple just before Cephas and I were reunited: "Tell Cephas that he has enough courage," he said.

The great man seemed to draw strength, visibly, from my words. 'You may need to remember that in Rome,' I said and he nodded. More tears were now falling from his eyes and he turned his head away in embarrassment. This time, however, I was not going to let his masculine pride get in our way. I put my arms around him and stroked his wiry hair as though he were my kin. And he held me, in return, with love.

I never saw him again but I heard rumours of his death in Rome. He was worthy of Yeshua's faith for his bravery was immense. He supported and helped so many people and he stood firm and strong as the rock he was named for. I am proud to have known such a man.

Some months after Cephas and the others had left, I started noticing that Apollonius's strength was beginning to fail. He was tiring more easily and sometimes he lost the thread of what he was saying. His abilities of concentration were failing, too, not so much that anyone else would notice and I said nothing to anyone but I could tell from Sarah's worried look sometimes that she was of the same opinion as I.

We dosed him with herbs and strengtheners and he thanked us with his customary courtesy and took all our brews. He smiled when Sarah spent less time at the Acropolis and as we made decisions which meant that neither of us would have to walk too far or stay out too late at night and he fell in with our plans without protest. One evening, when Sarah was with Prokne, my husband looked over at me and patted the seat beside him. That had always been his signal that he wanted what he would call 'a proper talk'. Often, in the old days, it had been advice on how to best act as a Roman wife or how to control my still-fiery temper. He had not done it for all the years we had been together in Rhodos and the gesture touched my heart. I sat beside him and he put both arms around me. At times like that I could forget our advancing years; we fitted so well together and so comfortably that we could have been any age; young lovers or old friends. Apollonius sighed. I leant my head on his shoulder and waited for him to speak. In front of us the fire crackled and spat, the wood being younger and damper than it should have been. Before it, on the hearth, lay an elderly dog, the daughter of the lop-eared hound that we had brought with us from the village on the south of the island. As I looked at her she thumped her tail gently in acknowledgement.

Still Apollonius did not speak but I knew what it was that he was trying to say. He knew. We spoke without words, understanding each other, saying how much we would miss each other and acknowledging that under the sadness there was still a deep joy that he would be going home.

'What will you do?' he asked as the flames began to sink in the hearth. 'I don't know,' I said. 'Stay here, I suppose. What else could I do?'

'You could go home,' he said.

'Home? Home is with you.'

'Home to Judaea.' As he spoke I lifted my head and looked into his eyes. I was surprised at the suggestion but so drugged with the sadness and the peace of the situation I could not react.

'Why?' I asked. 'What is there for me there?'

'Probably nothing,' said Apollonius with his dear smile. 'The question is more what can you take there! The impulse for your brother's teaching is heading throughout the Roman Empire. Someone has to hold the pivot point in the land of its birth.

'Someone will have to be the last to remember Yeshua. Why not you? You can teach, discreetly, and then there will be another root for the Word to grasp onto.'

I nodded and smiled up at him and we kissed, our embrace as familiar and comfortable as two halves of the same soul and deepening into the familiar wish to hold each other as lovers.

That night, after he slept, I got up and walked up to the Acropolis. Slowly, for I was not young any more, I climbed the steps up and up to the great Temple at the top. They knew me there and the guards uncrossed their arms to let me through.

It was a cold night and windy but there was warmth here; and I still felt the heat of Apollonius's body next to mine, my mind numbed with love and tenderness. I did not know quite why I had come to the goddess. I sat, just at her feet, and gentle tears slid down my cheeks. I had to face it; Apollonius had grown old. He might live another year; he might not. But sooner or later he would be leaving and he was content to go. One thing welled up inside me that would not be silenced. For a while I prayed, my pleas fervent but controlled.

'Theia?' Sarah's voice sounded soft and smooth in the silence. She knelt in front of me in one flowing movement and, despite my grief, I could see her beauty. Not physical; Sarah would never be a woman admired by men for her face or figure but she was a shining girl; a young woman of clarity and simplicity.

I held on to her arm; the old woman in supplication to the young.

'Luke must come home,' I said.

Sarah nodded. She held out both hands to raise me to my feet and led me to a seat in the alcove. Then she began an age-old ritual of worship for the goddess; the preliminaries of the making of a petition.

While she laid out the barley and the leaves, she spoke the Kaddish, the Jewish prayer of worship and joy, spoken in memory of the dead.

I knew she spoke it for Yeshua, for herself, for me, for Apollonius and for every soul alive or dead. Time was nothing when you lifted your soul to the level of Beriah, the heavenly world. We were all dead and all on the point of birth.

Then she took my hand again and led me to the goddess.

'Athena, Samael, Mars, Justice, grant our petition,' she said. 'We acknowledge that this command may bend the Universe and we submit to the balancing in return. If we transgress thy Law, we pay the price. But if this call is just and merciful in thy knowing then present it to the Holy One for judgement.'

She bowed and I did too, feeling the build-up of strength and light around us. Where I would wait for the angelics to contact me, Sarah had the authority to call them.

'Come,' she said with authority and led me to the colonnade that overlooked the ocean. Above us, the stars sparkled, the Moon having set.

'Speak,' said Sarah. For a moment I looked into her eyes. They were bright and sure and, yes, possessed. But not possessed by evil; far more frightening than that; they were crystal clear with light.

I turned to look out at the stars and summoned all my prayers and strength into my heart. The power built and built inside me and I whispered the Shemah. Beside me, Sarah echoed the words.

'Luke, come home to us! Come to Lindos! Come now!' I cried.

My words were lost in seconds but I knew that they were carried where they needed to go. If it were possible, if God truly willed it, he would come.

*

Nothing happened to give me the smallest indication that the prayer or command had been answered and Sarah and I did not speak of it. We both knew that the answer might well have been 'no.'

If Luke and his father were destined not to meet again I must accept it but, all the same, I fretted a little. It was hard. Very hard. I found it difficult to think kindly of Paul or of Barnabas for the estrangement between my son and me and it was not easy not to blame Luke either. The years we had spent together should have taught him not to judge others for having different perspectives from your own. But he could not even know if I were alive or dead, let alone where I might be. And did he even know his father lived?

That fact had already struck Apollonius. Within a few days of my visit to the Temple, he sat down and began composing letters. He wrote to Roman officials in Ephesus, Jerusalem, Alexandria, Antioch, Cyprus, Malta and Antioch as well as dozens of places I had never heard of. To each one he sent a little gift and a request that they keep their eyes open for a man named Lukas Apollonius of Alexandria, a Roman citizen and a physician who might be travelling with Paul of Tarsus and living and teaching with a new sect calling themselves Christians.

He implored them to inform this young man that his father Apollonius Lucius Sextus was not dead as he had feared but living in Lindos on the Island of Rhodos and would like to make contact with him. Then I did rest from my fretting; between us we had done all that we could do.

Once we had both acknowledged that the end was coming, my husband relaxed and, ironically, seemed for some months to be stronger. He was still very much himself, interested in study and debate and, although he finally gave up riding, we would still walk along the harbour's edge nearly every day.

News arrived one bitterly cold winter evening. No ship was expected that night and it was a battered hulk which limped into the harbour, guided by the lights set along its edge, rowed and crewed by men so tired they could not judge the wharf accurately enough. The sound of the prow crunching into the harbour side brought many of us out of our homes to see what was happening. The hull of the ship was only slightly damaged but the crew and the cargo needed to be taken off as quickly as possible to guard against the ship's sinking or water damage to the cargo. People living by the harbour edge usually came out to greet any ship that arrived—it was from merchants or the occasional Roman galley that we learnt our news of the rest of the world; of the birth or death of princes or of new orders from Rome.

The excitement of an unexpected ship crashing into the harbour wall added to everyone's interest. She was a smallish boat with only two masts, not the kind that usually braved these waters in winter, and she had been *en route* from Cyprus to Malta. The passengers were trades people and there were no women aboard.

Apollonius and I went down to the harbour to see if we could help. Apollonius took charge of the mail, as he always did when a ship came in. Even mail had to go through Customs—and it was a good thing that it did for that usually ensured that it found its way to the correct destination.

A captain was paid to convey letters all the way to their destination but there were times when an epistle would be sent via two or three ships or messengers. The likelihood of such mail getting through was always poor—why should people carry messages when there was no definite method of payment? Even if money had been sent with the letter in order to pay its transport further, it might well be stolen. However, a surprisingly large number of people did still attempt to keep in touch with others far away and, once a regular route had been established and a sea captain or the leader of a land caravan knew that the letters would be collected and paid for at the other end, fairly good links could be made.

I was standing, watching and talking with my neighbour Rosanna when I saw Apollonius coming back up the wharf towards me. His face was alight and he was walking more briskly than he had for months. 'It's Luke!' he called. 'A letter from

Luke!' And indeed it was. A long letter written from Ephesus and directed to Apollonius in Lindos. So Apollonius's own letters had borne fruit! Delighted, I sent a message to Rizpah to join us if she could and we went back to our home, resolved not to open the letter until we were warm inside with good light and settled enough to be able to concentrate. Apollonius gave it to me to read out but I passed it to Rizpah, who had arrived faster than a respectable matron should be able to run. My eyesight was still keen but I doubted that I would be able to read without weeping. Rizpah's practicality would serve us well but even she had tears in her eyes as she broke the seal and began to read out loud.

Luke had written the letter in three different segments. The first was an outpouring of delight to know that Apollonius lived. Rizpah stumbled a little as she read that first section and Apollonius sat with his head bowed in gratitude that his son was safe, well and eager to see him again. I wept like a child.

Luke did not forget me either and, had I not already been in tears, his gentle and affectionate salute to me would have ended all self-possession. 'I am glad to hear that God's grace has also reunited you with my mother,' he wrote. 'Since she and I parted I have thought of her often and, as she will have told you, not always with the greatest of clarity. Now, however, I hope I am older and wiser and I wish to impart to her my regret for any sorrow I have caused by my pride and assumption.

'Please kiss her for me and tell her that I love and esteem her, not least for the wonderful knowledge of healing which she taught me in my youth.

'My thoughts and prayers have been with you both, and for my friend and sister Rizpah, especially since I have learnt for myself what it is to have children of my own.'

Rizpah stopped reading as we all exclaimed with delight. Luke had married and had children! Well, so it should have been but with Paul and Barnabas's celibacy it might well not have happened.

'Read on!' said Apollonius eagerly and Rizpah spread out the papyrus again.

'My wife is Jemima, a Roman of Antioch, and we have two

sons, Apollonius, seven, Paulus, two, and a daughter Sapphira, who is six. They live with their mother and her family who are of a medical background and learned in both languages and history.

'They are members of the Christian community in Antioch and are content that I should travel as I do. Were it not for the importance of the teaching I would wish that I were home more often for Jemima is a good and virtuous woman and I love her well.'

There Luke changed the subject to the travels and work of the Christians and Apollonius asked Rizpah to scan the writing for more details of the family before she read the rest aloud.

'I don't think there is anything more,' she said. 'Wait, I will see.' We held our breath looking at each other and smiling with delight. It had never crossed my mind that Luke might have children!

Apollonius, to whom the blood line was more important than to me, was overwhelmed. 'Oh, to see them!' he said. 'Could we visit them?'

'Of course,' I said, swallowing down my fear of the sea. 'We must go.'

'Wait,' said Rizpah. 'Luke is coming here.'

'Here? When?'

'In the spring. At the very end he has added a note saying he has booked a voyage after the spring winds have dropped. He will come with a group of Christians to visit the community in Cyprus and will stop over here for several weeks. He says too that he wishes that he could bring his wife, but he doubts it. However he will do his best!'

The three of us could have danced with delight. The years fell away as we thought of seeing Luke again and exchanging all our news. Then, once I had prepared us all a drink of spiced wine, we sat again around the fire and Rizpah read us the letter in full. As she read, my exuberance died down a little. It was as though I was relating to this news on two different levels. I was glad to hear of the continuing success of the mission (for it was apparent that more and more people were becoming interested in Yeshua's story) but, from what Luke wrote about Ephesus, it was obvious that neither he nor Paul gave credence to women teachers. The priestesses of Artemis were all-powerful in Ephesus and had obviously often abused that power. Their magic was used to create lives that people wanted, not the lives which could best serve God and bring the greatest long-term fulfilment. Those who were attracted to Paul's teaching expected to be just as powerful as the priestesses were within the new religion (and it seemed that many who had been rejected by those who selected priestesses for Artemis were keen to find another outlet for their ambition). Their arrogance, promiscuity and refusal to tolerate different ways of behaving or new disciplines had nearly brought the whole Christian group into chaos.

Luke wrote that Paul had even pronounced that he would never allow a woman to teach again and, on hearing that, my heart was heavy indeed.

Apollonius squeezed me gently for he could sense, and identify with, my feelings and Rizpah broke off to sigh and shake her head. 'So we are beaten by our own kind at last,' she said. 'It is often so. Women are their own worst enemies so often. I see it with other mothers; they take whatever power is the easiest without thinking whether it's good or bad or appropriate to them. You can't blame them; women have so little power but, of course, they teach their children the same.

'Oh well.' She sighed again and continued reading. There was very little else of great interest. We did not know the names and places Luke mentioned, although we did notice that there was no mention of Barnabas until the very end and then just a note that he and Paul had parted company 'to work in different areas.'

'They've quarrelled,' I said.

'Not necessarily,' Rizpah had never been the quarrelling type and always thought the best of people.

'Barnabas knew his place was to be beside Paul, to provide the balance,' I said. 'He would not plan to break that partnership.'

'Perhaps Luke provides that balance,' said Apollonius but, remembering my gentle but sometimes fiery son, I could not see him acting as a foil to Paul. Still, we would find out more, come the spring.

That night I prayed that Apollonius might be spared until Luke arrived. Winter was never his best time; a cough, which developed during those long years in prison, would return each year in the cold, damp weather and this one lowered him so much that he had been spending whole days in bed. Once or twice he coughed up blood. I had access to enough herbs and salves to be able to ease the symptoms and I did all I could to allow the healing power to flow through me but it could only alleviate. What ailed Apollonius was the ravages of time and that will, ultimately, defy all medicine. But the letter from Luke had strengthened him. Although the winter was long and difficult, Apollonius's willpower, if nothing else, would have brought him through. Sarah also began to spend nights at home rather than at the Temple, rising before dawn to be able to complete her duties. At last, when the first rush of green and the calling of birds returned to Rhodos, we received another letter and, six weeks later, Luke himself arrived.

His ship docked in the early hours of the morning and our first knowledge of his coming was a knock on the door and Sarah's voice greeting a stranger doubtfully. We all rushed into the reception area and for a while there was nothing but glad greetings and half-hearted explanations, kisses and embraces.

To my relief, Luke was as willing to hug me as I was to hold him and there was no one without tears in their eyes by the time we had sent for Rizpah and her husband and all sat down to eat together. What a change there was from the slight young man who had left so many years before! This was a strong, thoughtful man who already had some grey in his dark hair but whose face was marked with laughter lines. My son, full grown, married and content. Jemima had not come with him but he had brought the next best thing, little portraits of her and the children done by some discerning hand in the Roman community. We looked at them long and hard and saw in them what we wanted to see. To me Jemima looked pretty and gentle (perhaps a little weak?) and the boys were images of Luke. Sapphira had the looks of my sister Salome; dark eyes and a graceful neck. I tried to feel some connection, and there was pride at least, but these strangers were only linked to me by blood. Sarah, Tobias and Alexander were far more real to me. They were all fascinated by their Uncle Luke and Sarah, especially, developed a great fondness for him. He found her magical, he told me—and when he heard her story he called it a miracle. 'Your own daughter re-born,' he said. 'So she is my sister.'

'But not through blood,' I said.

'Blood is not important,' he said and I sighed with relief that we were in agreement about that.

For Apollonius those were very special days. He kept the pictures of his grandchildren on his desk and never tired of hearing about them. He and Luke spent hours together talking and debating and getting to know each other all over again. If I had not been so delighted to see my son again I might have been jealous but Luke spent plenty of time with me too and we were good friends. However, friends have to be allowed to quarrel and we had many a heated discussion over the role of women in the teaching, about Judah and the stories told of him and about the different ministries of Paul and Cephas. One thing Luke did tell me, and that sheepishly, was that the stories about Judah had already escalated into his being a bad man from the very beginning. There was even talk of his being a thief.

'We do not start these tales, Mother,' he said. 'Believe me, I do what I can but it is known that Judah was in charge of the money for all the disciples and so many people hate and resent debt collectors, money changers and those who administer accounts that they throw their feelings onto anyone who has money, no matter how honest they might be.'

I sighed. So many years had passed now that I knew it was useless to fight the legend. There must be some reason for it, if only to make some people wonder why Yeshua would have chosen such a man to be one of the twelve. Surely anyone with any intelligence would think that strange? Perhaps that was the whole reason; to make people think with discernment and look behind the stories which were being told. And written. Luke's idea of bringing together four accounts of Yeshua's time was beginning to bear fruit.

'Many people are interested in contributing,' he said. 'People are writing letters with the stories in them and they differ so much that we really have to decide which are the right ones to tell. There's a group of us thinking of getting together in the next few years to work out a system. We need people who understand the mystical tradition underneath it all and so far there aren't many of those. People are very interested in Christianity but few are interested in the Judaism behind it. I think we need to preserve that too. So many of the gentiles who follow Paul are without backbone; they are all spirit and no reason. There are so many important disciplines in the teaching of the Tree of Life and we can hide them in the writings so that those who know will recognise them and others will still understand from the outer teaching.'

'Let those who have ears, hear,' I murmured.

'What's that?'

'That's what Yeshua used to say when he taught,' I said. 'He would speak in stories but the Pharisees or Essenes who heard him would understand from that phrase that he was talking of the universal wisdom and was not just another prophet.'

'Or Messiah,' said Luke with a grin. 'You'd be amazed how many of those there are nowadays! We've come across at least six. And so many people who prophesy and frighten people. Without the inner teaching it's very hard to tell who is performing the Lord's work and who is not. I am so grateful to you for teaching it to me, Mother. I can't tell you how much it has helped.'

'Then teach it to Jemima,' I said. 'And teach it to Sapphira.' But Luke's face clouded over. 'I couldn't,' he said. 'My wife does not need to know the inner teaching; she is content to let me speak and my daughter, well, it would make her different from the other girls and we would hate that.'

'But *I* taught you!' I said, exasperated. 'You have just thanked me for it! How will Sapphira's children learn if she doesn't know?'

'Her husband can teach the boys,' Luke said stubbornly. 'Mother, you are a rarity. You knew Jesus face to face. He taught you the Tree of Life. That's different. Other women don't need it.'

'He didn't teach me,' I said with dignity. 'God gave me the Tree of Life as a signal that women should receive it too if they want to.'

'And how many do?' asked Luke. 'Not many, I'll stake my life on it. Most women are content as they are. No, Mother, on this we will not agree.'

'But women should be given the chance!' I protested; but Luke was adamant. Part of me was shamed by the fact that in one respect he was right. Most women did not want to know.

Of course he wanted to see his parents again, but another reason why Luke had come to Lindos was to encourage the Christians in Rhodos and he was astonished when I had to confess to him that I had not made friends with them.

'But they are right here, in the city of Lindos!' he said. 'You *must* have come across them!'

I hung my head and said that we had not got on well and Luke laughed exasperatedly. 'You and your prejudices!' he said. But, this time, my prejudices proved to have some validity.

It turned out that three of the Lindos Christians were in jail— they had been discovered to be escaped slaves—and as these three had been the prime movers in the new religion the group had fallen into disarray.

Painstakingly, and with Apollonius's help, Luke sought out the group—and negotiated an amnesty for the imprisoned men. No one in the jail had reported anything of their faith or Apollonius would have heard of it before.

There were fifteen Christians who still kept the faith and Luke soon had them whipped into shape (or so he said). I went to see them with him once but, on his advice, again did not tell them of my link to Yeshua. Their mythology was clear on the point of Jesus' being betrayed by Judas and, as far as they were concerned, there were no brothers or sisters—like Helios, Jesus was born of a virgin.

'But she could have had children later,' I protested as I trotted beside my son's lengthy stride as we walked home. 'And anyway, I'm his cousin, not his sister.'

'Don't tread in dry camel pats!' said my son with a smile. 'The balance is very fragile here and it would just be too complicated.'

I had to agree.

As Luke's visit drew to a close two things began to worry me. Firstly, he and his friends had not made headway in the Jewish quarter. He was following in Cephas's footsteps there and anything he said to the Jews just confused them. If he had succeeded then, maybe, the Jews and the Gentile Christians could have worked together. Luke tried to bring them together five times but there was dissent and hostility on both sides. My son was not a good orator which did not help—and neither were the men who had come with him. They were all young, whereas Cephas had had the authority of age backing him up. For a while, there was an uneasy truce between the two sides but I wondered what would happen once Luke had left.

Secondly, I worried about Apollonius. He had so looked forward to Luke's coming; kept himself alive even for this return of the beloved son. When Luke left he would be deeply saddened and I did not want to see him fade away in grief.

God is merciful for that did not happen. Ten days before Luke was due to depart, and while we still had plans for many things we were to do together, Apollonius and I went to bed as normal, chatting about everyday things and scolding each other amiably about our long-held habits and customs. Before we slept we would always lie in each other's arms for a while but age and familiarity had long driven us to turn away and sleep apart, although still on the same mattress. That night Apollonius held me, with my head resting on his shoulder, and we talked happily of an outing we were to take with Luke and the children the following day.

For once, we fell asleep in each other's arms and it was in the deepest watches of the night that I awoke. I had been dreaming and dreaming in colour—radiant colour. What it was I dreamt I could not immediately recall; all I knew was that I had woken cramped and uncomfortable with my head still resting on Apollonius's shoulder. Gently I lifted my sleepy body away but my fingers touched something sticky which made me start and catch my breath. I whispered his name urgently but there was no response and the skin my hand touched was far too cold.

Shakily I reached out for the tinder box and lit a lamp. In its flickering shadows Apollonius lay, peacefully, with his eyes closed. The only jarring note was a trail of blood from his slightly parted lips. He would not have suffered but slipped away. No one could have hoped for a better death. No wife could have been more bereft.

'My love?' I whispered, in case the soul was still present, but there was an emptiness and a silence around the room. He had gone.

Then I remembered the dream. It was of angels; and with them had been a slender young man with dark hair and bright eyes. He had smiled at me and bowed and then merged into the joyful throng. I had never seen Apollonius as a young man but I knew it was him and I was glad.

I did not wake anyone; there was no point. Lovingly I wiped my beloved husband's lips and kissed them. Then I got up and, taking a blanket with me, I walked to the reception room where the fire was banked up overnight. The dog, lying in front of the still-warm hearth, awoke and thumped her tail at my entrance. I stroked her, feeling the warm living flesh, and tears began to course down my face. It was done. My life with Apollonius was finally over. Now I must face the grief and mourn the wholly appropriate loss of the man I had loved most in the world. Except one.

Thirteen

Rain had been threatening all day and the last leg of the journey had been dull, dispiriting and cold. It seemed as though the weight of the heavy grey clouds affected everything, slowing the boat's progress and filtering their way into body and mind and spirit.

We spent much of that last afternoon on the deck, despite the chilling wind and the obvious irritation of the sailors, for we had heard that those returning to the Holy Land could sense a difference in the air and the light as they approached and we wanted to feel that for ourselves.

Sometimes it is not easy to know when you do feel things or when it is imagination or illusion fuelled by hope or despair. One thing I do know is that if there is to be a sign or an offer of help, it will usually come when it is least expected or just as you have given up all hope and resigned yourself to receiving nothing.

We had been sitting at the prow, wrapped in our cloaks, with eyes straining as haphazard drops of rain began to spit through the following wind. I, always the impatient one, gave up first, turning away in irritation and discomfort. As I scrambled to my feet, a single shaft of gold and crimson light flashed in my face, blinding me for a moment. Then the clouds parted on the glory of the setting Sun and cascades of light flooded through the grey. That melody of song and strength, a rainbow, hovered in the air and water above and within me and I felt my heart jump in response. I turned and saw the land which had been hidden just moments before—and not just physical land but the distant silhouette of the heavenly Jerusalem, standing out clearly against the glowing hills.

'Can you see the way?' Sarah asked, still sitting calmly and waiting; accepting the expected message as a matter of course while I stood amazed and emotional. It was there for a split second; a pathway of red, purple, blue and white across the hills towards the Holy City and then it was gone, leaving just its resonance in our eyes. Ahead, instead, were the blackened shapes of buildings of the port of Jaffa with people hurrying and scurrying along the shoreline, doing what business they could before the storm clouds burst open above them.

The Sun was setting by the time our sturdy cargo ship sighed to a halt at the harbour wall and the sailors began their time-honoured routine of manoeuvring ropes and gangplanks; making her fast and beginning to unload goods from the hold. Our arrival turned no heads; nothing special was expected from this ship and no one cared but the merchants who would receive their wares and examine each piece with a critical eye.

Sarah and I stood, waiting and watching on the deck, our small pile of possessions rolled in waterproofed cloth at our feet. From a distance we could have been any two Jewish women arriving back; coming home. Except of course that ordinary Jewish women did not travel alone and ordinary Jewish women would not have left their country in the first place.

Anyone looking closer at the two of us would have seen distinct differences. There was no trace of Jewish blood in Sarah's face and the quality of the material of our clothing and its cut were both subtly foreign. We had eschewed all but the most basic jewellery but the tattooed kohl around our eyes and the smoothness of our hands marked us out as pampered foreigners.

No one handed us down as we climbed across the wooden planks to the shoreline. Paying passengers on a cargo boat carried their own food and kept to themselves. Women travelling alone took extra care.

A gang of young boys surrounded us as soon as we stepped

onto the wood of the harbour boards, clamouring to carry our bags for a shekel. Although we had little, what we did carry was too precious to give into uncaring hands and it was possible, if not inevitable, that the wily little porters would think a piece of baggage would be worth more on the open market than any tip a female might give. I refused their services in rusty Aramaic and two of them barged into us deliberately in disgust. Had we been weaker and more tired by our journey we might have been in trouble but we were both tall women with strong voices and eyes. A flash of fire and a couple of pithy words were enough to set the boys about their business with no further ado.

Sarah looked around her slowly, taking deep breaths of the air. She was always poised, always confident and, even in a new land, relaxed and strong.

'It's good air,' she said and I knew she was not talking about the tang of sea and fish and the wisps of wood smoke from the smoking sheds to the left. 'Clear. No other gods before me. Yes, I can feel how a faith like that could thrive here. That is, if everyone is agreed on the same god.'

She smiled, a tight, thin-lipped smile that, for a moment, looked harsh but it was Sarah's way to smile with her mouth first. If the pleasure reached her eyes then the joy was real; if not, she was about to become formidable. And by the gods, Sarah could be formidable!

We knew enough to search for lodgings away from the harbour where prices would be high and the inns and lodging places dubious. Our plans were simple; to find a home and to set up a pocket of the teaching as we knew it so the people who wanted it would be able to find us. If we could, we would try and ensure that it would continue after our death for the generations to come.

Rain began to fall in earnest just as I stepped off the wooden harbour boards and onto the soil of Judaea for the first time in more than thirty years. It was powerful weather, full of life-giving abundance for the parched country around us.

We found a boarding house away from both the harbour and the market area and, if the landlord found it strange that two women were travelling alone, he was still glad to rent out his best chamber for our private use in return for currency in gold. He brought us a hearty supper of fish, lentils and bread, apologised for the hardness of the mattress and even offered us wine. We paid a high price for our dinner for it came with a well-worn series of complaints about the Roman forces, the continuing rebellion and how life was hard for the ordinary man. It seemed as though the unrest had gone on for ever; prices rose continually; ordinary people suffered. He had said it many times before but a new audience fuelled his rancour. We listened; it is always good to know the views of the everyday people and we could sift from his complaint some of the essence of unease and discomfort that existed in people's lives. The food and the accommodation both seemed hopelessly primitive after the comforts we were used to but we had begun to become acclimatised on board ship and there had been many times for me when such a meal would have been thought a feast.

Even without the rainbow, there truly was something in the air of this land that brought strength, no matter how its inhabitants might quarrel or fight. To me, too, it felt powerful and clear; closer to God—just as it should be if it truly were the Promised Land. I wanted to sing a psalm or an anthem of recognition and, before we went to bed, I moved over to the window of our room and let the song rise and fall silently inside my head because there I could sing as loudly as I liked without disturbing or perplexing others in the lodging house and the tune could take what course it wished in worship.

The song warmed my heart and I felt stronger.

'How are you feeling?' I asked Sarah, who was sorting through our luggage. She, braver than I, had left behind her whole life; the chance either to marry and have children or to become the priestess of Athena for all of Rhodos.

As usual, her answer surprised me.

'I feel soft,' she said with a smile. 'Plump and pampered and out of condition. This is a lean country where nothing is wasted and every step must be assessed and considered. We have plenty of honing to do.' As she spoke, she drew a sturdy olive-wood casket out of my little roll of possessions and placed it on the table by my side. We smiled at each other and raised the fire-darkened and damaged lid to see, yet again, Yeshua's writing in the carving: '*Talitha Cumi*'—maiden, awake.'

It took two days to find a caravan travelling to Jerusalem and three more to undertake the journey. As expected, we faced resistance when it was realised that we were women travelling alone but, after we had stood firm, refused to see why we should have to explain ourselves and showed quite clearly that we could pay, we were accepted with a shrug which said it was up to us if we did not know the ways of the world. Our group of travellers included two Galilean families and three merchants complete with crowds of servants, camels and mule carts which gave us a little more chance of hiding so we might avoid the flurries of questions from the women who travelled with us. On the flat stretches, when we were allowed to ride on the merchants' carts, I spent my time staring hungrily at the almost-forgotten landscape of home.

We told them that I was a Jewish widow from Rhodos who wished to visit Jerusalem and they automatically assumed that Sarah was my blood-daughter.

'We must not even hint at your having any relatives in Judaea or we can be sure that, even after all this time, they will know someone who knows who you are and the Lord alone knows what stories will have been told by now,' said Sarah and laughed. It was a great adventure to her and my admiration for her courage grew every day.

We were blessed in that not one of the group we travelled with was intimate with the Jewish community in Rhodos. Even so, during the long periods of walking, we had to listen to long accounts from our sisters of how second cousins had once had a link with the island and acknowledge their surprise that we did not know that particular line. Our differences in manners and style were excused as being our foreignness and our modest demeanour passed for orthodoxy. I, at least, was a Jew and also had been the widow of a Jew. So long ago now, that I could hardly remember his beloved face.

We listened again to the rumble of discontent over the Roman treatment of the Jews; of the continuing rebellion and the armed forces in the hills who (according to the speaker) were thieves, martyrs, righteous men, collaborators or mischief-makers. What was clear was that Rome had lost patience with this province and had no intention of giving any quarter whatsoever to rebels.

'Is this different from when you lived here before?' asked Sarah. 'You said there was always trouble.'

'Yes, it's different,' I said thoughtfully. 'I think this is the beginning of the end times. Not the end of the world—not as the Christians are predicting it—but certainly something serious.'

The journey was taken at the slow pace of the loaded-down donkeys and impatience stirred restlessly inside me as we stopped early each night and set off again hours after the dawn. The idle chatter of the women irritated me, too, concentrating as it did on petty quarrels and offences mixed in with attempts to wheedle more information from us. Sarah's wonderful diplomacy covered for my intolerance and she made me laugh by asking me how Magdalene would have behaved, laughing out loud when I remembered the outrageous stories which my old friend would tell, making both men and women fall back with horror and never seek our company again.

Sarah carried a copy of Magdalene's scroll, painstakingly transcribed from the copy Rizpah had made for the library in Alexandria. Our own scrolls had been lost at sea but that was just the point of the libraries—to enable copies to be sent out to anyone who required them or, perhaps more accurately, who could afford them. Apollonius had been able to re-build our personal library steadily over our years in Rhodos and one of our trunks contained nothing but the written word.

The final night's lodgings on our journey lay only half a day from Jerusalem and, as we women lay together on the pallets of the long dormitory rooms of the road-side lodging house, Sarah and I were both aching for the morning to come. We said prayers together in a whisper and held each other's hands tightly; she excited at seeing this holy city for the very first time and me wondering what would be different and what would be the same about the most beautiful city in the world.

As I dropped off to sleep I marvelled again at this extraordinary woman who had chosen to share the final stage of my travels. I would have thought, if it were to be anyone, it would have been Rizpah but, with her marriage, that was not to be. And she did not want to travel again; life had been hard enough. With one adopted son and one natural-born one and a happy and comfortable life, she chose to stay and live out her life in peace. I did not begrudge her that; she of all people had earned her prize.

Luke had wanted to take us home with him to Antioch when he returned from Rome but Sarah and I refused point blank. Sarah, understandably, for she had a life on Rhodos of her own; me through what everyone else called my stubbornness. Rizpah thought (with some justification) that I did not want to go to sea again but it was more than that. Apollonius's words had found a place in my heart and, with his death, I knew it was time for me to go home.

'Mother, you cannot,' said my son who wanted nothing more than to make a home for me with his other kin. 'It's madness even to consider it. The whole area is virtually at war! You can't go alone.'

'I don't need to go alone,' I said. 'I have money; I can hire servants—or buy slaves.'

'You've never bought a slave in your life!' said Luke. 'I can't see you letting go of that old prejudice now. And it would be nonsense to set out on such a journey with new servants. None of the ones with you now will want to go.'

He was right about that. The few staff that we had were just as anxious for me to remain as Luke was for me to go with him. Paid work in a household was not easy to find; slaves were cheaper and easier to deal with and it was known that it was only to humour his eccentric wife that Apollonius had hired staff at all.

I tried to talk to Rizpah but she thought there were only two alternatives: stay or go with Luke.

'But I want to go home,' I said sadly.

Rizpah took my hands. 'Deborah, you are not young any

more,' she said. 'Your home is with your son. The travels are over for both of us. We have done what we can. We can do no more.'

You're wrong, I thought. I can do more. But I worried, too, that it might be stubbornness or just the effects of grief making me want to do what Apollonius had suggested.

'Lord, tell me what I should do,' I thought; but before the prayer was even formed Rizpah went on:

'You've never yet settled with blood family,' said Rizpah. 'Luke is your son; he is bone of your bone and flesh of your flesh. That's important, Deborah—more important than anything in the end.'

'No it's not,' I said, before I had time to temper my words. 'Blood means nothing in the face of Spirit.'

'Oh!' An exclamation of exasperation broke from Rizpah's mouth.

'Wake up!' she said. 'It's too late Deborah. You don't have so many years left yourself. Live them in peace where you can be the wise woman. Don't keep trying to blaze your own trail.'

I smiled at her and patted her hand. The conversation was over for me; and I knew that the way forward would be without Rizpah. I'd known that for a long time but it had never mattered until now. I would go to Judaea; somehow. In the heart of the grieving I felt something give; a release like a dove flying from within. This one I could safely leave to destiny.

'I'll leave it in God's hands,' I said with finality and stood up.

'That means you'll try to go,' said Rizpah. 'I know you.'

'Yes, you do know me,' I said. 'But not as well as I know myself. And I will go now to the Temple to pray.'

I think we said goodbye then and there. The routes had diverged one final time.

It never occurred to me that Sarah would be the one to make it possible—or that it would happen so swiftly.

She came and sat at my feet that very afternoon as I sat on a seat in the Temple of Athena trying to pray and failing. My heart was heavy and I felt confused and pulled in too many different directions.

'Mother, Prokne wants see you,' she said. I jerked upright. Sarah had always called me 'aunt.'

'What?'

'She wants to tell you something. And, Mother…'

'I'm not your mother Sarah,' I said quietly.

'Mother Deborah,' said Sarah, deliberately. 'I have made a decision. I'm not going to become priestess of Athena.'

'But my dear, it's what you've been working for for years.'

'No, it's not. You know it's not. Mother, I'm training to be in contact with God, not with gods and goddesses. These years have been wonderful but you know I've still studied with you and followed the festivals at the same time. I want to understand the Jewish faith more; I want to know about our forefathers and mothers; about our heroines and our villains. I'm sure the secrets of life are in all our stories. They have to be; the Greek gods are always at war with each other. With one God there need be no war; the war is only in our interpretations of the Holy One and the stories.

'Mother, I'll take you home if you want to go.'

I raised her hand to my cheek in gratitude. 'We'll see,' I said. 'It's in God's hands.'

We walked together to Prokne's room at the back of the Temple. I think I knew that it was bad news that was awaiting me but I was not prepared for the reality.

My friend embraced me warmly and sent her acolyte Julia for some hot tisane. She had letters on the table by her side and one hand rested on the scrolls as she began to speak. Sarah held my hand while she spoke. I just listened and felt a part of my heart break.

The news came from Rome; Prokne had many communicators and received an annual missive from her fellow priestess at the Temple of Athena in Rome. She told me as gently as she could but how can news of such deaths be anything but terrible.

Cephas had been crucified in Rome.

Paul had been executed after more than a year in jail.

'Paul's death is being kept a secret,' said Prokne. 'The Christians fear that it would end their cult if it were known. Fortunately, the officials did not regard him as important enough for his death to be announced to the public. But he is dead.'

I shook my head in horror. 'Who else knows?' I asked.

'No one,' said Prokne. 'My news comes fast and I had asked my colleagues to look out for these men'

'You knew they were in jail? You knew they were threatened?'

'I knew Paul had elected to be tried as a Roman citizen after being arrested yet again for Christian subversion. The last I heard he was being taken to Rome and the thought was that he would be jailed for a while and released again. He had been jailed before; it might not have meant anything.

'But there was a fire…'

'A fire?'

'A huge fire in Rome. The emperor blamed the Christians and, since then, they have been greatly persecuted.'

'Oh. I see. How did he die?' My words were trying to fill in spaces while my thoughts ran wild. I must tell Rizpah; I must tell Luke. I must tell Apollo… no, he was dead, remember, Deborah?

I began to cry, rocking back and forward in the seat. Both Prokne and Sarah knelt beside me, holding and patting me lovingly.

'I'm sorry,' I hiccupped. 'It's just…'

'It's not "just" anything,' said Prokne firmly. 'It's terrible news. Two men that you knew and you loved, both dead. And only because they chose to believe in a different god.'

'Not the belief, the teaching of the belief,' said Sarah quietly. 'The way of men to stand on rocks and preach! To create "I'm right and you are wrong" teachings and shout them louder than any other.'

'Sarah!' said Prokne sharply. 'Not now.'

'Yes, yes, it's all right,' I said, wiping my eyes. 'She is right after all.

'What will happen now? What will happen to Yeshua's teaching now?'

'There's John,' said Sarah. 'He is teaching, isn't he?'

'I don't know. I haven't heard any news of John for years. I suppose so but…' Somehow I could not see John taking the teaching out to the world in the way that Paul had done, for right or for wrong.

'Here's your drink,' said Prokne, taking the cup from her acolyte and nodding dismissal. She handed it to me and I cupped my hands around the warmth of the pottery. 'What is it?' I asked.

'No strange soporific drug,' said Prokne with a smile. 'Just something for shock and grief—with honey and lemon so it tastes good!'

'Thank you.' I drank deeply, gratefully taking the time to try and gather my thoughts.

'I will have this letter copied,' said Prokne. 'Julia!' The girl returned. 'Take this to the scribe on the Cheesemaker's street now and get it copied. Take this money and wait while it is done. Be swift.'

'Can I read it first?' I said.

'Of course.' Prokne handed it to me and I read hungrily for details.

"You wished for news of the Christians in Rome, particularly Simon Peter of Judaea and Paul of Tarsus. Of both I have news and not of the best. They are executed in Rome.

"Concerning the date of Simon's death I have little knowledge. I have but lately heard of it but the news is not new and may even be a year old; I cannot confirm. It is commonly believed that the general persecution raised against the Christians by the Emperor since the great fire led to Simon's arrest and trial. He was crucified with his head downward, that much is being spoken in the street. The word is that he chose that way so as not to be thought to seem worthy of his hero Jesus the Christos.

"Of Paul there are reports of a beheading in the last few weeks which is why I write with such speed. The news of both came to me together. Paul was tried as a Roman citizen so was executed as one. The Christians are not letting this news spread which is of interest to me. They do not appear to have faith that their god-worship will continue without this priest of Christ."

I handed the paper back and sighed. 'There is no doubt then?'

'There is no doubt.'

'So what do I do? What happens to this teaching now? Was Yeshua's life all for nothing?'

'If it is real, it will last,' said Prokne. 'But it will change and take on heresies without a strong leader. They may be what saves it, of course.

'And there is your son.'

'Yes, yes of course.' There was Luke. He and his friends would hold the teaching and take it forward. But only for the men.

'Mother,' said Sarah.

'Yes, my love?'

'There is us.' She looked at me with those clear grey eyes and I knew that we would be going home together.

I woke with a start in the depth of the night. That was not unusual for I was a light sleeper and any noise or movement was likely to jerk me back into the physical world. This time, however, it was a light that I had seen in my mind which gave the instruction to wake.

A word slid into my mind like fiery ice on the wings of an eagle as I saw the silver in my opened eyes as well.

'Gabriel.' It said.

'Agapetos!' I returned, in a whisper, 'Beloved!'

The message was brief and to the point: 'Remember. *Re*-member' and I knew I had to clarify everything I knew or had learnt in the last sixty years in order to face the final days ahead ... the night had turned and it was that time just before dawn when there is incredible stillness. All those years ago, in Alexandria, I had learnt how the Egyptians performed special ceremonies before the sunrise to ensure that the sun-god would appear and that life would go on.

This moment was one where you could doubt the coming of light. Those around me slept peacefully in the lodging house west of Jerusalem and, with a rush of memory still holding me in thrall, it would have been easy to believe that the night had gone on for twenty, thirty, forty years.

All that time; all that remembrance. As I lived it again, Gabriel's presence had held me and supported me. The cascade of images and sounds ceased with Apollonius's death, for the months afterwards were still clear in my mind.

I felt the celestial strength fill me for this final stage of the

Work. I did not have many years left to me but I did have a pupil—and such a pupil who would surpass me in every way—and I did have knowledge that would not be allowed to go to waste.

I got up and went to sit by the doorway of the dormitory. We were facing east and, as I began my morning prayers, I watched for the first glazing of light across the cloudy sky. It was followed by streaks of purple and crimson which turned the sky itself into a deep azure blue. Royal colours for a royal country.

As I watched, I seemed to see a parallel landscape in the sky itself with the heavenly Jerusalem deep within it, glowing like a golden diamond among its gardens and streams. This was the true Holy Land, the creation in the heavens where all knowledge and truth were stored and which could be visited in deep meditation whenever we wanted. This land would endure forever, whatever happened to the physical Jerusalem; whatever happened to the Jewish people or the country where they lived. As I watched, entranced, I felt the archangel's wings surrounding me again. It was like being held by a great bird of a thousand colours, fierce and yet so loving that even to think was a harshness within all that beauty. And yet there was a harshness here too. In my mind, as part of me concentrated on the illumination before me, I also sensed fear and anger in the world below. I half-saw, half-felt battles and slaughter with the Romans destroying all in their path and I shivered. Never had these visions been untrue. There was no point in reacting; all the angelics required, when such images were shown, was a commitment to whatever needed to be done.

I thought a question and in an instant I saw myself and Sarah at the settlement of Qumran. No, it was not Qumran, it was En Gedi. It was my land! The place I had owned and Barnabas had sold. Another question and the answer slid into my mind. 'Go to Jerusalem. The land is still yours.'

That made no sense, of course, but you do not question angels—it confuses them! They are only the messengers of *what*, not of how or why. Other spirits take care of that. I sighed deeply; there was so much work for us to do here. And then I must have slept, leaning against the door post, for the next thing I can remember was the glow of the morning Sun on my face and Sarah's soft voice greeting me and blessing the day.

We embraced and I told her my story.

'Yes,' she said. 'There will be trouble between Jews and Romans here. I can feel it too. Well, was there ever any other possible outcome of an occupation of an inassimilable people? You've told me time and again of Israel conquered and refusing to lie down.'

Dear Sarah! She made me chuckle. I thanked God for her company and her strength. We washed and ate and took our place in the caravan and began the last stage of our journey.

Fourteen

The old, familiar pall of smoke with its scent of burnt flesh was hovering in the wind as our caravan approached Jerusalem. My mind turned back to the very first time that I had seen this great and beautiful city, as a child of seven, when the stench of the Passover sacrifices had turned my stomach and blinded me to the beauty within its walls.

We had arrived on the Eve of Shivours and the reverent were already buying their way into cleanliness for the celebrations. Mixing with the other scents was the smell of poor drainage from too many people and animals and not enough hygiene. What a poor, parochial place Jerusalem was compared with Alexandria, compared with mighty, stinking Rome, but what beauty she had as well. I had tears running down my cheeks as we followed our companions past the houses and market streets outside the city walls and then to David's Tower and in through the familiar Jaffa gate.

'How many years is it since you were here?' said Sarah as we looked up at the Temple walls. 'Thirty,' I replied. 'Maybe thirty-five. I have been away for longer than I lived in Judaea!' I shook my head in wonder and then, parting company with our companions, we set out to find a lodging house where we could leave our belongings before venturing out to search for the city of my youth.

By nightfall I had discovered which streets had changed their wares, what differences there were in the standard of lodging and how the Temple was, on the outside, identical but strangely scruffy and cramped within the hallowed walls. More building had been going on but, even so, it seemed to me that there was a tired look to the great courtyard. The flowers, there and in the Court of the women, were fewer and scruffier than they had seemed to be before. Over the Temple itself there appeared to be an atmosphere of sullen hostility where before there had been excitement.

'It could be me,' I said, for I had been much younger and more vibrant myself when I had last been there and my descriptions of the Temple had reflected that. But it could also be the legacy of years of rebellion against Rome.

Before entering I had enjoyed the remembered familiarity of the women's bathing quarters and the Mikvah, now showing definite signs of wear and tear but friendly and bustling as always.

'With respect, older people do tend to remember things as having been better in their youth,' said Sarah with a dimple in her cheek.

'Humph,' I replied. But she was right.

It was all rather saddening even though I had never been a great lover of the Temple itself. There were ghosts there too. Not the happy times with Yeshua but of that last Pentecost where the Holy Spirit had come to the disciples and I had first learnt of Luke's existence around and within me. Now Paul, Cephas and Imma were dead as well as countless others barely remembered for nearly thirty years.

'I suppose there are some people here that you still know,' said Sarah doubtfully. 'It seems awfully lonely.'

She had put her finger on it. Jerusalem was lonely. It was also afraid. All around us the Roman presence felt threatening. Always, before, the riots and the troubles had blown up and blown over but now there was a aura of disquiet. I shivered as we passed the square where Magdalene died and Sarah put her hand on my arm.

'We must leave,' she said. 'It was good for you to come and see it again but our place is not here.'

But there was one more thing I had to do before I left Jerusalem and no possibility of doing it before the festival was over. We spent the night within the city walls but in the morning decamped to a small lodging well away from the city. Even as we were walking through the gate towards the valley of the cheese makers we heard the sounds of shouting and fighting behind us. Neither of us looked back but we increased our pace and did not breathe easily until we were safely on the edge of the city.

We rested and talked and counted our assets while we waited for the end of the festival. I knew that between us we had more than enough money to buy back the land at En Gedi—or at least something similar. Sarah was all for the idea and eager to get on the road. 'We will need a donkey too, she said. 'It's a long journey and you are not as fit as you were.'

I should say here that Apollonius had left us both well provided-for and my Jewish blood meant that I had dockets in my hand for money that I could collect from any money-handler here who would then retrieve the money from Rhodos, in his own time, through the amazing tribal connections that we Jews had. But all that would take time and the establishing of credentials so we had brought money with us, hopefully enough, for the moment.

As soon as the scribes arrived at the records house to open up after the festival I was there, waiting. I smiled to myself to see the men inside behaving exactly as they had when I had come so many years before in order to claim Judah's and my land. This time, too, I had to stand my ground and express my wish to buy some land several times before anyone would take me seriously. They had some new administration so I had to give my name and where I came from as well as making my mark on the document to certify what I had said was true. I said 'Deborah, daughter of Miriam and Joseph the Carpenter,' for that was the name by which I was known in this land, and gave my place of origin as Nazara. There was no point of talking of Alexandria or Rhodos; if I did there probably would be more time to wait while I was investigated.

I signed my name in Aramaic when asked to make my mark

and the scribe's eyebrows went up almost comically. He was less inclined to take me seriously when I asked him whether there was any land available in En Gedi and described the exact area I was looking for. 'I used to own that land,' I said. 'It was sold many years ago but I would like it back.'

Heaving a sigh for the trouble I was giving him, the scribe got up and went to the back room to look up the piece I mentioned to see what could be done. I watched him as he worked, slowly and probably carelessly, because I was a woman and had no right to accuse him of shoddy work. Then, as I watched, I saw the unmistakable signs of surprise in his posture. He got up and came back across the room looking angry and holding a piece of parchment in his hand.

'How dare you trifle with us!' he said. 'This land is already yours. Look. As you can obviously read you can see perfectly well that this has your name on it. This was bequeathed to you, then sold and then bought back on your behalf.'

I took the scrap of parchment from his hand. It said clearly that the land with its house and any stock remaining was returned to the possession of Deborah, wife of Judah, daughter of Miriam and Joseph, unconditionally. The writing was neat and could have been anyone's but, with a contraction of my heart, I knew it must have been Barnabas—or Joseph Barsabbas as he always had been to me. Why, I could not fathom; I was just grateful from the bottom of my heart.

I don't know what I said to the scribe; it could have been anything just to get out of that building with a copy of the precious deeds in my hand. I almost whooped with delight as I caught up with Sarah who was waiting outside the Temple precincts. 'Come on,' I said. 'We can buy a donkey. We can even buy two! And some goats and chickens and lots of grain—and a cart—and anything else we need!'

Four days later I had come full circle, standing on the plot of land where I had settled so many years before with Joseph Barsabbas, Rizpah and Magdalene and where Judah, my first husband, was buried. The land was overgrown and the little house dilapidated but it was just about habitable and the little stream still flowed clear and bright across the meadow. It took me some time to find the place for my memories had faded and the pathway to our home had long been clotted by plants.

'Why, it's a complete hideaway,' said Sarah. 'No one would ever know it was there. It looks as though no one has even visited it since you were last here.'

'Maybe they haven't,' I said. 'Perhaps the descendants of the very same goats are still here taking care of it!'

'They should be,' said Sarah. 'Isn't that the meaning of En Gedi—Spring of the Wild Goats?'

We never found them, if they were, but the two nannies in kid that we had brought from Jerusalem soon settled in, together with the chickens and the donkeys and the strange little floppy-eared dog we had seen cringing for a crust at a hostel on the way and adopted as a sentimental reminder of the happy years in Rhodos.

That night, while Sarah made the house habitable with a waterproof rug over one of the rooms and tended a stew of salt fish, onion and lentils, I made my way carefully to Judah's grave.

I couldn't find it. I could find the life-giving run-off from the Shulamit Spring that gave this part of the country so much fertility but the date palms and moringa trees seemed to be placed differently from how I remembered them.

Eventually I sat down by a clump of silver-leaved salvia. Magdalene and I had called it the Menorah Plant, because of its shape, and seeing that again sparked off a flood of tears from tiredness, memory and other mixed emotions. It was here that I had given birth to Luke; here that I had rebuilt a shattered life. I picked idly at the fern while I pondered.

Why was I seeking a grave? Why do we humans require markers and places of death to visit? The souls of the dead are not there. But I felt the inner longing for something familiar, even if only an unmarked mound in the grass.

'It's only something more to cry over,' said a voice in my head. A very familiar voice. 'Let it go my love.'

In my peripheral vision I could almost see him; Yeshua my brother, sitting peacefully, leaning against an old moringa.

'You're not alone,' he said. 'And you are right where you need to be.'

Oh how I wanted to turn and embrace him but he was only spirit.

'No I'm not,' he said, hearing my thoughts. 'This time you can hold me if you want to.'

I risked turning my head and choked when I saw him as alive as ever I saw him all those years ago.

'How do you do that?' I asked, with a child's curiosity. 'You are long dead.'

But then I realised that I didn't care. All I wanted was to be held in his loving arms again. With choking breath I hurled myself at him and wept unashamedly into the rough woven linen of his robe.

Yeshua put his arms around me and drew my head onto his shoulder. Gently he rocked me.

'I can't do it for long,' he said. 'And I can only do it at all because I understand the Laws of Creation,' he said. 'Form and physical being are the most fragile of the spectrum. You know that there is a place where the three upper worlds meet and a place where the three lower worlds meet?'

I nodded. Words were not going to come out in any understandable form at that moment. Instead I burrowed deeper into this physically-sound illusion and inhaled his inherently remembered, much-loved scent.

'Well I am standing at the centre of the three top worlds so I can reach down from Beriah to you—just,' He said. 'And you are at the centre of the lower three worlds and can reach up from there to where I am—just.'

'But I can smell you,' I said nestling into his shoulder.

'And I you,' said Yeshua.

Then we were both snorting with laughter just as we had done as children.

'Mother?' said Sarah and suddenly I was alone in the glade with only the flattened grass and the warmth that his body had left on the moringa's trunk.

'Sarah?' I said, dazed and irritated.

'Who was that? *Who was that?*'

'You saw him?'

'Of course I saw him. He was real. I saw him holding you. Tell me!'

'Is he still here?' I asked urgently. 'Can you sense him?'

Simultaneously we both sensed laughter and then silence. I put my head in my hands. Suddenly I felt deadly tired.

'It was my brother, Yeshua,' I said.

'Oh,' said Sarah, her eyes glowing. 'Oh, I see.'

'What do you see?'

'I see who he was,' she said. 'I didn't really know before. But if he is able to move between the worlds; no wonder they think him a god.'

'He's a doorway to God,' I said. 'Not God.'

'Yes, I know that,' said Sarah matter-of-factly. 'Supper is ready. I think we both should eat.

'Oh!' She stopped and knelt down by a grassy knoll covered with tiny white helleborine. 'Is this your first husband's grave? What lovely flowers. Did you plant them all those years ago?'

I swear the flowers had not been there before.

That night we talked until the Moon had set. We talked of Yeshua, the Tree of Life, the Exodus and the travelling tabernacle which became the image of the Four Worlds and we spoke, too, of the sacred legends of En Gedi; how David found refuge from Saul here and, later, spared Saul's life and how Solomon used its beauties to describe the beauty of one of his concubines.

But mostly we spoke of miracles and of what our work here was to be.

To start with, we and the animals all lived within the house itself for there was now no fencing to speak of and, until the animals knew and trusted us, they would be liable to roam. The donkeys and the goats we could hobble but we preferred not to. They, the dog and the chickens, however, soon learnt when they were well off and the problem was easily solved.

We spent a week just sorting things out and settling in, talking, thinking, meditating, praying and drawing in the dirt on the floor of the rooms—and discovering with joy the remains of old images drawn by Magdalene and Joseph. I looked for Yeshua and talked to him but there was no sign. But I held those moments in my heart as glowing treasure. I was not alone.

But once we were settled, the nightmares began. We both had them; images of men, women and children screaming and crying as they were slaughtered by solders. The first night we both awoke and held onto each other in terror.

'Where is it?' said Sarah.

'It was Qumran,' I said. 'We must go. We must go in the morning.'

Despite torrential rain, we went. It was half a day's ride down slippery paths and we got lost several times but we started at dawn and were at the edge of the community by midday. It had grown incredibly since I had last been there. There was even a kind of port leading out onto the Dead Sea and it was obviously a kind of market day for the people living in the settlements and tents around the centre of the town.

'What on earth do we do?' said Sarah. 'They'll think we are mad women.'

'Well they'll just have to think it,' I said. 'Some of them will listen.'

But on the first day they did not. We went to the centre of town and began to speak, calling out to the people that the Romans were coming; that their town was in danger and that they should, at least, send their women and children away.

There were a few of the traditionally-clothed inner order of the Essenes in the town. They obviously still preferred to live in the hills behind the town but those who were there were openly hostile and it was not long before there was an angry crowd surrounding us.

'And who do you think you are?' was the general gist. Strange women from nowhere, prophesying death and destruction! I, myself, would have found that hard to take. But we had to continue and do our best. Only when the first hand was raised, holding a stone, did Sarah catch my arm and hiss: 'Run, now! It's no use.'

We ran back towards the tethered donkeys and were barged

and elbowed by the crowd so that by the time we had reached the edge of the community we felt black and blue. There was nothing for it then but to retrace our steps as fast as possible and trail wearily home, cold, hungry and disheartened in the dusk.

'Well, we did our best,' said Sarah, sensibly, as we ate a cold supper after anointing our bruises with a rather inferior lavender salve bought in Jerusalem. 'There's nothing more we can do.'

But again, deep in the heart of the night, we awoke sweating with fear and with pounding hearts as the nightmare returned. For both of us it was identical and, even though we were able to talk ourselves calm and sleep again, it overwhelmed us a second time and by the dawn we were exhausted and panic-stricken. 'But we can't go back!' I said. 'But we must,' said Sarah.

And we did.

Sarah looked so calm as we made our way down to the settlement again. She had packed food and medicines in a shawl for she said we must stay in the area until we were heard. I felt the sweat of fear on the palms of my hands. Being stoned was a distinct possibility and this time I was not young and resilient. I did not want to die in vain but I had to face the fact that maybe that was what was being asked of me. If I died but they heeded the warning then that might serve the purpose of the Almighty. 'But if I live and they heed the warning, I can help them more,' I said to myself and to God, with gritted teeth.

This time the miracle happened; but not on the first day. The inhabitants of the town were, at least, curious as to why two women would return with the same prophecy when they had been so harshly treated only the day before. We spoke as calmly and logically as we could, repeating again and again that they could be safe if they would only leave the area. I saw some wavering; things had been bad with the Romans for some years now and what we said was entirely possible. We left before the crowd had a chance to turn nasty and retreated to a spot just outside the town where we could eat our olives and bread and discuss our strategy.

We did not have to do anything else. As we ate, some of the townspeople crept up on us and gathered around, asking frightened questions. We said perfectly honestly that all we had to go on was a vision and a series of nightmares but that we had come from Jerusalem lately and the atmosphere there was very unpleasant.

'But where would we go?' asked one woman who was holding the hand of a barely weaned child and who was obviously heavily pregnant. 'All around here it is desert. There is hardly anywhere to hide, let alone food for so many.'

'We have land; a place where you could shelter,' I said gently. 'It is green and fertile but it's half a day's walk away. It is hidden; no Roman would know where it was. You would be safe there.'

After a while the group dispersed and went back to spread our story throughout the settlement. Word of mouth would do what we could not. As she turned to go the pregnant woman said to me: 'How would we find you if we were to come?'

'We will wait,' I answered. 'For three days. If people come before then one of us will guide them to the hiding place and the other will wait here, then we will go. But if anyone wishes to come later all they need do is travel due north for half a day to the edge of the Salt Sea. There they should wait. We will come out from our land and seek them.'

We sat and walked and slept next to the community for three days and a small but steadily increasing number of people would come out to talk to us and even bring us food. They warned us to move a little further away for talk was running high against us within the community itself. It was beginning to be whispered that I was a former member of the Emmaus community and it seemed that my reputation had survived down the years. 'I expect I'm known as Lilith,' I said with irony and blushes and averted eyes showed me I was right.

'I don't think you have told me that story,' said Sarah with interest. 'We have time to spare so start at the beginning. I learn more and more of you, Deborah! I wish I had known you when you were young.'

I had noticed that since we came here she called me by my given name and not as her mother. It felt right. She was only sixteen but had a wisdom and a strength way beyond those years. And Prokne's training had stood her in good stead.

It assuaged my homesickness for Rhodos, for Prokne and for Rizpah as I told again of the time when Yeshua and I taught the Essene community outside Jerusalem and how the teaching of a woman had outraged the inner core of the group. One of them stoned me, knocking me unconscious, and the quarrels after that day led to the community remaining divided for many years.

'But that's when you met Magdalene,' said Sarah. 'I remember now. But I didn't know it was because you were teaching. How did you teach?'

I told her about the women's way of those days, of ministering at the Mikvah with herbs and knowledgeable advice. But how Yeshua also had encouraged me to answer the questions of the women outside of my work times; to sit and to wait for them to come to me. Not to preach but to answer; not to lecture but to listen.

'Like we are doing now,' she said with satisfaction. 'We wait.'

That night, as we slept curled up together in one rug, I dreamt of the stars and the night sky and of Judah walking among those stars with Cephas and Paul.

I was awoken by a male voice speaking my name. From the depths of sleep I thought I had slipped back more than forty years.

'Yes Joseph?' I said. 'I'm here.'

Then I sat up, blinking, while Sarah stirred beside me. A tall, spare, elderly man with white hair was standing over me. His brown skin gave sharp contrast to his white robe and silver beard and his eyes were quite alive in the weathered face.

I stared up at him speechless, still fourteen years old and over-awed by the leader of the Essene community at Emmaus.

'Yes, it is me,' he said. 'Your old friend. Back where he began.' And he smiled lovingly with light shining from his eyes.

For the second time I threw myself into the arms of a beloved. The years and the slight estrangement through Paul's influence dropped away.

'I thought you were in Cyprus!' I said. 'I thought you were dead! Everyone else is dead!'

'No, not dead. Desiccated, perhaps, but not dead.'

How I loved his dry sense of humour. We stood, holding hands like children, our eyes seeking every line, every moment on the other's face.

'And this is your daughter?'

I turned, clumsily, to Sarah. 'Yes—no! Sarah, this is Barnabas, my old friend from when Yeshua and I lived with the Essenes near Jerusalem. We used to call him Joseph Barsabbas. Remember?'

'I certainly do,' said Sarah bowing her head and then holding the old man's eyes curiously with her own. Some kind of force seemed to pass between them and both shone, there is no other word for it.

'I am Joseph again now,' said Barnabas.

'Oh.' I didn't know what to say but my forehead must have wrinkled in perplexity. To my mingled surprise and relief both Sarah and Joseph-Barnabas laughed.

'We are the same!' she said. 'We have had different names for different stages of life,' she said. 'I was born Sarah and then was called Keera but now I am Sarah again.

'Poor Deborah! She has never had another name so never been able to rebuild herself!'

'There's always Confused,' I said. 'I could easily be called that any day!'

So much catching up to do! So much to relate! And it was so wonderful to have my Joseph back. He glowed as he always did in the days when I thought he was the Anointed to follow Yeshua. That glow faded when we was with Paul.

'I had a job to do,' he said, before I could ask the question. 'I had to be the steel that tempered him; I had to be the guiding force that would make his work real. It was needed and I did it.'

'You knew he had died?'

'No.' Joseph's shaggy eyebrows dipped as he acknowledged his grief. 'I did not know. But it was only a matter of time before someone killed him. They killed Yeshua, after all.'

'He was nothing like Yeshua!' I said, my swift temper sparking.

'He was an ambassador,' said Joseph. 'Not the same but similar enough to be a threat. And how strange it is to be talking of him in the past. I hope he died well; with ease and in faith.'

'So many people now in the past,' I said. 'But isn't that what happens to us all eventually?'

'And we sit here with the future,' said Joseph, nodding towards Sarah who was kindling a fire to our right. 'She is shining, Deborah, shining. She is the lineage bearer now.'

I sat and looked at my adopted daughter and saw the light in her.

'Perhaps she is,' I said. 'But I cannot judge; I am too close. She still has much to learn.'

'No,' said Joseph. 'She may wish to learn theory but there is nothing she does not Know.'

I looked up at him in amazement and saw that he was totally sincere.

'Will you come with us away from here?' I asked. 'Did you hear about the dreams?'

'Yes,' he said, simply. 'I have followed you before and never regretted it. I will follow you now. And I will be able to bring others. Give me two days and I will bring whoever I can. I can feel in my water that your dreams are prophetic. It is a time of war.'

He sighed. 'Will we never learn?' he said.

'Who? Jewry or all of us?' I asked.

'All of us,' he said with a smile. 'How many years, Deborah? How many years?'

'Three or four thousand I should think,' I said, hugging my legs and resting my head on my knees. 'We are very young.'

'As are you,' said Joseph. 'You would sit like that at Emmaus. I remember it well.'

I watched him say goodbye to Sarah, and how they held each other's hands and talked earnestly before he took his leave, and a great contentment rolled over me.

'You are not alone, see, I told you!' said Yeshua in my ear. I closed my eyes and felt his arms around me. 'You can leave her safely with him,' said my brother. 'You will be coming home with me quite soon.'

My eyes snapped open with shock. 'But I'm much younger than Joseph!' I protested.

'Too much pampered living,' teased Yeshua. 'You are tired, my love, and you have done so very well. Joseph is honed like an arrow. He'll give Sarah a good ten years.'

'Will that be enough?'

'More than enough. Bless you Deborah. Your work is nearly done.

'Oh—and Deborah?'

'Yes?'

'She'll marry. It will be good. Let that worry go!'

I sighed and relaxed. That stupid, sensible, feminine fear that Sarah would be alone had sat, unbidden and unacknowledged, in my heart for years.

I think I slept then—or maybe I dreamed his presence; I do not know. But I did wake later, when the Sun was nearly half-way across the sky, to find Sarah playing with a baby gecko she had found on the broad leaves of a Sodom Apple and a beautifully-prepared lunch of toasted bread with oil and cheese, waiting on a palm leaf for me to wake.

Life could hardly get any better, I thought as I ate and then laughed out loud at the irony that the greatest joy of all was to be able to tell my adopted daughter that I had been told of my own death—and of her safety—and we could both be comforted and amazed in that knowledge.

We left on the third day with a group of twenty six including four families, six single men, including three from the inner group of celibates who came with Joseph, and two brave young women who left their parents and siblings. One of them, Tamar, was already partially outcast in the community for her wish to learn more and participate in her faith. She was an outspoken girl, and I wondered if she might be troublesome, but she was strong and willing to carry both children and possessions and, for now at least, we were glad to have her with us.

The people who came with us did not bring much. Apart from Joseph, who walked beside them with his long stride, wielding a knotted wooden staff more as a statement of strength than as an acknowledgment of age, they spoke repeatedly of returning home in a few weeks' time when the threat was over.

Sarah and I rather hoped they were right. Although we knew we were doing the right thing, we were torn between worrying whether our land could support so many and regretting our loss of privacy. Two of the young men, Achan and Micah, set to with a willingness to build a lean-to on the side of our hut and the women made a fire, gathered water and began to make a stew of vegetables, herbs and beans that they had brought with them. It was rather fun to exchange stories over the fire and eat the spiced food together while the children ran around, over-excited at this strange day. Micah had a pipe he had made and we sang songs and hymns until we almost fell asleep where we were from exhaustion. The next day, and for the eight following, one of us went down to the cedar trees to watch and wait for any others. Three came; the young pregnant woman, Leah, and her husband and son. The husband was not pleased with his wife for, as he said, she might give birth before they could go back and would be in danger without the help and advice of her mother and his. We reassured him that both Sarah and I were competent midwives but we all hoped that Leah would not go into labour. Already the little group was anticipating going home; the excitement and fun of finding fruit and vegetables and making meals on such a makeshift stove was beginning to pall and the women, in particular, were missing their own hearths and their own pots and pans. We were blessed in having Joseph with us for, without his senior presence, the men would have been starting to vie for position of leader of the group. It was annoying for us, though, that people asked Joseph for permission to dig or forage or walk; after all, this was our land not his.

'Ego!' said Sarah, ruefully, as we went off together to catch some of the delicious, tiny fresh-water shrimps from the Shulamit spring. We had to do this secretly for the others, being Jewish, would not eat shellfish and I had to admire Sarah for submitting to dietary laws she had never met before with such good grace.

'But we can be wicked because of our egos!' she said. 'And wicked is fun. Here's a beauty!' She snapped the shrimp in half, peeled off the outer casing and offered me the meat. I took it, having learnt by now not to defer when offered abundance. And Sarah caught another, even plumper, within a minute.

'It does depend on the kind of wickedness of course,' I said.

'Yes Mother,' said Sarah with a twinkle. 'And on whose definition the evil is based.'

Luckily there was too much to do, in order to feed such a throng, for people to be any more than bored as the days passed by. The men built fences for the animals which was a boon—and the little house was soon water-tight and snug again. Tamar had started several squabbles with the men because of her forthrightness but, although I had to speak to her quite sternly, I found I was growing to like her more and more. She asked intelligent questions and, when they were questions about the mystical tradition, she chewed over the answers and came back with more queries.

On the ninth day, eleven-year-old Mark went down to the cedars. He was back, heart pounding, out of breath and obviously shaken, in the fastest time possible.

'Come! Hurry!' he cried waving his arms about frantically. 'People are hurt. People are dying.'

It was one of those moments which seems to last a lifetime as we took in his words. So it had been true. There had been an attack.

'Why do I still doubt?' I muttered as I hastily assessed how many spare pots we had for fetching water and whether the fire could be split so that it could be heated more swiftly. The others stood paralysed for a moment; every one thinking immediately of loved ones, friends, relatives, who might have been hurt. Then with one mind they all, even Leah, began to run down through the cypress grove to the entrance of our tiny kingdom.

'Stop!' cried Sarah running after Leah and catching her arm. 'Someone has to stay here, to boil water and prepare what they can. Let the men go!'

She was talking sense and even Tamar saw it. Hastily we women gathered together all the pots and pans and sent Tamar and Rachel to the stream. Rebekah and Leah grabbed all the spare clothing so that it would be in reach for tearing and making into

270

makeshift bandages. Sarah and I milked the goats so that there would be sustenance for those who could eat and Susannah and her children searched for eggs and put them in the fire to roast.

It was not long before the first casualties arrived. Micah, Achan and Levi appeared, each carrying a wounded child. Behind them trailed a bunch of men and women, dazed, exhausted and too terrified even to speak, all being herded like cattle by both Phillip and Mark.

Tamar was a wonder. She left the seriously hurt to Sarah and me and settled all the others, giving them bread and milk and encouraging them to wash and rest.

'You can tell us later' she said again and again. 'For the moment you must just eat and tell me if you are hurt.'

Before we knew it, half of the meadow was filled with people. Later that night we counted forty seven new faces in all including children and nine of the celibate inner group. Somehow we managed to feed them all. When you think about it logically it was impossible; but the angels took care of us, just as they had served Yeshua and the multitudes who had come to listen to him. No one was so seriously hurt that their life was in danger, though I dreaded to think of those too sick to make it to our refuge. The men had already agreed to set out at first light to try and find any stragglers —and to confirm what had happened in Qumran.

What had happened was that the Romans had descended in their hundreds. Only the fact that the vibration of the horses' hooves could be felt in the ground had given enough warning for some to escape. Men, women and children dropped everything and ran in all directions. Most of them were overtaken and cut down as they ran.

'I don't understand. Why? Why?' they said, with tears falling down their faces. 'We lived quietly away from the city. We harmed no one.'

'But so many of you taught a doctrine of hatred and insurrection,' I thought, as I comforted all that I could. 'It was probably automatic; probably just bravado but it was heard and judged and the Romans took their revenge.'

I did not condone what the solders had done. How could I? It was horrific. When the men from our group returned, shaken and angry, the full measure of the disaster truly hit home. There was no one left. No one at all. The whole town had been burnt to the ground and there were too many bodies for the men to bury alone. Everyone had lost a loved one. Everyone had lost their home, their livelihood and their cattle. It was a terrible time for us all. Every able-bodied man went the next day to complete the digging of one great grave for the dead. Joseph conducted the service while the men kept guard around him in case the Romans returned. Thank the Lord we had fresh running water—a perfect Mikvah—for the cleansing of bodies and souls afterwards. There is nothing else I wish to say about those days except that they aged us all.

The work of the next few months was the rebuilding of shattered lives. All the settlements around us had been destroyed. Only the fact that our land was so well hidden and no one knew it was inhabited saved us. For months we would still find bodies as we searched the area for livestock or food. One way of knowing was to watch the circling vultures above. They increased in number greatly over the next months as the avian word spread around.

We got little news, for the trading which had gone on between villages had ceased completely. All we could assume was that the simmering resentment and rebellion that had been building for years had finally boiled over and retribution had been swift, harsh and thorough.

'But what of Jerusalem?' I thought—but the Essenes were taught to think Jerusalem corrupt so I kept the thought to myself.

Food was scarce; stores had been burnt and livestock killed or taken; we had to scavenge what we could. There were plenty of wild animals around—rock hyrax, ibex, sand partridge—and soon Micah, Phillip and Levi had made basic spears and bows and were bringing back game for the pot. We were very grateful, although it took the non-meat eaters more than two weeks to accept that this was a vital part of the nourishment that the Lord was offering. It was hard for them, raised as they had been to believe that the killing of an animal was wrong.

'Not as wrong as dying of hunger while the animals live on,' said Sarah, practically. 'You can be fussy next year when we have enough and our own crops to harvest but for now, just be grateful that we have male animals to eat and female ones to reproduce.'

Many of them held out for weeks but they grew steadily thinner. The celibates, all of whom apart from Joseph lived separately from the rest of us, had built their own hut as far away as possible and they suffered the worst. We had to be ruthless with them for if they ate more than their fair share of the vegetables and the eggs then the others would suffer as well. They also kept whatever roots and berries that they found for themselves, causing much anger for the rest of us were working as a community and sharing everything. Sarah and I were lucky, for we would eat the water shrimps so we could eschew some of our share but we all went hungry. We managed—just—but the celibates did not; two of their number died from malnutrition and the others were not even strong enough to dig their graves.

We all helped to bury the dead men but afterwards Joseph and Levi led a delegation to the surviving celibates, saying that they, too, were needed to work as hard as possible and their self-imposed denial was affecting us all. Seven men making themselves so weak that they were useless and a drain on the others was both unfair and unkind.

'The Law is overturned when it comes to the saving of life,' said Joseph. 'And not only are you destroying your own lives, you are hindering ours.'

It was in vain for the men's holiness was too great; they could not bring themselves to eat a modicum of flesh.

We had evolved our own way of killing, which was as humane as it could be, and we blessed and sanctified each animal before, during and after the deed itself. They truly were gifts from God, for without them so many more of us would surely have starved. Leah's son was born just two weeks after the massacre and brought both renewed fear for her and her husband over our hopes for survival but a glimmer of hope to the rest of us. New life was doubly precious now as it was a reaffirmation that all could be coped with; all could be healed with time. We managed to give Leah extra rations so that she would be able to feed her son. Luckily she was abundant in milk and the youngster thrived.

We lived very quietly for several months and then, once we had established routines of farming, hunting, gathering and cooking, the men who were fit enough set off for Jerusalem to find out what had happened to the rest of the country. To our surprise the group of celibates chose to go with them.

'Well, they will get better fed on the way!' said Joseph, speaking of our tradition of feeding passing travellers, particularly holy men.

'If the land is not razed,' said Tamar.

They were gone for six weeks and it was while they were away that our study and worship group began, for the women needed entertaining and to be kept busy so that they did not have time to worry. The remaining men were uncertain about this but Joseph, who had grown even leaner with harsher lines on his face, sanctioned it with the authority of a king.

He, Sarah and I began to teach and exchange knowledge with them and, within the hearts of nearly a dozen, it was obvious there was a hunger, a yearning for the feminine in worship. We arranged a service of dedication and remembrance for the dead and talked of the Shekhinah and the life to come. I showed them the diagram of the Tree of Life, explaining that this was the information given to Adam and Eve after their expulsion from the Garden of Eden and that it was a map for the road back to the heavens. If that time could not be called happy, with all its still sharply felt fears and griefs, it was calmer than it might have been and it bore fruit for the future.

The men came back with mixed news. Jerusalem was still standing but there was great unrest and nowhere was deemed to be completely safe. They had made a decision on their journey back and that was that they should set out south to new pastures, outside Judaea, where they and their families would be out of the battle between the Romans and the Jews. To stay would be madness, they said. To re-colonise in Qumran was possible but might be dangerous. The celibates, however, had decided to go back to their home, to build again, to atone for their evil which had brought destruction upon them and risk the consequences. They managed to persuade several of the others to change their minds.

Whatever their decision, Sarah and I did not argue; our little plot of land could not support so many long term and we were relieved that a decision had been made. Apart from the shortage of food, the squabbles were getting steadily worse and soon they were going to get out of hand.

To our joy and surprise, six of the women and nine of the men asked to stay with us. They were people who had gravitated towards the Essenes to try and learn more about their faith and they thought we had a good chance of building a little community which was open to ideas and thoughts. Tamar was one of them and also Leah with her husband and their two little children.

And so the last phase of my life began; the quiet years of teaching and writing. They were peaceful to me, as my body slowed and my mind grew more familiar with the higher worlds as earthly desires fell away. Sarah and Micah grew in friendship and companionship and Joseph married them at Hanukkah in the second year.

Joseph and I were Patriarch and Matriarch, living peaceably together almost like husband and wife but without that physical intimacy. There was no desire; for him that was his chosen path and I had been satisfied with my allotment of love. The world moves on and I was more grateful with every passing day for the blessing of a happy old age.

Yeshua and I talked sometimes; he would come to me in a whisper of the wind or as a scent or a touch. I learned to see beyond the persona of him that I loved to the divinity inside us all and peace reigned. I knew he talked with Sarah, too, but his voice was inside of her; and not just his voice; the voice of the all-seeing, all-loving Almighty was in this sacred daughter, this living embodiment of Shekhinah. Just some stranger's daughter, of unknown blood, met by chance on a swiftly-chosen ship on a voyage that might never have happened. Now I watched her with wonder as she easily mixed the work of the farmer, the love of the wife and the teacher of Truth.

Peace reigned in En Gedi, in the eye of the storm.

Outside of our little home turbulence raged unceasingly. The Jews were in full rebellion against the Romans and, on rare occasions when we went out into the world, we heard stories of atrocities and horrors which became almost commonplace. Somehow we knew we would be safe; that our tiny community was swathed in a cloak of protection. Inside we taught love and discernment, wisdom and understanding and, as my own health began, at last, to fail, I began to write my story.

I hope that our community will continue to live in peace and to learn; that the children will pass on our knowledge and that, somewhere, a tiny pocket of what we now call the Hidden Tradition will remain in this turbulent world. But if the community does not continue; if Sarah and Joseph should, at any time, choose to travel; whatever the outcome, whatever the choices, my story will still exist, hidden in the hills of Qumran until someone seeks it out and finds it. I have placed it in pots cast by myself inside some caves I came across quite by chance (though I know now there is no such thing as chance).

It is hard to say goodbye to my family in this world but I know it is time. For the past week Gabriel has been echoing in my dreams, calling me, showing me vistas of the life to come. There are many more tasks for me there but first there will be rest and reunion. I know that Judah is there and Apollonius in a world where there is no separation; no rivalry; no jealousy. I know that Yeshua is waiting to welcome me with Salome my sister, James my brother, Joseph and Miriam my father and mother. I know that Rizpah, too, has passed through to the other lands; I sensed it and I was so sorry until she and Magdalene came laughing into my dreams, teasing and encouraging me to follow them; to come home; to walk again with Cephas, Paul, Thomas and so many others, too, some of whom I do not remember in this life but whose presence will fill my soul with joy. I have done my best. I have done well enough. This time I did have the courage. I can be at peace.

As I leave this land, now Sarah's land, to take that last walk to eternity, one woman watches me go. Tears glisten in her clear grey eyes. It is Sarah's turn now. She will do well. No friend was ever truer. No child was ever more loved. The mantle of the Anointed One sits well on her shoulders.

May God bless her, and all my children.

It is done.

www.ingramcontent.com/pod-product-compliance
Lightning Source LLC
Chambersburg PA
CBHW011145070726
47591CB00015B/2267